Lost Among the Stars

by

Vicky Burkholder

Lost Among the Stars

Cover Art by *Debbie Taylor*

The Wild Rose Press, Inc.
PO Box 708
Adams Basin, NY 14410-0708
Visit us at www.thewildrosepress.com

Publishing History
First Edition, 2022
Trade Paperback ISBN 978-1-5092-4110-1
Digital ISBN 978-1-5092-4111-8

Published in the United States of America

Declan took in the woman sitting in front of him, from the long coal-black hair held back with a tie, to the expensive, but practical jumpsuit. She was everything Declan disliked—a bureaucrat of the worst type—stubborn, fiery, and determined. Of a certainty, she was neither old, nor wrinkled, but Dec wasn't sure about the coddling yet.

"There's no need to thank me. You handled the situation very well. However," his voice changed from silky smooth to one of warning, "in the future, please don't give my crew any orders without checking with me first."

Mandy stared at him. He could see the muscles in her jaw working. Fine, so she was angry. Dec wasn't exactly happy with the way things were turning out either.

"I wasn't aware I needed your permission to do my job. These people are my responsibility."

"And this ship and her crew are mine. While you're on my ship, you will follow my orders. Is that clear, Ms. Ki?"

Mandy stood, bracing her hands on the desk. "Like hell I will. You may be in charge of this ship, but I am in charge of this mission. Is that clear, Captain?" Without waiting for an answer, she stalked from the room.

Dedication

To my dad who taught me my love of reading and to reach for the stars. And the Bootsquad. They are my support and my inspiration always.

Chapter One

"Kora, what mail do I have? Prioritize them, please." Amanda Ki sat at her desk, and the black furball she had tagged Nuisance jumped onto her lap. She waited for the cat to settle down and absently stroked his head as the list of her emails scrolled down the wall opposite her. "Thanks, Kora."

"You are welcome. You have one high priority message, visual only, fifty marked urgent, one-hundred-twenty-two marked low priority." Kora, the compound AI's normally female voice came out as a deep bass, startling Mandy.

"New voice, Kora?" Mandy frowned. Had the voice been attached to a human, she might have been intrigued but coming from the AI, the deep tones became a reminder of her single status. Something she had neither the time nor the inclination to change.

"Yes, my dear. You like?"

"No. Please revert to your original voice and display visual message." Mandy checked the clock. She had ten minutes before the meeting she both anticipated and dreaded. The next thirty minutes would determine the course the rest of her life would take. Hopefully, off this god-forsaken compound that had become more of a prison than a home.

"Spoil sport." Kora's voice had returned to her normal generic female tone, and Mandy's display lit up.

1

"Thank you, Kora."

When the message appeared, Mandy's stomach lurched. She didn't need to look at the name to know the sender. Nor did she need to see the file. She'd seen the copy dozens of times before. The image of a man standing over her bloodied corpse held permanent residence in her mind. Miguel Alvarez. Mandy's hand clenched, and Nuisance meowed his disapproval before jumping down. "Sorry, Nuisance."

"Kora! Get me messaging security. Now!"

"Yes, boss."

Mandy tapped her fingers on the arm of the chair as she waited.

"Is there a problem, ma'am?" Trevor Howard, head of Tech Services, appeared on Mandy's wall monitor.

"Hell, yes, there's a problem! I thought you had security set so I wouldn't get any more messages from Miguel."

Trevor's eyes widened. "We did. We've got so many locks on your system, even I can't get in without your authorization."

"And yet, he managed. I received one of his calling cards a minute ago."

Trevor turned to the side, and she could see him checking different monitors.

"Can you trace the source?" Mandy asked.

"That's impossible." Trevor frowned, and Mandy's stomach clenched. "This shows in-house generation."

"Not as impossible as you may think." Mandy chewed her lip and fought off her nerves. "Work on finding the origin, Trevor."

"We will, ma'am. I'm sorry."

"I know, Trevor. I know." She glanced around the

office as a shiver shook her. If Miguel could break the computer codes Trevor had set, he could probably break the security codes to the complex. Was he watching her now?

"Colette?" she called to her calm, efficient assistant. Tall and athletic, Colette had more black belts than a department store and yet managed to keep Mandy's schedule from being too ridiculous. Her husband, Carl, ran the security section, and both were members of the Warrior class. Warriors were the elite of Aboolean society. Trained from a young age, they learned multiple forms of fighting, subterfuge, and security. Her purple and green beads tinkled in Colette's hip-length pure white hair. The bead colors defined what tribe each Warrior belonged to, and Colette and Carl belonged to the Guardian Division. Mandy had known Carl for a decade and trusted him implicitly. "You'd better get Carl down here."

"He's already on his way. Kora alerted me. You okay?"

Mandy swiveled around in her chair. "Yes. What time is it?"

"Five minutes after your meeting should have started. Kora's got them on hold. Malachi's talking to them about minor problems and will keep chatting until you're ready."

"Are you sure you and Carl don't mind shifting your services to Mali?"

Colette grinned and patted her obviously distended abdomen. "Gee, let me see. Would I mind moving out of an underground bunker for a chance to live on a private island with a nanny to help with the baby, a company paid house and a small staff to run the place, a private plane at our disposal, and, oh, yeah, all we have to do is put in some time each day doing what we're doing now but for your cousin? I guess we can handle that."

"And take good care of Nuisance."

"She's already marked Carl as hers. She'll tolerate me when he's not around but let him walk into the room and I cease to exist. I'm beginning to think she's going to be more of a challenge than Alvarez." She turned as Carl stepped into the room.

Colette waddled over to him, neatly sidestepping Nuisance when the cat streaked in front of her. She shook her head when Nuisance wove a pattern around Carl's legs, meowing until he bent over and scooped her up. "See what I mean?"

"Kora said you got another message from Alvarez—one generated in house," Carl said, his long hair and beads swinging.

"Yes." Mandy rose and moved to the front of her desk. She hated having the wide ebony piece between her and her friends. Murals of expansive vistas and minimal furniture decorated the huge office and attached apartment, but no matter how well done, at thirty feet underground and set up with the latest in security measures, the complex had become her world. Miguel enjoyed more freedom than she did.

"We did a quick physical search and found no problems, and tech is checking out their end. We won't know anything for at least an hour. You two okay?"

"Unless you consider I'm nine months pregnant and ready to pop, we're fine." Colette lightly punched her hulking husband on the arm.

Mandy chuckled as the wall screen opposite her

desk lit up. A dozen lawyers and managers stared back at her, and all but one of their faces held a frown. The lone holdout, her cousin, Malachi, toasted her with a tall glass. Mandy bit back a smile as she took in Mali's rumpled shirt and mussed hair, knowing he'd probably rolled out of bed less than five minutes ago, even though his local time was close to noon. Everyone except Malachi looked like they'd stepped out of a fashion magazine.

When had the company gotten so staid and formal? Yes, they had a lot going on. Between the pharmaceuticals, electronic and power systems, shipping companies, and more, there were a lot of branches to this large tree she oversaw. But size didn't negate the basics that her parents had founded the company under. People still came first—or they should. People and the betterment of all. Malachi understood this better than any of the other suits. He was also an organizational genius and could handle anything thrown at him, including this one extremely large company. Mandy studied her reflection in the glassy desktop. As usual, she had her waist-length hair pulled back in a braid, but she'd forgone her normal severe business suit for a comfortable skirt and tunic. There'd been a time when sober and dull had been her daily uniform. She was long past due for a change.

She listened as Mali argued with the suits.

"Come on, everyone, you know Mandy's right about this. She's the only one with the right training and power to get everything organized. Thompson, do you want to tell me you're willing to go off planet?"

The head of the Ki family pharmaceutical enterprises in the main city of Amalgama on Aboo tried to hide his look of shock and disgust with little success. His high-collared gray suit with navy trim marked him as a member of the judiciary class. Mandy saw far too many of those suit colors on her monitors.

"To a quarantined planet? No thank you. But Amanda has responsibilities he—"

"My biggest responsibility is to the people on Xy-Three," Mandy broke in on the conversation. "Ki Enterprises wouldn't exist if not for the opals and pharmaceuticals found in the Xy System. With most of the staff there either dead or too ill to do anything, they need someone who knows the business. The few people left are good, but they can't do everything."

"What about sending people from Xy-One?" another lawyer asked. "They're closer than we are."

"And off limits as well. Until we get this under control, most of the system is quarantined. Plus, our people on One have their hands full with the new discoveries there. They've got a red crystal that could be even more powerful than the blues and greens we've gotten from Xy-Three. I know your crystal people are excited to get hold of them. You want me to tell them to stop production?"

He looked abashed. "No, ma'am."

"But what if you get sick?" one lawyer protested. "You can't risk your life."

Mandy glanced up as her aunt, Taka Yu, strode into the office and broke in on the argument. "She won't get sick, and we aren't risking anything or anyone."

Barely five feet tall, Taka's presence commanded everyone's attention. Whether lecturing to groups of doctors or hip deep in test tubes and tissue samples, Dr.

Taka Yu was a force to be reckoned with. She wore her usual white suit with red and blue braiding but, unlike the lawyers, her top buttons were undone and her sleeves rolled up to her elbows.

"Since I'll be with Amanda, there's no need to worry about her continuing good health."

Mandy hid a grin at the wide-eyed shock on the suits' faces. Thanks to Taka's influence, and not a little of Mandy's power, they'd been able to pull this trip together faster than she'd believed possible. Taka had been working with the labs long distance, but according to the morning reports, they still had no clue as to the cause of the illness devastating the small population on Xy-Three, also known as Ki's Planet.

"How can you immunize against an unknown agent?" one lawyer asked.

Taka glanced at Mandy who gave a quick shake of her head. The people really were ill and dying, but the evidence she'd seen suggested industrial sabotage, not a plague. And she was pretty sure she knew who was behind the attack, but not the how. Security in all the Ki holdings had been quietly increased with people Carl knew and trusted. They reported directly to him. Mandy brought her attention back to Taka who had taken up the argument.

"We have some ideas as to what the problem might be, and Amanda and I will take all the necessary precautions. I've already put together the health services team, and Amanda has taken care of the other workers and supplies. We leave tonight."

Taka perched on the end of Mandy's desk. "Besides, in the long run, off planet and away from Aboo is the safest place for Amanda to be, and you all know this."

When Mandy had expressed an interest in leaving, Taka and Malachi were the only ones who hadn't argued. Miguel Alvarez wanted Mandy dead and would do anything to make sure he succeeded—including blowing up several of her factories and killing and injuring hundreds of people to get to her. In addition, there were the Luddites—a group of anti-technology fanatics who were always a problem where industry was concerned—as well as several other extreme groups and individuals. Running the largest energy and pharmaceuticals firm in five star systems tended to get you enemies.

She studied the faces in front of her. Most of them had been with various Ki Enterprises for years, but did she really know any of them? Were any of them working for Miguel or someone else? She shook her head. If she didn't get control of her feelings, she'd soon be suspecting Nuisance of orchestrating the conspiracy.

"Taka's right. I'm tired of sitting around waiting for Miguel to make his next move. I need to be proactive. Whether or not you approve, I will be leaving this evening with Taka. Malachi will be taking over as head of Ki Enterprises here on Aboo while I'm gone."

With Malachi in command, the company would remain true to her wishes of caring for the people before the business. His biggest problem would be dealing with the suits, but Mali would prevail. He had a rapport with people Mandy sometimes lacked. His quick wit disarmed them to the point where his opponents laughingly agreed with him before they realized what was happening.

"Any further problems should be referred to him." Mandy grinned at the faces on the monitors. "Don't worry. I'll only be out there for a year and will still be in touch even though Malachi will oversee day-to-day operations. Before you can file your quarterly statements, Taka and I will be back in your hair and causing you all kinds of problems." She signed off to a round of chuckles.

"Always leave 'em laughing," Taka said. "Did you get confirmation on your shuttle yet?"

"Yes. The governor gave us special permission to land here at the compound. Carl will check the ship over, escort me out, and we'll fly up to Pointe Noir Station. The *Phoenix* will be ready to go shortly after we arrive."

Carl returned to the room with Colette. "I've already talked to base security," he said. "They'll be waiting for you. On Pointe Noir, you'll have a guard and be in a secure area."

Mandy nodded. She'd put up with their security measures for now, but once she was on the ship, she'd be free, or as free as one could get on a spaceship. "Thanks, Carl." She rose and gave Colette a brief hug. "You'd better let me know when your son finally gets born."

"You watch your back out there. We have people in place who will act as your guardians while on board and on planet."

"Thanks. Now go on. I know you still have packing to do, and I hate long goodbyes." She sighed as her two friends left the room with Nuisance in a soft carrier.

"Mandy, honey, are you sure you want to do this?"

Taka asked.

Mandy picked up her briefcase and glanced around the office that had become her prison, her gaze ending at Taka. "Extremely."

Taka nodded, an impish grin on her face. "At least don't give me any crap about being back in a year. You and I both know that once you're out there, you'll never come back. You're too much your parents' daughter. Let the pencil pushers run the businesses."

Her aunt's laughter filled the room as Mandy opened her mouth for a quick denial but snapped her lips shut again when Taka waved a finger at her.

"You think you could hide your feelings from me?" She swatted Mandy's shoulder. "Now come on. We have a lot of work to do before tonight, and my shuttle leaves in thirty minutes."

"I thought you were going up with me."

"I can't. I want to do a final check of my medical supplies and finish getting the lab set up. I'll see you on board tonight after I've made my checks."

Chapter Two

Mandy stared out the shuttle's portal at the huge ship coming into view. Her home for the next three weeks.

"Quite a sight, isn't she?" Transport Commander Honan Lindell asked.

"That she is." Mandy glanced at the commander. Living on Aboo, she was used to being around the Warrior class, and Honan characterized his tribe perfectly. He was definitely different from her social status as a Master Merchant. Warriors were almost a separate species unto themselves. Tall with bronze skin and long bone-white hair woven with gold and black beads denoting his tribe as the Transport Division, he didn't speak much, but those gold eyes of his observed everything. He fit her idea of head of security for the ship as if the position had been designed specifically for him. She'd heard Honan and the first mate were a couple and let out a little sigh, then shook her head. A relationship with anyone was out of the question. She had too much to do, too many people depending on her. Besides, her last connection hadn't exactly ended in a stellar fashion. Instead of a wedding, Mandy found herself running from her own funeral and her fiancé dead, thanks to Alvarez. She refused to put anyone else in a similar position.

With an effort, she brought her attention back to

the ship.

Designed and built entirely in space, the *Phoenix* had none of the streamlined beauty of her atmospheric cousins. Actually, she looked like a whale but fulfilled the promise of being able to take on huge amounts of cargo, and Mandy admired the function if not the design. The ship had an excellent reputation, as did the captain—although she'd heard he could be a bit of a tyrant. But then, almost all captains had a tyrannical streak; having an arrogant attitude went with the job. But she'd never met a pure human before. Their species were rare on Aboo, and she was looking forward to talking with him.

"Let's see if I remember what you taught me," Mandy said to the commander as she studied the huge ship from her vantage point on the shuttle. "The lowest levels are where the holds and docking bays are. Mid-level contains engineering and environmental systems as well as the majority of the cold sleep pods. Top level is for crew and includes dining, recreation, living quarters, and medical. That's also where some of the cold sleep compartments are. Since most of the ship is cargo space or cold sleep areas, you only need twenty crewmen for each shift, and most of those are cold sleep techs and engineers."

"Good," Honan said. "Most people don't get beyond the first level."

"Most people didn't have a ship's captain for an uncle. My cousin Malachi and I practically grew up on ships, though not interstellar. Can you tell me why we had to shuttle everything over to the ship when loading from the station would have been faster and easier?"

"Orders from the station manager. We've done this

a couple of other times, especially when a crew comes in ill."

"I guess that explains the extra security." Security was so tight, *Mandy* had trouble getting through some checkpoints.

"Probably. Our last stop was Xy-Three, and some of the crew got sick shortly after, but this one looks like a quick fix. Nobody died, and they're recovering nicely, mostly thanks to your aunt. The extra checks are for your safety too. Security got a blip about some Luddite trouble."

Mandy snorted.

Honan glanced at her. "You don't think there's a problem?"

"If you knew how many times I've dealt with Luddite threats, you'd understand my skepticism. Nine times out of ten, they're nothing more than hot air."

"It's that tenth time we're worried about." He checked the panel. "Why don't you relax? We'll be there in a few minutes."

Mandy moved to a rear seat. She and Honan were alone on the shuttle since Taka had gone aboard the *Phoenix* several hours earlier to oversee the loading of the last of her medical equipment. Mandy relaxed and took advantage of the quiet time.

Honan was probably right about the extra security for health reasons, but she had a nagging suspicion the reasons concerned her more than a plague and Luddites. A health alert didn't call for checkpoints when were going out to the ship—only when coming in. She refused to think of what—or who—the problem might be. She didn't even consider the Luddites. They were merely nuisances. This had to be something much worse than a few fanatical saboteurs. She looked out the portal and sighed. Escape wasn't going to be as easy as she'd hoped. A few minutes later they docked, and she gathered her bags.

"Thank you for a comfortable trip, Commander. Can you point me in the direction of my cabin?" She studied the entry and the corridor stretching out from either side. She'd been expecting boring beige or grey, but these walls showed paintings from nature—waterfalls, trees, beaches, and more. She almost felt as if she was walking through a forest rather than a spaceship. The flooring was made up of standard industrial tiles with gray carpet, but the walls…definitely not standard. "Interesting walls."

Honan took her bags. "The paintings help you feel less confined, especially on long trips. They were the captain's idea. I'll show you the way to your cabin."

Mandy grinned at him. "Tell me, as my designated babysitter, do you get a break when we're finally underway?"

The corner of Honan's mouth lifted in a barely suppressed smile as he led Mandy down a corridor. "Actually, my duty ended as soon as we stepped on board. You're on your own here, ma'am. And welcome aboard."

"Thank you. And thank you for your help." Mandy wondered briefly about the captain. Although she really didn't want any special attention, she still felt slighted the man hadn't bothered to meet her.

As if he'd read her mind, Honan answered her unspoken question. "I apologize for the captain not being here. He had some last-minute problems to take care of on station."

He stopped outside a cabin and palmed open the door.

Mandy shot him a sideways glance. Psi abilities were rare, but not unheard of. She'd have to check the commander out a little more closely. "That's all right. And thank you for your kind attention."

"You're welcome, ma'am. I hope you enjoy the trip." He stood back, waiting for her to enter, then set her bag inside the door. "Ma'am."

Mandy closed the door and studied the space. There wasn't much to see—not even a porthole to look out of. *All the comforts of home,* she thought as she opened the storage cabinets. Softly textured, dove gray walls blended with darker, multi-hued gray carpeting and navy-blue trim.

She had a narrow mattress covered with a plain navy-blue spread situated on top of low storage cabinets. Another section of cabinets hung above, neatly boxing in the bunk. The opposite side of the cabin contained a personal bathing unit and dressing area. She had enough room between the two to stretch out her arms with a couple of hand spans of space left over. An open doorway led to an equally small sitting area with a built-in desk, shelving unit, and straight chair upholstered in the same navy material as the bed coverings as well as two upholstered armchairs. Not wanting special treatment, she'd opted for a mid-level cabin. She hated to think what standard berths looked like. Although tiny, the small space was still better than a cold sleep pod.

On closer inspection, she noticed signs of age in the worn areas of the carpet and nicks in the cabinets and shelves. The room had definitely been well-lived in. She opened her bags and stowed the contents in the storage cabinets.

Like the others traveling with her, most of her gear was packed in the hold. They had enough supplies down there to sustain them for at least a year. Hopefully, the medical specialists would be able to figure out what had infected her people—if anyone was left alive by the time they arrived. If not, her replacement crew would run the labs and management until new colonists could be recruited.

Mandy wrinkled her nose at the antiseptic smell left over from the medical cleansing the ship had gone through and wished she could open a window or something. She snorted. That wasn't likely to happen on a ship in deep space.

"Hermes?" She called to the ship's AI.

"Yes, boss?"

A medium range baritone voice answered her. The tone reminded her of what she remembered of her father's voice, and she swallowed hard against a sudden wave of homesickness. "Can anything be done about the aroma in this room? I've been in medical units that smelled better than this."

"You can set the environmental controls for extra filtration. You can also add a manual scented filter. Would you like me to request one from maintenance?"

"Thanks. I'd appreciate something light and forest-based."

"No problem, boss."

"Thank you. By the way, I like your name. Hermes is an ancient deity from Old Earth, isn't he?"

"Yes, ma'am. Hermes is considered the herald of the gods, as well as the protector of human heralds, travelers, thieves, merchants, and orators."

"Appropriate. Are there a lot of new crew?"

"Not counting your people filling out the lower tech jobs, there are actually only ten new crew. Unfortunately, many of the new people are rank tyros."

Mandy laughed. "Hey, careful there. I'm one of those rank tyros."

"Not according to my files."

Mandy pursed her lips. She'd hoped to avoid any special privileges that would separate her from the rest of the ship's personnel. "What do you mean?"

"I mean, boss, you own this ship, or at least one of your sub-companies does. And you've got some space experience, although not extra-solar. With your background, you could probably pilot this ship, with a little help from me, of course."

"Of course." Mandy sighed. If her luck held, nobody else would find out about the ownership. After all, she'd spent several hours tracing all the holding companies. She'd wanted to know who held responsibility for the ship.

"Does anyone else know about the ownership?"

"Unknown."

"Do me a favor and don't broadcast the information around. Oh, and Hermes?"

"Yes, boss?"

"Don't call me boss."

"Yes, boss."

Mandy fought to keep from laughing. She'd heard Hermes had a mind of his own. He was the most unique AI she'd ever met.

"Hermes? Can I get a listing of the personnel and their backgrounds? I didn't have much of a chance to see who's on board."

"Yes, ma'am. You can access those records on your monitor anytime you want."

"Thank you."

Mandy emptied the last of her personal items from her bags and carefully lifted out a small, well-wrapped package. She gently undid the packing materials and held up a small statue of a jaguar. Made of rare black chrystolian opal, her father had given the figurine to her before his final trip.

"Poppi, why must you go?" five-year-old Mandy asked.

Her father knelt beside her in the sand, his back toward the pounding surf. "This is my job, Kitten."

"Can you take me, Poppi?"

"Not this time, Kitten." He wiped a tear from her face. "Mandy, no tears. This is not a sad time."

"Why can't I go? Mommy's going."

"Because it's not your turn yet. Do you know about taking turns?"

"Yes, Poppi. You have to wait until everyone else has gone, then you get to go."

He laughed—a deep, happy sound. "Not quite, but that's a good guess. Besides, you like staying with Taka and Papa D. Now, I have a job for you while I'm gone."

"What, Poppi?"

He pulled a small statue out of his pocket and placed the figurine in Mandy's tiny hands. "I want you to guard this for me. Do you think you can do that?"

"Poppi! He's so pretty!"

"Like you are, Kitten. This is very special and comes from a place a long way from here. He will

watch over you when I'm not here. Will you take care of him until it's your turn to go?"

"Oh, yes, Poppi. Yes."

Mandy gently placed the statuette on the shelf above her desk. "I'm finally taking my turn, Poppi," she whispered before she sat at the desk.

"Hermes, ship's status, please."

"Yes, ma'am. Check your screen. Oh, and you have incoming messages."

"Thanks, Hermes. Put them through."

Most of the messages were routine but one flashed urgent. Mandy opened the file and froze as the picture of a bloody corpse formed on the screen. Her voice shook as she asked Hermes to trace the message.

"Sorry, ma'am. The message came from a public terminal on the station, but we can't determine if that was the origin. Do you want me to archive the message?"

Mandy clenched her fists in frustration. She knew the missive would never be traced. Like all the rest, every lead would dead end. "Yes, and you'd better send a copy to base security for routing to Fleet. Add the tag *Alvarez*."

"Done."

"Thank you."

Mandy closed the file. How had Miguel found her? Only moments ago, her cabin had seemed a refuge, now the walls closed in on her, similar to a cage with no escape. She had to get out. She quickly changed into a work suit and headed for the cargo bay. Hard physical labor would soothe her nerves.

****

Miguel Alvarez kicked over the body at his feet.

He reached down and tugged the ID bracelet from the man's wrist. "Sorry, man, but I need this more than you do." He dumped the body into the refuse rocket and sealed the hatch.

"May the sun god accept this sacrifice in his name," he intoned as he triggered the controls, putting the rocket in the queue to burn up in the sun.

He turned away and scratched at his face and arms. The medic had done an excellent job as always, but each time his reaction to the drugs they used to change his skin, hair, and eyes grew worse. Only the Utopia drug kept the itching at a tolerable level, but he needed more supplies. Fortunately, this would be the last time he would have to undergo the procedure. He had become an expert with makeup and artifice, but the genetic transformation was more secure than wigs and paint. All his plans were coming together. His final task was to remind the high and mighty Amanda Ki that she belonged to him. She should have been his by now, but Amanda thwarted him. Only she had the codes to the pharmaceutical labs on Xy-Three—codes he needed. Plus, she owned the company and so much more. And that wasn't right. He had the right to the money and products. Him. He held the power, not her. He would rightfully take over the companies. They would be his, as would Amanda. She would learn to obey. *Amanda would learn.*

He caught a glance of his reflection in a porthole and laughed. Who would ever suspect this red-haired, green-eyed man of being the infamous Miguel Alvarez? He absently scratched his arm as he pulled a small box from his pocket, plugged the wires into the computer outlet and dropped in the bracelet. "Okay, baby, let's see you do your stuff."

He tapped two keys and smiled in satisfaction as his new file came up on the screen. A few more taps and he checked the dead man's file. "My, my, Miguel, how you have changed."

He laughed as he disconnected the box and secured the altered ID around his own wrist. Whistling a light tune, he left the station refuse bay and headed for ship's maintenance. He had no problem slipping in with the other workers and floating out to the ship. After all, according to his ID, he'd already been cleared by security. A few minutes later, he settled into an airlock. The inner door opened, and he strolled on board.

****

Declan Chalmers drummed his fingers on the arm of his seat as he waited for the pilot to fly the short distance from the station to his ship, his mood as black as the surrounding space. Everything about this unexpected trip worried him. They'd barely arrived at the station before they'd been ordered to leave, and with most of his crew sick, he didn't like the alternatives he'd been given. Plus, security was in a snit about something, but nobody was talking. He rubbed his forehead, feeling a headache coming on.

Although technically a commercial ship, most of the *Phoenix's* crew were Fleet reservists who could be called up in an emergency, and this had been deemed one. In all his years of service, he could only remember this happening one other time—and that had been a disaster.

When he disembarked, Lt. Cmdr. Sarah Thomas, his second-in-command awaited him. "What's the word, Captain?" She fell into step beside him, her beaded hair swinging with her movement. Being the only pure human on board had never bothered him, but the new crew included not only Abooleans, but Orilians with their blue scales, webbed hands and feet, and nictitating eyes, and Surians with their coal black skin and gold hair. And he understood there were even more species in cold sleep. Fortunately, none of them required special breathing or foods they couldn't supply.

Declan glanced at Sarah and then at the corridor curving away from them. "The word is, we go. As of exactly one hour ago, we are under Fleet Command, and this is considered a Level I emergency mission."

Shock and dismay crossed Sarah's face as she increased her steps to keep up with his longer stride. "With three-quarters of the crew in quarantine? How the hell are we supposed to do anything?"

A tiny grin transformed Declan's forbidding face into one of almost boyish charm. Unfortunately, the look didn't last. "We use company staff as crew." He waited for Sarah's reaction. Nobody had ever heard of filling out a ship's crew with unseasoned landlubbers who'd most likely never been off planet, let alone in deep space. He wasn't disappointed.

"Company staff? As crew? On a Level I? You've got to be kidding! They're not even Transporters!"

Declan knew Sarah, like the rest of the crew, had nothing against planet-bound people, but they rarely took well to the stresses of deep space travel, which is why most of them traveled in cold sleep. And taking them into a Level I emergency situation was unheard of. Plus using non-transporters went against every custom the Abooleans followed. Your class determined your job, and you didn't veer into anything else.

"Seems the mission head has some influence with the Federated Council and pulled a few strings," Declan said.

They reached his office, and he sat heavily at his desk as Sarah pulled up a chair opposite him. Although he'd been in space for almost ten years and on this particular ship for more than half of those, no pictures marred the Spartan walls or knick-knacks cluttered the desktop.

Declan gazed out his porthole. He'd always felt any art would pale when compared to the sights he got to see out his window. A short distance away, the space station slowly revolved, the concentric rings and spokes making the base look like some giant spider's web. Pointe Noir station was the jumping off spot for travel from Aboo to almost anywhere else. Almost the size of a small moon, the base was like a small city with shops, medical services, security, restaurants, and more. Some beings who lived there had never set foot on land. He couldn't imagine never seeing mountains or oceans or forests. His love of the land was one reason he and others in the crew had painted the walls of the *Phoenix* with the scenes of home. Beyond the station, he could barely see the bubble-topped habitats on the largest of three moons and farther out—space. The dark solitude drew him. Aboo lay behind them, but he knew the lay of the land in his heart. He didn't need to see the planet to know what was there.

"There's not enough string in the galaxy to do that kind of pulling. Who is he anyway? And why us?" Sarah asked, bringing Declan's attention back to her.

"*She* is Amanda Ki, and why is because we're the

only long-range ship in dock." Amanda Ki sat firmly at the head of the richest family in the Five-Star Systems. Even the lowest person on the Ki Enterprises ladder stood well ahead of ninety percent of the federation population. He couldn't even begin to imagine the kind of power the woman wielded. Briefly he wondered what she was like. He rarely perused the financial news or social gossip. His lack of curiosity had less to do with interest and more to do with the pressing matters affecting him, his crew, and his ship. Ki was probably old and soft—someone accustomed to the easy life who insisted on being catered to. She'd find her time not so easy here on his ship. Coddling wasn't in Declan's nature.

Sarah's eyes widened. "Ki? As in Ki Enterprises?" At Declan's nod, she let out a low whistle. "Okay, so she does have enough string. But that doesn't explain the rest. Why can't they wait a week until the crew kicks this flu bug?"

Declan took a deep breath and exhaled slowly. "I guess you didn't get a chance to read the latest memo."

Sarah shook her head. "No. I came here straight from Health Services. Thought they'd never get done poking and prodding, but I've never seen them so tight-lipped. Do they know what hit us?"

"Health is saying possibly Cygnian Plague. That's why we've been ordered to stand at anchor away from the station and sent immediately into quarantine." CP had decimated an entire world before they'd brought the disease under control. Millions of people dead in days, thousands of others lingered, barely able to take care of themselves. Very few survived.

"What? Our crew? How? We were all immunized."

She studied her hands as if looking for the purple spots that marked CP victims.

"Health thinks a mutant strain, possibly introduced when we stopped at Three. Shortly after we left there, they sent word about the outbreak." Sarah picked up on his slight hesitation, as he'd figured she would.

"But?"

"But the problem could also be something else. Personally, I think they're using CP as an excuse. The only people sick are the ones who went planet-side at Three, and that was before we got to Secundus. Nobody on Secundus is sick, and none of the rest of us have shown any symptoms. The illness might be some kind of planetary contaminant specific to Three. If so, the planet could be interdicted."

"Council wouldn't like that. Interdict the Xy systems and there go their supplies of opals and the drugs. So, what does all this have to do with us?"

"With the exception of Ki, our passengers are health workers, techs, and security. We'll be taking them, along with a cargo hold full of medical and testing supplies to the Xy system. The trip is quarantine restricted. Once there, we don't come back without the cure or the reason behind the plague."

At least the reason made the trip palatable. Declan wasn't oblivious to the problems the colony had, but, thanks to them, he had his own to deal with.

Sarah sighed. "There go the plans Honan and I had to go to Aino Station." She frowned. "Why is Ki soiling her hands with this? She's got enough flunkies to do the work."

"From what I understand, the Ki family is taking on all financial and other responsibilities to contain this contagion. They also want to assure the rest of us that shipments of chrystolian opals and pharmaceuticals won't be affected since they have ample amounts stockpiled in safe areas. Ki will be taking over the administration until someone else can be found."

"How noble," Sarah said. "Can you imagine how much this is going to cost her?" She shrugged and flipped the stylus she held. "But then she doesn't have anything to worry about, does she?"

Declan held up a wafer-thin slice of opal about an inch in diameter. The light caught the bands of red, blue, and gold embedded in the black disk. He often thought the opals looked like a slice of space.

"Is that...?" Sarah stared at the disk—her eyes wide.

Declan handed the crystal to her. "Yes. Instead of the coils we requested, the company sent us this. I called them to complain, but the idiots in supply insist they'd sent the coils. Their records showed they sent coils, so that's what they sent. So I kept the opal—and picked up some coils on the rim." He took the wafer back, laying the mineral gently on the desk. "I can hardly believe a disk like this is worth more than what you, Honan, and I earn combined in a year."

"And Ki owns an entire planet full of this and more. Why *like this*?"

Declan pointed out a minute crack running through the disk, arms radiating out from the center. "See that crack? Something like this, in this shape, is only good for grinding up and mixing with polymers for low-grade use. You couldn't even run the bridge lights with this."

"What about our refits? Surely we aren't going to

go back out without at least a minor overhaul."

Declan rubbed the opal, as if summoning a genie. "The company decided since the *Phoenix* will be sold off for salvage after this trip, she wasn't worth the time and money."

Sarah jumped from her chair. "Not worth the money! We were lucky to get back to space dock in one piece this time. Do they know Ki is on board? They're risking her neck as well as ours."

"I never got the chance to tell them. They cut me off before I could say anything other than Fleet had commandeered us for an emergency trip. I think the accountant was too busy trying to figure out how he could sue the government and for how much."

"So they don't know Ki commandeered us?" A slight smile teased the corners of Sarah's mouth.

"Nope."

"And you're not going to tell them?" The smile grew wider.

"Nope." Declan grinned. "Let them explain how they let the most important person in several star systems go off on a ship in less-than-optimal operating condition."

Sarah shook her head and laughed. "I'll bet some heads will roll over that one."

"Yeah. But we both know they'll figure out a way to place the blame elsewhere, probably on us. Those bastards never get caught. Oh, there's one more issue," Declan said. He could tell from the wary look on Sarah's face that she anticipated the worst.

"You're going to be the liaison between the civilians and the crew and work closely with Ki. Your job is to keep them out of my hair."

"A babysitter? You want me to babysit some spoiled rich do-gooder?"

Declan winced at the glare Sarah shot him, thankful for the desk separating them, surprised the smoke alarms didn't go off. "Do you have a problem?"

Sarah swallowed hard. "No. If we are finished, Captain?"

Declan wondered if he'd pushed a little too hard. Sarah never called him captain unless she had to. "Since Health cleared you both, go find Honan and grab some shore time on station. Enjoy the time while you can. We leave in four hours."

He tapped a stylus on the desktop after Sarah left, mulling over his options, of which there were none. "Hermes?"

"Yes, Captain?"

"Has our main guest reported in yet?"

"Yes, sir. She stowed her gear, downloaded several messages, and is currently in the cargo bay. I must say she's not at all what I expected. Do you want me to page her for you?"

Declan had no idea what a computer would expect, and he wasn't sure he wanted to find out. "What the devil is she doing in the cargo bay? Never mind. Don't answer. I need to check with Donovan in the docking bay. I'll stop by cargo on my way."

"Yes, sir. Captain, a message just arrived. Station security wants you to contact them ASAP."

Declan sighed and ran his hand through his hair. "Get them for me."

"You're on, Captain."

Declan looked at the face on the screen. The head of station security looked as tired as Declan felt.

"What's up, John?"

"Not sure yet. Might be a problem, might be nothing. I'm sending you extra personnel and a special file explaining everything. You'll need to use Level I security to decode the file. Declan, I'm sorry to be so mysterious. You'll understand when you see the file."

Declan raised an eyebrow. "Can you at least tell me if this will affect departure?" Declan ran through all the problems a change in schedule would cause, the least of which would be informing Ki.

"I don't think so but use captain's discretion. This is serious. Watch your six, Declan."

"Thanks." Declan frowned as the circuit closed. John wasn't usually so close-mouthed about anything concerning security. And what could be worse than a Level I emergency? He wondered why the mystery as he called up the file. A few minutes later he leaned back in his chair, his fingers beating an agitated tattoo on the desk.

Chapter Three

Mandy jumped off a large pallet, landing lightly in the low gravity. She brushed a stray lock of hair out of her face. "Tom?" she called to a young man working the other pallets. "I thought there were supposed to be twenty pallets of survival gear. I only count fifteen."

He checked his manifest and sighed. "Yes, ma'am. Control says there's a delay."

"Another one? What's going on over there? Did you try to get them to hurry?"

"Come on, ma'am. They're Control. I don't tell them what to do, they tell me. At least that's what they said."

His frustration showed in his face. Mandy pursed her lips. "We'll see about that. Hermes?" she called to the ceiling. "Are you there?"

"Of course. How may I help you?"

"Would you get Control for me, please?" She tapped her headset.

"You're on."

She put on her best VIP voice. "Control? This is Amanda Ki. Where are those last pallets of survival gear?" Mandy cocked her head, listening to the curt reply on her earphone.

"There's been a slight delay for a personnel shuttle," a bored voice told her.

"I don't care who's in that shuttle—we're due to

leave shortly. We need those supplies so we can finish loading."

"I can't turn back the captain's shuttle. Your shipment is next."

"Oh. Okay. Thank you." Mandy closed the connection. Control didn't have to sound quite so smug, she thought. She tilted her head. The captain was already aboard, so who besides him or Taka rated VIP service? She grinned at Tom. "The shipment will be here in a few minutes. Any other problems?"

Tom shrugged. "Nothing major. Once those are loaded, we're all set. I appreciate your help with this, ma'am."

"Not a problem. I needed to get out of my cabin. But where is the rest of the crew? You were supposed to have two people working with you."

"Who knows? Like I said, nothing major. What about you? What are you doing down here in cargo territory, if you don't mind my asking, ma'am?"

Lading wasn't an easy job, and Mandy knew Tom didn't have much experience with ships. He came highly recommended, but he wasn't a spacer. Mandy studied the neatly secured cargo hold—if not, he could be. He certainly had the knack. "Restless I guess."

"Ma'am?" Hermes's voice interrupted them.

"Yes, Hermes?"

"You're wanted in the cold sleep area. A bit of a problem."

"So, what else is new?" she muttered. "Okay, Hermes. I'm on my way." She waved goodbye to Tom and hurried out. At a hub of corridors, she realized she was hopelessly lost. She stood there for several seconds trying to get her bearings, but all the corridors looked the same. She tried to remember the layout of this level. There was a single corridor between the hull and the inner rooms, one long corridor bisecting that down the middle, and at least a dozen or more connecting the outer one with that one. But which cross corridor would be the quickest way to cold sleep? "Um, Hermes?"

"Yes, boss?"

"How the devil do I get to the cold sleep area?"

"Follow the arrows. And I promise not to tell."

Mandy could swear she heard Hermes chuckling. A dark blue line appeared in the opaque paneling at the mid-line of the wall opposite her. "Thank you, Hermes."

She discovered the room was closer than she realized. As she went around the corner, a strange man rushing from the other direction ran into her. He immediately reached out to steady her.

"Oh! Excuse me. I'm sorry."

Mandy flinched from his touch, and he backed off.

"That's quite all right," she said as she tried to gather her composure. The man's badge showed him to be a maintenance tech. "Slow down and be more careful the next time."

"Yes, ma'am. I'm sorry, ma'am."

A short way down the corridor, Mandy felt a sensation on the back of her neck, like someone watched her. She looked back and saw the same man standing there, staring at her. She clenched shaking hands in her pockets.

"Can I help you?" Mandy asked, amazed her voice came out so clearly.

"N-n-no," he stammered and then went on. "I mean yes, ma'am. Can you tell me how to get to the crew's quarters? I'm late for reporting in and can't find my way around."

Mandy relaxed and chuckled to herself. Looked like the replacement crew had no more idea of their bearings in the big ship than she did. Besides, this pale-skinned redhead couldn't be dangerous. He looked like he should be enjoying a date with his best girl. Although the way he kept scratching at his arms was a bit distracting. "Ask the AI anytime you need help. His name's Hermes and he's quite smart."

This time she heard a definite chuckle coming from the ceiling and a red arrow appeared in the left corridor. "I believe if you follow that arrow, you will find your way."

"Thank you." He hurried off in the indicated direction.

"Cold sleep area around the next corner."

"Thank you, Hermes."

Mandy turned the corner and saw a large group gathered in the corridor. She shouldered her way through them to the doorway. The large, specially shielded room lined with rows of casket-like sleep pods always made her feel uneasy. All but the last few pods were filled—their occupants looking like pale corpses.

The technicians were prepping the last of the sleepers as Mandy arrived. Once in the pod, the technician would place the facemask in position and close the cover. An anesthetic gas put the occupant to sleep before the cold sleep chemicals took over, lowering body temperature and slowing down all biological functions almost to nothing. For those people who couldn't handle the procedure, the techs administered a light anesthesia before they entered the pod. Mandy wrinkled her nose at the chemical smell pervading the room, even with the air filters at full.

Two crewmen struggled with a tall, slender woman Mandy recognized as one of her technicians, Tina Andrews.

"What's the matter here? Who paged me?" Mandy asked the crowd.

One of the onlookers gestured for Mandy to join him. "I did, ma'am. I thought you could help before those heavy-handed spacers hurt her."

"No! You're not going to close me up in there!" The frantic woman struggled against the crewmen trying to restrain her.

"Tina!" Mandy reached out to put her hands on the woman's shoulders. Tina was a good head taller than her, but Mandy stood firm. "Tina! Calm down. Tell me what's wrong."

The woman's wide eyes locked on Mandy's. "Ma'am, please don't make me go in there. I'll die!"

Mandy looked at the nearest crewman. "Is there an empty room nearby?"

"The control office." He motioned toward a small room at the front of the area. "But I can't let you go in there. Only authorized personnel are allowed in there."

Mandy drew herself up to her full height, which still left her a few inches shorter than the tech. "What's your name?" she snapped.

The man's mouth tightened. "Smithers, ma'am."

Mandy frowned and pointed to her collar insignia of five stars circling five bars, indicating she was above everyone except the captain. "Well, Smithers, I'm about as authorized as they come. Move aside, and let me pass with this woman." Mandy kept her voice deceptively soft and low, daring the tech to argue.

Smithers looked at his companion for support, but the man chose that moment to avidly study the ceiling. Smithers turned back to Mandy, his face rigid with anger. He stepped to one side. "We'll have to report this to Captain Chalmers."

"You do that." Mandy motioned for Tina to join her. *Arrogant, condescending...where does he get off telling me what I can and can't do?*

She entered the tiny office and offered Tina a seat. As Tina pulled a cloth from her pocket to wipe the tears from her face, Mandy brought her profile up on the monitor. *First rule,* Mandy thought as she keyed in a command, *get her talking.* "Can you tell me what's wrong, Tina?"

"Look at those cold sleep pods, ma'am. I can't go in there. I thought I could, but I can't." She wrapped her arms around herself and rocked back and forth in the chair.

Mandy glanced at the screen. Tina's psych file seemed clean—no phobias. *What then?* "Why can't you go in there, Tina?"

"Because to go in there is to die. They call the procedure cold sleep, but death waits in those coffins."

Mandy caught her breath at Tina's depiction of the pods—so close to her own. She let Tina talk, injecting appropriate comments when needed as she searched the data. Finally, she found what she'd been looking for. Mandy could feel anger heating her face as she read the screen. *What the hell was wrong with the people who put the group together? How could they send a woman who'd lost her father and brother in a cold sleep malfunction into space? No wonder the woman panicked. That's what happens when you leave logic to the bureaucrats.*

Mandy sighed and briefly closed her eyes. There wasn't any purpose in getting angry. Tina would see her reaction and think the emotion was directed at her. They couldn't send the woman back and couldn't replace her at this point.

"You won't make me go in one of them, will you, ma'am?"

"Tina, when you signed up for this trip, you knew the passage would be in cold sleep."

Tina stopped rocking, her face mottled and red. "The company said we could choose. Besides, you're not going in cold sleep, and neither are some of the other techs."

Mandy studied Tina's tear-streaked face. "True. We're needed to fill out missing crew. What if we gave you a stronger sedative? Would that help?"

The woman's face got so pale Mandy feared she would pass out. *At least that would solve the problem.*

"No! You can't force me in there!"

"All right, Tina. Calm down. Let's see what we can do. Your specialties are hydroponics and exo-botany, right?"

"Yes, ma'am."

"Hermes, what can we do with those two?" Almost immediately a solution appeared on the screen. Mandy silently blessed the AI. "You're in luck. They're short a replacement tech in the hydro unit. Report to O'Malley in hydroponics. He'll get you settled."

Tina jumped up, a huge smile lighting her plain face. She grabbed Mandy's hand, almost crushing Mandy's bones in her exuberance. "Thank you, ma'am.

36

You won't regret this, I promise."

"That's all right, Tina." Mandy watched as the woman bounded out of the office. She shook her hand to relieve the cramp from Tina's handshake and turned back to the monitor. "Hermes? Thank you for the help. Please make the appropriate changes to the duty rosters."

"Already done, boss."

"Bravo. I enjoyed the performance," a deep voice interrupted Mandy.

Startled, Mandy looked up at one of the tallest men she had ever seen filling out the door to the office. She had a feeling if she stood next to him, the top of her head would barely come to his chest. He easily out-massed Mandy by a hundred pounds and, judging by the way his jumpsuit fit, without an ounce of fat. Like most career spacers, his dark hair was clipped close to the scalp, though he had a long, white, beaded braid behind his left ear. Almost like a Warrior. *Interesting.* Mandy glanced at the insignia on his uniform, similar to hers but with six stars, and realized that here, finally, was the captain.

Declan Chalmers exuded controlled power. Mandy recalled bits from the personnel file she'd looked up. The only child of esteemed scientists, he had graduated with honors from the Aboolean Science and Technology Institute before joining Fleet and heading for the stars. He'd been decorated and promoted for meritorious service almost as many times as he'd been demoted for insubordination and had opted out of active service and into the reserves seven years ago, when he'd been posted to the *Phoenix*. His new assignment, after this trip, would be to the exploration and discovery ship, the *Pythias*. Unfortunately, the file hadn't told Mandy anything about the man. And she really wanted to know.

"Thank you, Captain. There wouldn't have been a problem if my pencil pushers on Aboo had done their homework. Fortunately, this glitch was a minor one, easily solved."

****

Declan took in the woman sitting in front of him, from the long, coal-black hair held back with a tie, to the expensive, but practical jumpsuit. She was everything Declan disliked—a bureaucrat of the worst type—stubborn, fiery, and determined. Revising his earlier thoughts, she was neither old, nor wrinkled, but Dec wasn't sure about the coddling yet.

"There's no need to thank me. You handled the situation exceedingly well. However," his voice changed from silky smooth to one of warning, "in the future, please don't give my crew any orders without checking with me first."

Miss Ki stared at him. He could see the muscles in her jaw working. Fine, so she was angry. Dec wasn't exactly happy with the way this trip was starting out either.

"I wasn't aware I needed your permission to do my job. These people are my responsibility."

"And this ship and her crew are mine. While you're on my ship, you will follow my orders. Is that clear, Ms. Ki?"

Mandy stood, bracing her hands on the desk. "Like hell I will. You may be in charge of this ship, but *I* am in charge of this mission. Is that clear, Captain?" Without waiting for an answer, she stalked from the room.

Declan followed her from the room and stared at Mandy's retreating back as she marched down the corridor, a thoughtful expression on his face. He didn't know whether he wanted to kiss her or kill her. Of the two, the first definitely held more intrigue. He shook his head. The last thing he needed was to get involved with another woman, especially after the last one. The station manager could have his former companion, although from the way the two of them were entwined when he'd walked in on them, he already had. He quit his musings as Sarah joined him in the office.

"Hermes? Better send fire control up here," Sarah said.

"My censors don't detect any problems."

Sarah laughed. "Cancel the order, Hermes." She turned to Declan. "From the sparks flying off you two, I thought we'd have a blazing inferno. Looks like you struck a nerve."

Declan ignored her and turned as an older man joined them. He wore a Warrior uniform of black tunic, trousers, and knee-high boots, but his braids and beads encompassed all color combinations, showing his status over all Warriors. "Sarah, I'd like you to meet Master General Tyler Davis. General Davis, our Comm-Officer and my second-in-command, Lt. Cmdr. Sarah Thompson."

He bit back a grin when Sarah pulled her nearly perfect posture into even straighter alignment. He could tell from the way her eyes widened when he introduced the general that she recognized the name, if not the man. Amanda Ki and Taka Yu weren't the only VIPs they had on this trip. You didn't get any higher in the

Warrior class than Master General Davis. But then, who better to guard someone of Ki's importance?

"Sir."

"Lieutenant Commander." The general's voice came out deep and raspy, as if abused for many years. He nodded at Sarah and turned to watch Mandy's retreating back.

"Sirs, if you'll excuse me, I need to get up to the bridge," Sarah said.

"Go ahead. I'll be up shortly," Declan said.

"Quite the spitfire, isn't she?" Davis asked.

"Excuse me?" Declan wasn't exactly sure to whom the general was referring.

"Your mission commander, Amanda Ki."

"That's an understatement," he muttered, then paused. Something in Davis's tone told him he knew Ki on more than the surface level. He'd known the general for years, but their paths only crossed on rare occasions. "You know her?"

"Mandy does have her moments."

The way he'd said the name helped Declan remember. He'd known Davis had been a foster father to a young girl, the daughter of a friend, but Ki? He'd never known that. The general traveled in extremely high circles, he thought. "Mandy? General, you don't mean to tell me that—"he paused as Davis raised a warning eyebrow"—woman is the little girl you've been telling everyone about for years."

Davis chuckled. "I never said she didn't have a temper. Her father was my best friend. We remained friends even after he left the service. My one regret is I haven't been able to catch Alvarez."

"Does she know Alvarez might have been on the

station?" Declan asked. John's message had filled him in on the background between Ki and Alvarez. He'd also found out Ki had received a message here on the ship. Once he'd seen the file, he had to give her points for fortitude. You'd have to be a strong person to see something like that and not be rattled—and she'd been getting them almost daily for months. Maybe his initial assessment of her had been wrong. Yes, she was rich, but she'd had to shoulder the responsibility of her family's holdings when she was young and had the specter of Alvarez hanging over her. She'd have to be strong-willed to take on all that and survive. She was definitely not someone who needed coddling. He cocked his head. But maybe she could use a friend.

Davis shook his head at Dec's question. "No, and we're not even certain he was there. Mandy will have to be warned, but I don't think right now is a good time. Tell your AI to keep an eye on her, but circumspectly. I pity the next person she runs into, even if he's Alvarez."

"So do I, General. So do I." Declan turned away. Security had all their resources checking the station, but at least the ship was safe. He'd alerted Honan and Sarah, telling them to double-check all incoming personnel, making sure IDs matched the wearer. Thank goodness they'd been at space anchor and not tied to the station. The placement gave them an extra measure of security.

"How many Warriors do you have with you?" he asked the master general.

"I've commandeered the smallest cold sleep area and am going to bunk six there once the refit is done. I have another two dozen in cold sleep," the general said.

"Things could get a bit cozy for the six," Declan said, thinking about the tight space. They had enough room for a dozen cold sleep pods, but bunking six people? That could be an issue.

"They're Warriors. They'll adapt. Besides, maintenance did a good job of converting the space. There wasn't a problem putting all the pods in the one room?"

"No. We only use the secondary room if we need to. We moved the empty pods down to one of the holds. You don't think this is a Luddite problem, do you?"

The general shook his head. "They're fanatics, but not exceedingly smart. We don't know who is orchestrating this threat, but we have a good idea."

"Alvarez. Is he really that dangerous?"

"Yes. He's extremely intelligent and psychotic—a dangerous combination." Davis let out a sigh. "We're as set as we can be."

"In a way, we're lucky. By sitting at anchor away from the station, we've been able to screen the crew. Nobody could slip past John. He runs one of the best forces in space. Still, I'd rather know ahead of time." Declan glanced at his watch. "I've got to get going. I'll see you later."

He hurried toward the bridge. In less than an hour they'd be away from the station, and he could relax. Declan strolled onto the bridge. Although a large ship, this space was rather small. With the help of Hermes, they only needed three crewmen to man the bridge stations. Sarah sat at communications and internal systems. His best friend and first mate, Honan, took care of security and external systems, and Declan worked as navigator and pilot. Each could take over for the other and often did to keep their skills honed. They had a three-person crew to handle the off-shift, and several of the techs could step in when needed.

"Everything ready?" Declan asked as he slid into his seat.

"Aye, sir," Sarah said. "I already sounded the jump alarms and got final clearance from the station."

Declan keyed in the coordinates for the Xy system then double-checked them with Hermes. Even a minute error could send them spiraling off into unknown space.

"We jump in ten minutes." This was what he liked—a well-ordered crew and ship, no surprises. Like an unguided ship, Declan found his thoughts drifting to a slender woman with ebony hair and haunted eyes. He knew what caused the look and hoped she'd be able to relax here on the safety of the ship. He felt a little twinge of guilt he hadn't told Honan and Sarah all the details about the Alvarez file, but at the time, telling them hadn't seemed as important as getting away from the station. John excelled at his job. They didn't have anything to worry about.

So why was he?

He felt the subtle vibration as the ship changed from idling to full power. The Xy system was three weeks away, then who knew how long they'd have to wait until they found the cause of the plague? The illness had a ten-to-fourteen-day incubation period. Hopefully, the medical staff would make quick work of this since they appeared to know they were dealing with a mutant strain—or so they claimed.

Thankfully, this would be his last milk run. The exploration branch of the service held the real excitement—looking for new planets for colonization.

He'd been accepted earlier but had waited until Sarah and Honan could join him. They made a good team. He felt the surge as the ship entered into jump space and breathed a sigh of relief. Nothing could get them now. He looked around, wondering if Ki had ever seen a working bridge. They had six days of jump time to look forward to before the next junction. Maybe he'd invite her up. He had plenty of time to get to know Ms. Amanda Ki.

"Declan?" Sarah held her hand to her earphone and frowned.

"What?"

"I'm getting an audio message, but awfully garbled. I think it's coming from the station."

Declan stared at her. "You can't send communication in jump space."

One of the best communications people he knew, Sarah nodded. "Confirmed. The message is from the station."

"How?"

Sara shrugged. "Emergency beacon? I'm not sure. We've never gotten one in jump space before."

"Let's hear the dispatch." He listened, but there was so much static, he couldn't make the words out. "Hermes? Can you help clean the transmission up?"

"Attempting same already, Captain. The message is being scrambled locally."

"Locally?" His gut told him this definitely wasn't going to be a milk run. He listened again as Hermes tried to clean up the communique. Dec picked out an occasional word through the mess, but he did recognize John's voice.

"...Declan...dead crew...Ki...varez...ship."

Declan sat straight up in his seat—all sense of peace gone. "Hermes! Repeat the last pulse." He waited impatiently while Hermes worked on the message. An eternity later he listened in disbelief to the final words.

"…Alvarez is on board your ship."

Declan swallowed hard. He swung his seat around to face the others. "There's something you both need to know."

Chapter Four

How dare he, Mandy thought. *Who does he think he is, ordering me around like that! He's big and overbearing and far too...* "Damn. Of all the places and times for me to find someone interesting, but him? And now? Double damn." Mandy found a deserted corridor where she could be alone until she calmed down. She certainly wasn't going to take orders from someone who hadn't even bothered to introduce himself until now, especially when she was in charge of this mission.

She scrubbed her hands over her face, tired of the hassles, the delays, and the problems that seemed to have no solutions. For every delay, more people died. Didn't they know? Didn't anybody care?

The gray carpet muted her footsteps, making her wish she had a door to slam or anything to make some noise. Even the walls were textured to cut down on sound. She paced the corridor, her thoughts whirling. What was wrong with her? She was acting like a child, throwing temper tantrums, and storming off when she didn't get her way. She took a deep breath and exhaled. The last message from Miguel must have rattled her more than she'd realized.

She paused by a view port and gazed out, mesmerized by the scene. The blue and white jewel of Aboo slowly rotated beneath her, a shining beacon in the blackness of space. Somewhere down there was home. Would she see the purple mountains and blue seas ever again? She thought briefly of the friends and family she left behind, and of the people in cold sleep, trusting her to get them to their destination safely. The reflection of a face appeared in the glass, and she jumped, bumping into a man. She recognized him as the same maintenance man who'd asked her for directions earlier.

"Oh! I'm sorry. Are you all right?"

He laughed and brushed an imaginary speck from his immaculate suit. "Fine, ma'am. Since we seem to keep running into each other, may I introduce myself? My name is Damien Michaels."

Mandy held out her hand. "Hi. I'm Mandy. Amanda Ki."

"Oh, the big boss herself." Damien stood taller and looked down on Mandy, like... No. That wasn't possible. This man looked nothing like Miguel. Nothing. And he was much too young. Alvarez was nearly as old as Taka. This man appeared to be a little older than she was.

"What were you thinking about so deeply?" he asked.

"Nothing in particular, just everything in general," she said.

"I can imagine. You've been busy."

Warily, Mandy looked at him. "What do you mean?"

"Nothing much. I heard you single-handedly took on a crazy woman who wouldn't go to sleep, added her to the hydro crew, and had a run-in with the captain."

"She's not crazy, merely unsuitable for cold sleep. News travels fast."

"*Phoenix* is a small ship."

Mandy looked at the seemingly endless corridor stretching in both directions, crisscrossed by side halls and ringed with tubes leading to other levels of the ship and laughed. "Not everyone would call something this big, small." A warning bell rang. "Sounds like we're getting ready to leave. I've got to go. Maybe we'll run into each other again."

"Count on that. Ma'am." He gave her a two-fingered salute and headed off in the opposite direction she was going. She watched him go, not sure why he troubled her, but he did. For one, he was far too friendly with the boss. Most people meeting her would have greeted her and moved on, but not him. He stayed to chat, almost as if he knew her. She shook off her worries and headed for her cabin. She was safe here.

A series of announcements for different departments sounded over the intercom as Mandy checked her quarters then headed for the lounge/dining area. She listened to them absently, dismissing them as unimportant to her. She felt an increase in the subtle vibrations of the ship as the engines powered up for the jump and quickened her pace. A peek in the open lounge door confirmed her suspicion she wasn't the only one hoping for a last glimpse of home. Everyone not on duty stood or sat near the long observation portal, like a group of angels looking through the gates into heaven—or hell. Although crowded, a reverential silence pervaded the room.

Mandy wound her way through the chairs and tables scattered around the area and stood at one end of the viewing deck, gazing at the sight. The station was no more than a tiny speck of light in the distance. They were already past Aino and well on their way out of the solar system. Once they passed the asteroid belt, the view shields would close, and they'd jump.

"Beautiful sight, don't you think?"

Startled, Mandy turned toward a voice she thought she'd never hear again. "Pa…" She glanced around at the surrounding crew and changed what she'd almost said. "Master General Davis! What are you doing here?" A wide smile lit her face as she gazed at her foster father. He'd stepped in when Mandy's parents had died and, along with Taka, had raised her. Seeing him there was like putting a soothing salve on an open wound.

The general grinned at her and stepped up to join Mandy at the window. "You didn't think I'd let you go off gallivanting around the universe without me, did you?"

Mandy drew back and gave him a half-hearted frown. "I'm quite capable of taking care of myself, as you well know. After all, you had your Warriors train me!"

Master General Davis chuckled. "Yes, and you had every drill instructor in my unit screaming their frustration with you. I seem to recall an incident concerning a missing land transport and an underage driver."

Mandy blushed as she remembered the night she'd stolen a military transport vehicle from a bar and ended up stuck in a swamp—accidentally. The general had made her wash and wax every transport in the unit—by hand! She imagined she could still smell the harsh soap on her hands. "I needed to get home."

"We won't go into why you were late or the fact

you didn't have your license yet." He motioned Mandy to a seat.

Mandy pulled out a chair and sat where she could see out. She wasn't going to give up this last chance to see something familiar. "You still haven't told me why you're here."

"The same reason you are. We got word security on Xy-Three has been decimated by the plague. I've got a small troop in cold sleep."

He was lying. Every time the general lied, he rubbed his right thumb, and right now he was close to rubbing the skin off. Mandy clenched her fists beneath the table. She'd let Davis think she didn't know the real reason he was there. "Good idea. I was so busy putting together the techs and getting the ship and supplies, I never thought about that." Mandy relaxed as she watched the planets flash by.

"What about medical? Did you have trouble getting enough people?" he asked.

Mandy looked back at him and grinned. "I left those details to Taka." She bit back a laugh as the general looked around the room. Davis and Taka had enjoyed an on-again, off-again romance for most of her life.

"Taka's here? Where is she? In the lab?"

Her grin turned into a laugh. "How'd you guess? She commandeered one of the smaller cargo bays and turned the space into a lab. Nobody is allowed entrance without her express okay. If I know her, she's already hip deep in experiments and will probably have this problem solved before we get to Xy-Three."

It was Davis's turn to laugh. "I guess I'm not really surprised she's here. Wherever the worst health mess is,

Taka can be found there."

"Sounds like someone else I know." Mandy smiled softly at the older man. Their hectic schedules were the reasons the general and Taka had never gotten together.

"She only took over one bay?"

"She would have taken more, but this is a supply ship, and the rest of the space was taken up with those supplies. So, she commandeered one and built the lab to her liking. Unfortunately, this was the only ship available on short notice, so the refit was a challenge. Taka has multiple blood and tissue samples incubating with various compounds. And she wrangled more equipment than I've ever seen. She's been here a week, setting up. She told me she doesn't think the problem is a virus and not CP. We'll know more once we get there."

She paused as the shields closed over the portal and wondered why she hadn't heard the warning signal for the jump. "I'm glad you're here, Papa D. I feel a lot better knowing you and Taka are here to help." She fought to keep the trembling out of her voice.

"What's wrong, Mandy?" The general gently grasped her shoulder. Never a demonstrative man, the touch showed how much her foster father really did care.

Mandy stared at the people sitting around them, avoiding his eyes. "What could possibly be wrong? You and Taka are here, and I'm finally away from the lawyers and all the hassles. I've got some time to enjoy myself and relax."

"And? Come on, Mandy, talk to me."

"I never could keep anything from you." She sighed. "Before we left the station, I got another one of

Miguel's calling cards."

"Did you tell anyone?"

"Tell whom? Security? I sent them a copy, but you know as well as I do that by the time I got the message, he was long gone. Besides, there's no way he can be on this ship, and we're well on our way. I can relax for at least a little while, and so can you." She felt the subtle difference in ship vibrations as the engines shifted to jump mode.

The inexperienced people looked around the room, confusion on some of their faces. Mandy knew most of them were aware of what had happened but had never experienced a hyper-jump before and found the occurrence startling. The ship shuddered as if they'd run into something, and she felt a quick sensation of disorientation. Any longer and she—and a lot of other people—would have been space sick, not a pleasant experience.

Two crewmen lounging at a nearby table laughed at the newbies. "Look at the groundhogs. They don't even know what a hyper-jump is."

One man, a large, unkempt spacer with greasy stains on his jumpsuit oinked and hid his head under the table. "Look at me. I'm a scared little groundhog."

Tom, the cargo super Mandy had worked with, jumped up from his seat and advanced toward the crewmen. Mandy motioned for the general to stay seated and moved to block Tom.

"Tom, calm down. We don't want any trouble." She pushed against his chest as the crewmen continued to laugh.

"What's the matter, groundhog? Won't your mommy let you come over and play?" The larger of the two men taunted them.

Mandy put a hand on Tom's arm to stop him from doing something he'd regret. The man taunting them sauntered over to her. He was easily double Mandy's size, like Chalmers, but, where the captain was all lean muscle, this man ran to fat. When he got close enough to smell, Mandy had no doubt at all what he had spent his shore leave doing. He reeked of alcohol, cheap perfume, and hadn't seen the inside of a shower stall in several days.

"Is there something I can do for you?" Mandy asked, eyes narrowed and every nerve in her body stretched to the limit. She knew she had the capability of stopping the man, but she'd rather not use force if at all possible. Peripherally, she saw Davis taking Tom and the other crewman in hand.

The man stared at Mandy, making her shiver in revulsion. "Why don't you go back to whatever hole you crawled out of. Out here is no place for some fancy pants like you."

"Jenkins! To your quarters. Now." Declan's voice from behind her broke through the tension, startling Mandy. The captain glared at the unkempt man. "You're confined to quarters and on report. And you"—he turned to the other man—"are damn lucky I'm in a good mood. If I hear any more talk like that, you'll end up in the brig. Out." He watched the retreating backs of the crewmen, then turned to the others. "Please accept my apologies. We didn't have much choice in the crew we took on. Ms. Ki, General, would you please join me in my office?"

Although the words were couched as an invitation, Mandy had the distinct feeling they couldn't refuse. She followed Declan and the general into the corridor.

"What's up, Declan?" Davis asked.

"Not here." Declan dropped back to speak with Mandy.

Davis nodded once at him, and Mandy understood that whatever Declan wanted would have to wait until they got to his office.

"I know you haven't had much of a chance to explore the ship yet. Is there anything you want to know about her?" Declan asked Mandy.

She looked up at the man beside her. She'd been wrong about his height—but barely. She came up to Declan's shoulder, not his chest. Mandy had always been shy about her height—or lack thereof. Barely five feet tall, she'd learned to use abilities other than size to her advantage.

The captain moved with the easy grace of a natural athlete. A tiny dimple in his cheek showed when he smiled, which Mandy thought happened only rarely. His eyes were the color of the gray of the Carnbourn sea on a stormy day—a color no Aboolean with their gold-tinged eyes would ever be able to have. Except for the color of his eyes and the paleness of his skin, he could pass for an Aboolean from one of the northern clans. He had the height and build of those clans. She brought her attention back to his offer of a tour. "Thank you, Captain, but that's not necessary. Hermes has been assisting me where needed." She kept her tone light, to match his. Whatever he wanted them for in his office, he didn't want anyone else to know.

"I'm glad he could help." He stepped aside as the door swished open and gestured for Mandy and Davis to precede him.

"Hermes, put a privacy lock on my door and give us low white noise." He drew two chairs up to his desk and motioned Mandy and Davis into them.

"Done, Captain," Hermes said.

****

The general had seen the way Declan reacted in the lounge and found his actions amusing. The words had come from the captain, but his stance over Mandy had come from a man protecting a mate. Declan had never settled down. Davis also knew Mandy had never gotten serious about any one man. Although there'd been plenty of opportunities with suitors when she was younger. For some reason, after one or two dates, they'd all dropped her. He'd been there to pick up the pieces more than once as Mandy cried her heart out, wondering why nobody would love her. The idea of his two favorite people getting together intrigued Davis. He'd have to see what he could do to foster the feelings between the two. He wasn't above playing matchmaker.

"Okay, Declan, what's going on?" Davis asked. "I assume this has something to do with Alvarez."

"Yes. Although we can't be sure, there is a strong possibility he's on this ship."

"I'm not surprised," Davis said. He glanced at Mandy's suddenly pale face. He wanted to pick her up and soothe away her pain as he had when she was a little girl, but a lollipop and silly face wouldn't work with the woman sitting next to him.

"What I can't figure out is how he slipped in. We had security so tight a bacterium couldn't get through," Declan said.

Mandy twisted her fingers in her lap. "You don't know Miguel. He's a security and electronics expert. If a way existed, he'd find one."

"Who is this guy?" Declan asked, his head cocked to one side. "I mean, I've read his dossier, but the file doesn't explain what he wants with you."

"He wants control of the companies and me. Then he wants me dead," Mandy whispered. "Like my parents."

"Yes and no," Davis spoke up. "He's fixated on you because of who you are and your holdings, but he doesn't merely want your death. He won't be satisfied with only that."

Mandy swallowed hard. "What could be worse than my death? He's been torturing me for months with his insane messages."

Davis watched as Mandy struggled to compose herself. He turned his attention to Declan to give her time.

"My guess is, there's torture and then there's torture," Declan said. "From the looks of the message, I guess he's into some kind of ancient rites."

"Good eye," Davis agreed. "He uses ancient Boherean from the southern continent on Aboo, along with a conglomeration of other cultures and his own megalomania." He paused and turned to Mandy. "Actually, what you don't know is he's been sending you those messages for two years. Until he escaped the facility where he was being held, we were able to stop them from getting to you."

"How do you know all this?" Declan asked.

"Because I was on the original panel that put him away, and I'm on the panel keeping his case open. I probably know more about him than anyone. Some of what I'm about to tell you is still classified and must go no further than this room." Davis waited until both Mandy and Declan nodded.

"Alvarez wasn't only Ki's business partner. Originally, he was head of security on Ki's ship the *Shangri-La* and was an excellent officer. His wife, Drema, was the exo-botanist. They'd had a pretty successful run with the Xy system. Under the rules of entitlement, the crew staked out claims on various planets in the system. Most of them picked out pieces of Xy-One, but only Ki and Alvarez picked Xy-Three. Of the two, three was the more geologically active and scared off most people. Although there was evidence of past civilizations, there was no sign of current societies, unlike Xy-One and Two. Alvarez and Drema picked out a stretch of land on the northern continent while the Kis took two mountainous islands closer to the equator."

Mandy smiled, though he saw tears shimmering in her eyes. "They would. Mom and Dad always loved the mountains. Is that when they found the opals? Is that what started all this?"

"In a way. Xy-Three is where they discovered the opals and the plants. They came back to Aboo and filed their claims. Tests showed the potential for the opals in power and communications and the plants in pharmaceuticals. Since Drema had discovered the plants, Ki agreed to a partnership with them. He and Alvarez left active service for reserve status and went into business. Your father concentrated on the opals while Drema and your mother worked on the drug components. To say they were successful would be an understatement.

"The only dark spot was what happened to Drema.

On one of their trips to Xy-Three, she was working with a plant that had high potential in a variety of brain disorders. She was gathering some samples of white root when she accidentally scratched herself on a thorn. An hour later, she was dead. Alvarez was so mad with grief, he tried to kill himself with the same plant, but failed. The poison that killed Drema turned Miguel psychotic. Your mother put him in restraints and sedated him while your father took care of Drema's body. In accordance with her wishes, she was cremated, and her ashes scattered over the island. Alvarez found this out later. Your folks came back to Aboo as quickly as possible and got him into a facility. A month later, the medics declared him cured and set him free. What nobody knew was the toxins are extremely addictive and long lasting. One dose and you're hooked for life. There is no cure. The upside—if there is one—is the drugs remain in your system for a long time. Users don't have to have regular fixes, although the initial effects of the drug do wear off in due course. Unfortunately, the psychosis doesn't. The alterations in the brain are permanent and continue to mutate and change the brain. In Alvarez's case, he had enough in his system to last the entire time he was in rehab. After he was released, he broke into the labs and stole the entire supply. He bided his time and a year later went back to Xy-Three with your parents where he renewed his supply. They dropped off personnel and equipment and picked up a supply of opals. We found out later about the thefts. They were on their way home when the trouble began."

"What kind of trouble?" Declan asked.

"A sick crew." He held up his hand to keep Declan

from interrupting. "In this case, they had a legitimate illness—BX-16, an ancient illness, but still a problem in some places. But they couldn't figure out how the germ got on board. The filters were all clean with no contamination anywhere. Nobody suspected Alvarez at first. He took a shuttle out supposedly to check on an asteroid. The main ship blew up with all aboard. He was considered a lucky survivor—at least until later."

"How was he found out?"

"I can tell you that, at least in part, Captain," Mandy said. "When word got back to us, the estate people took over. During the investigation, we discovered Miguel had been embezzling money from the company almost since inception. All his holdings were forfeited to the partners. As my parents' sole heir, they came to me."

Davis nodded. "That's part of the story. There's more, but I don't want to get into those issues right now. I have everything on a data disk I'll give to you to study. Let's say, he's still psychotic and has no problem killing anyone who gets in his way. Declan, I'd like to use my men."

Declan shook his head. "Not yet. We know he's on board ship, but he doesn't know we know. If your Warriors start running around, he may do something worse than send messages. Right now, we still have the advantage."

"Good point," Davis agreed. "But your security crew is extremely small, and I know you don't have any surveillance or other equipment. So what do you want to do?"

"My first inclination is to move Amanda to more secure quarters, perhaps a cabin closer to mine, but that would tip our hand too. I'm going to start by having our doctor run a gene scan on all personnel who are awake. We'll say the tests are a precaution against the plague. Hopefully, we'll catch him that way."

"We have a good start, but I have a feeling catching him won't be easy," Mandy said.

"Hermes?" Declan said.

"Yes, sir?"

"Who's our replacement doctor?"

"Tricia Kirby."

Davis saw Declan wince and wondered what the story was there.

"My luck." As if he'd noticed the puzzled looks on Mandy and Davis's faces, he sighed. "A long story. Mandy, I'd also like to put a security watch on you."

Davis's goddaughter shook her head. "I don't want bodyguards following me around the place. That would really tip our hand."

"That's not exactly what I had in mind. Hermes, if Amanda uses the term…"

"Panther," Mandy said to his silent question.

"All right. When she says the word panther, you will raise the alarm and be quick."

"Aye, sir. Would you like active or passive interaction?"

"Passive unless extreme duress."

"What do you mean active or passive?"

"Hermes has the capability of activating several deterrents including sticky fields and sleep gas in small areas or wide dispersal. All are non-lethal but take effect quickly. If you are in immediate danger, he'll activate whatever he deems appropriate to the situation. Unfortunately, you'll also be caught, but then we'll have time to get you out of the problem."

Mandy nodded. "I agree. You've come up with a good plan, and I won't be hampered by security measures."

Davis knew she hated being hemmed in, and this would give her the freedom she craved, even if she was still contained within the ship. He'd be sure to get some of his people to keep an eye on her—circumspectly, but he wasn't leaving anything to chance.

"One other item," Declan said. "Once we get to the jump junction, I'm going to change course for Fleet Services on Crowley Station. The sooner I get rid of Alvarez, the happier I'll be."

"We can't do that, Captain," Mandy argued. "Xy-Three needs us. Any delays mean more people will die. I didn't think you were the type to run from a fight."

"I'm not. But that's why I'm changing course. I don't want any of those deaths to be on my ship."

"With what we've planned, there won't be. We have the scans, and we can wake up the Warriors if necessary. We have got to get to Xy-Three," Mandy insisted.

"As I told you earlier, this ship and her crew—all of her crew—are my responsibility. We will change course at jump junction. End of discussion."

Mandy stood and glared at Declan. "We may be done with this meeting, Captain, but we are definitely not finished with this discussion." She stormed from the room with her head held high.

Davis watched her leave and wondered at her temper. He'd known Mandy since her birth and had never seen her so strongly affected by anyone. He turned his gaze to Declan. The captain had been a colleague and friend for almost a dozen years and was normally calm under any sort of circumstances.

He rose, a smile on his face. Yes, there was definitely something going on between these two. "If you'll excuse me, Declan, I think I'd better go check on my people."

"What?" Declan continued staring at the door. "Oh. Yes. I'll talk to you later." He waved the general out of his office. "Hermes?"

Chapter Five

General Davis wanted to be in sickbay when Alvarez got scanned, but first he needed to stop by his cabin to get his favorite gun—an old-fashioned projectile weapon. Although, hopelessly out of date, he preferred the piece to newer versions. They were too clean, too neat. Killing was a messy business and should be treated as such. Besides, he liked the way the weapon felt in his hand. Technically, he wasn't supposed to have one without informing security, but there was no way this madman was going to get away from him again. He would make sure Alvarez paid for what he'd done all those years ago and the torture he continued to put Mandy through. An illicit weapon was the least of security's worries.

He'd get the data disk, drop the disk off with Declan, and then go to sickbay. He had a slight twinge of conscience as he thought about the contents of the disk. There were things he'd done to Alvarez he wasn't proud of, but given the same circumstances, he didn't think he'd do anything differently. He hoped Declan would understand, and he prayed Mandy would.

Davis opened the door to his quarters and walked into a nightmare. Furniture in the sitting area had been overturned, and what wasn't broken had been slashed to ribbons. He stopped inside the door and listened. Someone was in the sleeping area. As quietly as possible, he moved toward the wall dividing the two sections. He stepped over a broken chair but caught his foot on a leg and knocked the chair into the wall. He froze—waiting—listening.

No sounds came from the sleeping area. Long seconds passed. Finally, Davis took a chance and moved. He reached down to pick up the broken chair leg as a weapon. He straightened and came face to face with the lethal end of a long, curved knife.

"Well, well, old man. We meet again."

Davis identified the voice and knew immediately who this man was though he looked different.

"You don't recognize me, do you? Good. Because I paid some outrageously high credits to the medics who worked on me." He gave a small bow, kept his hate filled gaze on Davis's face. "Of course, I got the credits back when I killed them. Couldn't have anyone letting out what I look like now, could I?"

"Alvarez." He couldn't believe the man's transformation—even his eyes were a different color. Even knowing Alvarez as well as he did, there was no way he'd connect this man with the madman.

"Right on the first try, Master General." He motioned Davis over to the bed. "I'm sure you remember this." He pulled the high collar on his jumpsuit down, revealing a thin red scar at the base of his neck. "Compliments of your prison collar. I had the medic leave this as a reminder. Took Trella and me a bit of time to figure out everything, but, as you can see, we did. Trella sacrificed her life for the secret. She died screaming a curse on your name."

Alvarez backed up when Davis shifted his seat. "Uh-uh. I like you sitting right there. Funny thing about that collar. How could such an evil little device show up in the hands of one of our most outstanding citizens? What kind of deal with the devil did you make to get one?"

"You should know," Davis returned. He stared at the scar. He'd secured the collar around Alvarez's neck on the day of his sentencing. He'd pulled a few strings—surprisingly few—to get the highly secret device. That Alvarez had used the device on his own sister-in-law told Davis the depths of the man's insanity. He had no morals left at all—if he'd ever had them. "I thought Trella died in a plane crash."

Alvarez laughed—a harsh, bitter sound. "You liked our little ruse? The only person who died in the crash was a gullible missionary. Trella died in my arms from the poison your little device injected into her. She is now one with her sister Drema." He shook his head as though fighting off the memories.

Davis frowned. "Poisons? What are you talking about? The collar is mechanical, not pharmaceutical."

Alvarez raised an eyebrow. "Is that what you think? Well, I guess you don't know everything, do you, General? The leads can be directly linked to the nervous and circulatory systems. You can introduce whatever chemicals you want in the amounts you want, including the white root plant. Trella was experimenting with different combinations, trying to come up with a synthetic formula. The white root drug is ambrosia from the gods. Only those mortals selected by the gods can handle the effects. Unfortunately, Trella miscalculated the dosage, and the collar dumped too much into her system. She was like Drema in that respect. Her tests used up almost the last of my supplies. I wonder how well our dear Amanda will stand up to the test. Is she a mortal? Or is she one of the gods?

Davis clenched his jaw as a wave of horror washed through him. What had he unleashed? Even though he hadn't known about the full uses of the collar, the fault belonged to him. No wonder the labs had been so eager to release the device to him. They'd needed a living subject, and he'd handed them one on a silver platter, but the plan had failed when Alvarez escaped. Alvarez alone was bad enough but, with the collar in his possession, his madness would know no end.

"All right, General, I know you have the security codes to get me into the labs. Where are they?"

Davis carefully kept his face blank. Did Alvarez really know where the codes were, or was he fishing? Davis sat on the edge of the bed and watched for an opportunity to jump Alvarez. He knew he would only get one chance to alert security. His duty was to alert Declan. He also knew he was probably going to die. The feeling was nothing new—he had faced death many times in the past, but this time he wanted to take this monster with him. "I don't know what you're talking about."

Alvarez backhanded Davis across the face. "I'm not stupid, General. Where is the disk?"

Davis tasted blood. His only regret was he wouldn't be around to see what, if anything, would happen between Declan and Mandy. He waited for his opening and when one came, lunged, catching Alvarez in his midsection. Both men went down. The knife fell from Alvarez's hand and slid under the bed, out of reach. Davis drove his fist into Alvarez's face, feeling a satisfying crunch of bone.

Alvarez dug his fingers into Davis's eyes, forcing him up and off of him. He rolled to his feet and swung at Davis, connecting with a solid thump to Davis's midsection. He hit him again, using short, sharp blows that took their toll.

The exertion wore on Davis. He gasped for air, dragging each breath through fire-filled lungs. Although he'd kept in good physical shape, he hadn't been in a free-for-all brawl for years, maybe decades.

"Hermes!" Davis called out before falling under a vicious blow to his head. The room reeled, and he feared he was going to be sick. He looked up in time to see Alvarez's hand descending toward his neck. Clutched between two fingers was a long, dagger-like thorn. He had a pretty good idea what the thorn contained.

"Don't worry about anyone coming to your aid, old man. I disabled the system. Now tell me where the codes are."

Davis grinned, blood dripping from his mouth and nose. "You'll never hear them from me." He felt a sharp pain at the side of his neck. His last conscious thoughts were of Mandy.

Alvarez searched Davis's body.

"Nothing." He kicked Davis in the ribs. "Where is the bloody disk you old bastard?"

Alvarez went to the open air vent near the ceiling and climbed in, pulling the covering closed behind him. A few minutes later, he opened the grate over the vent in his quarters and jumped down to the floor. He quickly resealed the vent, tossed his screwdriver in the air, and neatly caught the tool.

"Well, Master General, you may have won this skirmish, but the war is far from over."

Chapter Six

Mandy chewed her lip as she glanced around her small cabin. What was wrong with her? She was never like this. She had to be reacting to the stress of events with Xy-Three and Miguel. What other explanation could there be? She needed to get rid of some of her energy. "Hermes?"

"Yes, boss?"

"Is there somewhere I can work up a good sweat?"

"There is a fully equipped gym next to medical."

"Thank you." Mandy stripped out of her jumpsuit and pulled on a pair of black shorts and a black sleeveless shirt. A few minutes later she entered the gym area. Hermes wasn't kidding when he'd said the gym was fully equipped. Inside the cavernous room, electronic weight bands hung from pegs near the door along with ropes, hand mitts, and a variety of equipment for the martial arts. Mats covered a quarter of the floor area with more stacked against the wall. Across the back was a lap pool and, ten feet above the floor, a jogging balcony ringed the wall. Opposite the pool was a gymnast's dream area with rings, balance beams, bars, and other equipment. Glancing around, she realized she wasn't the only one looking for a chance to work out as quite a few people were using the area.

She spotted a couple on the mats. She recognized Honan but not the woman with him. She was tall and slim, with well-defined muscles and wore her pale blonde hair in a short style setting off high cheekbones and wide-set eyes. She had Warrior beads woven into her hair, but the length and color marked her as from a different tribe than Honan. Mandy watched as the two performed a martial arts exercise. They were so perfectly in tune with each other she felt as if she was watching one person. They finished the exercise and bowed to each other before Honan turned to Mandy with a smile.

"Hello, Ms. Ki. Are you here to watch or to work?"

Mandy grinned back. "While I appreciate what I saw, I could use a good workout. Know anybody who could oblige?" She looked at the tall woman, sizing her up as an opponent.

"Forgive my manners," Honan said. "May I present Lt. Cmdr. Sarah Thompson, our com-officer and second-in-command."

Mandy dipped her head in acknowledgement. "Lieutenant Commander."

"Please, call me Sarah. With such a small crew, we rarely stand on ceremony."

"And I'm Mandy. Would either of you be up to some Thillo-toum or Gwallou?" She judged Honan's size. He was an expert in several forms of hand-to-hand combat and, if she'd read his dossier correctly, he was security chief for a reason. A champion fighter and well-versed in the kicking, punching, and more of the two forms she'd suggested.

Honan grinned at her challenge.

"Sarah, why don't you mediate while I see what our newest passenger can do?" He turned to Mandy. "Are you up for a battle?"

Sarah stared hard at Honan towering over Mandy. "You've got to be kidding. Mandy, this may be disloyal, but I've got to warn you, he's been Fleet champion in hand-to-hand three years running."

Mandy grinned back as she took up her stance on the mats. "Only three years, huh?" She bowed to Honan as he took up his stance opposite her.

****

"Captain?"

Declan looked up from the chart table where he worked. "Yes, Hermes?"

"I think you should see this." The view screen across the front of the bridge came to life. He sat down when he saw a wide shot of the gym packed with crew all watching something in one corner.

"What's going on, Hermes?"

Hermes zoomed in and Declan's mouth opened, then closed with a snap. As he watched, Mandy executed a feint and neatly flipped Honan onto his back but couldn't hold him. The crew erupted into cheers and jeers as Honan sprang up and then threw Mandy.

"What's the score, Hermes?" he asked as Mandy managed to get out of Honan's hold.

"Dead even."

"How long has the match been going on?"

"Twenty minutes."

Declan sat back and watched the match in amazement. He knew Honan's skills—he'd sparred with him often enough. From what he could see, Honan wasn't pulling back any more than he usually did in practice. "Hermes, give them five more minutes, then call Honan to the bridge. Tell him we have a Code 5. Oh, and make sure they break at a tie."

"Code 5? I cannot find a Code 5 in my data banks, Captain."

"I'd be surprised if you did. Code 5 is a win-win situation, especially with a woman, and is something Honan and I have used since we were at the academy together." He pursed his lips when Hermes chuckled. Declan watched the remainder of the match, keeping a close eye on Mandy. She was agile and strong for her size but, knowing she would fail, didn't rely on strength to overcome her opponent. Instead, she used her adversary's size against him. She was an incredibly talented woman as well as beautiful. Dec was almost disappointed when Hermes called for Honan, even though he was the one who'd ordered the end. He watched the two combatants bow to each other and then switched the screen back to normal security.

****

Sarah tossed a towel to Mandy. "You've got some amazing skills, Mandy. I enjoyed seeing him taken down a peg or two," she said as she grinned at Honan.

"I'll remember that on your next evaluation," Honan countered. "Mandy, this has been an honor." Honan bowed to her again as the gym quickly emptied.

Mandy bowed back also, and then rubbed her shoulder. "If you feel even half the times I connected with you, you're as sore as I am."

"Fortunately, only half of what you aimed had your full power behind them," Honan said with a grin.

Mandy chuckled. "I wasn't the only one holding back. By the way, don't you have to get to the bridge?"

"I've got time. Go hit the spa. I'll see you both in a while." He sauntered off.

Mandy turned to Sarah. "Spa? What's he mean?"

"What would you say to a hydro-massage?"

"I'd say I'd died and gone to Heaven. But what about Honan? I don't feel right taking one all to myself." Ships rarely had one of the specialized tubs on board. Having one on a cargo ship verged on the decadent.

"Not to worry. We've got two, compliments of the last guests we had on board." Sarah smiled at Mandy's questioning look. "Last year, the owner had a sudden urge to cruise around the solar system. He, his three partners, and their…um, special friends demanded we have the spas installed, as well as some other exotic amenities. That was an interesting trip."

"I'll bet." Their actions went against every precept in the Ki Company. Mandy filed the knowledge in the back of her mind. Maybe she should send Mali a note and have him look into who had been in charge of this ship. Meanwhile, Sarah led her to a small room off the gym. The room was bare except for a large tub surrounded by a blue and cream tiled bench.

"Here are the controls. I'll be back in thirty minutes," Sarah said.

"Thanks." Mandy turned on the taps and a thick, warm, cream-colored liquid filled the tub. She stripped her sweat-soaked clothes off and stepped down into the tub. Once she'd settled into a reclining seat, she turned on the jet controls. "Hermes?"

"Yes, boss?"

"What kind of music do you have in your library?"

"A wide variety. What would you like?"

"Something environmental with lute and windpipes." She closed her eyes as the music echoed softly in the small room. "Thanks, Hermes. That's perfect."

She relaxed into the fluid, letting the warmth soothe her sore muscles. She was half-asleep, lost in the music and her own thoughts, when she felt a cool breeze on her face.

"Sarah? Is my time up already?"

There was no answer. Mandy opened her eyes and looked around. The room was empty. She checked the timer. She only had five minutes left so she turned off the controls and reset them to drain and sanitize the fluid. Her muscles felt better, but she had the strangest feeling something wasn't right. She was finishing drying off when Sarah walked in.

"Thought you could use this," Sarah said as she tossed Mandy a bundle.

Mandy opened the pack to find a long deep navy-blue silken robe with cream trim and a high neckline, and slippers. The thoughtful gesture touched her. In her past, most people did favors for her because they wanted something in return. But she didn't believe that of Sarah. "Thanks."

She slipped the robe on, the material falling in soft folds to her ankles, and Mandy looked at Sarah with a smile. "Let me guess, this probably comes to your knees."

Sarah laughed. "Well, a little farther than that, but not all the way to my ankles. I figured you wouldn't want to put your work-out clothes back on."

"You're so right." Mandy picked up her clothes. She jumped as something small fell out and clattered to the floor. Mandy stared at the small, beaded necklace. A bright red feather stuck out of the beads.

"What's this?" Sarah asked. She picked up the

necklace and frowned at Mandy. "What's wrong?"

Mandy took the necklace in shaking fingers. "This...this is, um, a necklace made from monteri wood."

"Is that yours? And what's with the feather?"

Mandy's voice emerged as a bare whisper. "The necklace belonged to my father and is a family heirloom, sacred to the people he came from. I thought this was lost forever when he died. He never took the necklace off. This doesn't belong." She pulled the quill loose and stood there staring at the feather.

"Does the feather mean something?"

Mandy took a deep breath and exhaled slowly. "This is an ancient symbol of Aboolean sacrifice."

"What? I assume this wasn't there when you came in."

"No. Although, a few minutes before you arrived, I felt a slight draft I thought was you."

"You didn't see anyone?"

"No. I wasn't watching for anyone."

"Hermes," Sarah called. "Is Declan on the bridge?"

"Yes. Do you want me to get him?"

"No. Ask him to meet us in his office in fifteen minutes."

"Aye, ma'am."

Mandy gathered her clothes, checking carefully to make sure there were no more surprises. "Sarah, Hermes wouldn't by any chance have security cameras around, would he?"

"Yes and no. He has them, but not in this area, again, thanks to the owners. They said they wanted their privacy. Guess we're going to have to change that." She led the way to Mandy's quarters.

"Sarah, you don't have to stay with me," Mandy said. "I can meet you and the captain at his office."

"Oh, that's all right. I'm not doing anything else right now."

Her statement made Mandy suspicious. "Uh huh. I guess you're my designated babysitter." She watched a blush spread across Sarah's fair face. "So, what'd you do to get stuck with this detail? Must have been something really bad." She grinned when Sarah chuckled and palmed the door control on her cabin. A blast of frigid air hit her from the open door. "What the devil?"

Sarah stopped in the doorway. "Tell me this isn't your normal setting?"

Mandy shook her head and grabbed a blanket off the bed to wrap around herself.

"Hermes? What are the environmental levels for this cabin set at?" Sarah asked.

"Seventy-two degrees and forty-five percent humidity."

"What is the current reading?"

"Seventy-two degrees and forty-five percent humidity."

Sarah went over to Mandy's console. "May I?" Mandy nodded and Sarah keyed in a code.

"Maintenance." A bored looking crewman answered her call. Mandy thought he was the same man she'd run into earlier, but she wasn't quite sure. His one eye was slightly discolored, and his face looked like he'd tried to cover the mark with makeup. His lip was definitely swollen. He looked like he'd been in a fight.

"This is Cmdr. Thompson. I'm calling from cabin 10-A, and the temperature is absolutely frigid in here.

Can you check the environmental controls out?"

The crewman checked a palm pad. "We're having some trouble with several cabins in the surrounding area, ma'am. We're working on the problem and will get back to you as soon as possible. Thank you for your notice." The screen went blank.

"Working on the problem?" Mandy said. She gathered some clean clothes from her drawers. "They damned well better be working on the problem."

"Come on, you can change in my cabin," Sarah said. "And not as my assignment—but as my friend."

At that point, Mandy would have agreed to dress in the corridor in the middle of shift-change. "Thanks." She grabbed her clothes and followed Sarah. "Does this happen often?"

"The glitches have been getting worse. The *Phoenix* is an old ship, and the owners haven't bothered to do any upgrades, or even some repairs, in a while. We were hoping to get some re-fitting done while we were in space dock, but the owners refused. They claimed if Fleet wanted us so badly, Fleet could do the repairs. The regular crew knows all the little idiosyncrasies, but with all the new people, I expect malfunctions will be a bit worse."

Mandy winced at the slight on the owner. Why weren't repairs being taken care of? Spacers had to be away from family for sometimes years at a time, and they should at least be comfortable in their work. She was definitely going to have Mali look into the company. They got to Sarah's room, and Mandy stopped in surprise. Gone were the utilitarian gray and navy décor. Sarah's walls and ceiling were painted with scenes that made her feel like she'd stepped onto a desert plateau. Even the carpeting was soft shades of tan and brown interwoven with rust. One wall looked on a russet sunset while a full moon rose on the opposite wall. Instead of a box bed, Sarah had artfully arranged a pallet in one corner. She even had several live plants sitting in strategic spots.

Mandy looked at the room in awe. "This is incredible. The scene looks like the desert area around the Ethereal Wastelands on Aboo. Are you the artist?"

Sarah smiled and nodded. "I'm actually from the Wastelands. This is my ancestors' home. A short walk over that rise you see is the family compound. Time goes faster on these runs if you have a hobby. Among the regular crew we have chefs, published writers, musicians, and scholars with multiple degrees. We've got quite a group. I'm going to miss them."

Mandy slipped into her clothes, glad for the warmth of Sarah's cabin. "What do you mean you'll miss them?"

"This is our last milk run. Declan, Honan, and I will ship out with a few of the others to an exploration ship."

"I don't know whether to offer my congratulations or my condolences," Mandy said. She handed the robe back to Sarah. "But I do offer my apologies. I shouldn't have snapped at you like I did earlier. I don't know what's wrong with me lately."

"I'd say you have a case of plain old-fashioned stress. Anyone who's gone through what you have and still comes out smiling deserves to blow off steam now and then." Sarah stuck her hand out. "Friends?"

Mandy grasped Sarah's warm hand. "Friends." She followed Sarah out to the corridor. "Sarah, do we go anywhere near General Davis's quarters on the way to the captain's cabin?"

"Yes. His berth is two doors down from Declan's. Why?"

"I'd like to stop there first, if that's okay."

"Sure. We should probably let him in on what happened anyway."

A few minutes later, they stopped at the general's cabin. The door was slightly open, enough to peek in, but not enough to enter. Mandy looked down and saw a broken chair leg jammed in the door.

"That's odd," she said. She tried to open the door, but the panel refused to budge.

"Hermes," Sarah called. "Get Declan here now."

"Papa D?" Mandy called. She pulled at the opening, trying to get the door to move even a little. She tugged until her hands were slick with sweat.

"That won't work." Declan gently grasped her hands and pulled them away.

"So, get me in there!"

"Hermes, emergency override on the door to Cabin 2," Declan said.

Nothing happened.

"Hermes?"

"A-a-aye, C-c-captain?"

Mandy looked at Sarah who only shrugged in confusion.

"I need an emergency override on the door to Cabin 2."

"And who are you?" Hermes's voice dropped from a light tenor to a deep bass then changed to a sultry, but most definitely feminine voice.

Mandy could almost see waves of anger coming

79

off the captain. She wouldn't have been surprised to see him grab the door and force it open like she'd been trying to do.

"This is Captain Declan Chalmers and I want an emergency override on the door to Cabin 2. Now."

"All right. All right. You don't have to get huffy." This time Hermes sounded like a petulant child. An interminable minute later the door slid open.

Mandy quickly looked at the chaos in the living area but didn't see anything other than the mess. She moved into the sleeping area, which wasn't in any better shape. Drawers hung open, and clothing and bedding lay in a jumbled mess. On the far side of the bed, hidden from view, Mandy found Davis's inert form on the floor.

"Captain! In here! Hurry!" She knelt by Davis and checked for a pulse. The racing faintness when she found the beat scared her more than the bruises and blood trickling from his mouth and nose.

Declan knelt next to her and quickly checked the general over. He looked up at Sarah and nodded toward the door. "Sick bay! Medical emergency in Cabin 2." He waited a couple seconds. "Sick bay, do you read?" There was no answer. He punched a button on his wrist unit. "Sick bay, medical emergency in Cabin 2."

"They're on their way, Captain. Sarah alerted us."

The doctor and her aide arrived as Declan signed off. "What happened?" Trish asked. She looked around the room and answered her own question. "A fight? On your ship? Tsk, tsk, Declan, you're slipping."

Mandy looked up to see a dark-haired, olive-skinned beauty standing there wearing the white uniform with red and blue piping that marked her as medical personnel. The woman frowned down at her, eyes narrowed and mouth pursed. The hatred Mandy felt from the doctor was almost a physical force. Had she been less concerned about the general, she'd have wondered about the doctor's intense feelings. As far as she knew, she'd never met the woman.

"Enough with the sarcasm, Trish." Declan moved out of the way. "Master General Davis needs you. Take care of him."

Declan gently pulled Mandy away from the general. "Come on. Let them do their job."

Tears shone in Mandy's dark eyes, but none spilled over. She followed the captain out even though everything in her told her to stay. At the very least, she needed to tell Taka. She knew there was nothing she could do to help, and she'd only be in the way. The best way she could help the general was to find out who'd done this, although she had a pretty good idea. She righted the one chair not broken and sat down. Sarah stood at the dismantled com-unit, a tester in her hand. Mandy nodded to her. "So, what do we do now, Captain?"

"We? We will do nothing. You will go back to your cabin under guard and stay there. I will take care of this."

Mandy forced herself to remain in her chair. She took a deep breath and exhaled slowly. She refused to be locked up in her cabin like some kind of criminal, and if that's what the captain thought, he was sorely mistaken. She bit her lip as the doctor guided an anti-grav stretcher out of the other room.

"What's his condition?" Declan asked.

"Unknown. I'll let you know more as soon as I

do," Trish said. She glanced at Mandy then back to Declan. "I'll see you later, Declan."

Mandy caught the emphasis on the captain's first name, as she knew she was supposed to. The doctor was staking out her territory. Mandy glanced at Declan's face and bit back a smirk. The problem was, he wasn't willing to be in the doctor's territory. She turned her attention to the still figure on the stretcher.

"I'll get who did this, Papa D," she whispered. "I swear I will." She lifted her eyes to Declan. "I want to stay here."

Declan stared at her, one eyebrow raised. "No."

"I will not go back to my cabin."

"Yes, you will. If I have to tie you up and drag you there myself."

"Um, Declan," Sarah broke into the argument. "She can't go back to her cabin. At least not for a bit. That's why we were on our way to see you."

She quickly filled Declan in on what had happened at the gym and in Mandy's quarters. "Since I'll have to go over this cabin anyway and Mandy knows the general better than anyone, she might see something Honan or I would miss. Plus, she'll be safer with us than locked up alone in her cabin. Right now, we can't trust Hermes to know what's going on."

"I heard that," Hermes's regular voice came across the intercom.

"What happened, Hermes?" Declan asked.

"When and where, Captain?"

"Here. A few minutes ago. Your vocal processors had a glitch."

"Not according to my records. Everything is K.O.A."

"K.O.A?" Sarah mouthed to Declan. He shook his head.

"If you say so. Hermes, to be on the safe side, would you please run a Level I diagnostic of all your systems?"

"You corporeal beings are so paranoid. But if you insist."

"I do." Declan turned to Sarah. "She stays glued to you like a barnacle on a sailing ship. And you"—he turned to Mandy—"don't even go to the head without her. Understood?"

"Aye, aye, Captain," Mandy and Sarah said in unison.

Chapter Seven

Sarah could tell from the frown on Declan's face he didn't like his options, but he also knew he had no choice. All she could do to help him was her job. She watched Declan leave, shaking his head and muttering something about women. Sarah grinned at Mandy.

"Gee, I don't think he likes us much." She joined in as Mandy laughed.

"What's so funny?" Honan asked as he came in. "This doesn't exactly look like something to laugh at. And what's with Declan? He almost took my head off when I asked him how things were going?"

Sarah chuckled and motioned Honan in. "Let's say the captain hasn't been having a good day so far, and we're only a few hours into what is probably going to be a long trip." She filled Honan in on events, including Mandy's spa visitor and her cabin. "We need to go over this cabin to see if we can find anything."

Mandy looked from Sarah to Honan. "I guess you both know about Miguel. And I think we can all agree he's the one who did this, but we still don't know what he looks like right now. How are the scans coming?"

"Trish has finished with about a quarter of the crew and so far, nothing. The IDs all match the body scans," Honan said. "Declan has put the few Warriors who are awake on alert, although I'm not sure what they can do we already aren't." He looked around the trashed room.

"Any idea what he was looking for?"

Mandy nodded. "Probably a data disk or two. Papa D had all of Miguel's files as well as the control codes for the labs and farms at Xy-Three. Without them, Alvarez can't get to the white root plant."

"I thought white roots were safe plants," Honan said.

"Most of them are. But the ones with thorns and round leaves are dangerous, especially the thorns. That particular plant carries a toxic poison that is extremely dangerous, and there is no antidote. You either die or go psychotic. We have one farm where that strain is cultured under extreme security and where we're trying to find an antidote. All other plants are to be destroyed, roots and all, when found."

"Who else knows the codes?" Sarah asked.

"The managers on Xy-Three. Unfortunately, of the three, two are dead and, the last we heard, the third was in a coma. I'm the only other one. There's a set in my office back on Aboo, but I'm the only one who knows all the codes and the keys to opening them. Even with the disk, you still need me to put them in the right sequence."

Honan frowned. "Then you're a double risk. We already know he wants you dead, but he'll want the codes first."

"That won't be easy," Mandy said. "I couldn't tell you what they were if I had to."

"Excuse me?" Sarah asked.

Mandy lifted her hair and pointed to a tiny scar behind her right ear.

Sarah whistled. "I've heard of corporate bigwigs and special couriers being chipped, but I've never known anyone who actually has one. Of course, I don't know many corporate bigwigs."

"The chip was implanted after my parents died. I can access the information if I say the release string, but that's the only way. I have no idea what I know."

"Doesn't the not-knowing bother you?"

Mandy shrugged. "Not really. Whatever is in there isn't something I need to know except in an emergency, and this way there's no chance I'd ever forget the information or get mixed up or even let something slip. Who knows, maybe I talk in my sleep." She looked around the room. "So where do you want me to start?"

"Why don't you start in the bedroom?" Honan said. "If General Davis was going to hide something, that would be the most logical place."

"You don't mind if I mess up the crime scene?"

Sarah snorted, a most unladylike sound. "Really doesn't matter. We don't have any equipment. Medical can do DNA scanning, but that's about all. Since we're a supply ship, the company didn't think crime kits were necessary."

"Oh! I need to tell Taka. Hermes, can you get her for me?" Mandy waited a minute for Taka's voice to come over the intercom.

"What's up, honey?"

"Papa D's been hurt. They took him to sickbay. His room has been trashed, and he was unconscious." Mandy swiped viciously at a tear that dared to fall.

"Don't worry, honey, I'll go over there and see what's happening. I'll let you know anything. Is there anyone there with you?"

"Sarah and Honan."

"You stay with them and do what needs to be done

there. I'll take care of Tyler."

"Thanks, Taka." Mandy leaned her head against the wall, fighting for control. Taka would make sure the general was okay. There was nothing to worry about. She pushed away from the wall and straightened her shoulders. There was work to be done. She went into the bedroom and looked around. Where to start? Everything was a mess. "Start at the beginning," the general always told her when she needed to do something. She picked up a bed pillow and went to work.

A few minutes later, she had replaced the bedding, making sure the sheets and blanket were "tight enough to bounce a coin off of," as the general always said. She laid her hand on the pillow, remembering all the times the general had scolded her for leaving her bed unmade.

"You can tell you were brought up in a military household," Sarah said quietly. "Tell me about General Davis. Why do you call him Papa D?" She picked up several articles of clothing and handed them to Mandy to take care of.

Mandy appreciated Sarah's tact as she folded the clothing. All her money and influence, and she couldn't do anything to help the general. She'd never felt so useless. "He and Taka raised me after my parents were killed. Papa D was always after me to make my bed or fold my clothes a certain way." She looked down at the neatly piled clothes on the bed and chuckled. "I guess some of what he tried to teach me sank in."

Sarah re-inserted the drawers into the storage cabinets and straightened out the end tables while Mandy stowed the clothes. "You lived with both of them?"

"Yes and no. They lived next to each other and arranged their schedules so when one was away the other was there. We were together so often, the two houses might as well have been one anyway. I can't figure out why the two of them never got married."

"Sometimes the subject doesn't come up."

Mandy heard a touch of melancholy in Sarah's voice. "You and Honan?"

Sarah shrugged. "Yeah, well, some men can't be forced."

"And some are blind and stupid."

Sarah laughed. "Thanks. But part of the issue is his tribe. They're Argonians and aren't allowed to marry anyone outside the acceptable tribes. Being from the Wastelands like I am isn't exactly high on their list of suitable mates."

"But you're as much a Warrior as he is."

"Yeah, tell that to his family." She glanced around the room. "So, any idea where the general might hide a data disk?"

Mandy shook her head. "Something that small could be anywhere, and there's always the possibility Alvarez found the information already." She bent over to straighten the line of shoes next to the bed. Something bright caught her eye, and she pulled out the knife. "I seem to have found something, though."

"Honan!" Sarah called. "We've got something." Sarah motioned for Mandy to place the weapon on one of the end tables.

Honan came in and looked at the knife. "Nasty piece of business. Not something you'd expect a master general to have."

"That isn't Papa D's. He carries a small multipurpose set that fits in his pocket," Mandy said.

Honan ran a portable medical scanner over the knife. "No prints or any other identifying marks."

"No prints at all?" Sarah asked. "Mandy picked the blade up, so hers should be there."

Honan ran the scanner again. "None. Actually, I'm not surprised. I've heard of this material. This is a new substance that doesn't hold any prints for more than a few seconds. Here, feel the texture on the handle."

Sarah picked the knife up. "This is lighter than I expected and well balanced. But the handle is rough with an oily feel." She laid the knife back down and looked at her hand. "I get a weird feeling, like grease, but there's no residue."

"Exactly. We have no way of tracing ownership, but I can guess," Honan said.

"Look at the designs carved into the blade," Mandy pointed out. "They're like the ones on the messages Miguel keeps sending me."

"Agreed. Okay, we'll assume this is Alvarez's knife, so we know he was the one who attacked the general, but we still don't know who he is," Sarah said. "Are the bio scans on the crew finished yet?"

Honan nodded. "Trish finished them. With the exception of you two, Declan, and me. Everyone passed."

"I know I'm not Alvarez," Declan said as he joined the trio. "We either have a stowaway, or he's figured out a way to fool the scanners."

"Or he has a cohort among the crew," Mandy said. She held up her hand when the others would have argued. "I would never suggest anything of the kind if the crew were all yours. Three quarters of the crew is replacement, either with my people or new crew. How much do any of us really know about the people with us?"

Sarah nodded in agreement. "She has a point. Perhaps Mandy and I should look at the rosters. We can eliminate people that way, and we can look at the ones left more closely."

"Agreed. But I want you to work on the bridge," Declan said.

He turned to Honan. "Sarah's got a clever idea, but only if our problem isn't a stowaway. See if you can't rig something. At the very least, I want Hermes checked out manually. I don't like these glitches he keeps having. In the meantime, how are you coming here?"

Honan handed Declan the knife. "This is all we've found so far. We haven't had much time to really check."

Declan looked at the knife. "I've never seen one like this." He studied the room, his head cocked to one side. "You cleared the floor area, right?"

"Yes," Sarah said. "Why?"

Declan pointed at the air vent above the bed. The cover was slightly off kilter. "I'd say that might be how he got in and out."

Honan reached up. The grate came off loosely in his hand. "Looks like he was in a hurry. I'll get some samples. We'll do what we can, Declan, but you know as well as I do there's not a whole lot we can do."

"One action you can take is to have maintenance put security seals on all the air vents."

"All of them?" Honan asked. "That will take days."

"Have them start with the ones on this deck and

those with access areas large enough to accommodate a person."

Declan glanced at his watch. "Night shift is due to come on shortly, and I'll need to talk to them. Why don't you finish up here, and we'll meet in the officer's mess for dinner. We can figure out our next move later." He took the knife with him. "I'll lock this in my office."

Mandy saw the wide-eyed looks on Honan and Sarah's faces before they managed to stop them, and she wondered what had surprised them. She waited for Declan to leave before asking. "What's up? I saw your faces when he suggested dinner. I guess that doesn't happen often."

Sarah chuckled. "On truly rare occasions and then only under extreme duress. Declan hates formal dinners and only uses the officer's mess when absolutely necessary. We use the room when we have VIPs, but they have to be really high up there." She looked at Mandy. "I guess with your credentials, you qualify as one of the highest."

Mandy groaned. "Damn. I really hate when people feel they have to put on a performance for me. I don't want any special treatment, and I certainly don't want to be segregated from the rest of the crew and have fancy meals and all that crap. Can't you talk to him?"

Sarah smiled. "I'll see what I can do. But I have a feeling he's had this planned all along. I think I remember seeing Johnny B. heading there a few hours ago. If so, you may want to go anyway."

"Who's Johnny B.?"

"Only the best chef this side of Antares Station. Trust me, if Declan has him working, you're in for a treat. Hey, at least you don't have to wear a dress uniform."

Mandy looked at Sarah in horror. "Dress uniform? You're not serious."

"Yep. Standing orders from the company. We don't go into the captain's mess in anything less than full dress uniform."

Mandy sighed. "I guess there's no way around this, is there?"

Sarah shook her head. "Nope. Come on, let's get this finished and then we can go put on our party faces."

They went over every inch of the general's quarters and even tore apart his luggage in hopes of finding the data. All they found was his handgun and a small notebook Mandy tearfully grabbed.

"That's one of my father's diaries! Probably the last one. I thought they were all lost. How did Papa D get this? And why didn't he give the book to me?" She fingered the name embossed on the cover.

"Your father kept a paper diary? I've never heard of such a...hobby," Sarah said. She peered over Mandy's shoulder at the book.

"And you use a brush and paint to create a mural on your wall?" Mandy smiled though tears threatened. "Dad always said he loved the feel of pen on paper. Shipping costs to send them to me were ridiculous, but every time he went away, I could count on getting at least one of these books from him. Even now, I feel like I'm touching a part of him—as if he's still here."

"In a way he is," Honan said. "I believe his spirit watches over you. May I see the book?"

Mandy handed the book over and watched as

Honan leafed through the pages.

"What are these markings on the edges?" He pointed to random lines marked on several of the sheets.

Mandy shrugged as she took the book back. "Dad was always doodling. All his diaries have similar drawings." She leafed through, stopping at a page with a hand-drawn picture. "See, he loved to draw. This is a picture of the original shelter on Xy-Three. He's got scribbles like this everywhere."

Honan frowned and looked at the picture, then back at the doodling. "Would you mind if I showed this to Declan? I promise, you'll get this back as soon as possible. I want his opinion."

Reluctantly, Mandy nodded.

"We'll get nowhere else tonight," Honan said. "If we haven't found the disk by now, we probably won't. Why don't you two go get changed, and I'll meet you at dinner. I want to seal this room first."

Mandy stretched the kinks out of her back. "Sounds good."

Sarah walked Mandy back to her cabin. A young man in a black Warrior uniform stood outside Mandy's door. He came to attention when they approached.

"Mike? Mike Tremaine, is that you?" Mandy gaped at the young man.

"Yes, ma'am."

"What are you doing here? And what's with this ma'am crap?" Mandy was pretty sure she already knew the answer and was positive she wasn't going to like what he said.

"Standing guard, ma'am. I pulled second shift duty."

"Guard? Over what? You'd better not say you're guarding me."

The young man blushed. "Yes, ma'am."

"By whose orders? Not Master General Davis."

"No ma'am. Since he's not available, we fall under the direct command of Colonel Weiss and Captain Chalmers. We have strict orders from the captain that you are not to be without a guard at any time."

"Uh-huh. And exactly how many of you are there?"

"Enough to cover you twenty-four/seven, ma'am." He looked at Mandy and lowered his voice. "Don't be mad at me, Mandy. We all want to get the son-of-a…" He stopped when Mandy shot him a look and blushed again. "…gun who hurt the general, and we sure as hell aren't going to let anyone get to you."

"Michael Tremaine, you know as well as I do, I'm as capable as most of the people you have with you."

He grinned. "We know. But you're going to have a guard, ma'am. We were given our orders and, even if we hadn't been told, we'd still be here. You're one of us, and we protect our own. We've got guards on Dr. Yu as well."

Mandy sighed and shook her head. "No choice?"

"No, ma'am." He grinned at her.

"Do you still remember how to play Exo Oni?"

"I still remember how to lose Exo Oni, especially when you play."

Mandy chuckled and palmed open her door. "Thank you, Michael." She turned to Sarah. "Am I meeting you at dinner, or are we forming the parade here?"

"I'll be back here in thirty minutes," Sarah said.

****

Mandy yawned and slipped out of the emerald-green sheath she'd donned for the evening. Dinner had been delicious. Sarah was right. The chef was excellent. Mandy learned he was a hydroponics engineer and grew many of the fresh vegetables and greens they'd enjoyed. She'd met a couple more of the regular crew. Chane, an extremely tall, lanky man with a wicked sense of humor, was the second shift leader and an electronics expert as well as head of engineering, and O'Malley, a small, almost elfin man with a bald head and a perpetual smile. He ran the hydroponics and life support systems and was most grateful for the extra help Mandy had sent him. According to O'Malley, Tina was a godsend—or goddess. Mandy wasn't sure which word he'd used. Of her own people, the captain had been gracious enough to invite Tina, Taka, and Col. Judy Weiss, General Davis's second-in-command for this trip, a cold woman who'd barely spoken to anyone the entire evening.

The other dark spot to the evening had been the ship's doctor, Tricia Kirby. She'd been barely civil to Mandy, and when she wasn't glaring, she was trying to ingratiate herself with the captain. The fact that he wasn't buying the doctor's act didn't help matters any. Mandy had no idea why the doctor disliked her so. She knew they'd never met. Yet there was something vaguely familiar about her, but she couldn't figure out what.

Despite the colonel and doctor, they'd managed to have a good time. Mandy had been regaled with tales of the regular crews' escapades, some poignant, some dangerous, but all uproariously funny—at least that's the way Chane and O'Malley made them seem. After dinner, while they were relaxing over tea and coffee, the conversation had turned to the attack on the general. The doctor had been less than forthcoming with any information on the general's condition. What had surprised Mandy even more though was the colonel's attitude. Although she'd agreed the attacker had to be found, she hadn't seemed overly concerned about the incident. She'd even gone so far as to question the wisdom of the scans medical had done. The scans had shown nothing, and they were no closer to knowing who Alvarez was.

Mandy brushed out her long hair. "Hermes, do I have any messages?"

"Yes, ma'am. Sixteen."

"Give me sender and subject matter." Mandy listened to the list as she went through a series of stretching exercises. Most of the messages were general ship-wide ones she could ignore. A few she replied to, but one caught her attention and she stopped.

"Hermes, repeat the last sender."

"Sender is 'Alvarez.' Message topic is 'Who's next?'"

Mandy sighed, expecting the same type of message she'd been getting from him. "Is there a video attached?"

"Sorry, ma'am. The message is text only."

Mandy frowned. That was different. "Text? There's no picture?"

"No. Do you want me to display the text?"

"No. Audio only."

"The general was the first. The next is your choice. Give me the codes."

Mandy leaned her head against the wall. "Hermes, forward message to the captain marked urgent."

She raised her head as an idea occurred to her. She needed to stop behaving like a victim.

"Hermes, reply to message."

"Yes, ma'am."

"Go to hell. End message."

"Very good, boss."

Mandy heard the approving chuckle from the AI.

Chapter Eight

Mandy pulled the pillow over her head, trying to drown out the insistent buzzing. *I've got to remind Taka to get the screens fixed.*

A new sound reached her ears. This one was even more annoying than the mosquitoes. Suddenly, Mandy realized the noise wasn't due to pesky insects, but the repeated chime of her com-unit now added to her door alarm.

"All right! I'm awake! Come in."

Sarah burst in, followed closely by the captain and a guard. She yanked her blanket up as she caught the captain eyeing her thin top.

"Mandy?" Sara said. "I was getting worried. When you didn't show up for breakfast and nobody had seen you, I thought I'd better check. Then when I couldn't open your door…"

Mandy brushed her hair out of her face and sat up. "I'm fine. I overslept. I guess everything caught up to me. I'm sorry. But I don't understand why you had trouble with the door. I didn't put the privacy locks on."

Declan checked the door. "There doesn't appear to be a problem now, but I'll have maintenance do a check. If you're all right, I have other duties."

"Wait. Please. How's Pa…um, the general?"

Declan paused at the door. "Your aunt put him in cold sleep."

Mandy could see the sadness and the worry in the captain's face as well as something else. He wouldn't look at her. There was something he wasn't telling her. "I thought his injuries weren't serious."

"The physical ones weren't."

"But?" She was beginning to feel like she was paddling a canoe against a strong current.

"But the coma appears to be the result of some sort of systemic agent."

"Poison?"

"Yes. And the doctor doesn't know what kind."

Mandy hung her head. "I think we can all take a good guess, though. Does Taka know?"

"Yes, since she's the one who ordered cold sleep. They tested for traces of white root, but they came up negative. Now, I must go."

"Yes, of course. Thank you." Mandy waited for him and the guard to leave before getting up. "What's wrong with him? He seems a bit curt this morning."

"Declan?" Sarah said. "Gee, what could possibly be wrong? We've got one of the most powerful people in all the United Systems on board and a madman who's out to kill her. The top commander of the Warrior Caste is in cold sleep from an attack and poisoning. Three quarters of our usual crew has been replaced with new personnel who don't know the ship or the systems, and we're on our way to a plague planet. I'd say Declan is doing remarkably well."

Mandy chuckled. "Okay, I get your point. What time is it anyway?"

"Nine thirty."

Mandy dropped the shirt she'd pulled from a drawer. "You're kidding, right?"

Sarah shook her head.

"Damn. I've never slept so late in my life. You must think I'm some sort of lazy rich bitch with nothing better to do than lie around eating bonbons all day."

She quickly donned a pair of dark gray utility pants and the black T-shirt she'd dropped. A pair of soft demi-boots completed the outfit.

"Not at all." Sarah chuckled. She pointed at the regulation corners Mandy was folding her bedding into. "Especially since you were raised by a military man."

Mandy finished her bed and tackled her hair. In less than five minutes, she'd brushed the long waves out, braided the length, and wound the braid into a neat bun at the nape of her neck.

"Wow. How do you do that so fast?" Sarah asked.

"Years of practice. So, what's on the agenda for today?"

"First, you get some breakfast while I grab a second cup of coffee. Honan should be in the lounge about now. We can talk to him there."

Mandy followed Sarah out of her cabin. The guard came quickly to attention.

"At ease, Jean," Mandy said. "When nobody else is around, you don't need to treat me like brass."

The woman relaxed only slightly. "Yes, ma'am. Mandy? Do you know anything about the general yet?"

"I found out he's been put into cold sleep. He was poisoned."

The woman's eyes widened slightly. She quickly schooled her features into a neutral mask. "May I inform the others, ma'am?"

Mandy glanced at Sarah who nodded at her. "I don't see why not. The more people who know, the sooner we may be able to catch the man responsible."

"Yes, ma'am. We've also got a guard on Taka, although she wasn't happy."

Mandy laughed. "I'll bet. Tell me, did the Warrior who informed her come away unscathed?"

"I think his hearing will be back to normal in a day or two." Jean's smile told most of the story, then she sobered and looked up and down the corridor. The expanse was empty except for the three of them. "Mandy," she whispered. "Watch your six. There's something more going on here than this Alvarez business."

"What do you mean?"

Jean shrugged. "I don't know. Some of us have a feeling. I'll let you know if I hear anything specific." She straightened back to attention as a maintenance man came around the corner. "Have a good day, ma'am."

"Thank you, Lieutenant. You can take a break since I'm with Sarah."

"Yes, ma'am. Thank you."

Mandy fell into step next to Sarah as she headed for the lounge.

"Looks like you and the lieutenant know each other pretty well," Sarah said.

"Jean? We were classmates. Actually, apart from the colonel, I know all of the people the general brought along. I'm not sure how the colonel got put into the unit. She's not Papa D's usual second."

Honan waved to them from a small table near the door. There were only a few people in the room and most, like Sarah and Honan, were enjoying a light snack for break. Mandy strolled over to the counter and placed her order with the cook. While she waited, she studied the room. She hadn't really looked at the space well the last time. The walls and jump shields had been expertly painted with scenic murals, and she thought she detected Sarah's hand in the design.

The area to the left as she entered the door had a counter on which there were several urns with hot and cold drinks, and bins with a variety of pastries and fruits. Behind the counter was the open kitchen where two cooks worked.

The tables were set up for small groups of four but could easily be arranged to accommodate larger parties. The area in front of the jump doors was slightly raised and, although the platform was currently empty, she thought the area would probably make a good stage when necessary. Indirect lighting gave the entire room a soft ambience further enhanced with potted plants situated in various spots.

"Your order, ma'am."

"Thank you." Mandy picked up her breakfast and joined Sarah and Honan at their table.

"Ah, I see we have another health food nut among us," Sarah said.

"Excuse me?" Mandy asked as she dipped her spoon into her bowl. She took a taste of the concoction and sighed in pleasure. The dish was a combination of fresh rainbow fruit and grains layered with a smooth mixture of creamy Aboolean cheese and yogurt. The dish was light, creamy, and utterly delicious.

"Sarah is not into natural foods," Honan said. He speared a piece of rainbow fruit from his own plate and waved the fruit under Sarah's nose, chuckling when she turned away.

"Hey, I can't be blamed if my constitution was brought up on pre-packaged, over-processed convenience foods. They sustain the body."

"But not the soul," Honan countered. He looked at Mandy. "I am trying to change her, but believe I am fighting a losing battle."

"And you a Warrior!" Mandy chuckled. She had the feeling the argument was an old one. "Well, I guess I'll have to give you a hand. Hmmm. Let's see, maybe if we tied her up while she was asleep and then force fed her healthy food for the remainder of our trip…"

Sarah held up her hands in mock horror. "You wouldn't! No! A fate worse than death!" She took a huge gulp of coffee. "Caffeine, don't let me down."

Mandy and Honan laughed. Then the two chatted lightly while Mandy ate. Once she was done, the talk became more serious.

"So what do we do now?" Mandy asked.

"I'd like to go over the general's quarters one more time, and then you and Sarah can go to the bridge to work on the personnel rosters," Honan said.

"Sounds like a plan," Mandy agreed. She bussed her tray and joined the other two. A few minutes later, they stood at the door to the general's bedroom. Honan stopped her from entering.

"Mandy, I'd like you to do me a favor. You know the general better than anyone. You grew up with him, but did you ever travel with him?"

"A few times. Why?"

"Close your eyes and think. You're with the general, either in a hotel or a barracks room. Tell me what you see."

Mandy closed her eyes, took a deep breath, and

exhaled slowly. "He's got his duffle and a briefcase. Depending on where we are and why we're there, there will be one or two dress uniforms, a set of fatigues, and two sets of civvies. In his kit will be a regulation comb, razor, and toiletries. He will have three pairs of shoes— dress, boots, and workout." In the background, Mandy could hear Honan and Sarah going through the closet and drawers, taking inventory.

"Wait," Honan said. "You said *razor*. What kind?"

Mandy frowned and concentrated. "He was old-fashioned, like my dad. He preferred a straight edge to a powered one. He claimed the blade gave him a better shave and, in a pinch, could be used as a tool or weapon. He only used depilatories when necessary."

"You can open your eyes." Honan handed her a compact, black cordless razor. "Do you recognize this?"

Mandy turned the device over and over in her hands. "I've never seen this before. This isn't his."

"Maybe, and maybe not." Honan took the razor back, studying the piece like Mandy had. He pulled off the power pack. "We couldn't be this lucky, could we?" He took a small knife from his pocket and unscrewed a tiny screw under the power pack, then used the tip of the knife to pry open the body of the razor. Lying in the center of the cavity was a tiny data disk. He upended the disk into Mandy's palm.

"I believe we have found what we were looking for, thanks to you."

Mandy looked at the small disk lying in her hand and smiled. "Actually, thanks to Papa D and his habits."

She handed the disk to Honan. "I think you'd better take this to the captain. He'll want to see the information immediately."

"And you don't?"

"I don't need to know what's on the disk to know Miguel is deranged and has been for a long time." She paused and looked straight into Honan's eyes. "And I know he won't stop until I'm dead."

Honan nodded. "Declan is on the bridge, and since you're going there, I'll go with you."

"Actually, I'd like to stop by Taka's lab first."

"No problem. I'll walk you there."

"Honan…"

"Don't even bother arguing. I have not given you an option."

Mandy sighed but ceded the point. "Since we're going past the lounge, I want to stop in there and pick up some food for Taka. If I know her, she hasn't eaten more than a bite or two."

****

"Taka?" Mandy nodded to the guard outside the lab and waved Honan off. She stepped into the bay turned into a lab for her aunt. The area was so crammed with equipment, there was almost no room to move. High lab tables ringed the entire space, and a rack filled with equipment and shipping crates neatly divided the room down the middle. There was barely room between the racks and the tables for anyone to walk. Mandy heard a noise from the far corner.

"Back here, honey. Watch your step and come on in."

Mandy followed Taka's voice. She found Taka perched on a high stool, her eyes glued to a microscope. Mandy pulled up a second stool.

"Hand me that Petri dish," Taka said. Her eyes

never left the scope.

Mandy glanced around and spotted several dishes on the table. "Which one?"

"Sample C-2." Taka held out her hand and snapped her fingers.

Mandy quickly found the designated dish and handed the small container to her aunt.

"Taka? Have you checked on Papa D?"

Taka set the dish down and swiveled around on her stool. "The ship's doctor was right. He was poisoned. I'm glad you alerted me, though. The counteragent the idiot was going to give him was the wrong one. The drug wouldn't have hurt him but wouldn't have helped him either. I've taken over his treatment. If this sample pans out, I should have the antidote by the end of the day and have him up and around in another couple of days. Now, how are you doing? You look tired. Are you eating right?"

Mandy chuckled. Taka never changed. "I'm fine. And, yes, I'm eating right. Are you? When was the last time you ate?"

"I ate at that fancy dinner last night."

"Uh-huh. And if I know you, you haven't had a bite since." Mandy pushed the plate of food she'd brought toward Taka. "Break time. Eat."

"Hey, who's the person in charge here?"

"I am. At least, that's what the orders say." Mandy handed her a slice of rainbow fruit. "Now, eat."

Taka chuckled and took the fruit. "So, how are you really doing, honey?"

Mandy kicked her foot back and forth. "I feel so strange, Taka. I've lived so much of my life lately in Miguel's shadow. I've been protected, guarded, and secluded to the point I don't even remember what life is like to go somewhere alone. I adore you and Papa D, but I miss my parents. I feel responsible for those poor people on Xy-Three, and now the people on this ship. But what can I do? I feel so...I don't know ...inadequate."

Taka lay down the piece of cheese she was nibbling and took a sip of tea. "You will never and should never forget what he did to our family. They are part of who you are, and you will always carry them with you, but they are not the only part of you. You are so much more than your parents. You are a beautiful, intelligent, compassionate person. Just because Alvarez is here doesn't mean you're going to stop being who you are. I know a bit about what you're feeling. Every time I'm up against a new bug, I wonder if this will be the one I can't beat. If this is the one that will get away. Then I roll up my sleeves and get to work. If I let that kind of thinking take over, I've already lost the fight, and I refuse to do that. Your parents were the same— and so are you."

Taka reached out to hug her. "Now. You've interrupted me long enough. If I don't get to work, the antidote won't get made."

Mandy smiled through a sheen of tears. "You never change, Taka. Thank the stars for that. Don't forget to eat, okay? And take an occasional break?"

"Humph." Taka popped another slice of fruit into her mouth and turned back to her scope, but not before Mandy caught the hint of a smile in her dark eyes.

The guard escorted Mandy to the bridge and returned to Taka. Mandy stepped through the door and stopped. She saw the knowing look on Sarah and

Honan's faces as she scanned the area. The bridge was much smaller than she'd expected for a ship the size of the *Phoenix*. The elongated oval room was on two levels. The lower level held three seats behind three console panels. Behind them was a large table. The upper level curved around the back, offset by two steps. Along the back wall where she stood were various monitors and consoles, only two of which had chairs. The front half of the room was empty, save for the closed jump shields, and those were painted with an incredible forest scene that looked so real Mandy thought if she touched one of the trees she'd feel actual bark.

"I think we've managed to astound our guest," Honan spoke up.

"Astound is a good word," Mandy agreed. "Sarah, did you do the painting? The artwork is amazing."

"Thank you, but I can't take all the credit. The work was a joint effort from several of us."

"Exactly how long have you been on this ship?"

"Long enough." Sarah turned to Declan who'd been watching them. "Honan and I can take over nav for a bit, and Mandy can start on the personnel rosters while you study the disk."

Declan glanced at the small wafer. "Thanks. Things have been quiet here. That's the one good feature about jump space. Nothing much to do." He moved out of the center chair. "Sarah, why don't you take central while I look at this on the upper monitor. Honan, I'd like you to check out something else for me."

Mandy stood quietly while Declan talked to Honan. Sarah motioned for Mandy to join her on the lower level.

"So, any questions about our baby?" Sarah patted the console panel.

"Plenty. This big ship only takes three of you to run her?"

"Three humans and Hermes. Without him, we'd be in deep asteroid dust."

"Thank you, Sarah."

"You're welcome, Hermes. Since we're a supply ship, there's really not much to do. Honan told me you know the layout, so you know the biggest part of the interior is storage space. Once the holds are loaded, there's not much to do but put the ship in gear and go. We can monitor everything from right here. The consoles can be used separately or tied together and monitored from a single one or any combination of the three."

"Extremely efficient."

"The entire set-up was Declan's idea. When we first took over the ship, the bridge was a mess. There were the four stations here and ten more on the upper level. Working here was utter chaos with people tripping over themselves and each other. Declan had the engineers reconfigure all the consoles to be secondaries. The primaries are in the individual departments now. We can still monitor from here, but by moving them to the actual areas where they were needed, the work was much more productive. Now if there's an issue in hydroponics, they know right away rather than seeing something here, running down there, checking back here, and so on. Once Declan had all the kinks worked out, this layout became the template for all new supply ships being built."

Mandy looked up at the captain with new eyes. He wasn't merely a space jockey, but someone who knew how to get the best out of both his people and his equipment. He continued to impress her. "Didn't the owners balk at the refit?"

Sarah laughed. "Oh, yeah. In fact, they told him under no circumstances was he to *mess with an established system*. Their words. So, he went ahead and did anyway. And proved to them, not only was his system more efficient, but the change would save them thousands. He hit them in the credit column. And since his system worked so well, there was nothing they could do to him."

"I really hate people who can't go beyond the *but we've always done whatever this way* attitude," Mandy put in.

"I know what you mean. But what about you? You're in charge of a top company. Doesn't the business get in the way of innovation?"

"Yes and no. Finding new ways to utilize our products is important, but once established, we follow specific procedures from testing stage through production. Our employees are encouraged to experiment, and many do. One of our most lucrative products came from a maintenance tech."

"Yeah, but do you give them credit? Once Declan proved this set-up worked, the company integrated his system in all the ships. Declan didn't even get a thank you."

Mandy tapped her index finger on her lips. Somewhere in the hierarchy something was wrong. Everything she heard told her more about the owners—and what she heard wasn't good. "That's not the way

Ki Enterprises works. Anyone who comes up with a lucrative or viable idea receives a percentage of the profits from the application."

Sarah whistled. "Your maintenance tech must have liked that. Did he quit?"

"No." Mandy smiled. "He said he was happy with what he was doing, and now his family won't have to ever worry."

"His family? You take care of them too?"

"Not exactly. He was one of the first casualties on Xy-Three." She stared unseeing at the monitor. "That sounds so clinical. Casualty. The term sounds so blasé—so innocent—but doesn't tell you anything about the person. He had a family, grandkids. He loved what he did." She turned tear-filled eyes to Sarah. "And what about all the other casualties? There are hundreds. All those people. Now they're nothing more than numbers in someone's database. All those lives reduced to statistics."

She slammed her hand on the console. "I won't let that bastard rack up even one more casualty. I have to stop him. Now."

She swiveled her chair around to face Declan. "Captain, where are the personnel rosters?"

Chapter Nine

Declan considered the woman sitting in his seat. He'd heard most of what she'd said to Sarah—heard and understood the emotions behind the words. She was driven, which could be both good and bad. She would do what was needed to get the job done, but would her determination lead to mistakes?

He nodded for Honan to join Sarah. "You can use this monitor."

He waited for Mandy to change places with Honan. "Hermes, display personnel data on monitor five."

"Aye, sir."

A list of names appeared on the screen.

"Where do you want to start?" Declan asked.

"Hermes, eliminate all the women," Mandy said. "Alvarez can change his looks, but I seriously doubt he'd change his sex. He's too…self-absorbed to do that."

Declan agreed. "Also eliminate all regular crew. I've known those people for a long time. What's that leave us?"

"Nine." Mandy studied the thumbnail sketches. "Hermes, delete anyone over five-feet, eight-inches tall. Alvarez is short. He might be able to wear lifts, but he can't change his statistical height."

The list narrowed down to five—four crew and one Aboolean.

"Do you know the Aboolean?" Declan asked.

Mandy shook her head. "What about the new crew?"

"Hermes, delete Chuck Middleburg," Declan said. "I've worked with Chuck before. That leaves us with four: Damien Michaels, Steve Brake, Logan Spencer, and Ed Frieze." He turned to Sarah and Honan. "Do either of you know these guys?"

Honan punched the files up on his screen. He and Sarah checked them over.

"New to us," Honan said. "You want me to bring them in?"

"Take them to medical and stay with them while Trish runs another scan. Have her send the results here. Now that we have the general's disk, we can compare DNA. Tell her to put a rush on the results."

Declan turned back to Mandy as Honan left. "Hermes, put a security watch on those four. I want to know anything they do beyond normal ship's business."

"Aye, sir."

"Captain," Mandy said, "did the vent scan in General Davis's quarters show anything? I'm afraid I'm not familiar with what security does in these cases."

Declan raised an eyebrow. "Hermes, compare these files with the scans Honan ran on the VIP cabin. They should be in the medical database."

"Aye, sir."

Declan and Mandy waited impatiently for the results. Seconds turned into minutes.

"Hermes?"

"Aye, sir?"

"Have you run the comparisons?"

"What comparisons?"

Declan clenched his jaw. "I asked you to compare the scans Honan ran in the VIP cabin with the four personnel we have listed."

"I'm afraid I can't do that, Captain."

"Why not?" If Hermes had been a person, Declan would have been sorely tempted to punch him.

"I have no record of those scans."

Declan swung around to Sarah. "Please tell me you have a backup."

Sarah shook her head. "Sorry, Declan. We did a straight download."

Declan swung around in time to see the monitor screen go blank. "Hermes, what the hell happened to the files on this monitor?"

"What files, sir?"

"What files? The personnel files we were working on!" He ran his hand through his short hair.

"I'm sorry, Captain, I have no record of any such files."

Declan was ready to pull out wires. He stood and paced the upper level. "Hermes, please display a list of personnel."

A long list scrolled across the screen.

"Captain? I only recognize a few of these names," Mandy said.

Declan sat back down. "Because this is my regular crew roster. Hermes, where is the list of current crew?"

"According to my records, this is the current crew."

"What?" Declan frowned. "Hermes, what is the current date?"

"Current date is 235.2361."

"Damn. That's when we left on our last trip.

Hermes, what is our heading?"

"We are on route to Xy-Three. We are on day two of the first jump stage."

"Well, at least he's got that right," Declan muttered. "Hermes, what is your status?"

"N-n-no problems here, Catpin. All s-systems functioning at optimal levels."

Declan sighed. "Yeah, right."

He swiveled his seat around. "Sarah, get engineering to run a full manual diagnostic. I want that glitch found."

Mandy could hear Sarah speaking softly in the background. The captain was busy at another console. Feeling a bit useless, she turned back to her monitor and pulled up what personnel files she could. She filtered out the people who weren't currently on the ship and scanned through the others. Although she already knew a good bit about the captain, she pulled up his file and studied the data.

Mandy heard a noise and quickly closed the file.

"Don't worry," Sarah whispered in her ear. "I won't tell."

Mandy smiled, her face burning at being caught.

"Declan?" Sarah said a little louder. "I thought I'd take Mandy for some lunch. Or would you rather?"

Declan stood and stretched. "No, you two go ahead. I want to run some tests here. Could you have the cook send me something?"

Sarah nodded and ushered Mandy through the door. "So, you were checking out our illustrious captain. Find anything interesting?"

Mandy shrugged. "You know as well as I do the files only show the surface stats. They don't tell you

115

about the real person underneath. What's he really like?"

"Declan? He's smart, decisive, athletic, and a born leader. He can also be short-tempered, dictatorial, and whatever you do, don't talk to him before he's had his first cup of coffee in the morning."

Mandy laughed. "Sounds human enough." She entered the lounge and found the space definitely more crowded than earlier. Most of the tables were filled. People wandered between tables and food service areas. Although her breakfast hadn't been long ago, the aromas emanating from the kitchens set her stomach to grumbling.

She and Sarah placed their orders and looked for empty seats while they waited.

"Ma'am, over here."

Mandy saw Tina waving at her from a corner. She and O'Malley had two empty seats pulled up to their table. "Sarah?"

"Looks good to me." Sarah picked up her tray and led the way.

On their way to the table, Mandy saw a few places where crew and her people mixed, but for the most part, the tables were segregated. She wondered if there was a way to get more of them together. This trip was going to be rough enough without crew vs. staff prejudices getting in the way.

Tina and O'Malley pushed their trays aside to make room for Mandy and Sarah.

"Hi, O'Malley," Sarah said as she slid into a seat. "Hope we're interrupting something."

"Nothing that can't be restarted," O'Malley retorted. He turned to Mandy. "Ma'am, I can't thank you enough for sending me this angel. She can make anything grow. You should see the hydroponics room. She's got seeds started for plants I haven't even heard of and ideas for making the entire unit more efficient. She's a wonder."

Mandy hid a smile as Tina colored to the roots of her short blonde hair. This happy young woman was a complete change from the panic-stricken one she'd met in cold sleep. "I'm glad she could help. I wish some of the other crewmen were as enthusiastic about us being here." Mandy nodded toward the rest of the room.

"Don't you be worrying about them, ma'am," O'Malley said. "They'll come around. Most spacers keep their distance from grounders. That way when we have to say goodbye, there's no hard feelings."

Mandy caught a furtive movement and wondered if Tina and O'Malley were holding hands under the table. "I hope you're right, or we're going to have a rough trip."

She dug into her salad, relishing the fresh greens mixed with tiny sweet purple citrus fruits from Aboo, almonds, miniature egg rolls, and thin noodles—one of her favorite dishes. "I don't know what kind of a schedule the ship follows. I assume you follow Aboolean standard time."

Sarah nodded as she swallowed a bite of pizza. "Aboolean time is standard on Aboolean based ships. We have two twelve-hour shifts and usually run about twenty people per shift. Each rotation is four days on, three off. When we're in port, we keep a skeleton crew and monitor everything from the bridge. Also, we keep three bridge crewmen in cold sleep when we're out. They can be awakened in an emergency. All bridge crew are trained in all ships systems and have basic medical training so we can pretty much pinch-hit in any department."

O'Malley snorted. "Yeah, right. Don't let Sarah anywhere near my hydroponics lab. The last time she was there, she managed to kill off most of my stock."

"Not my fault if my green thumb is brown all the way up to my shoulder. And what about you? If I remember correctly, on your last rotation as navigator, you had us aimed straight for the sun instead of Thexadon. Thank the stars you were only doing a simulation, or we'd have burned up in the corona."

"Yeah, well what about the time—"

"Whoa you two!" Mandy waved her hand between Sarah and O'Malley. "I can see the problem's not going to be how to get your crew to work with our people, but how to get the crew to work with themselves."

Sarah sat back and laughed. "Point taken. Hey, O'Malley, what say we give these two groundhogs the grand tour?"

Mandy reached for her tea and felt a sudden case of vertigo that wrenched her stomach. The tea lifted out of the cup like a living entity. As suddenly as the sensation had started, the feeling stopped, and the tea splashed over the front of her jumpsuit.

"What the hell was that?" Mandy mopped ineffectually at her suit. Others in the room were in similar or worse states.

"I'd say the gravity had a hiccup," Sarah said.

"Some hiccup." Mandy paused as a general call to emergency stations sounded over the com. "I'd say the hiccup is more than we want."

"Yeah, well there's going to be one heck of a mess

to clean up all over. We'd better get to stations. Where's yours?"

"Here." Mandy saw Sarah hesitate. "Go ahead. I'll be fine." She looked up as her guard entered the lounge with Honan. "Look, Jean's here. You don't have to worry."

Sarah hurried over to the door and left with Honan. Many of the other crewmen, including O'Malley and Tina, also hurried out. When those with other stations had gone, Mandy was left with six crewmen and one awful mess. She pushed up her sleeves.

"Well, everyone, I guess we'd better get to work." She cocked her head, listening. She didn't hear anything from the kitchen area. "Do any of you know the kitchen crew?"

"I do, ma'am," one older man spoke up. "I'm regular crew, same as them. Name's Dawson."

"Dawson, can you go back and check on them while we get started in here?"

"Aye, ma'am."

As he left, Mandy marshaled the others into teams. "You and you, I believe there should be cleaning bots in those maintenance closets." She pointed to two doors next to the kitchen door.

"You two grab some cloths and clean off the tables. Sweep everything to the floors for now. What the bots don't get, we'll get later." Mandy recognized the red-haired man from maintenance. "You know where to get some I assume?"

He nodded at her.

"Ma'am?"

Mandy turned as Dawson came back in. "Both cooks are out of service. I've notified medical, but they're more than a bit busy at the moment."

"Are they hurt badly?"

"One's been burnt on his hands, arms, and face, and the other has a bad cut and bruising. I wrapped the cut, but he needs looking after."

Mandy looked at the lone crewman left. She vaguely remembered him as one of her people. "Do you think you and Dawson can rig up some sort of stretcher to get the cooks to sick bay?"

"I can do better than that, ma'am. I'm a med-tech. With a good first aid kit, I can probably do as much as sickbay at the moment."

Mandy nodded toward the kitchens. "Go." She looked at Jean. "Guess that leaves you and me." She picked up a plate. "The general would be most unhappy with us if we left such a mess."

"I haven't pulled K.P. duty since boot camp."

"Then we need to update your skills. We'll work on the trays, flatware, and other serving items. Salvage what you can, trash the rest. Fortunately, the dishes and glassware are of the unbreakable type." The two of them got to work.

Mandy moved to the upper level while Jean worked at the serving counter. She was almost finished with the half-dozen tables when she got the strangest sensation someone was watching her. She scanned the room. Jean was stacking dishes and cups that had survived. The two crewmen she'd sent for the cleaning bots had returned and were setting the programming. Another woman was scrubbing down tables.

Who was missing? The red-haired man. What was his name? Something Michaels? Damien. Then the realization hit her. His was one of the names on the brief list they'd had before Hermes went bonkers.

Mandy looked around. Michaels was kneeling behind one of the planters. Mandy couldn't tell what he was doing, but she thought he looked like he was stripping the lower leaves off the plants. She shook her head. She was letting her imagination fly away again. "Mister Michaels? Is anything wrong?"

He stood up and stepped out. "No, ma'am. I, um, thought I saw some glass back here and wanted to make sure." He started cleaning a table Jean had already finished.

"I believe you'd be more effective if you worked on a dirty table rather than a clean one." Mandy pointed to the middle of the room.

"Yes, ma'am. Sorry, ma'am."

Mandy watched him for a few minutes. He'd clipped the words out as if he were choking on them. Something about his voice was familiar, but maybe she felt that way because of their previous encounters. He swiped at a table, barely moving the surface dirt. "I have found that cleaning works better if you apply some elbow grease, Mr. Michaels."

"Yes, ma'am."

Mandy watched him for a minute. If his table cleaning was indicative of his maintenance work, no wonder there were problems. She'd have to say something to the captain.

An hour later, they had everything back to some semblance of normalcy. Mandy looked around the newly cleaned room, proud of the work she and her team had done. The med-tech and Dawson had seen to the cooks. Fortunately, the injuries weren't serious. They'd patched the men up and sent them to their quarters then joined the others in their cleaning.

Mandy sent the tired crew to their other duties, and she and Jean strolled back toward her cabin.

"What a mess." Mandy stretched the kinks out of her back.

"Yeah, but we got the job done. I hope our quarters aren't as bad." Jean stopped suddenly and stood at attention.

"Why weren't you at your post, Warrior?" The colonel's harsh voice rang through the corridor.

"Ma'am?"

"Your post is here at this door. Where were you?"

"At my emergency post, ma'am, in the mess hall."

"Emergency post? That's the most ridiculous excuse I've ever heard. Consider yourself on report."

Mandy stepped forward. "Colonel, I don't know where you've been for the past hour, but in case you weren't aware, we *did* have a ship-wide emergency and the lieutenant was at her post. In fact, if I'm not mistaken, her job is to guard me and, since she's been with me for the past hour, she was performing her duty."

The colonel sputtered, her face turning an ugly shade of red. "You may have everyone else fooled with your poor little rich girl routine, but I know better. People like you are the root of all our problems. You and your kind are a blight on the natural order. You're not even Warrior class. You shouldn't have been trained. You're not worthy. You and your companies should be banned from our worlds. The captain will hear about this."

Mandy stood aside and pointed down the corridor. "Be my guest. His cabin is that way. But you'll probably find him on the bridge right now."

The colonel marched away from them. Mandy watched until she was out of sight. The colonel's path wobbled from one side of the corridor to the other. She turned to Jean. "What was that all about?"

Jean shrugged. "I don't know, but watch your six with her, Mandy, especially after what she said. She's not well thought of by anyone under her command. Nobody knows where she came from or why she's on this mission and, with the general out, we can't talk to him." Jean looked around, then back at Mandy. "Do you want to bring her up on charges? I would be more than willing to be a witness."

Mandy shook her head. "Not yet. Let me see what I can find out about her. Unfortunately, since we're in jump space, that may not be much. Give me a minute to change into a fresh suit, and we'll go see your room. You can drop me off at the bridge after." She opened the door, not quite sure what to expect. Fortunately, only a little had been disturbed. She picked up the few items scattered on the floor and quickly changed into a fresh jumpsuit, then rejoined Jean in the corridor. "Lead the way, Lieutenant."

"Ms. Ki, please report to the bridge."

Mandy frowned at Jean as Hermes's voice came over the intercom. "Sorry, Jean. Duty calls."

"Not a problem. I'll walk you to the bridge first."

There was no use arguing with Jean—or any of the guards—so she'd better get used to having a shadow. What the devil had the colonel said to the captain? That had to be why she was being called to the bridge. She felt a twinge of unjustified guilt—kind of like being called to the principal's office when she knew she hadn't done anything wrong—this time.

Mandy stepped onto the bridge, narrowly avoiding being run down by the colonel. The woman didn't even glance at her. "Thanks, Jean. Go check out your quarters. I'll see you later."

The captain was sitting in the center seat. Sarah was on his left. She didn't see Honan anywhere around. "What can I do for you, Captain?"

Declan swung around in his seat. "Is the colonel always so acerbic?"

Mandy shrugged. "Your guess is as good as mine. I've never met the woman before this trip. I do know she's not endearing herself to her troops."

"She's not endearing herself to anyone," Sarah muttered.

"I recommended she go to her quarters. Unless I miss my guess, she was drunk," Declan said. "There's no excuse for such behavior from an officer."

"I noticed she was less than steady on her feet," Mandy added.

"Any more unsteady and she'd be passed out," Sarah spoke up.

Mandy walked over to one of the empty stations and sat down. She briefly debated telling the captain about the colonel's threat, and then decided not to. They had enough problems, and the colonel was so much hot air. "So what's happening? Why did the gravity go out?"

Declan ran his hand over his head, and Mandy could almost feel his frustration. She wished there was a way to help him but came up empty.

"We found several burnt out data cells in engineering. We've replaced what we could, routed around some of them, and repaired what was possible to repair. Unfortunately, what we did was a patch job at best. There are no guarantees."

"You mean the glitch could happen again?"

"Yes. I heard you did an excellent job in the lounge. Thank you."

Mandy wondered who had snitched. "I had mostly good people to work with. How are the cooks?"

"Both are fine, thanks to your med-tech. They'll be back at work tomorrow."

"Were there any other injuries?" Mandy asked.

"Several—all except a couple were minor, thank goodness," Sarah said. "The more serious ones will be fine though, once Trish is done."

"Now, back to our original problem," Declan said. "Honan got the scans from two of the four people on our list. We'll have to wait for sickbay to finish up with the current problem before we check the other two."

"I guess neither one was a match."

"No, so that narrows our choices down to two." Declan touched a pad on his console, and Mandy's monitor blinked on.

"I had one of them with me in the lounge," Mandy said. "He was less than effective at his job."

Mandy swiveled her seat around. She could see the location of both men as they went about their duties. The redhead was currently in maintenance. He was avidly watching something on his monitor. She thought he looked like he was playing some sort of game as he maneuvered the cursor around a path. The other man— a dark haired, older man—was in the hydroponics lab helping O'Malley seed a starter bed. As she watched, Honan entered the hydro area. "What about when

125

they're out of camera range?"

"We have tell-tales on them," Sarah said. "We can follow them anywhere in the ship."

"So we can relax a little. Does that mean I lose my shadows?"

"No." Declan shook his head. "Until we're absolutely certain one of these men is Alvarez, you don't go anywhere alone."

"Who else could he be?" Mandy looked at the man with Honan. He certainly fit the description—but that man wasn't him. She was sure of that. She forced her clenched fists open. Would this nightmare never end?

She noted the second man was on the move. He must have been out of camera range. She saw a small blue dot moving through a schematic of the ship. The dot stopped in the refuse area. Mandy checked the maintenance screen. Yes, there was a red warning light signaling a problem in the area. She watched as the dot moved around, and then stopped and then stayed in the same spot for several minutes.

"Captain? Aren't there any monitors in the refuse area?"

"No. Why?"

"I was watching the tell-tale on one crewman—I believe his name is Michaels—and the pointer stopped there and hasn't moved in several minutes."

Declan pulled up the screen. "Could be nothing. Maybe he's checking a data cell or something."

Mandy frowned. "Maybe, but I have a strange feeling about him. He's not exactly what I would call a conscientious worker. Are there any other crewmen in the area?"

"No." He looked over at Sarah. "How much do you

trust her hunches?"

"I'll go check."

Sarah left, and Declan motioned for Mandy to join him. He pulled her father's diary from his pocket. "I thought you might like to have this back." He tapped his lip with his index finger. "Mandy, did your father ever study any of the classical languages?"

Mandy cocked her head. "Yes. He had an ear for languages and spoke several fluently. I know he read both Quarterian and Xylean as well as several others."

"What about older languages, perhaps Abror? Those dialects predate standard Aboolean."

"I don't know, but I wouldn't be surprised. Why?"

"May I?" Declan touched the diary.

Mandy reluctantly handed the book back. What was the captain up to now?

"You said he was always doodling in his books he sent back. Did the books come straight to you?"

"No. He sent them to the general." She smiled. "That way, he could say they were a military expenditure and not be charged personal shipping."

Declan opened the front cover and flipped through the pages. "The doodling was always like this?"

Mandy studied the scribbling and shook her head. "I don't really remember. I never paid much attention to them. They were random drawings—weren't they?"

Declan held the pages together and bent them slightly, offsetting the edges. The random lines came together in a semblance of a pattern. "Have you ever heard of Aboolean runes?"

"They're what most of our language is based on, aren't they?"

"Yes. The word actually means secret. What if

your father wasn't merely sending you a diary, but was also sending a message to the general? One where only someone who knew the key could read?" Declan swiveled around to his monitor. "Hermes, display the Aboolean rune alphabet on my screen enhanced with the Standard equivalents."

The characters appeared on the screen. Mandy took the diary and held the book the way Declan had. The random lines took on a new meaning as she picked out individual characters. Her heart beat a quick tattoo. What if this was some sort of code? The diaries—did they all have a secret message? She rubbed her thumb over the markings. "Have you translated the code yet?"

"I haven't had time. I was hoping you could try."

"I'd be more than happy to." She grasped the book tightly, as if she could discern the secret through her touch alone.

"You wouldn't by any chance have any of his other diaries with you?"

"Yes. But they're packed in with my personal items in storage bay three."

"Maybe we won't need them. You can work at this station." Mandy took the seat he vacated as the intercom crackled to life.

"Declan!" Sarah's frantic voice screamed at them.

"Yes?"

"Help."

The line went dead.

Chapter Ten

Declan shot upright. "Sarah?"

He slapped a com-pad. "Honan, get a team down to refuse now. Sarah's in trouble."

Mandy watched him pace the bridge. She knew he wanted to be on his way to Sarah, but he was the captain, and without backup, he couldn't leave the bridge. Several interminable minutes crept by before Honan called them.

"Declan? I'm down here in the refuse bay. Sarah is unconscious. She's got a nasty lump on her head but is alive. I found Damien Michaels' body behind a bin. According to Trish, he's dead. She took the body with her. I thought I'd run scans while they're still fresh. This time I'll download one to Hermes and keep the other on a data file."

"Do you have any hard evidence? Any ideas what killed him or who attacked Sarah?"

"None. There wasn't anybody here when I got here. He didn't have a scratch on him. Trish said she'd check for poison."

"Are you okay?"

"Yeah."

Declan ran his hands over his head. "What else can go wrong?" He glanced at Mandy. "Don't answer that. Please don't answer that. I'd rather not know."

Mandy reached over and placed her hand on his

arm. "I'm sorry, Captain. I feel like this is all my fault."

Declan shook his head. "No. I have a feeling Alvarez had this all planned. First, the ship has problems. The *Phoenix* has been a good ship but needs a major overhaul. Anybody with access to the maintenance logs would know. The owners don't seem to care. They let repairs go until there's no other option. We've been doing the work on our own. There are so many jerry-rigged systems, I'm surprised we haven't had more problems. Second, we have a plague that's not a plague. Where did the illness come from? If we're dealing with a plague, why were only those who went down to the planet affected? Was all this some kind of ruse to get you and us there? If so, why us? How did he know we'd be the ship to ferry you? I feel like we're being manipulated."

"Welcome to my life. Do you know I've spent the last year in an underground apartment so secure, it's in the top five of places for the Federated Council to go in case of emergency? Anytime I go out, I've got more security than the head of the Council. This is the most freedom I've ever had, and I'm still caged more than Alvarez was. We reach the first junction in three more days. I know you wanted to change course to Fleet. Can you get them to meet us at Xy-Three instead? If I remember my coordinates correctly, we'll take less time to get there than if we go to Fleet."

Declan sat back in his seat and pursed his lips. He gazed at her and nodded. "Agreed. Where'd you learn to read a spatial map?"

"Remember who my parents were? I was following their routes from the time I could say landing pod. Captain? I have one more request."

"Yes?"

"Would you please call me Mandy? This ma'am stuff is a pain."

Declan laughed. Mandy thought he had a pleasant laugh, and she liked the way his eyes crinkled at the corners. He should smile more often, she thought. Although, granted, he didn't have much to smile about in the here and now.

"Only if you call me Declan. Shall we get to work?"

Mandy turned to her monitor. Maybe the captain wasn't as bad as she'd originally thought. He had a lot of problems, and everyone depended on him to solve them. That would make anyone terse.

She looked at her father's diary. "Declan? Can Hermes scan this in? The code will be easier to study if I don't have to keep holding the book."

"The table is a light table as well as extended monitor. Hold the book the way you want, and Hermes will do the rest."

Mandy took the book over to the large table behind their seats and held the coded pages against the surface. "Hermes, I need a scan and hard copy of the symbols."

"Would you also like a hard copy of the symbols to Standard conversion?"

"Yes, that's a good idea. Hermes? Can you translate the text?"

"He tried," Declan said. "We got nothing but gibberish. That's why I want you to look at what's there. Maybe there's something we're missing. Something you might know through your father that we don't."

"Perhaps, but I'm not sure. Maybe this was some

kind of code he and the general had worked out."

"You're still our best source. You know both your father and the general. If anyone can come up with something, you probably can."

"You're not asking for much are you?" She sat down, compared the characters on the monitor with the ancient Aboolean alphabet, and got to work, fascinated by what she saw. The language was based on a series of straight lines, which was good considering the way they were scratched on the edges of the pages.

"Hermes? Which alphabet are we using?"

"According to my analysis, the original."

"That figures. Have you tried translating to other ancient languages?"

"Yes, and all the modern ones as well."

Mandy sighed and kept working.

Sometime later—Mandy wasn't sure if the time past was minutes or hours—Honan joined her and Declan on the bridge. She rose from her seat, but Honan motioned her to stay still.

"Good news and bad," Honan said. "Sarah is awake. She's got a concussion and a nasty headache but will be fine. She has no idea who hit her. The attack came from behind. As for Michaels, according to Trish, he was poisoned. I had her run a scan while we were in refuse. Michaels was Alvarez."

Mandy's eyes widened in shock. She'd talked with him, joked with him, and even reprimanded him. All those times and she hadn't had a clue. "That red-haired, green-eyed man was Miguel? But how?"

"He had medical help. DNA recombination, surgery, and more."

"So, what's the bad news?" Mandy asked.

"Who killed him?" Declan said. "And who attacked Sarah?"

Honan nodded. "Our scans were inconclusive. Too many people were in and out of the section, and there were no signs of a struggle, no weapons or anything to give us a clue."

"But I'm free," Mandy whispered. Miguel was dead. Her mind reeled. She should feel something, shouldn't she? All those years—all those deaths, and everything came down to this. She closed her eyes and bowed her head. All she felt was relief. She was free.

"Maybe. We still don't know who killed him or how or why," Declan said. "I'm not certain this is over yet. From what I've read, this is a bit too easy—too pat."

Mandy snapped her eyes open and raised her head. "You worry too much, Declan." Even as she said the words, a niggling worm of doubt crept in. Declan was right. Alvarez's death had been too easy. She shook her head as hope took over. Miguel was dead. He had to be.

"Worry is part of my job description." Declan pursed his lips. "Honan, you said there were no clues. Can any of the scans you ran cut out at least some of the crew?"

"Maybe," Honan said. "I can work on that angle. Why don't you take a break? You've been in here all day. I'll watch the bridge for a while."

Declan stood and stretched. "Good idea." He turned to Mandy. "Do you feel like some exercise?"

"Sounds like a good idea. I'll meet you there."

"Wait, I'll walk you to your quarters," Declan said.

Mandy turned to him. "No. Please. I've been guarded for my entire life. I know this sounds silly, but walking to my own place with nobody watching over me is something I've dreamed of forever. Being on a ship surrounded by people doesn't make any difference. Let me enjoy this. Please."

Declan grinned at her. "Understood. I'll meet you at the gym in a few minutes. Enjoy your walk, Mandy."

****

"Hermes?" Declan said as he watched her leave. "Keep a close eye on her."

"Not a problem, Captain."

Declan turned back to Honan. "So, what do you think?"

"That you're right. This was too easy. Something's not right here."

"He's really dead?"

"According to Trish. She took the body and told me the results."

"So you didn't see her perform the tests?"

"No." Honan frowned. "What are you getting at?"

"I'm not sure I trust her findings."

"Is that Declan, the captain talking? Or Declan, the man?" Honan asked.

Declan leaned against the table. "I'm not sure. That's why I'm looking to you for help. Tell me what you think."

"If you're paranoid, so am I. But we're talking about Trish here. You've known her for the better part of a year, and not all of that time was good. Or bad. We'll get to the bottom of this, Dec. One way or another."

"Thanks. Right now, I'd better get moving."

****

Mandy ran through a warm-up routine while she

134

waited for the captain. When she'd gotten to her cabin, she'd been surprised to find the guard gone. News certainly did travel fast on the ship. She'd changed quickly and headed to the gym. There were a few people there, but not so many as to be crowded. She looked around, trying to decide what she wanted to do. The gymnastic equipment drew her, and she hopped onto the balance beam.

Mandy went through an old routine, half-remembered from college. She'd never been serious enough to make a team, but she enjoyed the challenge. She executed twirls, leaps, and even a back flip that had her wobbling for control. She did manage to stick her pike dismount.

She turned as she heard someone applauding in the background and found Declan watching her. He was dressed pretty much the same as she was, in form fitting shorts and sleeveless shirt showing off his muscles to good advantage. She noticed a tattoo circling his left bicep. The design reminded her of Honan's tribal beads, and she wondered briefly about the ink. In high humor, Mandy bowed to him.

"So, what's my score?" She noticed the teasing glint in Declan's eyes.

"For that? A 7.5 at best. You only did the one back flip and wobbled a bit when you landed. Although you stuck the landing, the move was a straight pike with no twists or other advanced difficulty. You performed a good basic routine, but nothing spectacular."

"Not spectacular?" Mandy bit back a grin. She might not like his assessment, but he was absolutely correct. "If you knew how long it's been since I've done anything like that, you'd give me at least a 9.0."

Declan cocked his head as if considering her request. "Eight point two five, and that's my final offer."

"Sold." Mandy laughed. "So, are you here to work or gab?"

She ducked as Declan threw a towel at her.

Mandy and Declan ran several laps on the upper-level track and went through a weight routine. When she finished an hour later, she was tired, but felt better than she had in a long time. She returned to her quarters, took a quick shower, and was heading to the lounge for dinner when she passed a door she hadn't noticed before. She wouldn't have noticed the entry now since the door looked like every other one in the corridor, but this one was slightly open, and she felt a wave of warm, humid air flowing from inside and the smell of plants. But she was nowhere near the hydroponics area.

"Hermes?"

"Yes, boss?"

"Is this a cabin?"

"Not exactly."

Mandy thought she heard a touch of reluctance in the AI's voice. "Is this a public area?"

"Yes, but…"

"Never mind, Hermes." She palmed the door pad and entered—then stopped. She was standing on what appeared to be a rocky ledge overlooking a miniature jungle. The warm, moist air smelled of rich loam and green plants, and she breathed deeply of the heady aroma. She turned to make sure the door was firmly shut.

The jungle was two levels deep. The stairs were

cleverly disguised as rocks. If she closed her eyes, she could almost imagine she was in a forest. Although there were no real trees, there were different varieties of vines and greenery trained over stakes and supports to give the illusion of trees. The silence was almost reverential. Mandy descended the steps slowly, enjoying the feel of the moist air on her skin. The space reminded her a lot of home when she could get out.

She reached the ground and followed the path through the growth. She pushed through a screen of hanging vines and stopped in surprise. Declan was sitting lotus style on a small bench, his eyes closed. This was the most relaxed she'd seen him since coming on board. She backed away slowly, so as not to disturb him.

"Don't go," Declan said, his voice low and soft. Hermes probably alerted him to her presence, and he'd heard her the minute she'd entered.

"I'm sorry, Declan, I didn't mean to disturb you."

Declan unfolded his legs and shifted to make room on the bench. "You're not. So what do you think of our room?"

"This is beautiful. Is this part of hydroponics?" Mandy joined him on the bench, curling her feet under her.

"We created this area four years ago. We spent the time during one trip to make all the plans and order the supplies and two more trips to do all the work. Everything you see here is bio-engineered to filter impurities from the air and give us back the maximum amount of oxygen with the minimum amount of resources."

"With all you've told me about the company, I'm

surprised they let you do this."

Declan shrugged. "What they don't know... If you look at the ship's schematics, this shows up as a specialty hold. Only a few people know this place is here."

"I'd say this is more than a hydro experiment. This is a place for rejuvenating the soul."

"Agreed."

"And I disturbed you."

"No, not really. I'm glad you're here." Declan realized he was glad she was there. Mandy fit this setting. She might be a powerful business leader, but he had a feeling she was more comfortable in a place like this than in a boardroom. "So, you've had a taste of freedom. How do you feel?"

Mandy trailed her hand over a nearby vine. "Strange. I've spent so much time being protected, watched, told what to do, where to go, and who to see. All with the knowledge that somewhere out there was a man who wanted me dead. Now you tell me he is, but I don't feel any different. Not really."

"He was once your parents' partner, a family friend."

Mandy shrugged. "Only until he was caught. The last few years, Alvarez has been a thorn in my side. And now, the threat is gone. Shouldn't I feel something?"

"Not necessarily. You are who you are. Just because this one aspect of your life has changed doesn't mean you have."

"Taka told me the same thing."

"Then I'm in good company." He cocked his head to one side. "You're close to Taka, aren't you?"

"Yes. She and Papa D are the center of my life."

"What about friends?"

"My life didn't really allow for many."

Declan shot her a questioning look.

"Oh, don't get me wrong. I had friends, but they were mostly military brats like me or carefully selected children of loyal workers."

"That sounds lonely."

"Sometimes. But what about you? You're a captain. That's not exactly a job that engenders close relationships. I know you have Honan and Sarah, but is there anyone else?"

Declan sighed and leaned against the back of the bench. "There are a few people among the crew I call friends, but you're right, the job doesn't exactly give you many opportunities to put down roots."

"And now you've joined E-and-D. May I ask why? You, Honan, and Sarah don't seem the types."

Declan smiled. "Thanks."

A red blush crept up Mandy's face. "You know what I mean. E-and-Ds are loners. No family, no ties."

"That's me." He shrugged. "Actually, I made the decision mostly to get away from here. Don't get me wrong. I don't regret my time with the *Phoenix*. She's a good ship, or she was at one time. Now, she's tired. We were given the option of signing on as crew of a new ship, but I'm conceited enough to not want to take a step down to security chief."

"What? You weren't offered the captaincy? That's absurd."

The shock on Mandy's face and in her voice made Declan feel somewhat better. "The new captain is the owner's nephew. He's fresh out of school with a navigator's degree and is full of himself. Funny thing is, when I took him out for a test run, he got space sick. Puked all over himself. Claimed I must have programmed in a rough ride."

"I can imagine. What about other captain jobs? I know quite a few companies are crying for experienced people."

"Yes and no. I was told by a couple of companies I had too much experience. They didn't want someone who knew more than they did running their ships."

"That's silly. One of the traits I tell my hiring people is to look for people who want to work, no matter what their background. Would you believe one of my clerks is a man with multiple degrees in literature and history? He's one of my best workers."

Declan frowned at her. "That's what I mean. He's got those degrees, and you've got him doing a low job. The downgrade's got to be hard on him."

"Oh, no, you misunderstand. He loves what he's doing. He spent years as a professor, dean, and head of his department. His family rarely saw him. On his breaks, he was forced to travel in order to do research. You know the old *publish or perish* routine. He finally retired but wasn't ready to sit around. According to him, he was looking for a nine-to-five, Monday to Friday job where when he went home, he was done. When he came to us, he was an old man. We almost turned him away, but I saw something in him. That was three years ago. Today, he's happier and healthier than he's been in years. I met his wife at our annual picnic two years ago. She couldn't thank me enough for bringing life back to him."

"You sound like quite a boss."

"Don't get me wrong. I have my problems, as I'm sure you do."

"You mean like Jenkins? Yes, we get a few of them through here every now and then. Fortunately, not often. Over the years we've actually built a pretty good crew. The trick is to get good people and then let them do their jobs. Like this place."

"O'Malley?"

"And others, like Sarah's painting or Johnny's cooking, or any of the other talents we have. We spend months out here. Our hobbies give us a bit of home to cling to."

"So why stay out here?"

"That's a good question. Quite a few of the crew were actually born out here, either on board ships or stations. For them, they don't have ground ties. For the rest of us, I don't know. When we're out here, we yearn for home. When we're home, we can't wait to get back out here."

"Could you ever be happy planet bound?"

Declan leaned forward, his elbows on his knees, chin in his hands. "I don't know. I have a place, a cabin really, in the northern mountains on Aboo, but I haven't been there in years. I think if I had something to keep me busy, I could be happy there."

"That's the draw for you then. You need action. If you were stuck as a desk jockey, you'd go stir crazy. This ship may be a well-oiled machine, but the little quirks keep you thinking and, when the machine runs well, you come up with places like this."

Declan chuckled. "You sound like a therapist." He laughed when she blushed again. "But you're essentially right. I don't like inactivity."

He heard her stomach rumble. "And you need some dinner. I'll walk with you on my way to the bridge."

A few minutes later, they both stopped at their destination. "Thanks for the conversation, Declan."

Mandy reached up to pull a dead leaf out of his hair at the same time as Trish was leaving the dining area. The doctor ran directly into Mandy, catching her off-guard and knocking her to the ground.

"Oh, I'm sorry, ma'am. Are you all right?" Her stance, with hands on hips and a frown on her face belied her soft words.

Declan helped Mandy stand. "Yes, I'm fine, thank you. And thank you, Declan." Mandy emphasized Declan's name. Two could play the same game. She turned her back on Trish and entered the lounge.

She saw Jean and several of the other Warriors sitting at a table grouping in one corner and elected to join them once she had her food.

"Hi, Mandy." Jean grabbed an empty chair and joined them at the table.

"Hi." Mandy set her tray down. "This sure beats the messes we used to get on the base, don't you think?" Mandy bit into a slice of bruschetta.

"Oh, I don't know," one of the men said. "There's something to be said for SOS."

"Yeah, that it sucks," another man tossed out.

"Let's hope this time we get to eat some instead of having to clean the mess off the walls," Jean said and received a round of chuckles.

"So what do you guys do now that our problem seems to have been solved?" Mandy asked.

"What do you mean?" Jean asked.

"Well, with Alvarez dead, you aren't on full alert anymore." Her statement met complete silence.

"He's dead?" Jean asked. "How? When?"

Mandy frowned. What was going on? "Earlier this afternoon in the refuse area. He was poisoned. But you guys must have known. There was nobody at my cabin earlier."

"The colonel pulled us off duty after the gravity glitch," Mike Tremaine said. "Although we all agreed to keep a watch on you, just in case."

Mandy was touched. These people were her friends. She'd grown up with most of them or knew them from her association with the general. She glanced around the lounge to see who was near them, but they were mostly alone in their corner. "What can you all tell me about the colonel? Does anybody know anything about her?"

Mandy caught sideways looks some of the group gave one another. They might not know any specifics, but she'd bet a year's income they knew something. "Look, this isn't a good place to talk, and I know some of you might not want to speak out of turn, but I think we'd better find out about the colonel. If you think of anything, drop me a note. And if you want to talk, you know where I live."

The talk turned to their arrival on Xy-Three and what to expect there. Mandy had never been to the planet but had more extensive knowledge than any of the Warriors so clued them in on conditions. If the specter of Alvarez, the general, and the colonel hadn't been hanging over them, she would have had a most enjoyable time.

Chapter Eleven

The next morning, Mandy woke feeling happier than she had in a long time. Alvarez was dead, and Taka was going to wake up the general. The nightmare that was her life was over, and her new life was beginning.

"Boss?"

Mandy stopped braiding her hair. "Yes, Hermes?"

"You're wanted in the lab."

"Thanks, Hermes. Tell Taka I'll be there in a sec."

Mandy finished dressing and headed for the lab. On her way past the lounge, she stopped in and grabbed an energy bar and container of fruit juice. She munched on the bar as she made her way to Taka's lab. *I wonder why Taka called for me.* Mandy shrugged. *She probably wants me there when Papa D wakes up.*

Mandy got to the lab and stopped, the power bar halfway to her mouth. Declan, Honan, and Sarah stood outside the door. Sarah had her arm around Taka's shoulders. Of the lab, not much was left. Everything from microscopes to monitors had been destroyed. Shattered test tubes and Petrie dishes littered the floor. Waves of heat rolled out of the room.

"Taka?" Mandy whispered. She went to her aunt and hugged her. "What happened?"

"We don't know," Sarah responded when Taka didn't. "Taka called us a few minutes ago. The lab was like this when she got here this morning. Everything's been destroyed."

A lump settled in Mandy's throat. "Even the antidote?"

Taka looked at her, pain evident in her eyes. "Yes. I can't bring Tyler out of cold sleep yet. I'll need at least a week to synthesize another sample. And that's after I get this mess cleaned up. That could take weeks. I might as well wait until we get to Xy-Three and use their labs." She took a deep breath and exhaled.

They all jumped as a high-pitched alarm went off.

"Everybody back. Now," Taka ordered.

She waited until they'd all left the destruction and palmed the door shut. "Captain? This room should be sealed off. The area should still be considered a biohazard. Nobody goes in or out without a suit, and I want each of you in sickbay for a checkup—now. Is there a way to close off this room from air circulation?"

"Hermes?" Declan called as the alarm stopped.

"Already done, Captain. I've put double seals on the vents. I've also taken the liberty of spraying the room with a generalized decontamination foam and sealed the door for two hours."

"Thanks, Hermes." Declan turned to Taka and Mandy. "This bay is one of the few areas we're able to do that to because the space is designated as a hazardous material bay. That's one corner the owners aren't able to cut. All ship's hazard bays have to have isolation capabilities."

"What about security cameras?" Mandy asked. "Can we get an idea of who did this?"

"Sorry, boss," Hermes said. "I've been checking my files. All I've got is static."

"If I ever find who's doing this, I'm going to seal him in a bio-hazard room," Mandy said.

Nobody argued.

****

The next few days fell into a routine. Occasional glitches kept the routine from becoming boring. Mandy spent most of her days on the bridge with Declan, Honan, or Sarah. While there, she worked on translating the scribbles from her father's diary.

"Hermes, shift the letters three positions to the right in the alphabet."

"You tried that," Hermes said.

"Okay, what about reverse order?

"You tried that."

Mandy leaned her head in her hands and stared at the gibberish on the screen. "Is there anything we haven't tried?"

"Yes."

"What?"

"The correct combination."

"Arrrgh!" Mandy ducked her head in embarrassment as Declan stared at her. "Sorry. This is so frustrating."

Declan joined her at her station. "I guess you've tried all the usual crypto combinations."

"Yes. And all the ones in your databases." She rubbed her eyes in frustration. "Maybe this is silly. I mean, Alvarez is dead so there's really no reason to work on this."

"I disagree. I think solving the code could be more important than we know. What's here doesn't meet the requirements of a normal scheme. That means this is personal. He was your father. Close your eyes and concentrate on him. Think about what he liked to do. Who were the people who were the most important to him? Did anything or anyone have any special significance?"

Mandy closed her eyes and thought back to her father. "I was pretty young when he and my mother died. I don't remember much."

"That's okay. Tell me what you do remember. When did he and your mother meet?"

Mandy shook her head. "We've already tried the dates they met, married, had me, birthdays, and holidays."

"What else? What did he like to do for fun?"

"He was always active. He liked to climb, kayak, hike, and bike, anything that took him outside, kind of like you. He also liked to read and do word puzzles."

"You're from the islands. What about the ancient Lanicam languages?"

"We tried those. No luck. And took everything we did and tried those in reverse."

"This can't be that hard. The key has to be something both he and the general had in common."

"They were great friends but didn't really have much in common."

"What about you?"

"Me? I didn't have anything in common with them. I mean, I loved to hike and go out with my folks and Papa D, and I did a lot of activities together with them, but…"

Declan shook his head. "No, not what you had in common with them. What if you are the common factor? What's your birthday?"

"March fifteenth. But we already tried that."

"The Ides of March?" Declan laughed. "I hope your middle name isn't Caesar." He tapped his finger on his lips. "Hermes, what can you do with the number forty-four?"

"Why forty-four?" Mandy asked.

"That was the year Caesar was killed."

"Who's Caesar?"

"Part of an ancient legend from some long-forgotten world. He was the ruler of an expansive realm who was killed by his best friend."

"Ouch."

As Declan returned to his chair, Mandy started counting letters and marking them down on a flimsy. "Hermes, try this."

Suddenly, the gibberish started making sense.

"Declan?"

"Yes?"

"I think I may have something.

Declan rejoined her at the monitor.

"Look." The jumbled letters shifted and coalesced into phrases.

"Unknown spy on board—confidential records compromised—coded message received on splinter faction—possible Luddite uprising on planet. Proceed with all caution."

Declan read the message. "They had Luddite problems?"

Mandy nodded. "We still do. As with all businesses, there are always those who disagree with something you're doing. We've had demonstrations, boycotts, and even sabotage at different times."

"Could these people be the ones who started the plague?"

"I wouldn't put something like this past them. The Luddites haven't been known for their passivity." Mandy stretched the kinks out of her back.

Declan pushed her toward the door. "Out. Now. Food first, then some R and R. And that's an order."

"But…but I'm finally getting somewhere with this!"

"And the solution can wait a little longer. You need rest. And food. Go."

Mandy executed a perfect salute. "Aye, Captain."

Declan turned back to Sarah. "Meet you and Honan in the lounge?"

"See you shortly," Sarah said as Declan joined Mandy.

****

Mandy looked around the almost empty lounge. "What time is shift change?"

"In about five minutes, and you won't be able to move in here. I suggest we get our orders in and grab a table while we have the chance," Declan warned.

Sarah and Honan joined them a few minutes later. Declan was right. Hungry crew quickly filled the lounge. Mandy noted the lines of division between the two crews had softened considerably. With a few exceptions, everyone was mingling comfortably with one another. She even overheard some good-natured ribbing comparing the two groups. Instead of fistfights, the joking engendered laughter. The overall mood was light and easy, unlike the beginning of the trip.

"I'm glad to see everyone getting along so well," Mandy said.

Declan nodded. "You've got good people with you who know their jobs. If we'd had our regular crew, we might not have had as many problems, but we're all coming together well."

"How long until junction?" Though she hadn't been in jump space often, she knew there were unmanned mini-stations where ships could stop to refuel, pick up messages, and more.

"Tomorrow afternoon. Then a second jump and another week in regular space to Xy-Three. We'll start waking up the rest of your people the last day. I assume you'll want them ready to go once we get there."

"Yes. I've already given Hermes the rotation for warming them. I'd like medical first, then security. The paper-pushers can wait until the last."

"Mandy, what do you know about this colonel in charge of the troops?" Honan asked.

"Not much of anything. I do know she's not well liked. I can't do much research until we get to junction. What do you guys do for information when you're in jump space?"

"When we're at station," Sarah said, "we upload as much as the company thinks we'll need. Unfortunately, we often run into situations like this where we need some vital information they didn't think was relevant to our trip, and we're left floundering until we get to junction."

"That doesn't make sense. You ought to have more than the surface records of everyone with you as well as trip details."

"We don't have the capacity." Sarah jabbed a piece of fish like she was harpooning a whale. "Something like this happens almost every trip."

"Let me guess," Mandy said. "The owners don't want to be bothered."

She pursed her lips as the others nodded. "I'm going to investigate every single one of those buffoons and then fire them all. There's no excuse for this."

She winced as Sarah, Honan, and Declan stared at her. "I mean, if I could…"

"Try again," Declan said. His voice was low but carried a tenor of accusation.

Mandy sighed. "I didn't find out until after I'd commandeered you that the company you work for is a sub-company of Ki Enterprises. Actually, there are several subs between you and me, but you're in there." She bit her lip. The expressions on the three faces across from her were definitely chilly. "Trust me, if I'd known what was going on, I'd have taken care of everything before we left."

"Would you?" Declan asked. "You have no clue what's going on in your companies, do you?"

Sarah placed her hand on Declan's arm. "Give her a chance, Dec. Ki Enterprises is a huge corporation with a lot of arms."

"Thank you, Sarah." Maybe she had one friend left, Mandy thought. "But that's not the way Papa D taught me to run the company. The business has gotten so that the lawyers and bureaucrats do all the business. I'm a figurehead so tied up in red-tape, I rarely see any of the real business."

She held up her hand to forestall the argument she saw coming. "Don't say what you're thinking. I know, that's no excuse. And trust me, when this is all over with, what you've dealt with will change. In the meantime, maybe we can work together. I can't fix what I don't know about. Make a list of what you think needs to be improved. How can we make life better for the spacers? My business depends on you guys as much as on the products. Tell me how to help you, and I'll do what I can. I can't promise everything will be done immediately, but I do promise to keep a lookout and do what I can. I've already composed a letter to Mali to start the inquiries."

The icy chill warmed up a few degrees. "If those words had come from anyone else, I'd take them as empty platitudes," Sarah said. "But I think I've learned a few facts about you in the past few days. You do care, and I trust you will make good on your promise. Don't let us down."

"I won't." Mandy rose from her seat. "If you'll excuse me, I have some e-mail to get ready before we get to junction."

Mandy made her way back to her cabin. Although the actual distance was short, that was probably one of the longest walks she'd ever taken. All the trust she'd built up, gone with one stupid slip of the tongue.

She palmed open the door and stepped in. A hooded figure rushed at her, knocking her into the corner of the desk.

"Panther," was all she managed to whisper before the room went dark.

Chapter Twelve

"Mandy? Mandy, can you hear me? Come on, Mandy, wake up."

Mandy heard Declan's voice as though a thick wall separated them. There was a bright light ahead of her, and she knew if she could get there, she could rest, but Declan wouldn't let her alone. There was something she had to do first. The light was so welcoming, so inviting. Why wouldn't he let her sleep?

"Mandy, wake up. Come on, Mandy." His voice sounded full of worry. About her?

She groaned. Her head felt twice the normal size, and her eyelids weighed a ton.

"Taka? I think she's coming around."

Mandy felt something cold on her arm and the sharp sting of a hypo-spray. The throbbing in her temples abated somewhat, and she cautiously opened her eyes. She quickly shut them against the painful glare of light. Her stomach threatened to empty, and she swallowed against the sour taste.

"Hermes, cut light to fifty per cent. All right, honey, you should be able to open your eyes now."

Mandy cautiously opened her eyes. She wasn't quite sure she wanted to move her head, so she settled for what she could see by moving her eyes. She appeared to be in sickbay. Declan stood on one side of the bed, flanked by Sarah and Honan. Taka stood on the

153

other side, up by her head, studying something out of Mandy's sight. Trish stood next to her looking grim.

"Declan?" Mandy whispered through dry lips.

"Shh. Lie still until Taka has a chance to check you out."

"Thirsty."

"Doctor? Can she have something?" Declan asked.

"Get a piece of ice for her to suck on. Although I gave her an analgesic, her stomach is probably touchy."

Declan pressed a small piece of ice into Mandy's mouth. Nothing had ever tasted as good.

"Are you in any pain?" Taka asked.

Mandy tested her senses. "Just my head."

"I'm not surprised. The painkiller I gave you should help. Can you move your arms and legs for me? Right leg first."

Mandy moved each of her limbs in succession.

"Good. Can you tell me your full name?"

"Amanda Rianara Oliana Ki." She saw the raised eyebrows on the faces around her and heard Taka chuckling. "Don't ask. Now you know why I go by Mandy."

"Can she answer any questions, Doctor?" Declan asked.

"A few, but she needs rest. We're lucky I'm not doing an autopsy. She's fortunate her attacker was in a hurry."

"What happened?" Mandy asked.

"We were hoping you could tell us," Declan said. "What do you remember?"

His voice was gentle, but insistent.

Mandy frowned. "I was with you in the lounge, then I went to my quarters. I opened the door and there was someone in there."

"Do you know who attacked you?"

Mandy floated through a thick fog, faces going in and out of focus around her. She could almost remember, but she was so tired.

"Declan, your questions will have to wait. She needs rest."

"We need her answers, Doctor."

"I'm afraid you won't get any today."

Their voices faded as Mandy drifted off into a dreamless sleep.

****

Mandy shifted restlessly. Something had disturbed her sleep. She heard voices behind the curtain separating her from the rest of the sickbay.

"You should have let her die."

"With the captain and that aunt of hers standing over my shoulder? Then we would really have had a problem."

"Never mind. Can you implant the chip?"

"Yes, but even then, the piece is still no good without the activation string."

"You don't worry about the string. I'll take care of that. Get the job done."

Mandy could hear rustling, but she was so tired. She tried to think what their words meant. There was something important she needed to take care of. Sleep overtook her again.

Sometime later, she woke again. Slowly but more alert.

She tested her limbs and felt the stiffness that comes with extended bed rest.

"Welcome back, honey."

Mandy gingerly moved her head. Thankfully, there was no pain. "Taka?" Mandy's voice came out as a harsh croak.

"Here, drink this. The liquid will help your throat."

Mandy sipped the proffered ice drink. She wrinkled her nose at the medicinal taste but finished the liquid under Taka's watchful eye.

"Three days," Taka said as Mandy handed her the glass.

"What?"

"The first questions a patient usually asks are 'Where am I?', 'What happened?', and 'How long have I been here?'. Since you know who I am, you probably know where you are. You know what happened or will as soon as you're fully awake. That leaves how long you've been here. So, the answer is, three days. If you're feeling better, you may sit up."

With Taka's help, Mandy managed the feat. The room spun precariously. She covered her mouth as her stomach threatened to erupt and swallowed hard against the rising bile and gained some semblance of control.

"The dizziness and nausea will pass quickly. Do you feel any pain?"

"No." Mandy watched as Taka checked her vitals. She had an IV-line attached to her hand. Taka removed the needle and covered the spot with a sealant.

"Do you feel up to visitors?"

"I guess."

Taka pushed back the curtain hanging between the two movable side walls, allowing Sarah, Honan, and Declan access.

"Welcome back, again." Sarah gave Mandy a quick hug.

"Thanks."

"Think you're up to some questions?" Declan asked.

"I'll tell you what I can, but I'm afraid there's not much. Taka said I'd been here three days."

"Yes. Can you tell us who attacked you?"

Mandy frowned, thinking back to the attack. "He came out of nowhere. I think I fell, but I really don't remember." She reached up to touch her head and found bandages on her temple and behind her ear. "What happened? Was I hurt?"

Sarah sighed. "We thought you were dead. Thank the stars Hermes alerted us when he did."

"Hermes alerted you? What happened to the deterrents?"

"Another glitch," Sarah said. "Hermes felt so bad, he went into diagnostic overload. He's barely spoken since then."

"Do you know who hit you?" Declan asked again.

Mandy shook her head and instantly regretted the action as the room swam again. "No. He wore a dark hood. I'd say he was a man, though, or a rather solid woman. I'm sorry, I really don't remember anything else."

"That's okay," Declan said. "We're grateful you're better."

Trish pushed aside the curtain. "Captain? You and Honan are wanted on the bridge."

"Thanks." Declan turned back to Mandy. "We'll see you later. Rest and relax."

After the men had gone, Mandy moved over so Sarah could sit on the bed.

"Uhn-uhn. Taka would have my head. How do you

157

really feel?"

"Like someone knocked me over the skull. There's no lasting damage, I hope." Her words came out as half-statement, half-question.

"You were lucky. From what we could gather, you must have hit your head on the corner of the desk. That's what knocked you out. Fortunately."

Mandy saw Sarah cringe. She touched the bandage behind her ear—the same spot where the chip was. A dismayed thought crossed her mind. "That would explain one bandage, not two."

Sarah sighed. "Whoever hit you took your chip. And not nicely. If we hadn't gotten there when we did, you'd have bled to death. Declan didn't even wait for the medics. He wrapped your head and carried you down here while Honan alerted Trish and Taka. Even so, we were awfully close to losing you."

Mandy couldn't even begin to imagine the scene. "I'll bet that raised a few eyebrows."

Sarah smiled, then sobered. "Understatement of the decade. There's been a pair of guards outside ever since—against the colonel's orders, I might add. You've got some exceedingly loyal friends out there. I think the colonel has put the entire squad on report. They're following Michael Tremaine's orders. He's been talking with Declan a lot. I have a feeling the colonel has effectively been relieved of duty."

"How can they do that?"

"We're on board a ship under a Level I emergency. The captain is pretty much the final voice, and the colonel can't do anything to stop him. If her orders countermand what he considers important to ship's security, he can negate them. If she continues to cause problems, he'll toss her in the brig."

Mandy cocked her head. "We should have reached jump junction. Did any of my messages get sent?"

"I checked your back-log and took care of everything in the send file. I also took the liberty of picking up any incoming and filed them for you for later."

Sarah's thoughtfulness touched Mandy. "Thanks. I really appreciate that. Sarah, you and the others have to know I didn't know about the company. I know that's no excuse, but I intend to see changes made."

Sarah patted her hand. "I know. And so do Declan and Honan. While we were in junction, Taka introduced Declan to Malachi, and they talked. He seems like a good sort. He was most concerned about you but agreed to take a look at the company and what needs fixed."

"Mali is good. That's why I put him in charge instead of one of the lawyers. If he said he'd check into the issues, rest assured he will. He may look like an easy-going wimp, but he's got more business sense than all my high-priced paper pushers."

"Why don't you quit worrying? We have other issues to concern us right now."

Mandy lay back on the bed. There was something she should remember. Something important. But the memory wouldn't come.

"You look like something's bothering you," Sarah said.

"There's something…like a dream I had. But I can't remember."

"Taka told us you might have some minor memory loss. If a few details of your dreams are the worst of what you can't remember, consider yourself lucky."

Trish stepped into the area. "Time's up, Sarah. She needs her rest." She tapped her foot until Sarah gave Mandy a quick hug.

"I'll be back later," Sarah said.

Mandy watched her leave. "Doctor? How long will I have to stay here?"

"Another day. I don't want you doing anything to risk breaking those sealants. Now, get some rest."

She did as the doctor ordered.

Mandy woke and stretched. The twinge of stiff muscles reminded her where she was and why. She cautiously sat up, relieved when the room remained stationary. Most of sickbay was an open area that could be sectioned off into various configurations depending on the needs. She had been given a private section. The wall at her head was the permanent one that held the displays. The two sidewalls consisted of accordion panels that folded into the permanent one. A stiff curtain spanned the space between them. The entire space was about the same size as half her cabin. The walls were a medium shade of blue Mandy knew was supposed to be calming, but all they did was depress her. She needed to get out of there.

She swung her feet over the edge of the bed. The tiled floor was cold beneath her bare feet. When she stood, several alarms went off, and she fell back onto the bed in surprise.

"I see you're awake." Trish entered the cubicle. "If you'll grant me a few minutes, I'll help you find your legs."

Mandy sighed and lay back on the bed. She recognized Trish's tone of voice. Taka used the same one when she was in doctor mode and there was no arguing with her. Mandy lay patiently while Trish checked the monitors and removed the bandages. She wondered where Taka was.

"You'll have a scar behind your ear, but your hair will cover that. The cut on your forehead wasn't as severe or as deep so should heal with no problems. You can get them wet, but take care combing or brushing your hair out for another couple of days. I also recommend nothing more than light exercise for a week. You lost a lot of blood and need to rebuild your strength. You'll probably feel some residual pain from the chip removal. The electrodes left some damage when they were pulled out. You might experience some short-term memory loss."

"But I'm okay?"

"Yes, you're fine."

Mandy looked up as Sarah peeked her head in the door. "Hi, Sarah."

"Am I interrupting?"

"No. The doctor was giving me my marching orders." Mandy saw the small bundle in Sarah's hands. "I hope that's clothes. I'd rather not walk around the ship in a hospital gown." She pulled at the light blue tunic over matching trousers.

Sarah laughed and stepped aside for Trish to pass. "Oh, I don't know, that outfit would make something of a fashion statement."

"One I'd rather not make." Mandy opened the bundle. She found a soft green jumpsuit that looked hastily cut down from a larger suit. There were also shoes and underclothes, none of which she recognized. She turned a puzzled frown on Sarah.

"This is lovely, and I appreciate the gesture, but,

um, you couldn't get my own stuff?"

Sarah stared at the floor, her face turning red. "Well, you see, there wasn't anything left of your clothes. This was the best we could do on short notice. You're not exactly standard size."

"Nothing left? What do you mean?" Mandy shrugged out of the gown and donned the borrowed clothing. She had to do some adjusting with Sarah's help, but finally had something she could go out in.

"We'd like you to put these on too." Sarah handed her a small box.

Inside the box was a pair of small round black earrings set in gold. Mandy pulled one out of the case. "They're lovely, but I don't understand."

Sarah helped her put them on. "They're not actually jewelry, although Chane designed them to look that way. They're sensors. With them, Hermes can track you and know not only where you are, but also if you're in distress. They were his idea."

"That was sweet of him." She looked up. "Thank you, Hermes." She waited, but there was no answer. "Hermes?"

Sarah shook her head. "The glitches are getting worse, and he feels pretty bad about what happened. Give him a bit, and he'll be back."

"Where's Taka?"

"Sleeping. She's been here ever since Declan brought you in. Trish finally ordered her out, and I think one of your med-techs slipped her a mickey."

Mandy chuckled. "That would be the only way to get her to sleep. I'm glad."

Sarah helped Mandy roll up the legs and arms of the suit and belt the waist. "Declan put a guard on her and on the general's pod. Plus, there have been two Warriors at the door here and either one of us, meaning Honan or Dec or myself, or one of the Warrior group were here in your cubicle the entire time. After Declan and I left you here, we joined Honan in your cabin. Whoever attacked you wasn't happy. They shredded everything—bed, blankets, furniture, and clothing. There was nothing left."

Her heart pounded, and Mandy was sure Sarah could hear the sound. "Everything?" What about her statue? The rest was minor and could be replaced but the statue…

"All but one item." Sarah dropped the statue in Mandy's hand. "I found this in a corner under the desk."

Mandy stroked the small carving. "Thank you, Sarah. This means more than you know. I don't care about the rest." She tucked the carving into a pocket.

"Is that what I think it is?"

Mandy pulled the statue back out and held the piece up for the light to catch. Sparks of red and gold burst from the depths making the cat look alive. "Yes."

Sarah whistled. "That's worth a fortune."

"This is worth more than money. My dad carved this on his first trip back—before we knew what chrystolian opal was." She tucked the figurine back into her pocket. "What's with the doctor? She was almost civil to me."

"You're a patient. She may not be the nicest person around, but she is a good doctor."

"So why does she hate me so much?"

"I don't really know. I'd guess because of Declan. She sees you as a threat."

"Me? I'm no threat. I'm not looking for any liaisons."

"Doesn't matter. You're young, pretty, rich, and have power. She wants what you have. Trish is a climber and doesn't let anything get in her way. She and Declan were an item for a few months. Surprised the heck out of quite a few of us."

"What happened?"

"Last trip, we were getting ready to leave, and Declan stopped in to see the base commander. They're fairly good friends. He caught Trish coming out of the commander's bedroom, sans clothing."

"She was with the commander?"

"No. His wife."

"Ouch."

"Yeah. Rumor mill says she's found someone else already, but nobody knows who. What do you say we break you out of this joint?"

Mandy stood up too quickly and grabbed the bed for support as the room wobbled.

Sarah offered a hand. "You okay?"

"Yeah. A little woozy, but okay."

"According to Taka, that's normal." Sarah grinned at Mandy's narrow-eyed glare. "Declan, Honan, and I were given a list of strict instructions to follow concerning your recovery. We adhere to them, or you end up back here."

"Okay, okay. I'll behave." The room settled back to normal. "Lead on."

Mandy followed Sarah out of the cubicle. Two Warriors stood outside the door. "Hi, Sam, Tony."

The men nodded at her and smiled. "Glad to see you up and around, Mandy."

They fell into step behind her and Sarah.

Mandy looked around at them, her eyebrow raised. "I guess I have no choice in this, do I?"

"No, ma'am."

"Yeah. All I need is a drum major's baton."

As they moved through the corridor, everyone they met stopped them and offered hugs or best wishes to Mandy. They got to her cabin, but Sarah kept going.

"Um, Sarah?"

"You've been moved. I was serious when I said there was nothing left. The room will require a complete refit."

Sarah led her to the VIP cabin next to Declan's. One Warrior stood outside the door, another at the next cabin. They came to attention when the parade arrived. Mandy sighed. Their concern and vigilance touched her, but all the fuss made her uncomfortable.

Mandy entered the room. Instead of the small sitting area and single bedroom, like the general's cabin, this was one large room with two single beds separated by a small table. On the bed nearest the door, Mandy recognized Sarah's blue silk robe. She turned to Sarah.

"Is there something else you want to tell me?"

"Um, I hope you don't snore?"

Mandy collapsed on the farthest bed. She hated to admit even to herself, but she was exhausted. "Okay, I've got a headache the size of Mt. Pitonas. I have no clothes. I've been moved to a secure cabin. I've got round-the-clock guards. And I have a roommate. Is there anything else I need to know?"

Sarah pursed her lips. "No, I think that about covers everything."

"Isn't this the cabin Taka had?"

"She's been moved to the general's quarters next door. Actually, she spends so much time in the lab, I wouldn't be surprised if she had a cot there. Most of the mess has been cleaned up, but as you know, all the samples were destroyed. Unfortunately, she had the only samples from Xy-Three so she can't do anything until we get there. I think she's been working round the clock on the antidote for the general."

"I didn't think she'd wait until we got to the planet. She won't stop until she finds the cure. Failure is not a term in Taka's vocabulary."

Sarah went to the storage drawers and opened them. "As for no clothes, we're working on that. One of your med-techs actually knows how to sew—with a needle and thread. Almost everyone donated something, and he's been busy altering what we got. He'd like to get your measurements so he can give you a better fit. Once we unload the pallets at Xy-Three, you can get to your own gear."

Their thoughtfulness touched her. "You guys are great." She yawned widely. "Oh, sorry. I don't know why I'm so tired. After all, I've done nothing but sleep the last three days."

Sarah rose from her bed. "Taka said you'd tire easily. Even though we're on the same level, our walk probably took a good bit out of you. I'll let you sleep, and we'll talk later."

Chapter Thirteen

The next day, Mandy rejoined the captain on the bridge and settled back at the station monitor she'd left only a few days ago. The interval away seemed like a lifetime.

"Are you sure you're up to working?" Declan asked, concern etched in his face.

"I may not be able to put in a full day, but don't expect me to sit in my room twiddling my thumbs either." She smiled when Declan nodded. If anyone understood her need for action, he would. "Have you made any progress on finding out who hit me?"

"Yes, and no," Declan said. He called a file up on his monitor. "This time we actually got a scan of fingerprints."

"That's good, right?"

"Yes, except for one problem. After we eliminated your prints, the only other ones we found belonged to me."

Mandy stared at the captain, then grinned. "Well, we know that's not possible seeing as you were with Honan and Sarah in the lounge. I think we've got more than a few credible witnesses who can attest to that."

"Thank you for your vote of confidence," Declan said with a wry smile. "Whoever is doing this is good and knows more than we do. Unfortunately, we don't have the equipment to do more than a basic investigation. Fleet investigators will meet us at Xy-Three, and we'll be able to take care of everything then."

"But you still have someone on board who's committed two murders, attempted another, possibly two," Mandy pointed out.

"Alvarez is dead," Sarah said.

"Is he?" Declan asked. "I've never been comfortable with that theory." He held up a hand to forestall arguments. "Yes, the man we thought might be Alvarez is dead. But whether he's Alvarez or not, we still have someone on board who's out for blood."

Mandy touched her head. The bandages had been removed, but the spots were still tender. "I'd say he got some. Sarah told me he pulled my chip out. I don't understand. The chip can't be used without the code string, and that's something only I know."

"For as many ways as there are to secure something, there are as many ways to get around one," Honan said. "Although I must admit, I've never heard of anyone beating a chip."

"So what do we do now?" Mandy asked.

"We go back to square one and start with the personnel again. This time, we don't leave anyone out," Declan said.

"Even you, Captain?" Mandy teased. "After all, we have evidence you were in my room."

"Maybe that was my clone. Lord knows, I feel like I could use one right now."

Mandy grabbed her desk as the ship shuddered. The glitches were coming more frequently and lasting longer. She checked what she could of the ship's status. According to the logs, engineering was keeping busy replacing burnt out power relays and tracking down system failures. Although she didn't understand a lot of what she saw, what she did see looked to her like they were fighting a losing battle. Hopefully, once they reached Xy-Three, they'd be able to power down the systems and do some real repairs.

She closed those files and brought up her mail files. There were dozens of get-well wishes from various crewmembers. She sent a thank you to each one. Malachi had sent a few communiques, and she flagged them for later replies. One that interested her more than the others was one entitled "Glenna Jones". Curious, she set the file aside until she could give the dispatch her full attention. The final one was sent after she arrived on the bridge. The subject was *get well* and had a generic ship address. She opened the file.

The message scrolling across the bottom said, "You got lucky—this time. Give me the codes."

"Declan?"

Mandy's voice came out as a bare whisper, but the others heard her. Declan responded first. He was at her seat almost immediately and saw the file. "Sarah, where was this file sent from?"

Sarah's hands flew over the console. "Hold One."

"Turn on those cameras." Declan turned to Honan who was already on his way out the door. The monitors remained blank. "Sarah, where are the cameras?"

"Sorry, Captain, I can't get them to function. I've sent in several ROVERs as backup. You should be seeing them now."

A fuzzy picture appeared on the screen and quickly cleared. Mandy took a minute to get the perspective. The camera angle was low to the ground and looking upward while moving. With her current skewed sense of balance, the view was disorienting. But the little 'bot was doing his job.

"ROVER 1," Declan said.

Mandy chuckled as an electronic bark answered Declan.

"Chane's idea of a joke," Declan replied to her laugh. "Scan mode, aisles one, two, three. ROVER 2, scan mode, aisles four through six. ROVER 3, scan mode, aisles seven through ten."

The view on the screen broke into three separate windows and they watched the aisles flash by.

"...don't like this..."

Mandy heard the voice and grabbed Declan's arm. "Aisle two. There's someone there—in the shadows."

"ROVER 1, silent mode, ears and eyes to maximum, aisle two. ROVERS 2 and 3, converge on aisle 2."

"Patience. You knew going into this, our plans would take time. Besides, I haven't seen you keeping up your end of the bargain."

"I told you, there are too many people watching. They've got guards everywhere, even in cold sleep. How am I supposed to do anything?"

Mandy realized she was probably listening to the person who had tried to kill her. And not only that, but there was more than one person involved. Unfortunately, she couldn't tell if they were men or women. Did Alvarez have accomplices who would continue to carry out his threats even after his death? She shivered in spite of the warm room. Declan placed a hand on her shoulder, and she welcomed his touch.

The voices were horribly distorted and the picture

on the screen grew fuzzy as she watched. The other two pictures were still clear. "Is the system glitching again?"

"No. They must be using a leash—an electronic masker," Declan explained.

A sudden alarm made Mandy jump. The distorted voices continued.

"We've got company. Get out of here. I'll talk to you later."

Mandy watched as a shadowy figure loomed over the camera. "Ah, ah, ah. Bad doggie." Was all they heard before all three screens went blank.

"Sarah, replay that last bit and see if you can enhance the person," Declan directed.

Mandy waited with Declan, her hopes sinking as Sarah shook her head. The voices sounded familiar, like something from a half-remembered dream. She concentrated on her memory, but nothing came to her.

"I can't clean the feed up," Sarah said. "I can't find any record. The ROVERs are all blank, and the feed was zapped."

"Declan?" They heard Honan's voice over the speakers. "I've got a team with me. Can you give me any guidance?"

"Last we heard they were in aisle two. The ROVERs are all dead."

"The cameras have all been fried. We're working on a temporary set-up."

The monitor came back to life with a view of Honan's face. "One of the Warriors has a portable. He'll feed from that."

As Mandy and Declan watched, the small troop swarmed over the bay, but they found nothing except three ROVERs damaged beyond repair.

Declan slammed his hand down on the desk. "Damn. I'm getting tired of this. How the hell did they get out of there? Honan, leave a guard detail there and have the rest check any possible avenues of escape."

"Aye, Captain."

Declan grabbed the edge of the desk as the ship shuddered again. "Sarah?"

"Every hour on the hour, Declan. I've gotten so I can set my watch by them."

"Any other glitches?"

"Minor ones in environmental control in the docking bay and lighting in engineering control."

"Have Chane check them out."

"He already has, Declan."

"Then have him check them again. I want to know what the hell is happening to my ship." He ran his hands over his head and Mandy heard—and understood—his frustration. She wished she could help him, but there was nothing she could do.

"Aye, Captain."

Declan left the bridge without a backward glance.

"Well, now you've seen him at his worst," Sarah said.

"I'd say he has good reason." Mandy swiveled her seat around and opened the Glenna Jones file. When she finished reading the information contained within, she pulled up another file and compared the two, then blew out a long breath. A few minutes later, she sat back and chewed her lip. She turned around in her seat. "Sarah? I have a file here you all might want to see."

Sarah scanned the dossier, sat back in her seat, and whistled. "No wonder she didn't like you. How many other enemies do you have floating around out there?"

Mandy shrugged. "Who knows? People in power tend to collect death threats as easily as other people breathe. What I want to know is how she managed to get on board with security so tight?"

"I wonder if she's one of Alvarez's cohorts. That would explain the security breach," Sarah said. "Declan needs to know this."

"I need to know what?" Declan strolled back onto the bridge. He looked slightly less angry than he had when he'd left, and Mandy wondered if he'd visited the garden.

"Why the colonel has been less than cooperative. She was on the fast track for promotion when Master General Davis caught her in an illegal arms deal. Seems she played both sides of the fence during the Aino uprising, supplying both combatants with military weapons. She got sent to a penal colony, then disappeared a year ago. Suddenly she shows up here with a new name, forged credentials, and a new look. Plus, she has ties to the Luddites. She's one of their leaders."

"So how do you know for sure the colonel is this Glenna Jones?"

"She's cagey, but not too smart. I checked the DNA on her ID with what's in the file. She's the same person."

"Hermes? Get me Honan."

"Aye."

"At least we can solve one of our problems," Declan said. "I wonder if she was the one who attacked the general?"

"I thought we agreed that was Alvarez," Mandy

said. "I don't see the colonel using the knife we saw."

"Not necessarily. Without the equipment to even do a basic investigation, we can't even prove the master general was in the room. We have his fingerprints we can test and DNA, but that's all, and we've seen how those can both be manipulated."

He turned as Honan entered the bridge. "Honan, I'd like you to take two Warriors and place our recalcitrant colonel under arrest. Throw her in the brig and post a guard. Oh, and you don't have to be nice. She's neither an officer nor a lady."

Mandy caught the smile on Honan's face. She guessed the colonel had been a major thorn in their sides and the relief was heartfelt. Mandy's stomach rumbled, reminding her she'd gone too long without a break. "Declan? I'm going for some lunch."

Sarah jumped up. "Wait, I'll go with you."

Mandy snorted. "You think I don't have enough guards? I need a babysitter too?"

Sarah feigned a hurt look. "I don't know what you mean. I'm hungry."

"Yeah, right. Okay, shadow, let's go."

Mandy stepped into the crowded lounge behind Sarah and in front of her two guards. The silence started at the door and spread through the entire room as every eye in the place focused on her. One Warrior on the upper level stood and started clapping. Quickly, the entire room erupted into cheers.

Mandy dipped her head to hide the blush she could feel and waved at the crowd. She and the others placed their orders and looked for an empty table.

"Here, ma'am." The same Warrior who had led the ovation offered his table. "We were pretty much done."

His companions nodded and gulped down the last of their meals.

"Thanks," Mandy said.

"Thank you. We owe you for getting rid of the colonel. Though she wasn't too happy."

"How many of you were needed take to bring her down?"

The man feigned a hurt look. "You think one of us couldn't do the job? Actually the security chief— Honan?—put a hold on her we can't wait to learn. Had her marching in front of him with barely a fight. Good thing he wasn't in front of her. The look on her face would have frozen him in place. We're rotating guard duty on her and, believe me, she's not getting any privileges."

Mandy looked at Sarah who only grinned. "News does travel fast around here."

"Nothing's faster than the grapevine express."

They enjoyed their meals and the conversation.

After lunch, Mandy retired to her room to rest. Her lack of energy frustrated her, but she knew she'd have to behave or risk ending up back in sickbay. At least, by confining the colonel, she'd accomplished something before giving in to exhaustion.

****

The shuddering had become routine, and still the engineers hadn't been able to find a reason. Mandy returned to the bridge the next day after lunch and walked into a sauna. The temperature had to be a hundred degrees and the humidity almost as high. Honan had stripped down to shorts and a sleeveless shirt, but sweat soaked the material. A central floor tile had been lifted off the lower level, and Mandy heard muffled sounds from beneath, most of which was unintelligible.

Mandy fanned her face. "Whew! Who turned up the heat in here?"

"Environmental claims this glitch isn't their fault. Declan wants to make sure we haven't sprung a coolant leak or something worse," Honan said. He joined Mandy and Sarah on the upper bridge and wiped the sweat from his face.

"Under the floor?"

"There's an arrangement of low access tunnels under the entire bridge, and they are the only way to get to the systems in here. We have wall panels in the rest of the ship, but not here," Sarah explained. "The problem is access. Maneuvering room is a bit tight down there."

"What about the ROVERs?"

"We tried, but they keep dying on us. They get about halfway in and stop. Nothing. No video, no audio, no nothing."

"You need the human touch," Mandy said.

"Yes. Declan, Sarah, and I have all been down, but the space is a tight fit."

"What about me?" Maybe her size could finally be an advantage instead of an irritant. "I'm a lot smaller than any of you. Could you tell me what to look for?"

"Declan?" Honan called. "What about putting Mandy down there?"

Declan's head popped out of the hole. "Are you sure you're okay?"

"I'm fine. Taka gave me the once-over this morning and passed me, as long as I don't do anything too physical. Walking around a tube is fine."

"Who am I to argue with the great Taka Yu?" He climbed the rest of the way out and wiped his hands on his shorts. Unlike the others, he was bare-chested. A fine sheen of sweat showed off sculpted muscles, and Mandy drew in a breath as she tried not to stare. Honan was fit and good looking, but Declan…. The heat she was feeling had nothing to do with the ambient temperature.

"Besides, I'm tired of playing snake," Declan said as he grabbed a bottle of water from a nearby cooler.

"Give me two minutes to slip into something more fitting," Mandy said. The jumpsuit she wore was another hasty job and much too loose to wear in tight quarters. She thought she might have something that would work better. She ran back to her cabin, Sarah close behind.

Mandy worked at getting out of the too-big garment while Sarah searched the drawers.

"Look in the bottom right one. I believe there's a pair of shorts and a sleeveless top in there," Mandy said. "I think one of your crew—Malick?—donated them."

Sarah pulled out the clothes. "Malick is small, but not quite as small as you." She tossed them to Mandy.

"Not to worry. She claims they're tight on her." Mandy donned the dark shorts and top. They weren't tight, but they were by no means as loose as the other pieces. "Suitable?"

"Perfect," Sarah said. She led the way back to the bridge.

"I've got your snake," Sarah said.

Honan gave Mandy a headpiece with a mike. There was a small camera attached above the earpiece. "This

177

is two-way, so we won't have to yell at each other. We've also put another ROVER down there. You can run him manually."

"What am I looking for?"

"That's part of the problem," Declan exclaimed. "We don't know. Try for a different color or size or shape than the surrounding conduits. Look for cracks or leaks or anything that doesn't seem to fit. Everything down there is white or light gray and smooth piping with no extraneous protrusions. The space is immaculate. Ready?"

Mandy sat on the edge of the opening. "Ready."

She held up her hands, and Declan lowered her to the floor below.

"There's not much light down here and it's hot—a lot hotter than up there." She wiped a trickle of sweat from her brow.

"There's a light panel on your right at about shoulder height," Declan said.

"Your shoulders or mine?" Mandy heard a round of chuckles.

"Press the bottom switch."

Mandy found the panel and hit the switch, and pale light flooded the area. She had headroom, but barely, and her shoulders were almost to both walls. The men would have been extremely uncomfortable negotiating the tubing, and she admired them for having tried as much.

She saw the ROVER and switched on the robot.

"How's the pick-up?" she said into the two-way.

"Fine." Declan's tinny voice came through the device.

She studied the maze of conduits carrying wires,

coolant, and all the other pieces of machinery that kept the great ship going. The tube curved off in both directions. "Which way do I go? And how far before the ROVER quits?"

"Try to the right. We don't know how far or what's going on, so be careful."

Mandy looked at the close quarters, all her senses on edge. "Not a problem."

She crept through the tunnel, checking the conduits and keeping an eye on the ROVER. In some spots she had to slip sideways through tight spaces. She kept an eye on her surroundings and on the ROVER. The little robot skidded to a halt and let out a high-pitched squeal that reverberated through her headset.

"Ouch!" Mandy tore the headset off and rubbed her ear. Using her toe, she nudged the immobile ROVER back, cutting off the noise. Her ear was still ringing.

She put the two-way back on. "Declan? Can you still hear me?"

He didn't answer.

"Declan?" Mandy yelled back toward the opening. "Are you all right?"

She barely heard Declan's voice. "Except for an earache. The ROVER's completely dead, and so is the mike."

"Do you see anything unusual?"

Mandy stared at the maze surrounding her. "As if I'd know," she muttered.

She saw a small black cylinder attached to one of the conduits that didn't fit in with the rest of the piping. "I might have something," she yelled.

Without any forethought, she reached for the cylinder and pulled. Sparks flew, and she received a jolt

that landed her on her backside.
 "Damn!"

Chapter Fourteen

Mandy shook her head. Both ears rang, and her arm was numb from the hand all the way up to her shoulder. She heard a noise behind her, glanced back, and broke out laughing.

Declan was on his hands and knees, scurrying as quickly as he could toward her. The other set of hands and knees she saw could only belong to Honan. Sweat dripped off Declan's face.

"I guess if you're laughing, you're all right," Declan said. "She's all right!" he yelled.

"I think I've found your problem, gentlemen." Mandy stood and pointed at the black cylinder. "I do suggest you don't touch that gadget. Packs a heck of a jolt."

Declan tried to get past Mandy, but the close quarters made the move impossible. Mandy put her hands on her hips, smiling at the men kneeling in front of her. "I always did want to have men kneeling at my feet, but this isn't exactly the setting I had in mind."

She glanced at the tube. "This space makes a giant circle around the bridge, right?"

"Yes," Declan agreed.

"Good. You can stay here and study our bug. I'll go around and get you the tools you need."

She moved off easily, chuckling as the men grunted and shifted into sitting positions. A few minutes later, she stepped into the square beneath the opening. "Sarah? Could you give me a hand?"

Sarah's face appeared, blocking the light. "Grab on." She helped Mandy from the tube. "What's going on?"

"There's a small black cylinder, about six inches long and one in diameter attached to one of the conduits that's dangerous to touch. Declan and Honan will need some tools for removal."

Mandy grabbed a bottle of water from a nearby stash and drank deeply. The heat and humidity hadn't abated any. In fact, if anything, the air felt hotter than ever. Sarah had set up portable fans so there was at least some air moving on the bridge. Mandy picked up a towel from a pile on the table and wiped the sweat from her face.

Sarah pointed to a small box. "This should have what they need." She handed Mandy an AV unit. "Put this outside the dampening field on close-up mode, and I'll monitor from here."

"No problem." Mandy jumped back down into the hole.

"This time don't touch anything," Sarah said as she handed Mandy the tools.

Mandy rubbed her still-tingling arm. "Don't worry. I'm not planning to."

She rejoined Declan and Honan as they strained to maneuver in the tight space. Stifling a grin, she set up the video unit and handed Honan the tools. "Have you figured the mechanism out yet?"

"Yeah," Declan said. "We call it a leash, but this one's got some extra punch."

"So I noticed." Mandy watched as the two men

tried to work, bumping their heads and other body parts on the tubes. After the fourth muttered explicative, an idea occurred to Mandy.

"Honan, since you've seen the leash, is there a way you can talk me through the dismantling?"

Honan paused and stared at her. "I wish I'd been born a pygmy."

"Ah, but then Sarah would be continually looking down on you."

"You'll have to get past me," Honan pointed out. "Guess we'll have to go back to the opening."

Mandy studied the pipes over her head. "How secure are the conduits?"

"Very, why?"

"Lie face down on the floor."

Honan frowned but did as she requested.

Mandy grasped two conduits and used them to support some of her weight as she quickly walked up Honan's legs and back and stepped lightly off his shoulders. She heard muted laughter coming from the AV monitor, and Declan had a huge grin on his face.

"Okay, bosses, what do I do?"

Following their directions, Mandy unhooked the cylinder and stowed the offensive piece of equipment in a protective sleeve. She wiped her sweating hands on her shorts and finished the job by wrapping repair tape around the conduit.

"Mandy, did you see any more of these babies on your circuit through the tube?" Declan asked.

"No. At least not on the surface. But I didn't take the time to really search. Do you want me to take another walk around?"

"Yes, especially now that you know what to look

for. And you can take the AV unit with you. If that goes dead, we'll know there's probably something there."

"Declan? Is the way we came in the only access point to these systems?"

"No. But the only one that's easy to get to—if you call this easy. The other way is through the hold, but I don't think that way's ever been used. You have to climb almost the entire height of the ship through the maintenance tubes to get here."

Mandy thought back a few days. "I'll bet someone has—and rather recently."

"Anyone using those access points would have shown up on a monitor," Declan said.

"A maintenance monitor, right?"

Declan nodded.

"What if he was a maintenance person and somehow got around the monitors?" She pointed at the bagged cylinder. "This guy is no dummy. He's had us running around in circles ever since we started this trip."

Declan tapped his finger on his lips. "You may have something. Let Honan and me get back above, then you can go around and see if there's anything else down here."

Mandy laughed as the two men crawled while she walked back through the tube.

"You don't have to make that look quite so easy," Honan muttered.

Mandy waited as Honan pulled himself out of the hole, then stood aside for Declan to do the same. She clipped the AV set to the collar of her shirt and walked the circuits. She found one more cylinder and quickly disengaged the piece the same as she had the other one.

The rest of the tube was clear.

"I only found this one. Was pick-up clear on the monitor?"

"Except when you were near the leash," Sarah said. "I'd say we're clean. At least the temperature's a little cooler."

Mandy chugged another bottle of water. Cooler air was coming through the vents, but bringing the bridge temperature down to any semblance of normalcy would take time. "Where are Declan and Honan?"

"On their way to the holds."

"What can you get to from there?"

"If you know where to go, practically everywhere."

"I'd say whoever did this knew where to go."

"Sarah?" Declan's voice came over the speakers. "Turn your monitor to my remote pick-up."

Sarah did, and the hold came into focus. The view bobbed around, high above the floor. "Um, Declan? Either you've grown a bit, or something is going on with the camera."

"Neither."

The picture moved along showing the tops of the pallets. Several items floated by.

"There's no gravity down here. Atmosphere is okay, but there's no footing. Honan went to get some gravity boots. I'm checking some of the maintenance tubes now. I'd say someone has been tampering with them. The seals are all broken."

"How bad are we talking?"

They could hear Declan grunting in the background. "Damn. Bad. Really bad."

Mandy could see cylinders attached to almost all the conduits. "Declan? Do you need me down there?"

"No. I want Chane to work on this. He's the best one for this job. Sarah? Get a crewman down here to tie down the loose cargo."

"Will do. Anything else?"

"Damn. Damn. Double damn."

"Declan? What's wrong?" Sarah asked.

"Sarah, what's our heading?"

Sarah turned to the navigator's station. "On course for Xy-Three. Why?"

"I'll be there shortly and explain."

The screen went blank. Mandy stared at Sarah and Sarah stared back. "I wonder what that was all about?"

Mandy frowned. "You don't think…"

"That we've got navigation problems? No. We were on course when we passed through the junction."

"But that was three days ago. What if we are off course? Is there any way to check our position manually?"

"Yes, but you're talking a real hassle here. For a manual navigational check, we'd have to drop out of jump space, get a fix on the stars, and chart our position on actual printed charts. If Hermes is compromised, we won't be able to use him to verify any of our data."

"But you can do one manually, right?"

Sarah shrugged. "I've never done a manual check. Honan and Declan have."

"I have what?" Declan strode onto the bridge.

"Done a full manual navigational check," Sarah said.

"Yes, I have, thank goodness, because that is exactly what we're going to do."

Sarah stared at him. "I'm not going to ask if you're serious 'cause I know you wouldn't joke about something like that. What do we need to do to get ready?"

"We'll be dropping out of jump space, and people will feel the change, so we'd better warn the crew. And we'll need to download the star charts for this area of space. We don't want to drop out in the middle of an asteroid field or worse."

"Hermes, give me the star charts for our current position and all flanking systems."

"Aye, Captain."

Mandy hadn't heard the AI's voice since she'd left sickbay. "Hi, Hermes."

"Hello, Ms. Ki. I'm glad you're better."

Mandy heard a definite tone of contrition in his voice. "Hermes, you weren't to blame for what happened to me. In fact, if you hadn't alerted the captain when you did, I'd probably be dead. You actually saved my life."

"I did?"

"Yes, Hermes, you did," Declan agreed. "Now get those charts for me."

"Aye, aye, Captain." The AI's voice sounded happier than he had a minute ago.

Declan turned to Honan. "Have Chane get teams together and coordinate repairs. I want to know what systems are affected and by how much."

He sat down at the console and put on a headset. "Attention all hands. In thirty minutes, we will be dropping out of jump space in order to take care of some routine navigational maintenance. This should not take more than an hour. You will be notified prior to resuming the jump. Thank you."

Mandy stayed out of everyone's way. There was

really nothing she could do but watch. Suddenly Sarah held up her hand while holding her earpiece with the other.

"Declan? Security says the colonel has escaped. She freaked out when she heard the announcement and fell to the ground, as if she'd passed out. When the guard went in to check on her, she clobbered him and took off. The Warriors are searching for her now."

"Tell them to keep me apprised."

Sarah nodded and relayed the information. She joined Mandy on the upper level. "Give me a hand."

"What can I do?"

"Once Hermes gives you the hard copies of the charts, lay them out on the table according to file number, low to high."

Mandy sat down and got to work. Sarah was working on different files on her monitor. As the charts printed out, Mandy laid them out on the table. She soon had three stacks of flimsies piled up.

"Done, Declan." Sarah swiveled around in her chair.

Declan nodded. "Coming out of jump space now."

The ship shuddered violently, as if they'd run into something. People were thrown to the floor or against walls. The lights flickered and went out. The emergency lights came on after an eternity in the dark.

Declan climbed back into his seat. "Is everyone okay?"

Mandy rubbed her head, which was sore but seemed to be in one piece. She settled in her seat. "I'm okay."

"Bruised, but fine," Sarah said.

"Fine," Honan said.

"What happened?" Mandy asked. "That didn't seem like a normal drop from jump space."

"That wasn't," Declan said. "Sarah…"

"Already checking." She held her hand up and listened to her earpiece. "Several broken bones, a lot of bruises, especially in engineering. Two critical, one dead. Life support is out on the lowest level. Emergency support only on this and engineering levels. Engineering reports serious damage to the jump drives, possibly from some kind of bomb. Definitely sabotage. Right now, we're at a dead stop. They don't recommend trying anything until they assess the damage."

"Tell them to work on life support first. Send everyone who's not doing something vital to quarters. I don't want people running around like crazy. And then I want to know what the hell happened."

"Aye," Sarah said.

Declan turned to Honan. "We might as well take care of what we stopped for. Open the view doors."

Honan manipulated the console, and the huge doors surrounding the bridge opened.

Mandy gasped as the roof and three walls disappeared, revealing a clear canopy. The view was like being in the middle of space without a spacesuit. She stepped down to the lower level and walked over to the windows like a sleepwalker.

She heard Declan whisper something behind her. The emergency lights went out, and she was left standing in the middle of space.

"Wow. I've never seen anything so beautiful," she whispered. Stars surrounded her. To her left, in the distance, shades of green and pink shifted in a gaseous cloud. Having never been out of her home solar system, she didn't recognize any of the stars from this vantage point.

"I'm glad you think so," Declan said. "When people first see this view, they either love or hate what they see. There's no middle ground. If you love the view, you're a spacer and always will be. Even if you spend your entire life on the ground, you'll never get this view out of your mind."

"I've never seen anything like this."

"And never will. The *Phoenix* is the last of her kind. The newer ships don't use view ports like this. They use cameras and screens."

"That's their loss, then," Mandy said. She walked around the bridge, feeling like she could reach out and embrace the universe. The emotion was empowering and humbling all at the same time. She sighed and turned back to Declan. "So, where are we?"

"That's what we're about to find out," Declan said. He walked back to the table and flipped a switch that turned on a soft backlight on the table. He pulled down one of the charts. "Here is where we started, and here is where we're supposed to be."

He pointed to a spot in the lower right corner of the chart, then to another one midway up the chart.

"And here is where we're going."

He pointed to a dot in the upper left corner. He picked up a ruler and drew a line between the three points.

"We should be able to see these constellations from here." He pointed at a spot outside and frowned at the map. "I don't see that nebula anywhere on this graph."

Honan studied the chart, holding the flimsy up to

try to match them up. "Or those constellations. I'll take these." He picked up the stack on the left side of the table.

Declan studied the constellations outside, comparing them against the maps on the right side of the table. He discarded one after another as nothing matched.

Honan wasn't having any better luck.

"Hermes, give me any charts surrounding Xy-Three."

"Hard copy or monitor?"

"Screen monitor."

As Mandy watched, one of the windows turned opaque and a star chart appeared.

"Okay, people, we're looking for anything that matches."

All four of them searched. Declan brought up page after page, but nothing matched the view from their windows.

"Hermes?"

"Aye, Captain?"

"We could use a hand with navigation."

Honan interrupted him. "Declan, we may not be able to trust him. We still don't know his systems haven't been compromised."

"We don't have a choice. We'd need weeks to go through all the charts. Hermes, check our position."

Hermes whistled. "Where are we? Jeeze, you go into diagnostic mode for a few days, and look what happens. You solids go and get yourselves into trouble. And what did you do to my jump drives? And life support? What have you people been doing?"

"Hermes." Declan's voice was filled with warning.

"Find the appropriate star chart."

"Already working, Captain. Give me a few minutes."

Declan paced the bridge. Nobody spoke a word.

"Captain?"

"Yes, Hermes?"

"We have a problem. Has someone been fiddling with the navigational controls?"

"Possibly. Why?"

"We're not on any of my charts."

"Have you checked them all?"

"Aye, Captain."

"Declan, how can we be sure?" Honan asked.

"We'll have to take his answer on faith. Hermes, can you give us any indication of where we are?"

"According to my calculations, there was approximately a ten-percent deviation from our original course."

"That doesn't sound too bad," Mandy offered.

Declan shook his head. "Not when you're talking around the block, but out here, ten degrees can mean the difference between habitable planets and unknown space. In case you haven't noticed, space is rather large. Here, watch."

He pulled out a clear flimsy and drew a line down the center. At one end of the line, he put a dot labeled Aboo. At the other end, he put Xy-Three. "Okay, this straight line is an approximation of our path."

He borrowed a compass from Honan and marked a ten-degree mark west of the original point. Using the origin and the deviation mark, he drew a line until the mark went off the page. The upper end was nowhere near Xy-Three.

"Do you see?"

Mandy nodded, subdued by the visualization.

"Okay, that's if we went off the Y axis. Don't forget this is space. We have multiple axes. This is a flat representation of a three-dimensional problem. We could be anywhere along hundreds of vectors. Plus, we were in jump space, which makes the distances even more pronounced."

Sarah returned, and Mandy joined her. They watched Declan and Honan drawing lines on the charts. "What are they doing?"

"Charting out a ten-degree deviation from the jump junction."

"Why there?"

"We can be pretty sure we were okay at that point since we got all our messages and everything. If they plot from there, we can get an idea how far off we are."

Mandy and Sarah watched the men for several long minutes. They kept shaking their heads and checking other charts. Finally, Declan sat down and ran his hands over his head.

"Hermes, are there any Fleet beacons in range?"

"No, Captain."

Declan sighed. "Hermes, do any of the near stars show up in your data banks?"

"No, sir. While we've been talking, I ran a diagnostic of my navigational systems. I cannot promise they haven't been compromised. I detect anomalies—gaps in data—that may affect my analysis. And the jump data doesn't compute with what we should have. We might have overshot our destination."

Chapter Fifteen

"Oh, this just keeps getting better and better," Declan muttered. The lights came on, and they all blinked in the sudden glare. "Hermes, are there any G-class stars within cruise distance?"

"I assume you want less than a year travel time?"

"Preferably."

Declan paced the bridge while they waited for Hermes's answer. An arrow appeared on the screen.

"I believe this one has what you need. There are several planets orbiting, two at optimal distance, however I cannot tell if they are viable. My sensors are at their limits. You would need to send probes."

Sarah held her hand to her ear. "Declan?"

"Hmmm?" He was busy studying the charts.

"The jump drives are gone. There's no possibility of repair. Engineering found the remains of a bomb. They were able to salvage enough to take a look at the remaining components. They think our second drop from jump space triggered the explosion."

She had Declan's direct attention. "What can they give us?"

"Partial cruise control, and that's if you don't do anything fancy. The best they can do is half-power. They're holding the engine together with duct tape and wishes."

"Tell them to do what they can. Thanks."

"That sounds like a Luddite tactic," Mandy commented.

"Yes, but why now?"

"They wanted to strand us at Xy-Three. Think for a moment. The colonel escaped after you made the announcement. If this hadn't come up, our second drop would have been at Xy-Three. She needed to get to the bomb in order to stop the detonation before we dropped out of jump space the second time. Only she was too late."

"Makes sense." He turned back to Honan. "Set a course for that system and pray there's something habitable there."

"What are they talking about?" Mandy asked Sarah.

Sarah turned sad eyes to her. "Finding a habitable planet where we can live."

"What? What do you mean? Why can't we turn around and go back?"

"Because there's no *back* to go back to," Declan said. "Our jump drives and navigational systems are gone. We could spend years trying to get within hailing distance of a Fleet beacon— providing we even head in the right direction. Our only chance of survival is to find a planet where we can live until we can figure something out."

Mandy was thinking furiously. She could tell from the dismayed looks on Sarah and Honan's faces Declan was telling the truth. They didn't like the situation at all but accepted the reality. Could she do any less?

"How long until we get to that system?"

"At least two months."

"What about supplies?"

"We'll have to go to a skeleton crew and put everyone who isn't essential in cold sleep. We'll run everything from here and shut down life support except this level and engineering. The next few weeks—or longer—are going to be hard on everyone."

Mandy sighed. "How can I help?"

"There's not much you can do," Declan said.

Mandy shook her head. "Declan, I'm an organizer. You, Sarah, and Honan will have your hands full finding a place to set down. Let me take care of getting us ready for the two months—and beyond."

She waited for Declan's nod. "If I can have Sarah for a bit, we'll have your personnel schedule inside thirty minutes."

"You don't need to work that fast," Honan said. "We do have some time."

"No, you don't," Mandy said. "In addition to organizing people, we need time to get them all into cold sleep. And you have to think about supplies. If we're going to emergency mode, that means no cooking. We'll have to go to emergency supplies. What do you have on hand, and where are they? We also need to think about moving everyone into closer quarters in order to not strain the systems. And…"

"Stop!" Honan held out his hands in surrender. "Okay, I give. Now I know why your businesses are so successful."

"Not so successful we can't make mistakes. If I had been more diligent, we wouldn't be in this mess."

"Mandy, you can't possibly think this is your fault?" Sarah asked.

"Of course I can! Because of me, you had to go to Xy-Three. One of my companies sent you out in a compromised ship. And because of me, Alvarez and the colonel are on board. Thanks to those little toys someone planted on systems already damaged, we've ended up here. How can this mess be anything but my fault?"

Silence met her words.

"Actually, the connecting thread I see is Alvarez," Declan said. "If anyone is to blame for this mess, Alvarez is. Now, enough of the blame game. We have work to do, people. And I have an announcement to make."

Mandy listened with one ear as Declan made the announcement. He didn't soft-soap their problems, but he didn't make everything all gloom-and-doom either. She had to admit he was a good leader. He laid out the facts, the problem, and the solution. She almost envied the people already in cold sleep. They were unaware of the problems surrounding them. She pulled up the personnel files and with Sarah's help got to work.

Thirty minutes later, she sent the file to Declan's monitor. "Captain, personnel file coming over to you now."

Declan looked the list over and made a few changes. Almost all the people staying awake were members of his regular crew. "I see you've put yourself on the sleeper list. I'd like you kept warm if you don't mind."

"I don't understand. I can get supplies organized, and then I'm done until we reach the system."

"Actually, keeping you with us is a security issue. We haven't found our killer yet. Putting you into cold sleep puts you in jeopardy. In cold sleep, you're more vulnerable, unable to protect yourself, and we can't have a guard on you. We already have one on the general, and even putting your pod next to his would still put a strain on personnel."

Declan smiled at her. "Don't worry, Ms. Ki, you won't be idle. You're going to work as hard as the rest of us."

"I wouldn't think differently. I know you're going to post the list, but I'd like to ask a favor first. Could you ask my people to gather in the lounge? I'd like to talk to them. You spacers may understand this as a necessary step, but my groundhogs won't."

"Not a problem." Declan checked his watch. "Is fifteen minutes okay?"

"Fine. And thanks."

Mandy moved to leave the bridge but stopped when Declan called to her.

"Aren't you forgetting something?"

She frowned and looked around. "I don't think so."

Declan joined her. "Your escort. You're still not to go anywhere without one of us."

"In light of what's happening, that seems sort of silly, but if you insist."

"I do." She hated to admit that having him at her side made her feel better. He made her feel…a lot. But right now, she had a job to do.

****

Twenty minutes later Mandy stood on the upper level of the lounge looking out at the assembled group. Behind her, the jump doors were open, allowing a clear view of the vastness of space. Several of the people sported slings or temporary patches. More than a few showed multiple bruises, and a couple limped. They filled up the chairs, and some used the tables and counters as seats.

"I'd like to have your attention, please," Mandy spoke into the portable mike Declan had given her. He stood near the door—close enough to be available for trouble, but far enough away to show she was in charge. By putting her on the upper level, directly opposite him, they were assured all attention would be on her.

Mandy looked over the group. Although the largest majority were her people, there were more than a few crewmen mixed in the group as well. She and Declan had talked about the assembly and the arrangements. *Keep your attitude light*, she thought, *but don't leave anything out. They deserve the truth.*

"As you've heard, we have a problem. Due to a malfunction with the navigation systems, we are off course. In addition, our jump drives are gone and can't be repaired. We won't be able to get to Xy-Three."

She watched their stunned faces for signs of trouble. She expected the voices—some loud, others troubled—and waited a few minutes for them to quiet down.

"Why can't we turn around and go back?"

Mandy smiled. That was one question she was prepared for, thanks to her asking the same one earlier. "Because we don't know where we are. None of the visual star systems show up on any of the charts. And, unfortunately, it's hard to go back when you have no frame of reference. We could end up at Xy-Three, or we could float into another unknown sector—this one without a place to land. That and without jump drives, the trip would take us years—perhaps decades—to get back. I don't think any of us wants to end up a floating ghost ship."

"Is there any good news, ma'am?" one young woman asked.

"Possibly. There's a planetary system not too far from here. We're going to head for there. If there is a viable planet, we'll set down and settle in until we can figure out something."

"How long will that take?"

"Two months." Mandy waited for the babble to die down. She raised her hands for quiet. "That raises some other problems."

"Only some?"

"Yes. Due to the damages and the length of the trip, we're going to need to turn off power to most of the ship. We'll also need to go to emergency supplies. In order to conserve supplies as much as possible, especially since we don't know what we'll face if we even do find a planet, we're going to go to a skeleton crew."

"Ma'am?" Tina stood.

"Yes, Tina?"

"Does that mean we'll be going to cold sleep?" Tina's voice came out as a bare whisper.

"What'd she say?" one man from the back yelled.

"Tina asked if we'd be going cold sleep. The answer is yes. All but a dozen crew will be going to sleep." Her reply met with dead silence.

Tina stepped forward. "Then—then I volunteer to be the first."

Mandy appreciated the amount of courage Tina showed in stepping forward.

"Tina," she began, and then stopped as singly, and then in groups, everyone in the lounge stood.

Their acceptance overwhelmed Mandy. She

cleared her throat and held up her hands for attention. "Thank you all. This isn't the trip we all signed up for but is what we need to deal with now. We were prepared to go into the unknown—this is merely a slight change of variables. Those of you who will be staying awake, pack your gear as well. We'll all be moving to close quarters. You'll find your reporting schedule or assignments posted on your room monitors. Be sure to secure all personal possessions. If any of you have messages to send home, file them now. We'll be sending several communications buoys back toward what we hope is home."

"Yeah, maybe our grandkids will read them," a male voice called from the back of the room. Silence settled over the group.

Mandy looked at the crew. They were strong, adventurous types or they wouldn't have signed up for the mission in the first place.

"Well, folks, we set out to rebuild a planet. Looks like we're going to get that chance, but not exactly in the way we planned. What we face will be a challenge, but I know you are all up to the job, otherwise you wouldn't be here. Think about what's happened. You've all become members of the elite Exploration and Discovery division. We will be the first of our kind to set foot on a new planet. For those of you with scientific interests, imagine the possibilities—unknown plants and minerals. Maybe one of you can be the discoverer of a new source of energy even better than chrystolian opals."

That elicited a chuckle from many of the people.

"We'll be facing new experiences few people even dream of. I'm not saying what's coming will be easy, but our adventure will be exciting. Rest assured the captain will do everything possible to get us to safety and to let others know where we are. Thank you."

Mandy caught Tina's eye and motioned for her to wait. She made her way through the crowd, answering questions and calming nerves. The room slowly emptied, leaving her, Tina, and Declan.

"Ma'am, I meant what I said earlier," Tina said.

Mandy smiled at her. "I know. And I appreciate the gesture, but that won't be necessary. You'll be staying warm."

"Why me?"

"Because you and O'Malley are the two best hydro techs we have." Mandy chuckled when Tina stopped wringing her hands. "I wouldn't be too happy if I were you. You may regret not going into cold sleep. You're going to be terribly busy over the next couple of months."

Tina's wide smile spoke volumes. "I don't mind, ma'am. I'd work around the clock if I can stay warm. Thank you."

"You're welcome. Now go on. There's a lot to be done before we get started and not much time to get everything done."

Mandy glanced at Declan leaning against the wall. He hadn't changed out of his shorts and shirt, but even in the casual outfit, he looked every inch the captain.

"So what do you think?"

"I think I understand why you're a leader. You know what to say and how to say it so your people are willing to do what you want. Hell, *I* was almost ready to sign up for cold sleep."

Mandy laughed, a good feeling for a change. With

everything that was happening, she hoped they'd be able to keep positive. That would be the only way to get through the next few months.

She and the captain headed back toward the bridge. "Declan, what happens if we don't find a viable planet?"

"Then we send more communications probes out in a variety of directions. We'll rig solar sails, put the *Phoenix* into orbit, and put the entire crew in cold sleep. We will become that *ghost ship* you spoke of."

A shiver of fear ran down Mandy's spine. "How long can we stay that way?"

"In theory, indefinitely."

"In theory."

"Yes. But a solid supposition I'd rather not put to the test. How much do you know about finding a planet?"

Mandy shook her head. "Just the basics. I'll leave that to you. You're the ones trained for exploration. You find me a place, and then stand back and let me go to work." She fingered the statue in her pocket. Ever since the attack, the figurine was never far from her hand. "Declan, would having a piece of opal help with the power?"

He shook his head. "Wouldn't matter if I had an entire mountain of opal. Our drives were never upgraded for opal. Why?"

Mandy pulled the statue from her pocket and held the piece up. "Then I guess you have no use for this."

Declan goggled at the statue and whistled. "That's opal? I thought this was some kind of polymer. May I?"

He held out his hand, and Mandy placed the carving in his palm. "He was a gift from my father before he left on his last trip. The opal is pure in case you were wondering."

"Does anyone else know about this?" Declan handed the figurine back to her.

"Sarah. Oh, and Taka and the general."

"Good. Don't tell anyone else. And thank you for the offer. I wish we could use the opal, but I'm afraid we don't have the equipment."

Silently, Mandy let out a sigh of relief. Although she was willing to cede the gem, if necessary, she was glad she didn't need to.

The next few hours flew by as everyone got to work. While the med-techs prepared the pods for cold sleep, Honan and Sarah made sure rooms were secure and helped the ones who would stay warm to move to new quarters.

Mandy worked at her monitor on the bridge. As each crewman was placed in cold sleep, she checked his or her name off the list. Even though there were at least two months of travel ahead of them, everyone worked with a sense of urgency.

Declan programmed and launched a probe. Hermes had given him a rough chart of the system, and he pored over the map, picking the most advantageous route.

Mandy was scrolling through the monitor banks, making sure all the remotes worked when she caught a blip on the security monitor. Moving through the hold.

"Declan?"

"Yes?"

She could tell from the abstracted way he answered that he heard her only on a minimal level, and she needed his full attention.

"Captain?"

Declan raised his head from the charts. "What's wrong?"

"I thought you took the security trackers off the questionable crew after we found Alvarez."

"We did."

"Then why do I have one of the blips moving through the hold?"

Declan jumped to the upper level and bent over the monitor. He touched several buttons, but the blip remained.

"Honan? Where are you?"

"Crew's quarters. Why?"

"We've got a security tag moving through the hold."

"That's not possible. We removed them all."

"Did you? Even Alvarez's?"

Honan hesitated. "No. Trish took the body before we could."

"What happened to the body?"

"Trish put him in a cold sleep stasis unit until we got to Xy-Three."

"Could you check? And check the hold."

"I'm already on my way. Have Sarah check the stasis unit."

"Watch your six, Honan."

"Yeah."

Declan called Sarah and told her what was going on.

"I'm in engineering right now, Declan. I'll get up there as soon as I can."

Declan and Mandy continued to watch the blip move around the hold. Suddenly the indicator stopped. They waited impatiently for Honan to get to them.

"Declan?" Honan's voice came over the speaker. He sounded a bit winded.

"Yes?" The blip shifted slightly.

"I found your security tracker on the colonel—or rather, her body."

"What? How did that happen?"

"No clue."

"You said *body*. Are you sure she's dead?"

"This knife sticking out of her chest makes my conclusion pretty definite. Chane took a quick look around but didn't see anyone. What do you want me to do?"

"Get medical to take care of the body."

"Declan?" Sarah called, interrupting them. "Everyone that's supposed to be in cold sleep is accounted for."

"Thanks, Sarah. Meet Honan in the hold. He'll fill you in there."

"Aye."

Mandy checked her lists. "Declan, ninety per cent of the sleepers are down. That leaves the people who are staying warm."

"Or a stowaway."

"I thought you rigged something to check that."

"With all the glitches we were having, we were never able to get the system to work."

"So you're sticking with the stowaway theory? You don't really believe that do you?"

"No. But I don't have any better theories." He ran his hand over his head. "And right now, we've got other issues to think about. Honan and Sarah will see to the latest mess."

"While I don't condone violence, I can't say I'll

mourn the colonel's passing much."

"In that, we are in complete agreement. Good catch on the monitor."

"Thanks."

Declan went back to his charts, and Mandy returned to scanning the monitors. A tiny icon in the lower corner of the screen alerted her to a message, and she pulled up her mail.

"Turn back or die."

Mandy swiveled her chair. "Declan? I've got a calling card."

Declan looked at the message. "This was sent from the hold before Honan got there." He shook his head. "The sender is long gone. I think this time Alvarez fouled himself up as well as us. I was thinking he sent us off course on purpose, but I'm not so sure now."

"He had no way of knowing about any of the previous problems you had. He might have been sabotaging the ship, but I don't think he planned on the issues being this bad."

"So we've found his little toys, he's running low on his drug supplies, and we're off course for the only source of those supplies. That means he'll be more desperate than ever."

"And he'll be after you as well."

Declan frowned at her. "How do you figure?"

"You're responsible for changing course. All he wants from me is revenge—and the codes for Xy-Three. But we're not going there. That leaves revenge. I realize that's a strong motive, but not as strong as his need for the drugs. He needs you to get him there. He'll want you—or the ship. He has to have control. Is there any other way to run the ship than here at the bridge?"

"Engineering. Hermes?"

"A-a-a-aye?"

Declan sighed. "Never mind." He turned to his console and input information. "I'm putting a level one lock-out on all navigation systems. They can't be changed without my codes."

"Welcome to my life, Declan."

"We'll get through this. He hasn't won yet."

"And with any luck, he won't." An idea occurred to Mandy. "Declan? Could the colonel have been the one to plant the cylinders?"

Declan shook his head. "Things like that aren't standard Luddite style. The bomb, yes, but not this level of sophisticated electronics."

Mandy could understand his logic, but the explanation didn't sit well with her. "I wouldn't totally discount them. Granted, all the actions they tried against me in the past were less than technical, but that doesn't mean they couldn't change tactics. In a guess, I'll bet the colonel was working with Alvarez. When the bomb went off, he saw her actions as unsuccessful. I don't think he'd take the failure lightly."

She swiveled back to her monitor. "When will we get information back from the probes?"

"Not for a few weeks. How's the list coming?"

"Almost done."

Chapter Sixteen

Mandy checked the lock on a door and moved to the next one. The dim corridor stretched into darkness, the doorways on either side making darker blocks in the silent gloom. In the shadows across from her, Declan checked those rooms and spaces.

The weeks on the ghost ship had stretched into a sameness that was starting to get to everybody. Tempers were often short, but quickly gotten over. The twelve-member crew had become fast friends over the weeks. She glanced at Declan. Some of them even closer than friends. Though they hadn't been able to act on their growing feelings, over the weeks she and Declan had formed a fast friendship that was more than she could have hoped for. Every time she looked at his trim form, her heart sped up. And the heated looks he sent her let her know he felt the same. But they forced themselves to stay separate. The close quarters and lack of privacy afforded them little opportunity to share more than a platonic relationship. She wondered briefly what kissing him would be like and quickly tamped down the thought. In that direction lay danger.

Originally, Declan and Honan had programmed the ROVERs to perform some of the routine security checks like the one she was now doing, but on occasion, they did a manual inspection to do a headcount of the ROVERs. Besides, the irregular checks helped break up the tedium of the trip.

Out of the corner of her eye, Mandy thought she saw a motion. She peered into the gloom but couldn't see anything.

"Declan, I thought I saw something. Five doors down, your side."

"Hermes, raise lighting in corridor C to fifty percent."

Mandy blinked in the sudden brightness. After weeks at quarter light, half-light seemed harsh. She and Declan searched the corridor but came up empty.

"Sorry, Declan. I guess my eyes are playing tricks on me."

"I'm not surprised. We're all tired. Hermes, return lighting to previous setting."

"Lights up, lights down. M-m-make up your mind."

"Hermes, you know you're not supposed to be vocal," Declan said.

"That does not compute. Please rephrase."

"Hermes, go to vocal dormant."

The lights dimmed and nothing further came from Hermes.

Mandy stretched. "How bad is Hermes?"

"Bad and getting worse. Chane has stripped him down to minimal levels. There aren't enough good circuits left to even restore his backups. At this point, he's more computer than AI."

"I miss him." She chuckled. "Do you believe that? He's not even a real person, and I miss him almost as much as I do Papa D and Taka."

"Not so odd. I feel the same way. Hermes is actually more a part of this crew than many of the people we have with us. Hopefully, we'll be able to eventually restore him."

Mandy checked the last door. "We've finished this corridor. I'd like to splash some water on my face before we get busy with the probe data."

Declan glanced at his watch. "Shift is ending." He stopped outside his door. "You've already put in a full day. You don't have to be there for this."

"I've been waiting for this for weeks. If you think I'm going to sleep, you're sadly mistaken. I'll see you in an hour." Mandy opened her door and was surprised to see Tina still there. She had joined Mandy and Sarah as a third roommate in the large room, but working opposing shifts meant they rarely saw each other.

"Hey, Tina, running a little late, aren't you?" Mandy shrugged out of her jumpsuit.

"Not really. O'Malley's running some tests, so I've got a few minutes. How's everything?"

"Same old, same old." Mandy loosened her braid and finger combed her hair. "We'll be in probe range in an hour. I want to get a quick shower and go up to the bridge. I'd like to be there when the data comes in. Have you eaten yet?"

"If you can call one of those meals eating. I'll be glad when this is all over. A person can only take so much re-hydrated food."

Mandy laughed. Hydroponics, like the rest of the systems, was kept at minimum levels, which meant no fresh fruits or vegetables beyond what they'd eaten in the first weeks. Anything fresh had been consumed early on, leaving emergency meals for later. The current quality of their food had become a source of jokes and regret for the crew. The pre-packaged meals were nourishing for the body, as the manufacturer promised, but they lacked nourishment for the soul.

"Have you noticed any more rations missing?" Mandy asked. Tina was in charge of the food supplies. Several times, she'd reported discrepancies in the counts.

"No. I can't imagine why anyone would willingly steal those items. They don't make sense. What about the other missing items?"

"We haven't been able to come up with any leads. There are only twelve of us awake, and we know the thief isn't any of us. And Chane and Honan have been running regular bio-scans, but they're always negative."

"What all is missing?" Tina asked.

"Mostly food, but the problem isn't only the missing stuff. The lights are going up and down at weird times, odd glitches in the computer system—or at least odder than normal—and the feeling someone is watching you."

"I know that one. It gives me the creeps."

"Declan's had us running checks day and night, at irregular intervals, hoping to catch someone. Whoever is doing this is always one step ahead of us."

Tina glanced at her watch. "I'd better get going. See you later."

"Yeah. I'll probably be up on the bridge the rest of the day. Say hi to O'Malley for me."

A brief time later, on the bridge, Mandy slipped into an empty seat next to Sarah on the upper level. Declan, Honan, and Chane sat in the central seats. Several other people sat around the upper ring. She wasn't the only one anxious.

"Any news on the probe yet?"

"Coming in now," Sarah said.

Mandy stared at the information scrolling across the screen. Of the ten planets orbiting the star, three were possible landing sites. Of those three, the fourth and fifth planets looked the most viable.

Mandy and Sarah watched the readouts for almost an hour until Mandy's stomach reminded her she hadn't eaten supper.

"You want to join me for some dinner?" she whispered to Sarah.

"Sure." Of all of them, Sarah was the least affected by the loss of fresh food. She actually enjoyed the pre-packaged meals.

They arrived at the lounge, logged in, and picked up two dinners from the locked supply. Mandy pulled the heating tab on hers.

"Gee, what taste-tempting delight awaits me tonight?" She sniffed the warming repast and wrinkled her nose.

"Can anyone join you, or is this a private party?" Declan asked as he and Honan walked in.

"If that pad you're carrying shows favorable read-outs, you not only can join us, I'll serve you dinner myself."

Declan grimaced. "That sounds like a threat." He opened his own meal reluctantly.

Mandy studied the report. She wasn't an expert on what made a planet habitable, but she knew enough to be able to read the data.

"So, what does all this say?"

Declan pointed at the more important aspects. "These readings are from the fourth planet. There's a breathable atmosphere. No signs of habitations. The gravity is a little heavy. The land to water ratio is okay, but there's only one large continent. I'm concerned about the axial tilt, though."

"Why?"

"Too much tilt gives you extreme seasonal changes. You could go from blizzard conditions to searing heat with no moderated changes. That causes problems with growing crops and living conditions. And these figures here"—he pointed to a group of numbers—"show high concentrations of dust and sulfur in the atmosphere."

"Sounds like volcanic activity," Mandy said.

"Yes. Which may account for the lower temperatures in the western hemisphere. The concentration of atmospheric dust is highest there."

"What about the eastern half of the continent?" Sarah asked.

"Good temperatures, but the visuals show almost no vegetation."

"That's not good either. If conditions were favorable for plants, they might sustain larger life. No vegetation means problems."

"Valid points, but we may have no choice."

"When will we have the scans from the other planets?"

"Tomorrow afternoon." Declan caught Mandy's stifled yawn. "Why don't you get some sleep?"

Mandy hid another yawn behind her hand. "If I know you, you haven't slept much either. You ought to follow your own prescription."

He laughed as Sarah and Honan yawned. "I think yawning is contagious. I'll see you all tomorrow."

Declan stood and glanced at Sarah. "Relax, you

two. I'll walk her home."

He stopped outside Mandy's door. "This trip hasn't turned out to be anything either one of us expected. But I'm glad you're here." He leaned against the wall and smiled down at her.

Mandy smiled back as he reached out to stroke her cheek.

A sudden noise in the corridor startled them both. Declan looked down at the dark stain spreading across his chest.

"Damn."

He crumpled to the floor.

"Hermes!" Mandy screamed. "Get help. Declan's been shot."

She knelt next to him and tried to stanch the flow. A trickle of blood bubbled from his mouth and nose. "Don't you leave me, Declan Chalmers! Don't you dare leave me."

Honan and Sarah arrived, followed closely by a med-tech and a Warrior.

"What happened?" Honan said.

Sarah pulled Mandy away from Declan. "Mandy, tell us what happened."

Mandy stared at Declan, willing her strength into him. He couldn't die. He was the captain. He had to get them to safety. She stared at the blood on her hands. Declan's blood.

Sarah palmed open the cabin door and steered Mandy inside. Honan spoke quietly to the med-tech and Warrior, then followed Sarah and Mandy. He shut the door on the sight of Declan's body.

Sarah got a wet cloth and wiped Mandy's hands off. "Mandy? Can you tell us what happened?"

Mandy looked at her, tears streaking her face. "We were standing there. There was a noise and he…he…"

"That's okay, Mandy. Did you see anyone?"

Mandy took a deep breath and exhaled slowly. "No."

"Enough!" Honan exclaimed. "We're done with this. Sarah, I'm going to tie all the monitors to the bridge. You and Tina can watch all the systems from there. Keep one monitor on sickbay. Everyone else is going to join me. We're going to do a room-by-room, level-by-level search of this ship."

"That'll take you days," Sarah said.

"I don't care if I have to spend the rest of my life looking. I'm going to find our ghost and take care of him once and for all."

The intercom beeped. Honan punched the switch open. "Honan here."

"Sickbay here. Thought you'd like to know. The doctor is working on the captain. He's alive but beyond that, I don't know. I'll keep you informed as to his condition."

"Thanks." He turned to Mandy. "Did you hear that?"

Mandy nodded, tears streaming down her face. "Yes. Thank you. Honan, I want to be on the security team." She held up her hand as he opened his mouth to argue.

"You know I'm good in a fight. And this is more my fight than any of yours. I suggest you agree because I'm coming whether you agree or not."

Honan flashed a small smile. "I could always throw you in the brig."

"But you won't."

He shook his head. "No, I won't. Sarah, go to the bridge and wake everyone who is in warm up stasis. We're doing this now."

****

Honan looked over the tiny group of people. They were armed and grim like Mandy.

"We'll break into two groups. Chane will take one team and start in the holds and work his way up. I'll take the second group and work this level. There are six of us. Tina and Sarah are on the bridge, and there are three people in sickbay—the captain, the doctor, one med-tech, and a Warrior. If you see anyone else, capture him or her if you can. If you can't…do what you must."

He handed them portable radios. "These are tuned to the same frequency as Sarah's headset. We can communicate with each other without going through the ship's systems. Watch your sixes, everyone. This guy is a killer. Don't take any chances."

Honan sorted them into two groups. Chane and his team took the lift to the lower level.

Honan had Mandy and O'Malley with him. "We'll start here. I'll take the rooms on the left, O'Malley on the right. Mandy, you watch the corridor. Nobody gets past us."

"Hermes, lights to fifty percent," Mandy said. She moved into position, laser rifle at the ready.

The first room was Declan's office and cabin. Honan went through the area quickly. They made their way slowly down the corridor. As they finished each room, Honan sealed the door with a security seal. Both he and O'Malley searched the lounge, kitchens, gym, and spas. In sickbay, they were gratified to see Trish

217

out of the surgical bay.

"How is he?" Mandy asked.

Trish pulled off her gloves and mask. "He's still unconscious from the anesthesia, but I expect a full recovery. The shot nicked a lung, which I've repaired. Fortunately, the shot missed his heart and any other vital organs. He needs rest. He should be up by tomorrow afternoon but will need to be on minimal duty with a lot of rest for at least two weeks. I gather you haven't had any luck on your search yet."

"No," Honan said. "Seal the door behind us." He looked at the Warrior. "If anyone tries to come in, subdue them as necessary."

"Aye, sir."

Before they left, Honon relayed the news to the search teams, and they continued on their rounds. By the time they returned to the bridge, they'd found an abandoned still, a stash of weapons, one crewman who had left food—now rotted—in his locker, and other contraband, but no killer.

From the reports they were receiving from Chane and his group, they weren't having any better luck.

"Chane? We're heading to the engineering level. We'll meet you there," Honan said.

The teams regrouped on the middle level. Honan directed Chane's team to the left while he, Mandy, and O'Malley went right.

They were crossing the docking bay when Mandy caught a movement inside one of the shuttles. She grabbed Honan's arm and pointed. He nodded and motioned her to take the right side while O'Malley manned the docking bay console.

"Chane," he whispered. "We may have something.

Docking Bay Two."

Honan crept toward the shuttle. He reached the door and nodded for O'Malley to open the hatch. When he did, a man rushed out, knocking Honan over.

"Stop!" Mandy yelled. The man kept running. She aimed her rifle for a spot mere inches in front of his feet and fired.

The man jumped and dashed in another direction as Honan caught up to him. Honan kicked the man's legs out from under him, and he went down in a sprawling heap.

"Move, and you're dead," Honan warned. He pulled the hood off the man's face.

"Jenkins?"

Mandy recognized the man who'd caused trouble at the beginning of the trip. He was thinner, but not by much, and his personal hygiene hadn't improved any since the first day.

Honan hauled him to his feet as Chane and the others arrived.

"Chane, check the shuttle." Honan pulled Jenkins' arms behind his back and wrapped a set of binders around them. He also attached a looser set around the man's legs.

Chane came out of the shuttle carrying several food trays. "Well, we know who's been taking the food stores. We found a stash of rotgut in the hold. Judging by the empty bottles in here, I assume he's been going there regularly."

"Why are you here, Jenkins?"

The man glared at the team. One of the men hauled off and hit Jenkins in the stomach.

Mandy winced. She didn't approve but didn't

blame the crewman. She felt like hitting something herself.

"I got rights!" Jenkins gasped. "Commander, you can't let him do that to me."

Honan stood in front of Jenkins. He was a good head taller than the man and in much better physical condition. He made a show of handing Chane his weapon and flexing his hands.

"Then I suggest you tell us what you're doing down here instead of in cold sleep."

Jenkins looked at the angry faces surrounding him and licked his lips. "I wasn't going to let you close me up in one of those coffins to float for the next couple of centuries. If I'm going out, I'm going in style. As soon as we get enough power for the bay doors, I was going to take the shuttle and head back home. I got people waiting for me. I got important stuff to do."

"Like killing the colonel? Or attempting to kill the captain?"

Jenkins blanched. "The captain's dead? That weren't me, Commander. I ain't no killer."

Honan nodded to Chane. "Take him to cold sleep and put him out." He turned to Jenkins. "If you're lucky, I may remember to wake you up."

Honan turned away. "The rest of you are dismissed. Thank you for your help."

Mandy walked with Honan toward the bridge.

"You don't think he's the one who shot Declan, do you?"

"No."

"Do we search again?"

"No. We've lost the edge. Whoever was responsible is back in hiding. Probably in plain sight—

remember the air vent in the general's cabin? I don't have enough sensors or ROVERs to check them all and, even if I did, he'd probably find a way around them. We may stop searching, but we won't stop looking."

He looked at Mandy. "Are you okay?"

"Yes. I think I'll get some sleep. And I suggest you do the same. We're all going a bit stir crazy."

"Yeah." He stopped outside Mandy's door. A dark stain on the carpet reminded them both of what had happened earlier—as if they needed a reminder.

Mandy stepped over the spot and entered her cabin. "Good night, Honan."

****

After eating breakfast, Mandy and Honan went to sickbay. Declan was sitting up in bed, complaining loudly to Trish. For her part, Trish kept right on doing her job, ignoring anything the captain said to her. Mandy glanced at Trish, then looked harder. There was something wrong, but she wasn't sure what. Other than a slight puffiness around her eyes, she looked the same as always. Trish looked up and caught her staring. Her glare would have melted titanium. Mandy turned back to Honan.

"If Declan's that grumpy, he's probably going to live," Honan said.

"Oh, I don't know," Mandy quipped. "Looks to me like he should stay there at least a day or two more."

Honan grinned at Mandy. "Or a week. We'll have Trish knock him out, and we'll take over the ship. Think of how peaceful the bridge will be."

Mandy touched Honan's arm and cocked her head to one side. "Better yet, let's put him in cold sleep. That way, we won't have to worry about him at all."

Honan nodded as if considering her idea.

Declan glared at the two of them. "If you two are done discussing your mutiny, would you mind telling me what's going on?"

Honan glanced at Trish.

"He'll be fine as long as he rests for a few days. No strenuous activity. He's staying here until this afternoon to give the patches a chance to meld with his tissue." She looked at Declan. "Do as I say, and you'll be out in time for dinner. Don't, and I may take the mutineers up on their ideas." She turned and left the area.

Mandy bit back a laugh. She knew exactly how Declan felt. "Relax, Declan. We've managed to not wreck the ship in the last few hours, so, I'm sure we can keep her going for a few more."

"Oh, that makes me feel so much better." Declan turned a sour frown on Honan. "Tell me you found the cutthroat responsible for putting this hole in my side."

"No. We did, however, find Jenkins stowed away in shuttle bay two. He's responsible for the missing supplies."

"I thought all crew was accounted for in cold sleep."

"They are. Once they were done putting you back together, I had the med-tech do a visual inspection of the cold sleep pods. I don't know how, but Jenkins's pod was rigged so the monitor showed he was in there. And before you ask, his was the only empty one."

"What about the new probe scans? Are they in yet?"

Honan shook his head. "They're due to be in later this afternoon. Right now, all's quiet and as normal as can be expected under these circumstances. Not exactly what we had planned on, right Dec?"

A wry smile flitted across Declan's face. "No, my friend, but at least we're together in this mess. I wouldn't want anyone else here."

Honan grasped Declan's arm. "I'll talk to you later."

Mandy watched him leave. The two men were a lot alike in many ways. Both were quiet, intelligent, and strong with a strength that went beyond the physical. They had stood up to all the problems with cool-headed competence and determination. She admired both of them, glad that if she had to be stranded somewhere, she was with them.

"I guess this means we'll be canceling our workout session," Mandy teased.

"I'd say that's a pretty good bet. How are you doing?" Declan asked as he settled against the pillow.

"Me? I'm fine. I'm not the one who was shot."

"No, you had your head cracked open." He gave her a wry chuckle, then sighed. "Have you had any more messages since this happened?"

She shrugged. "To be honest, I haven't even looked. I guess I've been a bit reluctant to see what he has to say now."

"They're only words, Mandy. They mean nothing if you don't let them." He reached for her hand.

His hand engulfed hers, the warmth spreading up her arm. She studied his fingers. They were long and slender, but strong—like him. "I know. You must think me the world's worst coward."

"Not at all. I don't know many people who could go through what you've been through and still come out with their sanity intact, as you seem to have."

"How do you know I'm not some raving lunatic and this is all a façade?"

Declan laughed, then winced and clasped his side. "I think we'd all know by now. We've had more than our share of lunatics on this trip to compare you against."

Trish pushed aside the curtain and glared at them. "If he's going to get out of here this afternoon, he needs his rest."

Mandy squeezed Declan's hand and left the room. She reached the corridor and realized this was one of the first times on board she didn't have someone with her. The dim corridor curved away into the darkness, and she shrugged back a shiver of nervousness.

"I've wanted my independence, now I have some." She looked at the empty corridor stretching away in front of her and shuddered, then headed for the bridge.

Chapter Seventeen

Sarah looked up as Mandy slid into her seat on the upper level. "I was going to come for you. Everything okay?"

"Yes. Trish kicked me out, and I managed to get here all by myself and in one piece, I might add."

Sarah chuckled. "Thank goodness for small favors. Declan would have our heads if we let anything happen to you after all this time." She turned back to her monitor.

"Honan?" Mandy asked. "Did Trish look all right to you?"

"I didn't notice anything wrong. Why?"

She shrugged. "Probably nothing. I thought she looked a little off, but you know her better than I do."

"We're all a little off at this point, and she was fresh from Declan's surgery. She's probably tired, like the rest of us."

"Probably." Mandy brought up the supply files on her screen and ran through the inventory. In a way, they were lucky. Since they'd had no clue what to expect on Xy-Three, they'd brought pallets of supplies that would enable their survival on another world. They had equipment suitable for testing air, water, and ground systems as well as plants. In addition to the testing kits, they had purification systems that could supply the entire crew with drinkable water under a variety of conditions.

They had huge tents that would have served as self-contained decontamination units and would now serve as temporary shelters. And they had enough food supplies for the entire crew for at least a year.

There were other supplies as well. Mandy made notes as to the order in which they'd need the items. Three hours later, she was putting the finishing touches on an inventory of the pallets listed in order of importance when the pungent aroma of fresh coffee drew her attention.

She looked around and saw Declan sitting at the next station. He had two mugs of coffee and two ration dinners. Mandy saw Sarah and Honan also had drinks and dinners in front of them.

"Thought you all could use a break. If I know the three of you, you've been up here since you left me in Trish's clutches."

Mandy sipped gratefully at the hot beverage he handed her. "You're one to talk. If I remember correctly, you're the one who's gone without sleep waiting for the probe data to come in."

"Guilty as charged."

"I thought you were supposed to be resting."

Declan pointed to a medical patch on his arm as he sat in the seat next to hers. "Trish knows exactly what my condition is. She wouldn't let me leave without this blasted contraption."

"Mandy thought Trish looked a little off this morning," Honan said.

"She was. She had a black eye. Said she'd slipped and hit her head on her bunk."

"And you believed her?" Mandy asked.

"I didn't see a reason not to. I'm here. I'm alive and on the mend. She had ample opportunity to take me out and didn't."

"Thank the gods for that." Mandy touched Declan's hand and smiled. "What do you think the odds are on us finding a good planet?"

"You can answer that about as well as I can. Exploration and Discovery doesn't find many viable planets even with their extensive resources and fancy toys. We're going into this blind, with a crippled ship and people on board who don't want us to get there."

Declan swiveled his seat around. "Speaking of which, has the data arrived yet?"

Honan grinned. "Patience, Dec. The report is due in about an hour."

Sarah looked up from her monitors. "Can someone tell me where we're going to live if we do find a planet?"

Mandy winked at Honan. "What? You mean you don't like sleeping under the stars?"

"Uh-uh. Not me. I want a place with walls and a roof over my head."

Mandy laughed. "Well, at first, the walls will have to be made of canvas. After that, I have an idea, but I want to see what you three think. This may sound a bit absurd, but what about using the *Phoenix*?"

Declan frowned. "In case you weren't aware, we'll be lucky to get to a planet. Even without the problems we have, landing this baby is impossible. She wasn't built for that."

"I know. There is absolutely no chance of repair, is there? Even with time?"

Declan shook his head. "No. We couldn't even

make repairs with the full services of space dock. The engines have to be completely replaced. And there are so many other problems, the refits would end up costing more to repair her than building a whole new ship."

"So the ship is basically salvage." Mandy held up her hand to forestall the arguments she saw on their faces. The subject was a hard one for them to hear, but they needed to. "I'm sorry to have to say that, but am I wrong?"

"No." Declan's shoulders slumped.

"So what happens to the ship?"

"The solar sails won't hold her out here forever. The orbit will eventually decay, and she'll crash."

"Then I suggest we strip her down. The wall panels are all made of high-quality polymers that are easily removed. We can use the shelving braces in the holds as wall supports and use the wall panels to build walls. We can use whatever good wiring there is for new wiring. We can transfer all the furnishings downside, so we have beds, tables, chairs, and all the other paraphernalia we need for living. Since landing the ship isn't an option, why not use what we can?"

Declan looked at Honan and Sarah. He tapped his fingers on the table. "That's going to take an awful lot of work."

"We'll have the manpower available. Besides, what else will the people have to do while waiting for transport downside?"

"She's got a point," Honan said. "We can start with the holds and work our way up. With no gravity, the pallets can be stacked atop one another, and we can start dismantling the shelving. Once that's done, we can work on the wall panels."

"Once we've got everything shipped down to the planet, we can also use the packing crates and pallets," Mandy said. "I'm not saying we'll win any awards for design, but I think we can cobble together a decent settlement from what we have."

"Sarah, wasn't one of our engineers also an architect?" Declan asked.

"Yeah." She tapped her lips with her finger. "I think Jimmy Webb. He's in cold sleep."

"Have medical warm him up. Explain to him what we want to do, and see if he can come up with plans. We probably ought to have a team start dismantling furnishings and non-essentials. Warm up whomever he needs, but no more than six."

Declan turned to Mandy. "Much as I hate to admit, you've got a good idea. We'll see what Jimmy comes up with. Besides, if you think about this, we'll have the best-furnished tents in the system. Now, did you ever check your messages?"

Mandy looked at her lap. "Um, no."

"So look at them now, while I'm here with you." His voice came out gently, and he lightly gripped her shoulder. "You'll be okay. I'm here."

She sighed, appreciating his concern. "Aye, Captain."

She pulled up her mail. There was only one—from Alvarez. She displayed the message. This time the corpse had Declan's face and voice.

"Your luck has run out, and so has your time. I am one with the gods, and we will have you."

Mandy laid her head on the desk.

Declan did a quick search. "This one originated in the docking bay." He turned to Honan. "I thought you said Jenkins was holed up in there."

"He was." Honan rose from his seat, a grim look on his face. "Sarah, come with me." He opened the weapons locker, pulled out two laser pistols, and handed one to Sarah.

"We'll be back shortly."

Declan deleted the file. He touched the back of Mandy's neck. "Mandy? I'm sorry. I shouldn't have pushed you to look at that."

Mandy turned her head to look at him. "This isn't your fault, Declan. So many people have been hurt because of me. Maybe I should tell him to come get me. At least then everyone else would be safe."

Declan's eyes widened, and he drew back from her. "You're not serious."

She looked up at him. She was so tired. "Why not? I'm supposed to be a leader. All I've done is lead this crew and ship from one disaster to another."

****

Declan didn't know whether to wrap his arms around her or kick her. He settled for getting up and pacing the bridge.

"Listen to yourself. I've never heard such selfish crap in my life—and I've heard a lot. So you're going to give up and let Alvarez have you? What about those three hundred people in cold sleep? What happens to them when you're dead?"

"They'll have you."

"I'm not their leader. You are. Miss Amanda Ki. Daughter of Tanabe Ki. Foster daughter of Master General Tyler Davis. Niece of Master Physician Taka Yu. I may be the captain of this ship, but you are the one those people are going to be looking for when they wake up. Don't you remember the lounge when you told them about what had happened? Every single one of those people rose up to follow you. They weren't looking at me. They were looking at you, their leader."

He stopped pacing and glared at her. "So you want to give up and let that bastard win? He killed your parents. He nearly killed the general, you, and me. Is that what you really want?"

Declan stopped and watched her, knowing the instant she'd made her decision to fight. Her chin went up. Her back straightened, and a look of determination settled into her face.

"No. I don't want him to win. But what can we do? We've checked everything that can be checked, and still we're getting nowhere."

"Yes, but not for long. He's been able to evade us here on the ship, but once we get to the planet, he won't be able to land without a shuttle, and we control them. All we have to do is get through the next couple of weeks, and he's ours."

Her laughter had a tinge of hysteria, and then she sobered. "Now who's the one who's delusional? The next couple of weeks? We'll have to warm up more med-techs and open another sickbay."

Declan shrugged. His words had had the desired effect. She was ready to fight now.

"We'll do what is necessary." He turned to the monitor. "Right now, I think we have work to do."

"Declan?"

"Yes?"

"Thanks."

Declan smiled and sat down at the center seat as Honan and Sarah returned. He studied their faces, seeing what he'd expected—unfortunately. "Don't tell me, let me guess. Nothing."

Honan slid into his seat with a sigh. "Nothing. There was a chance someone had tampered with the shuttle, but what we found could have been left over from Jenkins. We never checked after we caught him. I've added an extra security lock on all of them. I talked to the others and strongly suggested none of them go anywhere alone and also took the liberty of arming them."

Declan nodded. He approved of Honan's actions. The people who were awake were cool-headed and wouldn't shoot unless completely necessary. But they wouldn't hesitate to use the weapons either.

"Thus, we begin," Mandy said, as she took the pistol Honan handed her.

"I assume you know how to use one of these?" Declan asked.

Mandy nodded as she checked the charge and power levels. "General Davis made sure of my weapons training. Doesn't mean I like them, but I know how to use one, with accuracy."

The monitor tuned to the probes beeped, startling everyone.

"The data from the fifth planet is coming in," Sarah said. They all gathered around the monitor. Volumes of data streamed across the screen.

Declan pulled the data up on his monitor, slowing the rate so he could study the information. He read off the pertinent data for the others.

"The planet has approximately a twenty-six-hour day, a diameter of roughly 8,000 miles at the equator, east to west rotation. Atmosphere is close enough to

Aboo normal to be of no difference. There are two small moons. Geologically, the planet appears stable. There are no indications of increased atmospheric gases and matter. There is also no evidence of towns or other constructs. Water to land ratio is acceptable with most landmasses being large islands. Abundant vegetation."

He turned to the others, a smile on his face. "We got our first break. I think we've found a place to live."

Everyone grinned widely.

"How long until we get there?" Mandy asked.

Declan checked the figures. "Eight days." He rubbed his hands together. "Okay, folks, we have a lot to do in the next week. But first, I have an announcement to make."

"At least this one will go over a bit better than the last one," Mandy said.

Declan chuckled as he thumbed the communications control. "Attention, all hands."

Mandy listened as Declan told the crew about the planet. This nightmare trip would soon be over.

Declan finished his announcement and pinged engineering. "Chane? How're the engines?"

"Iffy. We should be able to hold them together for a while longer. We'll get you there, and then we can rig solar sails for orbital power. I'm assuming you want any extra resources for the shuttles?"

"Yes. They're our top priority right now."

"Right. Coast downhill if you can."

Declan chuckled. "I'll see what I can do. Thanks, Chane."

"Aye, Captain."

Declan swung around to Mandy. "You have the inventory and personnel lists ready?"

Mandy sent him the files. "I finished this morning. In a way, we were lucky we were prepared for fighting a plague. We've got more with us than a normal supply run, and people who know about testing for all the little nasties that can make us sick."

Declan read over the personnel lists. "This looks good except for one item."

"What?"

"You've only got four shuttle pilots."

"I didn't forget. That's all the pilots listed."

"I've got twenty regular crew who are qualified on our shuttles. Since we won't need them for other duties until we're on land, we can use them as pilots. We have four shuttles—two personnel, two straight cargo—and can rotate the crew among them. Once the personnel are down, the other two can be converted to cargo."

Mandy checked the list he sent her. "What about your other crew? I know some of them are qualified in multiple areas, but I don't know what they are."

"I'll look over the list and get back to you, but overall, this looks good."

Declan swiveled around to Honan. "I assume Jenkins is locked away in cold sleep?"

"Yes. Chane was there and made sure there was a security lock on his unit. That's one character I'd like to forget to wake up."

Declan rubbed his side. "I agree. You're certain he wasn't the one who fired the shot?"

"We can't be positive, but personally, I don't think he has the guts to do something like that. He's a braggart, but he's a coward."

"I was shot from the dark," Declan reminded him.

"I know, but I still don't think shooting someone is

234

his style. And you were shot with an old-fashioned projectile weapon—the general's gun."

"I had the gun locked in my safe," Declan retorted.

"*Had* is the operative word. I checked. The data disk is missing too."

"So, he has the codes."

"But not the key," Mandy said. "And they won't do him any good now. We're nowhere near Xy-Three and can't get there."

"Since you're here," Honan continued, "I'd like to follow up on the cold sleep pods. Sarah and I can run a check on them while you catch up here."

"Sounds like a plan. How's Hermes doing?"

"I'm doing fine, thank you," Hermes said.

Declan grinned at Honan. "I thought your databases were full of holes."

"When did I say that?"

"Never mind. Continue monitoring those areas you can and keep me updated."

"Aye, Captain."

Mandy watched Declan move to the lower level and sit down. He was definitely moving slower and favored his right side, but she supposed after being shot, that was normal. She knew if anything was really wrong, Trish would be on him faster than anyone would believe possible—at least she hoped so.

"Join me?" Declan pointed to the seat Sarah usually occupied.

Mandy turned off her monitor and joined him. "How are you feeling?"

"Like I've been shot." Declan shrugged. "I've felt worse, but not by much."

"What do you say we get back to the personnel

rosters?"

"Slave driver." Declan brought the list up on his monitor, and they got to work.

****

Mandy looked up as the night shift pilot strolled onto the bridge. "Gee, are we at shift change already?" She hadn't realized how much time had passed.

"Yep. Time for you two to get some rest. Declan, I passed Honan and Sarah in the corridor. They told me to tell you the cold sleep pods are secure, and they did a security check of this level."

"Thanks. Everything's quiet here. See you tomorrow." He rose and stretched, then winced.

"Yeah. Get some rest. I'm not ready to break in a new captain yet."

"Thanks." He turned to Mandy. "Shall we?"

Honan and Sarah met them at Mandy's cabin. They were standing in the corridor, leaning against the wall, when Mandy and Declan strolled up.

Declan pulled Mandy to a stop. "I know that look on Honan's face. He's up to something."

Honan schooled his face into a façade of innocence. "Me? I was saying goodnight to Sarah."

"Uh-huh," Declan palmed open the door and stood aside for Mandy to pass.

"I'll see you tomorrow."

He turned toward his cabin. Honan followed close behind as Mandy and Sarah watched from the doorway.

Declan stopped and so did Honan. Dec turned to Honan. "And where are you going? If I remember correctly, your cabin is that way." He pointed in the opposite direction.

"Yeah, well funny thing about that. My cabin is,

um, having problems. Since you're the only one with room…"

Declan raised an eyebrow. "You can't seriously think you're going to bunk with me."

"Yep. Shall we, roomy?" Honan strode past Declan.

Mandy covered her mouth to bite back the laugh that threatened. She and Sarah stepped backward and let the door slide shut. Mandy leaned back against the panel and let the laughter burst out.

Sarah collapsed on the bed. "I don't know who I feel sorrier for, Honan for having to put up with Declan, or Declan for having to put up with Honan."

"I'm guessing you and Honan decided on this."

"We talked about this while you were in sickbay with Declan. We actually talked with Chane and the others too. From now on, everybody has a partner."

"Sounds good to me." Mandy yawned. "Right now, though, all I want to do is sleep."

The next day, Mandy spent the morning working over the personnel rosters and supply lists with Sarah, Declan, and Honan.

"We have about two-dozen people to warm up initially," Mandy said. "Six each of the cargo techs, pilots, and Warriors. Since cold sleep recovery takes twenty-four hours, we'll need to start warming them up tomorrow."

"We'll start with the cargo specialists," Declan said. "They'll have the hardest work and be needed the soonest. Then pilots and techs last. After that, we'll work through the rest of the people in the same order. With power so low, we can only warm up a dozen at a time."

Mandy stood and stretched the kinks out of her back. "Right now, I could use a break. How 'bout a cup of tea?"

"Make that coffee, and I'll join you," Declan replied.

Mandy wrinkled her nose. "That mud you serve here isn't fit to be called coffee. Wait until I get my personal effects out of storage, and you'll see what real coffee is."

"Don't tell me you used personal space to pack coffee," Honan said.

"Freshly ground, freeze dried, vacuum packed, straight from the Aboolean highlands to you."

Honan frowned. "I don't see how you can drink any of that. I tried coffee once. That brew is vile."

Mandy and Declan looked at each other and laughed.

"I guess our brew is an acquired taste," Mandy said.

"One I'll never acquire. I'll stick to tea."

"I've had some of your tea," Declan said. "Tastes like weeds."

"I guess my brew is an acquired taste," Honan deadpanned as Mandy and the others laughed.

Mandy and Declan each got a tray in the lounge. Declan stacked ration meals on his while Mandy got mugs of coffee and hot water for tea.

Back on the bridge, the foursome relaxed with their meals.

"How are we with food supplies once we get there?" Declan stirred his coffee and blew the aroma toward Honan.

"Not a problem," Mandy said. "Since we didn't

know what we'd be getting into at Xy-Three, we packed enough to sustain the crew and remaining survivors for at least a year. That will give us time to set up hydroponics huts. Hopefully, we'll be able to supplement our supplies with indigenous vegetation," Mandy said.

"We'll need to test everything," Declan responded.

"I know. The pallet with the portable labs is one of the first on the list. The biggest problem is logistics."

"Why?" Declan asked.

"Those pallets were some of the first in. They were extras in case of problems with the labs on Xy-Three. I'm going to need help to shift cargo."

Declan frowned and tapped his lip with his finger. "Even if we woke up cargo crew today, they wouldn't be able to do physical work for a couple of days. How much shifting are we talking about?"

Mandy turned to her monitor and brought up the schematics of Hold Three and the dispersal of pallets.

"Which pallets contain the portable labs?" Declan asked.

Mandy checked her manifest. "That would be pallets 10-A, B, and C." She punched in the numbers, and three squares lit up.

Declan and Mandy studied the chart. "That's not as bad as I thought," Mandy said. "You, Honan, and I should be able to get to them without too much trouble."

Declan stared at her with a raised eyebrow. "How long since you worked in a suit?"

"A what?"

"A suit. Or did you forget there's no air, minimal heat, and no gravity in the holds?"

239

She had forgotten. She knew enough about suits to survive in an emergency but had never worked in one. "I guess I'll monitor from here."

"So will Declan," Honan said. "O'Malley and I will shift the cargo."

Declan stared at him. "Don't you dare—"

Honan held up his hand. "Declan, this is one time you're going to listen. You've got a patch on your lung. You need to give yourself time to heal. You are not going into the holds to move crates, even if the cargo is weightless."

Mandy rose from her seat and stood next to Honan. She could tell from the look on Declan's face he wasn't happy. She thought she also saw a twinkle of amusement.

"Declan," Sarah said as she joined Honan and Mandy. "You know Honan's right. We'll do what needs done. You stay here with Mandy. We'll grab O'Malley and have the job done in no time."

Declan sighed as he looked at the three of them. "I can see I have no choice in this."

"None," Mandy affirmed.

"I could cite the three of you for mutiny."

"You could try," Honan said. "But then I'd get Trish to declare you medically unfit for duty and take over anyway."

Declan chuckled, then winced. "Okay, okay, I cede. Get out of here."

Mandy slid into the seat next to Declan after Honan and Sarah left. "They're good friends. How long have you known them?"

"Forever. Honan and I were roommates at the academy. We met Sarah there and have been friends ever since. The last seven years, we've been together here on the *Phoenix*."

"You're lucky." Mandy stared at the starscape in front of them.

"What about you? Didn't you have trouble leaving your friends behind?"

"What friends? My two best friends were my bodyguards. Truly, the Warrior troops you have in cold sleep are probably the closest friends I have. I grew up with quite a few of them. We attended the same cyber-school activities on the base and trained together. Other than them, there really isn't anyone. The Ki name doesn't leave much room for close relationships, especially when you have a madman trying to kill you, or Luddites blowing up your cars, or paparazzi trying to get whatever dirt they can on you for the tabloids, or politicians trying to gain your favors, or any one of a thousand other people looking for a handout or favor.

"Papa D and Taka did what they could, but can you imagine having a sixteenth birthday party and the only people who come are military or bodyguards? The security scans alone are enough to scare away most people."

Declan saw the loneliness in her face, heard the longing in her voice. She had all that money and power, more than most people could even dream of, but all that wealth and power hadn't brought her anything but trouble.

"Well, ma'am, in less than a week, we will be landing on a new world, one where you won't have any more money than the rest of us. You can start a whole new life. Let's see—how would you like to dig latrines?"

His words brought the desired effect when Mandy chuckled.

Chapter Eighteen

People were everywhere. Mandy maneuvered the short distance to her cabin through the knots of crew and specialists newly warmed. The noise assaulted her ears, and even the half-light in the corridor seemed harsh and glaring after almost two months at quarter power. She reached her cabin and opened the door to the quiet within. Sarah was sitting at the monitor working on charts.

"I never thought I'd miss the quiet of a skeleton crew," Mandy said as the door slid shut against the din. She crossed the room and flopped on her bed.

Sarah switched off the monitor and swiveled around. "I know what you mean. I went to lunch today, and the dining area was so noisy, I almost turned around and left. A few weeks ago, I wouldn't have thought anything about the racket. There were enough empty tables I would have thought the place deserted, but now even half full is almost too much. How many are warm?"

"Only the first three groups, but after all this time short-staffed even that many seems like a lot more. Declan doesn't want to start on the others until he's sure about the planet. How are you coming with sleeping arrangements?"

"They're not going to be pretty. There's almost no privacy. I've got mattresses spread out in the gym and, by now, the lounge. We've used every available inch of floor space. We can't even build bunks. Jimmy's commandeered all the supports. He's got everything laid out according to size in the aft hold."

"At least we'll only have to cope for a couple of days—a week at most—until we get set up on the planet. The emergency tents won't be much better, but they'll do until we get shelters built."

They both turned as the door chime sounded.

"Enter," Sarah said.

A blond man Mandy didn't recognize pushed a small cart into the room.

"What's this?" Mandy asked.

"Since we don't have a lounge anymore, everyone gets their meals wherever their quarters are. This is the allotment for this cabin."

Sarah took the cart. "Thanks."

The man left, and Sarah checked the cart she'd set against the wall. "Looks like enough for a day or two. You hungry?"

"Yeah. I didn't get a chance to eat dinner. How 'bout you?"

"No. Honan and I ate earlier. You go ahead. I want to grab a quick sonic shower. I sure will be glad when I can take a real water bath again. Sonics get you clean, but they don't feel the same."

"Amen." Mandy picked up the top meal and grimaced. "Great. Chicken stew with biscuits. If this meal ever saw a chicken, I'll faint."

"Oh, I don't know. Maybe one walked past the factory once."

Mandy loosened her hair and finger-combed the length while she waited for her meal to warm. "Yeah, right. Go on. I'm going to eat then hit the sack. I'm dead on my feet."

Mandy grimaced at the slightly bitter flavor of her food. "If I ever get hold of the person who makes these, I'm going to force feed them to him."

A short time later, Sarah emerged from the shower. "Did you say something?"

"No. I was merely commenting on the wonderful tasty treat I just finished."

"Yeah. And Ki opals are just another piece of rock."

****

"Poppi! No! Don't leave! Poppi!" Mandy screamed. She clawed at the door, desperately trying to find a way out. "Where are you Poppi? Mali?"

Sarah jumped from her bed, shaking off sleep. "Lights!" She quickly scanned the room not certain what had happened. She shook her head, trying to shake off the grip of sleep and saw Mandy trying to break down the door, panic and confusion evident in her eyes and movements.

"Mandy? What's wrong?"

Mandy turned to her. Her eyes were wide, and she acted like she didn't know who Sarah was. She crouched in the corner in a defensive stance.

"Hermes! Get medical here!" Sarah tried to get close to Mandy. "Mandy. Listen to me. Calm down."

She worked her way around so she stood between Mandy and the door. Her friend's face was blank—no recognition at all. Suddenly, the door opened, and Mandy kicked out, catching Sarah in the ribs as Declan and Honan rushed in.

Honan bent over Sarah as she grasped her side.

245

"This is one factor they don't teach you in class," Sarah gasped. "How in the world do you get under the guard of an expert who's gone over the brink?"

Sarah looked up as Trish came in.

"Trish, take care of Sarah," Declan ordered. He crept toward Mandy. "Sarah, any idea what happened?"

"No. She was screaming something about someone named Poppi leaving her. I don't think she knows who we are or where she is."

Declan nodded. Mandy had told him about her father and their pet names for each other. He knelt in front of her, holding out his arms. "You're all right, kitten. Poppi is here. I'm not going anywhere."

Slowly, he coaxed Mandy into his arms, and then grasped her so Trish could sedate her. As soon as Declan's arms tightened, Mandy struggled violently, managing to deliver some well-placed kicks, and Trish wasn't able to inject the medication. His side felt on fire, and he was sure he'd undone the patch on his side if not the one on his lung. But he could still breathe, so he ignored the pain.

"No! Stay away!" Mandy looked at Declan, her eyes wide. "Can't you see? Don't you see what she is?" She ran for the open door, but Declan caught her before she got there.

Honan joined Declan in trying to capture Mandy. He received several bruises and a black eye for his troubles. Finally, they pinned her down so Trish could administer the drug.

"Give that five minutes," the doctor said as Declan and Honan tried to hold Mandy down.

Mandy kicked him in the shins, and he grunted. "For such a small person, she sure packs a wallop."

Finally, the drug took effect and she collapsed into a semi-conscious state.

"Poppi?"

Declan gathered her into his arms. "Relax, kitten. You're safe."

Mandy's head drooped into sleep.

"Trish? How's Sarah?"

"Three broken ribs. I'll get her to sick bay and take care of them." She turned to go.

"Um, Trish? Don't you want to know what's wrong with Mandy? I know I do."

Trish walked over to Declan. On the way, she glanced at the food cart next to the door.

"Looks like she's high on some drug. You know how flighty rich people can be. That sedative should keep her asleep for the rest of the night. If there are any problems, let me know."

Declan watched the doctor leave. He looked at Honan. "Tell me I'm imagining what I saw. Did she seem like she was less concerned about this than she should be?"

"You're not imagining anything. Did you see the way she looked at this cart? Plus, she didn't even ask about you. That beating Mandy gave us had to have hurt more than just her punches."

Declan struggled to get to his feet, Mandy still in his arms until Honan took her from him. He gently laid her on her bed, and Declan drew the blanket over her.

"Why is this cart here? We've been eating in the mess, not off carts."

Honan picked up the food container from Mandy's dinner. "There are three dinners here, but only one's been eaten." He sniffed at the container and winced.

"I know these dinners aren't the greatest, but this one smells worse than usual. How much do you want to bet there's something wrong with this?"

"I'd say that's a pretty even bet. I'd also say our illustrious doctor already knew about what that something is. Has Taka been warmed yet?" Declan asked.

"Yes. She was in the last group this afternoon. She's probably still recovering."

"Get her. I want her to check Mandy and those food packs. And let's keep this to ourselves."

Declan studied the woman in the bed while he waited for Honan and Taka. He winced as he brushed against the bed. He'd have more than a few bruises to remember this night. As for Mandy, she slept on, blissfully unaware of the damage she'd done.

"Who did this to you?" Declan shook his head. "Check that. I know who did this. But who is he?"

He looked up as Honan returned with Taka in tow. She had an old-fashioned black bag with her that she set down and went immediately to Mandy.

"Any idea what happened?" Taka put two fingers on Mandy's neck.

"Possibly," Declan said. "I'm not sure, but I think the food may have been tainted."

"Tell me exactly what she was acting like."

"She was wild, like she didn't know any of us or where she was. She kept calling for Poppi and said Trish was some kind of monster."

"Looks like she did a good job on you and Honan." Taka glanced at Declan's side and shook her head. "Do you know what Trish gave her?"

"No. She said something about a sedative and that

Mandy would sleep the night through."

Taka opened her bag and pulled out a piece of equipment Declan had never seen before. She held a small black box about six inches square. On top was a keyboard and small screen. On two sides were slots of various sizes. She set the box on the nightstand.

Taka pricked one of Mandy's fingers and squeezed a drop of blood onto a slide. She slid the sample into one of the openings. She also took a scraping from the food container and inserted that in another slot.

"Now we wait," she said.

"What is that?" Declan asked. "I've never seen anything like that before."

"And you never will. This is something I've been working on and seems like as good a time as any to test my experiment. You're looking at a self-contained portable testing unit. I can pretty much tell you everything about yourself from one drop of blood. I can check for poisons, drugs, diseases, and deficiencies. I haven't had a chance to run real-time tests yet. Lab, yes. Real life, no."

"So how do we know if it works?" Declan asked as the machine beeped.

Taka checked the screen. "I'd say we have our answer. According to this, Mandy was given a powerful hallucinogenic drug as well as the sedative. I don't like the level of drugs in her system. They're a bit too high for my comfort."

She dug in her bag and pulled out a hypo spray. "I'm going to give her a counteragent. That should bring the levels down."

She set the control and administered the drug. The machine beeped again. "You were right about the food.

That's the source of the drug. Any idea who's responsible?"

Declan rose from where he sat. He didn't remember ever being so angry. "Not yet, but I will. Honan, stay here with Taka and Mandy." He clenched his jaw to the point where his teeth hurt.

Honan grasped Declan's arm. "Declan, are you sure you want to do this? I can question her."

Declan took a deep breath and exhaled. "No. This is long overdue. Take care of them."

"I will."

Declan strode through the corridor, not seeing anyone or anything. Fortunately, at that time of night, the space was mostly deserted. He reached sickbay and stalked in. Trish was finishing with Sarah. Declan motioned the med-tech over. "Can you finish here?"

"Aye, Captain."

"Doctor, I want to talk to you."

"Declan, I'll be—"

"That wasn't a request, Doctor."

Trish looked at him, shrugged, and turned Sarah over to the med-tech. "Okay, Declan, what's so important you can't let me finish with my patient?"

Declan ushered the doctor into her office and shut the door. "What do you know about the drug used on Mandy?"

Trish walked around her desk and fiddled with several data disks lying there. "Nothing. Why?"

Declan leaned on the desk. "Cut the crap, Trish. I've seen your innocent act one too many times to be fooled any more. Did you put the drug in the food?"

"No."

"Do you know who did?"

She glared at Declan. "What if I do? I won't tell you. That little bitch is nothing. Nobody will care who she is. I know where the real power—and the money—is. Why don't you join us, Declan? Once we're in control, you'll have anything you want. You want a new ship? You can have one. Power? Money? Women? Everything will be ours. Turn this ship around, and you can have a share."

Declan looked down as a piece of the desk snapped off in his hand. Another victim of the owners' penchant for cheap materials. "You don't get it, do you? We can't turn around. The ship won't last more than another week, if that long. The *Phoenix* is dead, Trish. And we will be too if we don't find a good planet to settle on."

Trish laughed, a high-pitched eerie sound with an edge of panic. "I know that's the story you've been feeding everyone, but that's not the truth. Am I right, Declan? I'll bet you know exactly where we are. Tell me, did she put you up to this ruse?"

"I don't know who's been feeding you this line of bull, although I've got a pretty good guess. This isn't an elaborate scheme. We are in serious trouble. And you're in deeper than anyone. Will you tell me who you've been working with?" Declan really didn't expect her to answer, but he held out a sliver of hope until he saw her eyes. He'd thought he'd seen a glimmer of fear, but her expression quickly changed to hatred. Had he ever really known her? And she'd been the one running all the scans. No wonder they hadn't found Alvarez.

"No. I don't believe you, Declan. He told me you'd try to get me to go along with you. I won't. You deserve what will happen, and I'm glad. The almighty Declan Chalmers. You think you're better than anyone else. Well, you're not. You had your chance, and you refused. Miguel was right about you. You are nothing."

Declan moved around the desk. He grabbed her arm and twisted it behind her back. "In that case, Doctor, I am placing you under arrest for the murder of Glenna Jones and the attempted murder of General Tyler Davis, Amanda Ki, Sarah Thomas, and myself. If you're lucky, you'll stand trial on our new home planet."

Declan dragged her out of the office. The tech was finishing with Sarah.

"Sarah? If you're feeling okay, can you accompany me to the brig?"

Sarah stepped down from the exam table. "Aye, Captain." She shrugged into her tunic and pulled her weapon.

Declan ignored the startled looks they got from crewmen as he escorted the doctor to the brig.

"Do you want me to post a guard?" Sarah asked once they'd sealed the cell door.

Trish glared at him from the middle of the cell. "No. I really hope her friend comes for her. We both know how much he likes failure."

As he turned away, he caught a true expression of fear on the doctor's face.

"Declan, you can't leave me here alone."

"Tell me who Alvarez is."

"I…I…can't, Declan. He'll kill me."

"That's your choice, Trish." Declan motioned Sarah through the door.

"Declan!"

Trish's voice followed them into the outer office. Declan shut the door behind him. He moved to the monitor and punched in a code. His shoulders slumped as he left the brig.

"Declan? Are you okay?" Sarah asked.

"Yeah. I want to check the stasis pods before we go to your quarters."

"You think Trish was lying about Alvarez being dead?"

"Yes. She's been lying a lot. Plus, she's been the one running all the scans. No wonder we haven't found Alvarez."

They reached the small room off sickbay that served as a lab and, when necessary, a morgue. There were two pods within. Declan checked the first one, which contained the colonel. The second one was empty.

Chapter Nineteen

Declan palmed open the door to Mandy's cabin. Honan stepped out and held a finger to his lips. The door swished shut behind him.

"Mandy's still out. Taka fell asleep a few minutes ago." He looked Sarah over.

"How are you?"

"Sore, but okay. You look like you've been in a fight."

He chuckled, then winced as he touched his eye. "We all do. How'd you do with Trish?"

Declan motioned toward his cabin next door. "Let's talk in there."

Honan nodded, then frowned at Declan's side. "You're bleeding."

Declan looked down. There was a small patch of blood on his shirt. "I'm fine."

"You're not fine," Sarah said as they entered the cabin. "Take off your shirt." When Declan didn't move, she cocked her head at him. "That wasn't a request, Captain. Either Honan and I take care of you here, or we send you back to medical. Or I get Taka over here."

Declan sighed but took off his shirt. "I think only the outer patch is bad. I'm not having any trouble breathing."

Sarah nodded and cut a strip of cloth from his shirt. "Fine. This will suffice for now. But I want you in medical if the bleeding doesn't stop or if you have any trouble."

"Fine." He grabbed a clean shirt from his closet but didn't miss the way Honan's eyes kept straying to Sarah or the protective way he stood over her once they were in his office. Actually, ever since that first incident with Sarah, Honan had been acting rather protective. After all this time, maybe Honan was finally realizing how important Sarah was to him. Sometimes, a little danger brought out the best in some people. And maybe out here, away from his tribe, he could finally act on his feelings. Then Declan thought about Trish. Danger could also bring out the worst in someone.

"Trish is in the brig." Declan flipped on his monitor and swung the screen around for Sarah and Honan to see. They could see the doctor lying in her bunk, one arm thrown across her eyes. In a corner of the screen, they could also see the interior of Mandy's cabin.

"In addition to the cameras, I'll have a secure feed that Chane is putting together for me that is supposedly immune to leashes. I've also set the bio monitors to maximum. If anything larger than a flea tries to get in there, we'll know."

"Did she say anything?"

"Plenty, but nothing we can use. She's convinced this is all some kind of elaborate hoax. What do we really know about her? I mean, I know she's got the medical credentials, but do we know anything else about her? And yes, I know I hooked up with her for a short time—"he paused when both Honan and Sarah snorted"—Okay, so a week, and I admit, the attraction was purely physical. I got out as fast as I could, once I realized she wasn't my kind of person. Unfortunately, I know almost nothing about her."

Honan drew his chair closer. "Actually, we know more than you realize. While you were taking care of the doctor, I did a little digging. After a bit of hacking, Chane and I managed to get into Trish's personal files. What I found didn't make much sense until Taka got a glimpse of them."

"Taka? What's she got to do with this?" Declan asked.

"She made the connection between Trish and Alvarez. I was reading through Trish's entries and kept coming across two names—Drema and Trella."

Declan held up his hand. "I recognize the one name—Drema. The general mentioned her. She was married to Alvarez."

"That's what Taka told me. Trella was Drema's sister and, according to Taka, so is Trish. She changed her name and ID. Anyway, Trella died in some kind of plane accident. Trish is the last one of her family. Alvarez gave her the idea she should come on to you. Her...um...preferences didn't lean that way, but she complied for her sisters' sakes."

Declan cocked his head, then snorted. "That explains some of her actions. But why do what she did?"

"To get control of the ship and get to Xy-Three under their rule. Trish was the one who poisoned the water there. Alvarez promised her she'd be head of the pharmaceuticals once they took control. By the way, if there's anything good to be said about this whole mess, we know the poison is short-lived. The people left on Xy-Three are most-likely safe by now."

"That will relieve Mandy." Declan ran his hand through his hair. "Money and power. This whole mess is because of that?"

"You know as well as I do those are pretty potent motives," Honan said. "Especially this level of money and power. Add in Alvarez's drug-induced paranoia, and you've got a full-blown conspiracy."

"Well, we know Alvarez is alive and kicking, but we still don't know who or where he is. Trish wouldn't talk. Scratch that. We know he was Michaels, but who is he now? Trish could have helped him change his looks," Declan said. "Should we do bio scans again?"

"Taka already suggested that. She's planning on getting them started tomorrow. With fewer people warm, they shouldn't take as long."

Sarah frowned at them. "What about the guy who delivered the cart to our room? I didn't know him. If I'm with Taka, I might recognize him again."

"What did he look like?"

"Medium height, stocky build, but not fat, dark blond hair, brown eyes, spoke with a slight lisp. He was wearing a standard issue suit and a maintenance badge."

"He can change clothes as easily as he changes identities. Remember, when he first came on board, he had red hair and green eyes," Declan pointed out.

"Yeah, but I still might be able to see something." Sarah hid a yawn behind her hand. "Sorry. The tech gave me a painkiller. I guess the drug's taking effect."

"Plus, we've had a long night," Declan said. "Okay, you start with Taka in the morning."

He looked at Honan and Sarah. "Tell you what, why don't the two of you stay here for what's left of the rest of the night? I'll stand watch next door."

Sarah grinned her thanks.

Declan nodded to the guard standing outside Mandy's door and quietly let himself into the room. Taka woke when he entered. He put his finger to his lips and motioned for her to go back to sleep. He stretched out on the bed closest to the door. Tina was on night shift and wouldn't be back for several hours. Declan listened to Mandy's deep, even breathing— overlaid by Taka's gentle snores.

Declan lay there thinking about Trish and all she had done. They would have no place to imprison her once they got settled. He could put her into a cold sleep pod, but that was only a stopgap solution. Depending on the lay of the land, perhaps they could isolate her and Alvarez away from the main colony. They'd give the two enough supplies and equipment to survive on their own and let them go. The more he thought about the idea, the more he liked that plan. Maybe some honest-to-goodness hard work would change those two. Maybe. But he had his doubts.

****

Mandy woke slowly and stretched. She'd had the oddest dreams—nightmares, really. Something about monsters and her father and cats. Weird. She looked around the room. That was strange. Where was Sarah? Then she saw the clock. Stars! She was late. Why had Sarah let her oversleep? And where was Tina?

She jumped out of bed, splashed some cold water on her face, and pulled on her clothes. Less than fifteen minutes after waking, she strolled onto the bridge. Declan was sitting at the center console, Honan to his right. Both were absorbed in something on the monitor.

Sarah was nowhere in sight.

"Good morning," Mandy said. Honan and Declan turned to her. Mandy stopped in mid-step and stared back. Honan's left eye was swollen and discolored, as was his lower lip. Declan didn't look much better. His right cheek showed signs of bruising, and there was a cut over his eye.

"I'm sorry I overslept. Um, did I miss something? You two look like you've been in a brawl." She continued on down to the third console.

Declan swung around to her. "You really don't remember?"

Oh-oh. Mandy sat hard on the chair. "Remember what?" Her voice shook. *Please, God, tell me I'm not responsible for this.*

"What's the last thing you remember from last night?" Declan asked.

"Sarah and I talked. I ate some dinner while she got a shower, then I went to bed."

"You don't remember anything else?"

Mandy shook her head. "I had the strangest dream. Really bizarre. I dreamed about my father and some sort of monster whose face kept melting. Everything's all so hazy."

"You weren't dreaming. You were hallucinating," Declan said. "Your meal was drugged."

"Drugged? How? By whom?"

"Trish. She's been working with Alvarez."

"I thought he was dead."

Declan shook his head. "That's what they wanted us to believe. He's definitely alive and wandering the ship. Taka is running scans on all personnel again."

"You don't seriously think you'll find him that

way, do you?"

"No." Declan sighed and ran his hand through his hair. "But what other choice do we have?"

Mandy tapped her lip with her finger. There was something…a niggling thought at the back of her mind. "Maybe there's another way. Remember my chip? I think Trish transplanted the device into Alvarez."

"Why do you think that?" Honan asked.

She cocked her head and frowned. "I'm not really sure. Maybe something from a dream."

"Your last dream broke three of Sarah's ribs," Declan said.

Mandy blinked at him and felt her face flame. "Oh, God. Is she okay? I'm so sorry. I know how inadequate that sounds, but I really am sorry."

Honan grinned at her. "Sarah is fine. She's with Taka, helping with the scans. At least now I know how much you were pulling your punches during our sparring match."

If anything, Mandy's face burned even more. "Why haven't you two gotten your injuries taken care of? And Declan, what about your side? Did I tear open the patch?"

"To be honest, we haven't had time," Declan said. "Well, except for my side. Taka took care of that first. The rest is superficial. And before you ask, Taka told us to let you sleep as long as you needed. You had a pretty good dose of drugs and sedatives. But about this chip…"

"Is there a way you can check for that? He'd have a scar of some sort behind one of his ears."

"Is the chip detectable by a basic bio scan?" Honan asked.

"Yes. The hardware will show up like any other piece of internal devices."

Honan swiveled around to his monitor. "Sarah? How many crew have you gotten through?"

"Only ten," Sarah said. "The process is slow."

"Tell Taka you don't have to do the full scan. A basic bio reading will do. You're looking for Mandy's chip. All you have to do is a head scan, and you should be able to see the embedded chip."

They watched as Sarah turned from the monitor, presumably to talk to Taka. "Taka says scanning for the chip will take us an hour or two instead of all day. I'll get back to you when we have something. Oh, how's Mandy?"

"Embarrassed," Mandy said. "Are you really okay?"

"I'll be fine. What happened wasn't your fault, Mandy. Trish did this to you." She signed off.

"How are they certifying they've tested everyone?" Mandy asked.

"Sarah has the rosters. Everyone not accounted for in cold sleep has to come past her. The Warriors are making sure they do," Honan said. "Anyone not accounted for is tracked down."

"You won't find him," Mandy said.

"He can't get away from us this time," Honan argued.

"Trust me. You won't find him."

****

Five hours later, her words proved true. His was the only name on the rosters not accounted for, and a ship-wide search had turned up nothing. Four extremely frustrated friends settled in Declan's cabin with their dinners.

"I don't understand how he keeps eluding us." Declan stabbed his mystery meat.

"Remember the air vents?" Mandy held up her hand to stop their interruptions. "This is a big ship with thousands of places to hide. For all we know, he's already changed his appearance and ID—again. We won't find him until he wants us to."

"I don't understand how you can be so blasé about this," Sarah said.

"I'm not. But I've lived with Alvarez in my hair for a long time. We will catch him, but not yet. He's not done playing with us yet."

"How can you be so sure?" Declan asked.

"I'm still alive."

Her quiet words silenced the others. Mandy toyed with her food, not really hungry. She'd become leery of eating even the sealed meals, subsisting mostly on crackers and nutria-drinks from Taka. "Has Trish told you anything?"

Declan pulled the brig up on his monitor. Trish was in her bunk, one arm lying across her eyes, the other on her stomach. "She hasn't eaten, spoken, or even moved."

Mandy stared at the monitor. Something didn't look right to her. "You say she hasn't budged since you put her in there?"

"No. Why?"

"Has anyone checked on her?"

"I had a guard take in her meals."

"But did the guard check her? Did he say anything to her? Did she even acknowledge his existence in some way?"

Declan shook his head. "Not that I know of. What's bothering you?"

"I think she's dead."

Declan and the others sat up and stared at the monitor. "What? That's not possible."

"I'll bet she either had something on her she could take, or Alvarez slipped something in. But she's dead."

Declan strode out of his cabin—the others close behind. When they arrived at the brig, he turned off the alarms and stepped into Trish's cell. She didn't move. He checked her pulse and breathing.

Mandy could tell from the way his shoulders slumped that her guess was correct. She jumped when Declan slammed his fist into the wall.

"She's dead?" Honan said.

"Yes. And not only that, but she's been dead for a while. Rigor has already set in. You'd better notify Taka we need her to do an autopsy. I want to know how and when she died." Declan turned and stormed out of the brig.

Mandy checked on Trish. Having worked with Taka, she knew a few facts about dead bodies. "Honan? You're not going to need Taka. I can tell you what you need to know. She didn't die of any exotic poison or anything like that. Somebody broke her neck."

Honan shook his head. "That's not possible. Declan had this place set so nothing or no one could get in here without setting off the alarms."

"That's only if they came in the front door. What if they came in the back window?" Mandy pointed to a square of floor tile that didn't quite line up with the others. "What's under the floor?"

Honan sighed. "That's where all the wiring,

plumbing, and other conduits run. But there's a security net between the tiles and the access. One that's supposed to be impervious to attack. And before you ask, yes, the space with the conduits is large enough to get through—if you're not a big person."

"And Alvarez isn't. Plus, we know he's an expert at getting around impervious systems. I assume the alarms were set to go off only if someone came in from the outside. They couldn't be set in here because Trish was here."

"Declan's not going to like this," Honan said.

"There's nothing to like." Mandy went to the monitor. "Hermes, can you show me where Declan is?"

A small dot showed up on a schematic of the ship. Mandy smiled. She wasn't surprised. "Honan, you and Sarah drop me off there on your way to see Taka. I'll talk to Declan."

A few minutes later, Mandy was descending the trail to the floor of the garden center. She found Declan at the bench she knew he loved to go to. He was sitting there, head in his hands, shoulders slumped. She'd never seen anyone look so dejected. She settled on the bench next to him.

"Are you all right?"

Declan sighed and looked at her. Worry lines marred his forehead, and the creases at his eyes had deepened.

"Yeah. I will be."

"I understand you and Trish were close at one time."

"I wouldn't exactly say that. She might have wanted to think so, but there wasn't much substance there. I'd known her for a couple months, dated her for a week, but never really knew her. All that time, and I never saw anything wrong."

"You saw exactly what she wanted you to see. Declan, this isn't your fault. You and Trish were both victims. You have to let go of what she did to you. You can't let her actions get to you, or you will continue to be a victim. If she was the right person for you, she'd have thrown off Alvarez. She'd still be alive and would still be with you. The fact that she isn't should tell you the relationship wasn't right."

Declan looked at her, pain in his eyes and on his face. "I know you're right. But still…" He looked back at his hands.

Mandy lay her hand on his arm. She wished there was a way to help him but knew he had to work through those feelings for himself. "I know, Declan. I know."

They sat there without saying anything for a few minutes, then Declan the captain took over Declan the man. He stood and brushed imaginary dust off his pants. "We've got a lot to do before tomorrow. Guess we need to get to work."

Mandy climbed the steps ahead of him. "What's our agenda for tomorrow?"

"We'll load the shuttle with supplies and personnel at 0800 and head downside," Declan said. "Sarah and Honan will stay up here and handle this end. Once we've found a place to set down, you and your team get to work, and we cross our fingers."

"Sounds like a plan," Mandy said. She'd be glad to get her feet back on stable ground. Although the shuddering in the ship had stopped, she knew as well as the others, the ship wouldn't last much longer. Systems were failing all over the place, and Chane was hard-pressed to keep the ship running as smoothly as he did. She hoped they could hold out for the few days they'd need to do the tests and get a basic camp set up.

Chapter Twenty

Mandy checked the emergency supplies in the landing shuttle. The craft was a miniature version of the ship. The top level could hold twelve people with the cargo area beneath the decking. With the seats and flooring removed, the shuttle could be converted into a lab or living quarters.

A gray-haired man stuck his head in the hatch. "I've finished with the cargo manifests and everything's standing by, ma'am. I can have this shuttle ready to go as soon as I get the word. Do you want me to start removing the seats?"

Mandy frowned at him. "Why? We're taking this one down. Shuttles Two and Four are straight cargo. By the way, I don't believe I've seen you around. What's your name?" She gripped the handle of the weapon holstered at her waist.

"I…uh, I'm newly warmed, ma'am. My name's Mark Andrews." He turned his head as though listening to something. "Oh, sorry, ma'am. I'm being called to the cargo bay."

Before Mandy could stop him, he was gone. She hustled out of the shuttle but didn't see him anywhere. "Mike?" She called to her ever-present shadow. "Did you see that cargo man?"

"Yes, ma'am. He seemed to be in a hurry. Is there a problem?"

"There might be. Contact Honan and see if he has a crewman named Mark Andrews and give him the guy's description. There's something about him…"

She paused as Declan entered the docking bay. "Hang on, Mike. Declan? Do you have a crewman named Mark Andrews?"

Declan frowned. "I don't recognize the name, but I've got quite a few new crew. Problem?"

"Maybe. Maybe not. Might be paranoia. Especially with those initials." She nodded to Mike. "Go ahead and notify Honan, in case I'm not totally crazy."

Mike left, and Mandy turned to Declan. "The guy was helping ready the shuttle. I didn't recognize him, although he did seem a little familiar, but he gave me the creeps."

"Honan will check on him. Anything else I need to know? I'll give the shuttle a quick look to make sure we don't have any of Alvarez's surprises."

"Okay. We're good to go as soon as my people get here. I've got Taka and eight techs in addition to you, the pilot, and me. The cargo bay is filled to capacity with testing equipment, supplies, and two shelter tents." She paused as a group came into the bay. They were chatting excitedly. She did a quick head count.

"Looks like that's everyone," she said. Declan nodded at her and ducked through the door into the shuttle. Mandy waited until the group had gathered by her. "Okay, we're all ready to go. Take your seats and strap in."

"Miss Ki?" one of the techs asked.

"Yes?"

"Why can't we take the ship down? Then we wouldn't have to shuttle everything."

"Because this ship's not built for atmospheric pressures. Newer ones can handle the pressures on planet, but this one can't. She'd be crushed and burn up in the upper atmosphere before we even reach the ground."

The woman's face paled. "Oh. Okay."

Mandy checked each person off her list as they entered the shuttle. These were all people she knew. They'd been with her company for many years and worked well together. In addition, they were experts in their fields. She climbed aboard and strapped in directly behind Declan.

"Is everything clear?" she asked.

"I could only do a quick surface check but didn't see anything."

Mandy nodded, and Declan turned back around. He and the pilot went through their checklist. Finally, the shuttle door closed, and Mandy felt the engines power up.

The *Phoenix's* huge bay doors opened, and Mandy felt a surge of excitement. A slight vibration thrummed from the deck up through her body as the pilot lifted off. The craft slowly exited the ship and turned to the planet beneath them.

The passengers in back were able to see outside by way of the monitors positioned around the cabin. Mandy watched through the front window as the bay doors slid shut and they pulled away from the *Phoenix*. The planet, almost as beautiful as Aboo, grew larger in the viewing window.

"Does the view from out here ever get old?" Mandy asked. The scene mesmerized her. She realized the normally chatty techs had also grown quiet.

"Nope." Declan smiled back at her. "No matter how many planets, moons, or even space stations you see, the sight from out here is still incredible."

"There speaks a true spacer," Taka said. She was in the seat next to Mandy.

"Do you have an idea for a landing site yet?" Mandy asked.

"We're going to aim for one of the larger land masses in the western hemisphere," Declan said.

The pilot maneuvered through the atmosphere. He was good at his job as there was truly little buffeting as they descended.

Suddenly, the ship lurched. If not for the straps holding her down, Mandy would have been unseated. Declan and the pilot were busy at the controls, and they didn't look like they were enjoying themselves. Mandy didn't think now would be a good time to ask questions, so she bit her lip.

The view through the window spun wildly. Landmasses appeared, then mountains, growing larger and larger. She swallowed against the bile rising in her throat and glanced back at her people. Several of them had a definite greenish cast to their faces. One man muttered quietly to himself and made a religious warding sign several times.

Finally, the crazy motion steadied, and the ship leveled out. On the monitor, Mandy could make out individual branches on trees below them. The possibility of a crash had been far too close.

Declan blew out a long breath and turned to face Mandy and the others. "I know you have questions. Unfortunately, I don't have the answers. We had a simultaneous malfunction of several systems but were able to reroute to secondary systems. We are under control for the moment and should be landing as soon as we find a good spot."

Mandy pulled up her seat monitor. "Declan? What about that land mass in the upper right quadrant? That one looks promising."

Declan checked his screen. "Could be a possibility."

He punched the coordinates into the panel. "Low and slow, Mitch," he told the pilot.

"Aye, Captain."

They flew over the large island, studying the surface. Mandy could tell from the look on Declan's face the verdict wasn't good. "Can you tell me what you're looking for?"

"A relatively level area with good water supplies and vegetation."

"So, what's wrong with this one?"

"You've got nothing here but flatlands and little vegetation. The few trees all have branches facing the same direction."

"That could be the way the native flora grows."

"Agreed. But that could also mean storms and winds that sweep constantly over this land. With no hills to break up the storms, what little vegetation there is adapts, leaning away from the worst. Also, the land is relatively low, which means flooding could be an issue." Declan turned to Mitch. "Let's head for that mass in the lower left quadrant."

Mandy checked her read-out. "That's got some pretty nasty cliffs."

"This from someone who was raised in the Aboolean islands?" Declan chuckled. "Actually, from what we've been able to gather, they're on the windward side. That makes them good protection. Judging from the vegetation, there's still enough moisture on the leeward side to get good, tall growth."

The huge island was roughly circular in shape. The mountains Mandy had mentioned were highest in the west, dwindling to rolling hills in the north and south. They sloped to a bowl shape in a central valley that gently leveled out to the sea on the eastern slope. Several large creeks and a small river fed a teardrop shaped lake at the southern end of the basin.

They did an aerial survey, looking for a place to land. Declan pointed to a large, relatively flat area near the eastern shore. As soon as they landed, the scientists unbuckled and went to work. They tuned their monitors to the external sensors and probed for airborne contaminants or anything that spelled danger. They compared the new data with the preliminary data from the probes they'd sent out from the ship.

"How's the air look, Pete?" Mandy asked a short, bald man. He was a combination meteorologist/koniologist and could tell to the smallest micron whether the air would be safe.

"Give me a few minutes. I want to be certain of my results."

Mandy, Declan, and the others waited impatiently for him to finish his tests. Finally, he raised his head from his work.

"The air is breathable with no known pollutants or poisons that could be detrimental to our health. Do you want me to do a personal test? I could go out for a while, then we'd know for sure."

Mandy shook her head and grinned. "If you're so

sure that you're willing to risk your own precious neck, I'll take that as positive proof we're good. We'll keep our fingers crossed there isn't anything unknown out there."

She turned to the others. "What about the rest of you?"

"Our scans show no evidence of animals larger than a Aboolean wildcat in the vicinity. Most of what I've seen on the monitors is small, but the shuttle probably scared away the natives."

"Vegetation is abundant, but no jungle. Looks like the plant life you'd find is a nice deciduous forest. I'll know more once I can get out there."

Mandy listened as each one gave a short report. She knew the reports lacked detail, but the most important fact was everything seemed safe. She turned to Declan.

"Well, Captain? You heard the experts. What's your call?"

Declan put his hands on his knees and pushed to a stand. "Mandy, you're with me. The rest of you stay here." He turned to the pilot. "Mitch, you're in charge until we get back. If there are any signs of trouble, get this craft and crew out of here."

"Aye, Captain."

Mitch cycled the inner door to the airlock open and handed Mandy and Declan a supply of sentinel posts to deploy around the ship. Declan handed Mandy a sidearm and pinned a small circular pin to her collar. "This is a two-way. Mitch will monitor us from here."

Once they were in the airlock, Declan closed the inner door and cycled open the outer one.

The first detail Mandy noticed was the smell—

cool, crisp, and moist, like a clear spring day after a shower.

"Fresh air!" Mandy closed her eyes, face tilted toward the sun, letting the warmth flow over her. She took a deep breath, savoring the taste and feel of the first fresh air in months. The sensation was a heady feeling but sobering at the same time. They were about to step onto a planet no Aboolean had ever walked on. She opened her eyes and caught Declan gazing at the sky. Unlike most of Aboo, no smog obscured the clear azure expanse.

Declan nodded at her, and they stepped down from the shuttle, scanning the area for signs of danger. He motioned for Mandy to take the left side while he went right. They searched the area for a distance of approximately 300 feet out from the ship, setting up sentinel posts at ten-foot intervals and activating them. The posts would alert the camp to anything larger than a rabbit entering the area.

They had landed in a large meadow bordered by tall forests on two sides, low hills to the north, and the sea to the east. A small stream flowed through the area giving them access to fresh water for testing and, with luck, drinking. Long, soft grass covered the ground broken only by an occasional grouping of large shrubs.

"Looks like you picked a good place to set up camp," Mandy said. "We can do most of our testing here, and the forest is close enough for more extensive testing later."

"I guess we should let the rest out of their cage," Declan said. "Mitch?"

"Aye, Captain?"

"Everything's secure out here. You can start setting

up camp."

"Aye, sir."

Almost immediately, the lock cycled open, and the crew bounded out of the ship. Mandy watched as each one paused at the top of the ramp and took a deep breath.

"Can you believe this? We're actually standing on a new world—a place nobody's ever seen before. Now I know how the First Ones must have felt." Stacy, a small redhead in charge of botany said, referring to the mythical settling of Aboo. She set down a portable lab table almost as big as she was and studied the area, her eyes wide, and with a huge smile. "Think of the papers I can write on this!"

She turned to Mandy. "Where do you want us to set up, ma'am?"

Mandy glanced around. "Use the shuttle as a base, and set the lab tents on the aft end. Rob, you and Pete set up the mess tent near the front. We'll form an open-ended box. Is there anyone other than me who will want to sleep outside the ship?"

Mandy laughed as she got an army of hands waving in the air. "Okay, we'll need a sleeping base and shelter. Set that on the end of the mess tent. For the time being, we'll keep medical equipment in the ship. Taka, you can set up your lab in there. Any questions?"

There were none. "All right, people, let's get to work."

****

A few hours later, Mandy took a break from setting up sleeping pallets and looked around. The camp was completely set up, and the scientists were already busy with their various specialties. Where possible, they'd opted to let the sides of the tents open, allowing for air circulation. There wasn't much more for her to do. At this point, letting them do their work was more important, so she stayed out of the way. She glanced at Declan restlessly prowling the perimeter like a caged tiger looking at the forest beyond, and she joined him.

"What do you think?"

"So far, everything looks good, but I'll wait until this evening to give Honan the go-ahead on warming all the personnel. I want to be sure this place is as good as I hope." He swatted his neck. "One thing's for certain. There's an insect life."

Mandy checked the small welt on his neck. She looked around and saw her aunt in the first lab tent. "Taka! I think you'd better check this."

"What the devil do I need a doctor for?" Declan protested. "I have a damned mosquito bite."

Taka, hands on hips, glared at him, not daunted by either his size or position. "Mandy is exactly right. Until we know more about this planet, anything, no matter how small, is potentially dangerous. In fact"— she raised her voice so everyone in camp could hear her—"if any of you has so much as a hangnail, I want to know—immediately!"

Mandy hid a grin at the look on Declan's face. Taka was right, and he knew so. He meekly sat on a camp chair so Taka could check him. Sitting, he was still as tall as she was standing, but there was no doubt as to who was in charge. Taka took a small scraping from the bite, sprayed an antiseptic on the welt, and disappeared into the ship.

Mandy knew Declan was feeling as restless as she was. "How would you feel about a little exploring?"

"Good idea. Get your gear, and meet me here."

Mandy checked in with Taka first. "What's the prognosis?"

"So far, no problem."

"Any reason Declan and I can't go for a hike?"

Taka glanced at Mandy, an impish grin on her face. "Behave yourselves. I'm not set up for a nursery—yet."

"Taka!" Mandy blushed furiously. She grabbed her gear and headed for the door. Taka's laughter followed her the entire way.

****

Only the rustling of their passage through the underbrush broke the quiet of the forest. Occasionally they heard strange noises they assumed were animals or birds. Huge trees filtered the sunlight marking the ground with a patchwork of shade and light. Dark humus softened their footsteps and filled their nostrils with a rich, loamy aroma.

Mandy stared at the huge trees that dwarfed anything she had ever seen on Aboo. "This is a beautiful place." Even her hushed voice sounded obscenely loud in the stillness.

Declan sat on a fallen log. "I'd forgotten how much I missed this."

Mandy joined him. As he wrapped his arm around her shoulders, she leaned against him. "What do you miss?"

He swept his arm around, encompassing the forest. "This. The smell and feel of fresh air and the forest. No matter how you recycle, filter, and clean canned air, there is still a smell that can't be erased."

He leaned back and closed his eyes for a few minutes. Suddenly his eyes opened. He stood, his head tilted to one side, a look of concentration on his face.

"Do you hear something?"

Mandy closed her eyes, listening to the sounds around them. Leaves rustled in a slight breeze. Something stirred in the branches overhead. Behind that, she heard the faint sound of rushing water.

"That sounds like a waterfall," she said as she rose from the log. She and Declan scrambled through the underbrush until they came out at the edge of a wide, rock-filled creek. The water tumbled from a high cliff down a series of miniscule pools to a small pond. A bright ray of sun showing through a break in the trees created a misty rainbow over the falls. They stood and gazed at the scene for a few minutes, hands entwined.

Mandy sighed and pulled away from him, slipped off her knapsack, and pulled out sample bottles. "As much as I would love to wade in, I guess we'd better do this right and take samples back for testing."

Declan sighed and reached for a pair of gloves. He handed her a pair as well. "You're right. I don't like to admit that, but you're right. Here, give me some of those bottles, and I'll get aquatic plants while you work on water and whatever else we find."

They worked in companionable silence for a while, enjoying the view and the work. Mandy watched as Declan collected various samples, meticulously labeling each bottle with the place and time of collection.

"Where'd you learn to do sampling?" she asked.

"My mother is a botanist and my father a marine biologist. I think one of the first lessons I learned was how to collect. My first words must have been 'container labeled'."

Mandy laughed as she wrapped each sample and

settled them into containers. "Somehow I don't picture you as the scientific type."

"I know. I was a great disappointment to my family. Instead of a scientist, they got an adventurer. But what about you? This isn't exactly a routine job for the head of a big corporation."

"When I wasn't with Papa D and the Warriors, I was with Taka in the labs." Mandy finished her bottles and sat down to enjoy the view. Declan joined her. "I know you've got a place in the Argonian mountains. Is that where you're from?"

"No. I grew up in Yalla. The northern reaches are an incredible place to be a kid. Thick forests, fog-enshrouded rocky coasts. Heavy snows in the winter, cool summers."

Mandy could imagine him as a young boy, scrambling through the Yallan forest, tossing stones across one of the cold lakes or fishing the coasts. "So why not have a place there instead of Argonia?"

Declan shrugged. "Honan has land that borders mine. When the land next to him came up for sale, I bought the acreage. Seemed like a good idea at the time. Besides, my folks were gone by then, and there wasn't anything left in Yalla for me."

"Sounds like you had fun there, though."

"Yes and no. My father didn't believe in wasting time with hiking or camping. At least, not unless they included something of scientific interest. My mother was a little more understanding."

She revised her earlier idea. Rather than rambling about for fun, he probably had to account for his time with studies. "Are they the only family you had?"

"Yes."

"Where are they now?"

"Last I heard, they were on Alpha Centauri Nine. They'd been invited to head a multi-year study at the university there."

"Harper's Planet? I'd heard that's mostly a water planet. Your dad must be ecstatic."

"Both of them are. From what Mom said in her last missive, they've found a marine plant that actually shows some signs of intelligence. They'll spend the next few years on that discovery alone." He looked around. "We've gotten the samples we needed. Let's go downstream for a while, then cut diagonally back to the camp."

"Sounds good." Mandy packed away the last of the kits and hefted the heavy pack to her shoulder.

"Why don't you let me take that?" Declan asked.

"I can handle this myself."

"I know, but you know you can accept help once in a while."

Mandy chuckled. "Accepting help is one of my many failings. When I was younger, Mali was always telling me I was too small to do anything, so I went about doing everything. To this day, I don't know if he said so on purpose to see how far I'd go."

"You miss him, don't you?"

"Yes. Mali was one of the few people who treated me as a person. To think I'll never see him again…" A single tear escaped, and she swiped the drop away. Declan came to her and pulled her into his arms. "He probably misses you too. So you'll have to make do with me."

"Make do?" She grinned up at him, then sighed theatrically. "I suppose if I must."

"Brat." Declan gave her a quick kiss, took the heavy knapsack from her, and handed her his lighter one. "If it will make you feel better, you can carry mine."

"Gee, thanks. I feel so much better now." Mandy shouldered the pack and led the way.

Chapter Twenty-One

They climbed over huge downfalls and around granite-like outcroppings until they came to a large lake. The clear blue water lapped gently at the narrow, rocky beach. Mandy watched several small fish darting about in the shallows chasing long-legged insects skipping over the surface. Farther out, a flock of birds glided, feathered in brilliant blues and greens.

"This looks like a good spot for a lunch break," Declan said. "We'll stop here then head back. That should get us to camp well before dark."

Mandy opened Declan's knapsack and pulled out their rations. "Red beans and rice with cornbread and fruit or savory stew with biscuit and fruit?"

Declan grimaced. "Some choice. I'll take the rice."

Mandy inspected her meal, looking for any signs of tampering. She was still leery of eating any of the meals.

"If you prefer, I'll eat the stew," Declan said.

Mandy shrugged. "I know I'm being silly, but I can't get past the fear."

"Your fear isn't silly. Actually, the fear is good. Only a fool would dismiss what happened to you. We were lucky she dosed you with a normal drug and not poison. Do you have any of those energy bars Taka came up with?"

"No. She ran out of the ingredients." Mandy sighed

and popped the heating ring on her dinner. "Remember, if anything happens, I'm not at fault."

Declan rubbed his shin. "Believe me, that's one point Honan and I will never forget. Where the devil did you learn some of those moves? They weren't taught at any of the classes I ever attended."

She chuckled. "When the teachers finished with me, Papa D called in some favors. I, and several of the Warriors we have with us, learned some, um, shall we say unconventional ways of fighting? Some of them known only to the elite Warrior class."

"Unconventional doesn't begin to cover what you did. Would you mind teaching me some of them?"

"Once we're all down here, I'll get a couple of the others and we'll show you, Honan, and Sarah what you need to know." She checked her meal, but the food wasn't quite warm yet. "So what's our next step?"

"We do a flyover to see if we can find a site suitable for settlement."

"But what if the tests don't pan out?"

"I have a feeling they will. Besides, if we get one done now, we'll be one step ahead and may be able to begin transporting supplies down by tomorrow and people a few days later." Declan stretched out his legs and leaned against the log. "This is a beautiful place. I wonder, though, about the absence of larger animals."

"Ben said the lack of animal life was probably from the noise of the shuttle landing. I'm sure there's nothing to be concerned about."

Declan held up his hand for silence. He indicated with his eyes that something was behind her.

Very slowly, Mandy turned her head. Two large feline animals stood in the middle of the path leading to the lake. One, slightly larger than the other, stood in front, its long tail twitching back and forth. The cat sniffed the air as if trying to figure out their scent.

The animal was about the size of a small Aboolean mountain lion so about waist high on Mandy with mottled rust and tawny coloring and startling blue eyes. The other, smaller one was darker and more subtly colored, and Mandy assumed a younger version— mother and child. That made them more dangerous. The mother would probably attack anything that appeared threatening.

Out of the corner of her eye, Mandy saw Declan slowly slip out his weapon.

One step at a time, the big cat approached them, ears pitched forward. Mandy calmed her breathing and sat as still as possible. The cat sniffed at her and the food containers. She stuck a pink tongue into Mandy's food, shook her head, pawed dirt over the container and continued to the lake to drink. The smaller one joined its mother. Mandy almost choked on her laughter as the youngster played in the shallows, chasing small fish and bugs. The mother's attention never left her or Declan. They sat there for several minutes until a loud roar sounded from deeper in the trees. The mother answered and bounded into the trees followed closely by the cub.

Mandy let out her breath and stood, stretching a cramp from her leg.

"That was interesting," Declan said as he holstered his weapon.

"At least we know there's large animal life." Mandy grimaced at her ruined dinner. "Intelligent, too."

"Let's hope that's as large as the animals around

here get. I think we'd better head back. We don't want to meet papa." He held out his meal toward her. "Here. I wasn't hungry anyway."

"Liar. Share?" She held out a spoonful of beans and rice to him. Rather than take the spoon, he opened his mouth. Mandy chuckled as she fed him, then took a bite herself. The next bite went to Declan. She wasn't sure when their play turned from something fun to something serious, but by the time they finished the meal, her heart was thumping a bit too fast for comfort.

They sat there, staring at each other until Declan took the empty container from her hands and set the dish aside, then leaned in close to her and kissed her.

The kiss started light, then grew deeper, more desperate. Without moving his lips from her, Declan lifted her and pulled her into his lap where Mandy could feel his desire. She wanted this. Wanted him.

A roar from the forest, too close for comfort, pulled them apart.

"We should go," Declan said as he stroked her back.

"Yeah. We should." Mandy didn't move.

Another roar, closer this time, had them both moving. They cleaned the remains of their meals, keeping an eye on the woods, and headed in the opposite direction from the roars and back toward camp. They arrived back at the camp near sundown, hungry, but with no further incidents. The camp was a hive of controlled activity. Taka was breaking out food packs while Mitch secured the area for the night. There was an air of camaraderie and light-heartedness around the area.

"I was beginning to wonder about you two," Taka

said.

"We got sidetracked by a kitten and his mother," Mandy said, fighting off the heat scorching her face.

"She means a mountain lion," Declan countered. He set the full knapsack on the lab table. "Is everything secure for the night? I don't want Junior bringing the entire family to see what's new on the menu."

While Declan talked with Mitch, Mandy emptied their packs, arranging the specimen bottles for biology, hydrology, and the other sciences. She studiously avoided Taka but should have known better.

"Mandy?"

"Yes, ma'am?"

Taka stared at her, not saying a word, one eyebrow raised, and Mandy felt her face heating up all over again. "I need to get the rest of these samples out."

"Amanda Rianara Oliana Ki."

Uh oh. All three names. "Nothing happened, Taka. So stop, okay?"

"You could do worse."

"I already did." She looked Taka in the eye. "Don't push, okay?"

"I only want what's best for you, honey."

"I know." She hugged her aunt. "Now, come on." She raised her voice. "Time for a break, everyone. You need to eat."

She garnered several chuckles. Like many avid researchers, meals and personal hygiene tended to fall to the wayside when something new came by. As they gathered at the makeshift tables, Mandy listened to the chatter. Most of the talk was general, relating to differences or similarities between the new planet and Aboo.

"I hope this is one of the last ration packs I have to eat," Mitch said when he and Declan joined them.

"What kind of plants did you bring back?" Stacey asked.

"Who cares about plants? I want to know more about those cats!" Ben, Stacey's husband argued.

"You're both star-kissed. Tell us about the lake. Did you find the source? Did you bring back samples so we can compare that water with the water from our stream?"

Mandy laughed as they argued. Each specialist felt his or her area of expertise was the main area of importance.

"Tell you what, why don't you tell me what you found out today and we'll go from there? Stacey, how's the plant life look?"

Stacey beamed like a little kid let loose in a candy store. "So far, what we found is compatible with our biology, so we can use some of the flora as food. The only oddity I've found I don't know about is a complex protein in a tuber I dug up. Though the root doesn't appear to be dangerous, Taka and I are running some more extensive tests. A couple of plants are poisonous, but that's to be expected. Even Aboo has its share of deadly flora. I'll post descriptions and details. I'd really like to do more testing farther afield," she finished, a tremor of hopeful excitement in her voice.

Mandy nodded, knowing she and Declan would have a full report and analyses on their pads. "Soon, Stacey. Ben, what about animals?"

"Small, fur-bearing, feathered and scaled, split between carnivore, insectivore, and herbivore. I'd watch out for the local equivalent of a lizard, though.

Meat-eater type with a voracious appetite and no fear of something bigger." He held up a bandaged finger. "I'm not sure yet, but there's a possibility the animals have a pack mentality. After this one grabbed me, I saw several others getting ready to pounce. This particular lizard is about six to eight inches long. You'll know by the bright purple coloring. There's nothing bigger around here—except for your kitten. Lots of insect life, which is good. I'd like to go farther inland though. We probably scared off most everything when we landed."

Mandy listened as each specialist gave a quick summary. So far there was nothing that would keep them from settling here and establishing a home. She said a silent prayer of thanks. Finally, something seemed to be going right. The sunset turned the sky glorious shades of gold, peach, and aqua. Mandy looked to the east where the darkening sky was highlighted by the glow of twin moons. The others followed her gaze, staring at the sight, lost in individual thoughts.

"Welcome home, folks," Mandy whispered.

They finished their meals quietly and broke into groups. Mandy joined Declan and Mitch in the ship.

"How's everything look so far?" Declan asked.

"Good," Mandy said. "Unless these new samples turn up something really strange, we can go ahead. Normally we'd take weeks, if not months, on the tests, but we don't have that luxury, so we'll have to hope for the best. What's our timetable?"

"We'll spend tomorrow testing and exploring for a permanent site. This may end up being the best area, but I remember a plateau to the north I'd like to check out. If we decide this place is a go, Mitch and I will ship up the next morning to coordinate the shuttling."

"Did you find the problem with the shuttle?"

"Mitch found two electronic tubes he disengaged. Alvarez may be a genius, but he's not terribly imaginative, thank goodness. So far, he's sticking to the same type of gadgetry. We missed them on our first scan, but we won't make that mistake again."

"What time do you want to get started?" She stared at Declan, her heart beating a rapid tattoo, wanting nothing more than to be alone with him. But that wasn't going to happen. They had responsibilities that took priority.

"When you get up," Declan said.

"I warn you, I'm an early riser."

Declan grinned. "So am I."

"And I'll bet Taka will beat us both. Good night, gentlemen."

Mandy found her pallet and unrolled her sleeping mat and blankets. She lay there listening to the sounds around her—the muted discussions of the crew, strange pipings and callings of night animals and, in the distance, a roar she recognized as the cats. In the background, she heard the familiar calming sound of the surf, and she fell soundly asleep.

****

Mandy woke slowly, savoring the taste and feel of fresh morning air, heavy with dew. She took a deep breath and smelled the distinctive aroma of fresh coffee brewing. Her mouth watered in anticipation.

"I was beginning to wonder if you were going to sleep all day." Declan stood over her.

Mandy glared at him. "It's barely past dawn."

"Not a morning person, are you? Coffee's hot.

Help yourself."

"Pompous ass," she muttered. Shivering in the cold air, she quickly pulled jeans and a warm shirt on over the shorts and tee she'd worn to bed. There was something to be said for climate control. She grabbed a cup of coffee and joined Declan and Mitch at the table. "This is good enough to be mine."

"That's because the brew's the same as yours." Mitch yawned. "At least, that's what Taka claimed. She's the one who made the mix."

Mandy eyed Declan who was suddenly interested in the top of the table and laughed. "I told you she'd beat us both up. So how are we handling today?"

The scientists joined them, singly and in pairs as they woke to the aroma of coffee. Declan smoothed out a printout of the island, holding the flimsies down with small stones. They ate breakfast and discussed the lay of the land and the best way to explore the environs.

"Are you still going to do a flyover?" Mandy asked.

"No. Honan was able to get more details for us from the ship. I have maps for each of you on your pads."

"So what would you like us to do?"

"Mandy, I thought you and I would take the northeast route along the beach so we can check out that plateau. Pete, you and Toni can head for the lake we saw yesterday. I'll draw you a rough map. Ben and Stacey will take the southern route, and Tom and Sam can head northwest through the forest. Mitch and Taka will remain here to monitor the teams and for emergency purposes." He handed out pins similar to the one Mandy wore. "We'll all be linked to the ship, but not to each other. I want each team to check in at one-hour intervals and meet back here no later than 1700."

Taka handed each team member a pack. "Each pack contains enough food and water rations for the day as well as med-kit, emergency signal, and sample collection kit. Don't do anything foolish."

"Yes, ma'am." They all chorused and laughed as Taka chuckled.

"Ready?" Declan shouldered his pack and handed Mandy hers.

"When you are."

They turned north from the camp and climbed a low dune covered with rough grass and small trees. The light brown sand was coarsely grained, studded with small pebbles that crunched under their boots. When they reached the top of the dune, Mandy stopped and stood gazing at the waves breaking on the beach. A line of debris—grasses, reeds, shells, and driftwood—showed the high-tide line. A light fog shrouded the coastline giving everything an ethereal quality. This was nothing like the soft, sandy beaches of her home, but was close enough to cause a pang of homesickness. In the near water, several birds floated, bobbing on the waves, and occasionally ducking down and coming up with wriggling fish.

Mandy closed her eyes and listened. She heard the surf breaking on the rocks, birds crying in the distance, the wind sighing through the trees. She took a deep breath, cherishing the cool dampness, the salty taste. She opened her eyes and looked around at Declan. He was hunkered down, examining the rocks.

"Everything okay?" Mandy asked as she joined him.

"Yeah. I was thinking how much this was like home."

Mandy chuckled. "I guess we've got more in common than we know. I was thinking the same way. Oh, the beach is different, and I'm not used to this chilly fog, but the ocean sounds the same and smells the same."

"This is exactly like the beach where I grew up—rocks, fog, and all. You could be hiking around a small lake, like the one we were at yesterday, the weather as clear as can be and fifteen minutes later, you're shrouded in fog so thick you can't see your feet."

"That might be a good place for the Orilians to nest during mating time. They like rocks and water."

"This works then. You have a lot of diversity in your group. Do they all get along well?"

"For the most part." She shrugged. "There are occasional issues, but nothing you don't get in any group. Don't you have other species within your crew?"

"Some. But almost the entire group is from the Warrior Transport tribe. Not a lot of diversity there. When we work with other tribes, though, we get other beings."

"So how did you, a pure human, end up in the Warrior tribe?"

He chuckled. "You can blame that on Honan and Sarah. I spent a lot of my vacations with their families and, after graduation from the academy, I was inducted into Honan's tribe."

"But your hair…um, didn't that cause a problem?"

Another chuckle. "As a human, I'm allowed certain…unusual traits. The elders aren't in love with my short hair but allow the deviation because of my position as captain." He rolled up his sleeve and showed her a ring of tattooed beads around his bicep. "These are my tribal beads."

"I noticed that before and wondered about the design."

"Sarah did the design, and Honan did the inking."

Declan stood and brushed his hands on his pants. "Guess we should get moving."

He moved closer to her, and she caught her breath. "Yes, I guess we should," she whispered.

Declan bent down and captured her mouth with his. She wrapped her arms around his neck and kissed him back.

The roar of the surf, calling of the birds…everything disappeared from her senses except the man with her. He pulled away from her, leaning his forehead against her. "We really should go."

"Yeah." Briefly she wondered how far they would go. Not on a hike, but physically. Though not here. Not out in the open in unknown territory, but eventually.

Declan clicked his com unit. "Mitch, this is Declan. Mandy and I are going to head inland."

"Copy that. You're the first to check in."

"Understood. Let me know when the others do."

"Yes, sir."

The beach narrowed to a rocky strip that forced them inland, climbing steadily. The incline leveled out to a large plateau that sloped gently upward toward the northern hills. The fog had burned off, and the sun shone hotly on them. They looked around the area, judging the site for a possible settlement. A wide creek fed by several smaller streams flowed through the area. They waded through knee-high grasses and skirted around shrubs covered in tiny white flowers. Scattered around the meadow, Mandy saw patches of other types of wildflowers in every shade of the rainbow. Her botanists would have a field day cataloging all the new flora.

"This looks like a good spot," Declan said. "The area is relatively level, has a good water supply, easy access to the ocean and yet high enough to prevent storm damage from any surges, and has protection on the windward side by the hills."

"Why here instead of the meadow we landed in?"

"Mostly because of the elevation. I noticed some indications of flooding down there. Since we don't know what the seasons are here, we don't know if there's a wet season and what effect that might have on the lowlands. This area is higher so we probably won't flood, but not so high that altitude would be a factor. The lower meadow can eventually be used for agriculture. The spot is close enough for easy access and, according to your scientists, the soil is good for growing, with a rich base under the plant life. We can erect storage units there and housing up here."

"But what about flooding?"

"We'll deal with that when we have to. This is to start with. We'll make changes as necessary along the way."

Declan found a large, relatively flat rock and spread out the aerial survey map he had. He sketched in the details and his suggestions of building placement with input from Mandy. They stepped off areas for the proposed building plots.

"We should probably erect a community building and medical facility first," Mandy said. "We can use that as temporary shelter until we get individual ones erected, and later use the space as a gathering place and offices. That one building should anchor the village, but at the center or at the end?"

"Central, especially if medical is going to be a part of the space. I'd like to keep as close to a square layout as possible. That shape is better for protection than a single street layout."

Mandy nodded and scanned the meadow. "I believe the far side of the creek would be better than this side. The ground doesn't appear as rocky and is slightly uphill from the water so if we get heavy rains, any rising will miss the town."

Declan nodded and sketched the layout on the map. "I'll get Mitch to get a detailed holo of this area when we head back up tomorrow." Declan's communicator beeped.

"Captain? Do you copy?"

He glanced at his watch. "He should have contacted me before this." He clicked his unit. "What's wrong, Mitch?"

"Sam and Tom haven't reported in, and I can't raise them. They were heading northwest, into the mountains."

Mandy checked the map. "Declan, if we cut due west, we might cross their path."

He nodded. "Mitch, call in the other teams. Have Ben and Pete—" He paused as Mandy shook her head. "Hold on, Mitch."

"Have Ben and Toni go. Toni has experience in tracking and wilderness work."

"Mitch? Have Ben and Toni take their trail. Mandy and I will go west from here to see if we can cross their path. Keep trying to raise Sam, and have everyone stay alert for a signal. Contact me every half hour."

"Aye, Captain."

As Declan talked, Mandy repacked their bags, putting their emergency equipment in one bag and sample kits in another. She cleared a small hole near the rock they were using as a table and tucked in the bag with the samples. "Declan? What about a fly-by?"

"Wouldn't work. The area they headed for is here." He pointed to the map. "That stretch is heavily forested. Plus, we don't want to use fuel unless we have to. This'll have to be a foot search. Ready?"

Mandy nodded and took the lead, setting a pace that would cover ground quickly without overtiring them. These were her people, and she felt responsible for them. She thought about Tom, the tall, young man who was invaluable as a supply hand as well as an expert geologist, and Sam, a gifted scientist and good team leader. She prayed they were safe.

A short time later, she and Declan stood at the top of a cliff looking at a dizzying drop. "We can't go around. That would take too much time."

"I guess we go down," Declan said.

Mandy pulled two ropes from the pack and looped one around her waist and legs into a Swiss seat. Declan checked her knots and secured her rope to a sturdy tree.

"Rappelling." Mandy backed over the edge of the cliff and dropped, pushing off the rock face. A minute later she was at the bottom of the cliff and undid her rope. "Clear!"

She held the second rope steady as Declan rappelled down the precipice. As he touched bottom, his communicator beeped. "Declan here."

"All the teams are back, and Ben and Toni left a couple of minutes ago. Still nothing from Sam and Tom, and nobody's seen any flares."

"Okay. Keep me posted. We ran into some rough terrain and may be longer than anticipated."

"Aye, Captain."

Mandy checked their compass and pointed the direction through a thick stand of trees stretching out of sight in both directions. Declan took the lead this time, breaking through the underbrush until the shrubs thinned out enough for them to walk together. They hiked in silence, maneuvering around huge dead falls, climbing when they couldn't go around. They crossed small streams and skirted huge monolithic rock formations, standing as silent sentinels in the forest. They startled different species of small animals, but nothing as large as the cats they'd seen the day before. The trees towered above them, forming a thick canopy high above the forest floor. The late afternoon light didn't penetrate the dense cover, and they broke out hand lamps. Mitch checked in with them every half hour, but no sign had been found of the hapless pair.

"I wish we had more time to explore this area. There are some interesting formations around here. I wonder if there are caves," Mandy said.

"We'll mark this area for prime exploration after we get the shelters set up. If there are caves, we may be able to use them for shelter or storage. I'd like to see more of that myself. This area reminds me a little of home, except for this moss." Declan shone his light over the ground cover cushioning their steps in the deep forest. The growth gave off a light cinnamon scent.

"We certainly don't have anything like this on

Aboo. I love the color—more blue than green and so soft." Mandy bent down and ran her finger through the thick carpet.

"Ouch!" She jerked her hand back and went to suck her finger. "And has thorns!"

Declan grabbed her hand before she could get her finger to her mouth. "Don't do that. We'll have to tell Taka." He pulled on gloves, reached down, and carefully picked some of the plant and tucked them in a pocket of their bag. He pulled out the first aid kit and sprayed Mandy's finger with a general antiseptic.

"Declan, I have a stupid thorn prick."

"And all I had was a mosquito bite. And think about Alvarez's wife and her plants. We're in terra incognito here, and everything is potentially deadly. Since we can't easily get back to camp, you'll let me know if you start feeling anything funny?"

"Aye, Captain." Mandy offered him a mock salute, but she knew he was right. Something as simple as a thorn prick could kill.

They were maneuvering across a large log spanning a rushing creek when the communicator beeped. He tapped the button. "Declan here. Do you have them?"

"Ben and Toni found them. Tom took a fall and landed on the flares. Sam lost his communicator, and Tom's malfunctioned."

"How's Tom?"

"Broken arm, sprained ankle, and bruised ego, but otherwise okay. I've sent Pete out with the anti-grav sled to bring them in. What about you two? Want a lift in?"

Mandy shook her head. "Save the fuel. We're too

far out to start back. We can camp here for the night and head back tomorrow morning."

Declan nodded and relayed their plans to Mitch.

She scanned the area for a likely campsite finding a spot up from the creek between two small trees. She cleared the ground of small rocks and twigs and shook out her thermal blanket.

Declan joined her. "Looks like a good spot." Using some vines, he tied a long branch between the two trees and threw his blanket over the branch.

Mandy helped him peg the edges to the ground with some rocks.

"Hand me your jacket," Mandy said as she untied hers from her waist. She and Declan had shed them some time ago as the hike warmed them. She tied the jackets together and, using first-aid tape, secured them to one end of their makeshift tent.

"Do we dare make a fire?" she asked.

Declan had been busy clearing a fire ring and gathering kindling and wood. "We really should. If this is anything like my home, the temperature could get cold tonight, plus for safety in case there are any animals. Looks like you know what you're doing camping. I assume that's thanks to the general."

"He took me out when he could. Plus, I spent two summers with the student corps in college and did cold climate survival, among other challenges."

"Sounds like you were planning to join the corps." Declan stacked the kindling in the center of the ring and lit them.

"I wanted to, but Papa D changed my mind."

"The general? I'd have thought he'd be the one to get you in. Or did he keep you out because of your business concerns?"

Mandy pulled two ration bars out of the bag and a bottle of water. She handed one of the bars to Declan.

"Me joining the corps had nothing to do with the companies. That was the one time Papa D and I had a huge fight. I'd actually signed up but, before the papers could be processed, he came storming into the recruiting office and tore them up. I thought he was going to tear up the recruiter. I'd never seen him so angry. He didn't say a word to me, just dragged me out of there, hauled me to Taka's, and left. I didn't see him for two months."

"And you never talked about what you did?"

"No. By the time we saw each other again, other events had happened, and there didn't seem to be a point to dredging up old history."

Declan crumpled the wrapper from his bar and tossed the paper on the fire. "Funny thing about history. If you don't take care of issues like that, they tend to come back and bite you in the ass."

"You and Trish?"

"Yeah. I keep asking myself what I could have done differently."

"Probably nothing. You're as much a victim of this mess as I am."

Declan stirred the fire. "That doesn't make what happened any better." He shrugged. "Why don't you get some sleep? I'll take first watch."

"You don't want to join me?"

He grinned. "Oh, honey, you don't know how much I want to join you, but not tonight. Unfortunately."

Mandy snorted and crawled into the improvised

300

tent and pulled the blanket close around her. Declan sat outside, near the fire. She lay on her stomach and stared at the flames. "Declan? I know what Trish did isn't easy to accept, but you have to…"

She stopped as Declan held up a hand. He pointed to the bushes beyond the fire. Mandy saw a slight movement.

"Where's your weapon?" she whispered.

"In my leg holster. I don't want to move any more than necessary. What about yours?"

"Here. But you're in line of sight. I can slide mine to you behind your back."

"Okay."

Mandy inched her pistol toward Declan.

Before Declan could retrieve the weapon, an animal emerged from the shadows. With the exception of his startling blue eyes that shone in the firelight, the cat was darker than the surrounding forest. He was also easily twice the size of the two animals they'd seen the day before. Declan slowly unfolded his legs and moved his hand toward Mandy's weapon, but Mandy stopped him.

"Wait."

She didn't know why, but she felt the cat was no threat to them. And she was certain this one was the male. She held out her hand toward the cat. Slowly, one step at a time, he circled the fire and approached her, keeping a wary eye on Declan. He sniffed Mandy's hand, cocked his head at her, and nodded at her, then snorted and left as silently as he had arrived.

Declan pulled out his weapon as Mandy retrieved hers. "That was a damned foolish thing to do. What if he had decided you were the latest menu choice?"

"I wasn't. I can't explain how I know, but he wasn't here to hurt us."

"Do you think he's intelligent?"

"Intelligent, yes. Sentient? I don't think so, but I don't know. All I know is we passed his test."

"We'll have to warn the others."

"I hope nobody gets trigger happy."

"Only those who have a solid reason will be armed. I guess we need to talk about how we're going to set up the village, government, and all that nonsense."

"That will be one of the points we'll go through at our first town meeting. We'll need to set up a council and draw up some rules."

"That could take some doing."

"Not really. Remember, most of the people we have with us are scientists. With all this new territory around us, they're not going to want to be bothered with bureaucracy. The Warriors under you and the general can act as security. I don't really envision here being much different than what we had on the ship, but we'll have to wait and see."

"Sleep on the matter. I'll wake you in four hours."

Chapter Twenty-Two

Mandy and Declan strolled into the camp to the sound of cheers, cat calls, and whistles. Mandy ducked her head and hurried to the ship to check on Tom. "Taka?"

Taka met her at the door. She took Mandy's arm and guided her to a seat. "Tom's fine. He has a simple fracture, no complications. Now sit."

"Okay, okay, I get the message." She told Taka about the moss. "Declan gave the plants over for testing. I haven't had any problems, no funny feelings, no hallucinations or anything."

The botanist stuck her head in the door. "The moss is safe, Taka."

"Thanks, Stacey." She turned to Mandy. "You're free to go, unless there's something else we need to talk about?"

Mandy hugged her aunt. "There isn't. Thanks, Taka." She rejoined Declan.

He handed her a signal gun. "Take a look."

Mandy checked the gun and found a crack at the base of the firing mechanism. "This has been tampered with."

"So have all the rest. None of them will fire. Fortunately, none of the rest of the supplies appears to have been modified."

"What about the shuttle? Has Mitch repaired the

damage from Alvarez's little toys?"

"As far as we can tell. We won't know for sure until we're airborne."

"Nice. Have you told the others about the plateau yet?"

"No. I thought you'd like to. Besides, I need to contact Honan and Sarah and talk to them." He stared at her but didn't move any closer. They both had roles to play and would keep their personal lives as separate as they could.

Mandy smiled. "Thanks." She put two fingers between her lips and let out a shrill whistle. She motioned everyone over to a table where Declan had spread out a map. "Three miles north, there's a plateau with everything we need for settlement. There's plenty of fresh water, easy access to the sea, level ground, protection from storms, and room for expansion. We'll be setting up a permanent site there."

She watched their reactions. They all seemed excited by the prospect, but she saw a few shadows. That was to be expected as well. This wasn't what they had planned on. "We'll be establishing a landing site on the northern perimeter and move camp up there as soon as we can get packed."

She paused as Taka came out and handed around small cups. Mandy eyed the non-descript contents and noted the blank expression on Taka's face. She knew that look. Taka was hiding something. "What's this?"

"A toast—to a new world, a new home, and drinkable water."

A cheer went up as each person downed his or her cup of water. Mandy sipped hers, savoring the slightly mineral taste. She saw Declan leaning against the shuttle and raised her cup in a silent salute. He returned the gesture.

"Okay, everyone, we've got a lot to do. Let's get packed up and get ready to move."

While everyone went to work, she joined Declan. "How's everything topside?"

"Chane's got the solar sails rigged, but he's holding his breath. There's no power at all to the lower level, second level only in engineering, and intermittent losses on the first. The construction teams have been busy stripping what they can and getting everything ready for shipment. Honan has two cargo shuttles ready to go. I told them about our little problem, and he and Chane checked the shuttles out pretty thoroughly. Found a few more, but nothing vital affected. I guess we managed to stay ahead of him on this one. The med-techs are warming people up according to your schedule. I figure three days to have everything and everyone moved down here."

"Any luck finding the crewman I saw before we left?"

"No. Honan has the Warriors standing guard on each shuttle and at all entrances to the bays, including the vents. Nobody gets in or out without passing inspection. The extra steps are a pain, but nothing else has happened since he started the procedure."

"But what do you do when the last shuttle comes down and he's still up there?"

"As far as I'm concerned, at that point if he still wants the ship, he can have her. Of course, he won't be able to go anywhere or do anything because nothing will be left but the shell. Chane and his crew have even figured out a way to get Hermes down here."

"Don't pat yourself on the back quite yet, Declan. I've been under his thumb for too long for me to believe this will be over so soon and so easily. He's not done with us yet."

"I agree, but he's no longer in control. We are."

Mandy bit her lip. She didn't want to argue with Declan, but she didn't share his optimism. "Have the techs warmed up Papa D yet?"

"No. Taka wanted us to wait until the last wave for him. That way she could be there to monitor him when they wake him."

"I thought she'd purged all the poison."

"She did, but the general isn't a young man. She wants to make sure of everything."

Mandy nodded. If Taka was there, she knew the general would have the best chance ever of coming out whole and hearty. She joined the rest of the teams to help pack up and move. Rather than use the shuttle for the short hop, they loaded everything on two anti-grav skids and moved the camp that way. They needed three trips to get all the gear moved but, by midafternoon, they had the equipment hauled over and the new camp set up. Since they could no longer use the shuttle as the base of their area, they formed the six long tents into a U on the south side of the creek. The medical tent formed the center base with the mess tent and sleeping quarters on one side and the labs on the other. They left the north side of the creek open for building.

While they worked, Mitch took off for the *Phoenix*. By the time they had the new camp set up, the first cargo and personnel shuttles had arrived. Declan directed the newcomers where to unload the supplies.

"Team One, you can set up the sleeping tents

adjacent to the one we already have erected," Declan instructed. He looked around for Mandy. "See Ms. Ki for specifics. I believe you'll find her in the mess tent.

"Team Two, since the communications tent is the smallest, set that one up in the open end of the quad. Team Three, set up the supply tent outside the mess tent. Team Four, we'll be erecting the permanent buildings on the north side of the creek. Start laying out the materials there according to your directives."

With everyone working together, they soon had the shuttles emptied and were on their way back to the ship. In short order the new tents were erected. They were stowing supplies when the next shuttles arrived. As each new group arrived, they joined their designated teams, and the work went faster. The last shuttle of the day arrived minutes after sunset. Once they had everything unloaded, Mandy called a general meeting in the central area of the quad. Everyone had their dinner rations, and she figured now was a good time to make announcements. More than three-quarters of the people were hers.

"We made a good start today," she said. "But we have a lot of work ahead of us. Since we don't have monitors for you to read for announcements, we'll use this time for dispersing information. We'll have time for questions and answers after I finish. I know you've all been made aware of what happened. This isn't exactly what you signed up for, but I don't think you'll be too disappointed. Our initial teams have already cataloged more than a hundred new flora and fauna, and that's without even trying. We have a new village to establish and a new world to explore. This may not be Aboo or Xy-Three, but what we've seen so far is nice, and I think we'll do well here. Right now, the facilities are primitive, but we're going to work together to change that.

"Team leaders, you will be responsible for indoctrinating new crewmen into your teams. There will be little privacy, so I ask all of you to put on your best faces. For you new people, we know the water is safe. We don't know all the plants, insects, or animals. Check the lists daily for updates on what can and cannot be used or touched. We'll keep the updated lists posted in the medical, lab, and mess tents. Oh, and before I forget, the latrine is downwind." She pointed a bit south of the tents, and everyone chuckled.

"We've got three days to get all the supplies and personnel down. The next few days are going to be hectic at best. You're going to be sore, tired, and frustrated. Keep your emotions bottled or take a cold swim. I don't want to have to break up any fights. We're talking survival here, folks. Until we've got everyone down and can establish a working council, we'll abide by ship rules. Any infractions will be dealt with swiftly. Are there any questions?"

Mandy fielded the couple questions, but for the most part everyone was content. With few exceptions, everyone was working well together. She hoped that would continue as the remainder of the people joined them.

Her hopes didn't last long.

****

"Ma'am, we have to have the grav sleds this afternoon, and this idiot won't let me have them."

Mandy looked up from her terminal as two men barged into what was loosely called her office in one corner of the communications tent. The electronic specialists had managed to give them working monitors, but the system was primitive at best. *Here we go again*, she thought. Her hopes for everyone to get along hadn't lasted long. Tempers flared, and frictions between ship's crew and her people grew until she was afraid they'd have a civil war.

"Hermes?" At least Chane had been able to get a portion of Hermes up and running in their temporary offices. Hearing his voice was like hearing an old friend. She hadn't realized how much she'd missed him. He wasn't as powerful, but he was there.

"Yes, boss?"

"Show me the sled schedule."

"No problem. You might want to look at the supplemental information."

Mandy quickly scanned the information and smiled. "Thank you, Hermes." She turned to the complainer. "John, you were given the chance to schedule the sleds the same as everyone else. When you didn't send back the form, you were given the next available slot."

"I never got the message," he blustered, red-faced.

"According to this, you not only got the message, but signed the note—with a flourish. Also, you haven't looked at any of your messages today at all. You're supposed to check the boards after breakfast and lunch. If you took the time to read them, you'd know what was going on."

"I don't have time to look at everything that comes across the boards."

"Then I'll put someone in charge who does. Stop bothering the sled drivers. They'll come to you when you're scheduled and not a minute sooner. Now get out of here and do your work."

Mandy swiveled around in her chair and looked at the map tacked to the board behind her desk. She listened to the two men leaving and shook her head. The past few days had been full of similar problems, and she was tired of the bickering, the setbacks, and the work. She couldn't remember the last time she'd had a moment to herself, let alone any time with Declan. He was as busy as she was, if not more so.

"Hermes? Thanks for the info. And welcome back."

"No problem, boss. Although I am feeling a bit lightweight."

"Hopefully, we'll have you up to your usual self once we have the buildings established and better power running. Can you show me our fuel usage for the sleds?"

She checked over the information. They were going through their supply at a faster rate than they'd anticipated. No matter how closely they monitored usage, the level was always lower than they calculated. But they had plenty of other supplies. The assembly teams already had the shell of the community building erected and the skeletons for medical and labs. By the end of tomorrow, they should have the interior pretty well finished and a permanent place set up for Hermes. She'd looked over the structure earlier. Like all the places planned, this one was a single story high and slightly larger than the combined area of the gym and lounge on the ship. Individual offices lined the two sides with a large gathering area in the center. At one end of the auditorium was a raised stage. Attached at right angles to the sides of the structure were the lab and medical wings. Numbered crates were stacked on skids near the areas they belonged to, and the cargo people were constantly handing her updated lists of what had been brought down and where each pallet was. Mandy was more than a little impressed at how much had been done in such a short time. All the planning she and the others had done over the long, quiet weeks in transit was paying off now.

There was only a skeleton crew left on the ship, those who would do the final dismantling. So far, everything had gone smoothly. She couldn't wait for the final shuttle of the day to come down. Taka and the general would be on that one. She'd talked to him earlier. He sounded wonderful. He was working with Honan and Sarah on security. Nobody was getting through without a thorough check.

"Mandy?" Declan stuck his head around the temporary panel that served as her walls. "Have you got a minute?"

She rose from her chair and stretched. "No, but what do you want?"

"The team would like to give you a tour of the newly finished community hall and your new office."

Mandy stopped her movement, leaving her arms raised high in her stretch. "Finished? They're finished? How in heaven's name did they get the building done so fast?" She stepped around the crates and boards comprising her desk and joined Declan.

"We asked for volunteers. Everyone that could joined in."

He led the way across the pontoon bridge spanning the creek. The building sat at the top of a small rise.

311

Wider than tall, the wings stuck out to either side. Mandy bit back a smile at the colors. The walls were a conglomeration of wall panels from various parts of the ship in colors of gray, tan, white, and blue. Someone had obviously thought ahead and managed to put the colors into some semblance of a pattern, but in front of her was probably the most unique building she'd ever seen.

Declan pushed open the front door with a flourish and ushered her in. The team of builders sat on the stage taking a well-deserved break. They stood when she and Declan entered.

"Sit, sit. You've earned the break," Mandy said. "Declan will show me what you've done."

She looked around. The large communal room held carpet in the same shades of blue and gray as the ship's corridors. Mandy recognized the mural from the Captain's Mess along the back wall. Along each side were four offices, and Declan opened the door to one close to the stage and escorted her in. Inside was a real desk with a swivel chair backed by a small window, a table, and two guest chairs. On the desk was a full monitor and a small wooden sign with Amanda Ki carved into the surface. Maps of the area were tacked to one side wall. On the other two walls, Mandy recognized part of the mural from Sarah's quarters. Their thoughtfulness touched her.

"This is lovely." She turned around to find members of the team peeking in the doorway. "Thank you all. This is wonderful."

"Wait 'til you see the rest, ma'am. We've even got a PA system set up. No more yelling."

"My throat thanks you," Mandy said amid

chuckles. The lack of amplification in the open quad had been a problem. "I'd say this calls for a celebration. How 'bout if we have a party here tonight?"

She looked to Declan for confirmation, and he nodded at her. "I think we've all earned a little R-and-R."

Mandy and Declan left the building and walked around the area. Foundations for future construction were laid out in neat squares. Crates of supplies for each were stacked in appropriate spots. The village was a fascinating mixture of high-tech and primitive. They'd used what they could from the ship and, where something else was needed, improvised. Mandy and Declan were passing one of the building areas when she noticed one of the crates was broken.

"Declan, that one crate is damaged. Has anyone checked out the contents to make sure they're intact?"

Declan checked the crate. One side was broken out. He checked his pad. "Strange, nobody noted the damage earlier. I'll have someone check."

"No problem. We've had others that sustained some damage. Moving this much equipment this fast isn't easy on the cargo or us. Some equipment is bound to get banged around."

Mandy spent the remainder of the day in her new office listening to the sounds of construction going on outside her window.

The evening's festivities did much to alleviate the building tensions. The cooks had even managed to come up with a cake. Hermes provided the music, and there was much laughter as the crew danced and joked until late into the evening.

****

A week later, Mandy was in her office trying to make sense out of the declining fuel allotments, food supply usages, lab resource requests, and a dozen other details that never got done. Over all of that loomed the specter of Alvarez. With only four people left on board a ship that was nothing more than a skeleton, they had to assume he was here on land with them. But where?

She hadn't even been able to see Taka and the general for more than a few minutes here and there. Taka was busy with the scientists testing everything, and General Davis was overseeing security. With the last wave down and still no sign of Alvarez, they weren't taking any chances. The general had his warriors checking supplies and people daily. Mandy shook her head and turned back to her desk. A knock at her door interrupted her—again. Whoever was there would have to go away. "What now?"

Sarah poked her head in the door. "I can come back later."

Mandy smiled and waved her in. "No. Come on in. I could use a break. What's up?"

"Did you forget about our hike?"

Mandy blushed. "Oh, Sarah, I did. I'm sorry. But I don't see how I can leave right now. I'm up to my ears in work."

"I thought you'd say that. This is the fourth time you've canceled."

"I really am sorry, but there's so much to do."

Sarah shook her head, smiled, stuck two fingers in her mouth, and let out a shrill whistle. As she did, the lights in Mandy's office went out and her monitor went dead.

"Sarah? What's going on?"

One of the electronic techs stuck his head in the door. "Sorry, Mandy, the power went out in this area. Tracking the glitch down could take a couple of hours."

Mandy snorted. "A couple of hours, huh?"

"Yep."

"I don't suppose there's anything I can do to help?"

"Nope."

"I'll also bet any terminal I try to use is going to mysteriously go down."

"Funny thing about that," Sarah said with a grin. "I'd say there does seem to be a distinct possibility. Sounds like some kind of selective virus."

"Okay! Okay, I get the picture. When do we leave?"

Sarah handed her a backpack. "Immediately."

"Am I at least allowed to talk to Jean?" The perky Warrior had turned out to be an excellent aide.

"If necessary, but be quick."

Mandy knocked at Jean's office door and stuck her head in. She noticed the lights and monitor were working perfectly here. She glanced back at the tech who only shrugged and grinned at her. "Jean? I'm going out for a while. Can you check on the progress of the hydroponics building? They're supposed to be up and running this afternoon."

"No problem, Mandy. Have a good time."

Mandy joined Sarah, Honan, and Declan. The weather was clear and cool with a light breeze blowing. They climbed a slight rise, and Sarah stopped and turned Mandy around so she could look down on the village. "Mandy, look at what has been accomplished in a couple weeks, and all because of you. I don't know anybody who could have done as much in as little time.

You deserve a couple of hours off."

Mandy looked over what had been an empty plateau a short time ago. There were temporary shelters, a medical building, hydroponics and greenhouses, the meeting hall, and labs all laid out in neat squares with plenty of room for expansion. People bustled about, working to make what they could of the situation. She swallowed hard against the lump in her throat. No, the island wasn't Aboo, but the settlement was definitely becoming home.

"Good people working as a team did this, but I get the point. Which way do we go?"

"I thought we'd head northwest to the cliffs," Declan said.

Mandy nodded. Their destination would be a good hike of several hours. They traveled over increasingly rough terrain, marking the map they carried for future reference. Finally, they stopped atop a high cliff overlooking the ocean. Mandy sat on the edge, gazing at the surf breaking on the rocks far below. The wind whipped her hair around, and she could taste the tang of salt in the air. A bank of dark clouds hung low on the horizon.

"You were right, Sarah. I needed this." Mandy sighed as she munched on a ration bar. "I didn't realize how much."

"Taka did. She practically ordered us to get you out of your office," Declan said.

"She should talk. I'll bet she hasn't left medical since they opened the new wing."

"I don't know about that. I saw her and the general walking around the compound last night, and I don't think they were talking about business," Sarah said.

Mandy laughed. "Good. Maybe I'll finally be able to get the two of them to settle down together."

"I think that's a given," Declan said.

"Have you heard anything more from Chane?" Mandy asked.

"Chane and three of his men are all that's left on the ship, and they're coming down this afternoon. There's nothing left but the shell, and we've even salvaged parts of that."

"So what we thought about him being down here already is probably true. But we scanned everyone boarding the shuttles. You had more security than I've ever seen. There's no way he could get through."

"There's one way. One we never thought of, but he did. Remember the damaged crate?"

"What…" Mandy thought about the crate she and Declan had found. "You don't mean he had himself shipped down as cargo? He'd never survive. They were in the holds with no life support."

"We found an environmental suit crammed in the shipping carton along with some ration bars and bottles of water. He had protection, food, and water. He's been down here for several days."

Mandy felt the tension she'd released building back up again. "Does Papa D know?"

Declan nodded. "Yes. And so do the other Warriors. They've been told to be on the lookout for anyone who doesn't seem to be fitting in. Unfortunately, that description can apply to several people. Tensions between the cold sleepers and crew are getting worse."

"I know, but what can we do, short of knocking their heads together?"

"I'm not sure anything can be done. We can't force people to get along."

"I'll try talking to my people again. I'll say something at tonight's meeting. And I'll try to get out more, keep a closer eye on what's happening." Mandy peered at the clouds moving toward them. "Right now, we have another issue to deal with, and unless I miss my guess, we're going to get wet well before we get back."

Sarah glanced at the distant clouds, shading her eyes from the bright sun. "What do you mean? There's only that one bank out there, and meteorology hasn't warned us about anything."

"If this is anything like the storms back home, that bank you can barely see will be upon us quickly since there's nothing out there to slow the storm down. Not only that, but from the looks of those clouds, I'd say this is going to be a bad blow. Look at those waterspouts spawning off from the energy. We'd better get back. Now. I hope I'm wrong."

The return trip was quicker than the hike out, but not quick enough. The first chill drops hit them as they reached the northern edge of the plateau.

Mandy had to yell to be heard above the rising wind. "Declan, Honan, the tents will need to be reinforced. They're not stable enough for a hard blow."

Declan nodded his understanding. He handed her his pack and took off at a ground-eating trot followed closely by Honan. Mandy and Sarah shouldered the extra packs and broke into a slow jog.

Chapter Twenty-Three

The camp was a hive of controlled activity as everyone worked to secure supplies and shelters from the increasing storm. Lightning crackled around them, followed by deafening thunder. The rain poured down in sheets, soaking everything in minutes. Mandy found Declan with a group tying down the last of the shelters, fighting the wind with brute strength.

"Is everything else secure?" she yelled.

"Yes. Everyone is gathered in the hall. There're five injuries—none are serious."

Mandy nodded and headed for the hall. There was nothing she could do to help Declan and plenty she could do at the hall. She fought against the wind, struggling to maintain her footing. The pontoon bridge bobbed and bucked in the rising creek.

In the hall, Mandy looked at the knots of people milling around. Someone handed her a towel she gratefully accepted. She wiped her face dry and wrapped her dripping hair. The cooks had set up a table with warm drinks, and she grabbed a cup of coffee.

"Where's Sam?" she asked one of the men at the door. He pointed at a group gathered at the front of the hall. "Thanks." She joined the smaller group.

"What've we got, Sam?"

"A storm."

"Very funny."

"Actually, I can't give you much more than that. Our station isn't due to go on-line until tomorrow."

"What about the probe Chane was going to set into orbit for you?"

Sam looked at his feet, the ceiling, anywhere but at Mandy. Mandy got a sinking feeling in the pit of her stomach. "Sam? What's going on?"

A young man Mandy barely knew spoke up. "We don't need those space jockeys. Mr. Kingsley's the best there is."

"Sam?" Mandy was amazed her voice came out so calmly.

"There's only one probe, and that's situated on the far side of the planet. The others are no good."

"What did you do?"

"They input a little virus."

Mandy raised her eyebrow, staring at him until he blushed and looked away. "A little virus in a system that was already compromised. In other words, we have no weather coverage and no way of knowing how bad this blow will be."

Sam, shamefaced, nodded. "This is my fault, ma'am. I should have stopped them before they went this far."

"Yes, you should have. As for you"—she glared at the young man—"due to your stupidity, we are without vital information. We're in the midst of a blow, and we have no idea how big or bad this storm may be. This planet and all natural systems are unknowns. I hope you haven't signed our death warrants. As of this moment, you are dismissed from the weather group pending a full investigation. Since everyone is busy, you can help with the injured and explain to them why we had no warning about this storm. Sam, I don't care what you have to do, but as soon as this blows over, you and your team will get that station operational."

"Yes, ma'am."

She turned her back on the group as the door blew open and Declan ushered in several people. Mandy hurried over as the men struggled to close the door against the wind.

"Is that everyone?" she asked.

"Yes. What do the weather people say about the storm?"

"You don't want to know. Excuse me, I have something I have to do." She left Declan, strode up to the stage, and activated the PA system. "May I have everyone's attention?"

The crowd quieted down until Mandy heard nothing but the storm outside. "I was going to call a meeting later tonight, but since we're all here…" She waited for the chuckling to subside. "We need to discuss some issues. First of all, the weather. Due to a problem, we have no idea how bad this will be or how long the storm will last."

"Those stupid space jockeys did this. They screwed up everything."

Mandy heard the comment come from the back of the room where a group of her people stood. Angry retorts followed from the crewmen. Mandy sighed and wondered if she should open the doors and leave. Let them survive on their own.

"This is not their fault. It's mine." Total silence met her announcement. "I take the blame for letting rumors rule. I'm sure you'll find out soon enough through the grapevine how this happened. We do have a problem, though."

"The last time you said that the ship went out of control."

Mandy searched the crowd for the voice but couldn't see anyone talking. She saw others looking around also. "The ship went out of control due to sabotage by the same person or persons responsible for killing our people on Xy-Three. If not for the captain and crew, we'd all be dead."

"They do not deserve to live. You pander to them. You've had everything given to you. You own—but you do not control. You don't know the true power."

The voice, familiar yet different, jeered at her. She didn't need to see him to know who he was. She knew all too well.

"I know enough to know we need one another to survive. We've found good friends in both groups."

"Especially you." The same voice, but a different direction. Others were looking around, trying to find him. "You could have had everything, but you chose not to."

Mandy spun around as the voice came from behind her. Declan and Honan jumped on the stage and searched the shadows but came up empty.

"You're right, I have made friends, but I'm not the only one. We depended on one another in space. We were able to work together there. We can do the same here. All we need is cooperation."

She needed to keep him talking, give the others a chance to find him. Honan, Declan, Sarah, and the Warriors were systematically going through the crowd, searching.

"Not with them. Their fate was decreed by the

gods—as was yours."

Honan was scanning the PA system speakers. A loud shriek from Honan's sensor startled the people around him. He climbed onto a chair to reach the speaker. Mandy and everyone else in the room watched as he opened the plate. He reached in and pulled out a small audio unit.

Suddenly, the lights went out, leaving the room in total darkness. "Everyone, please remain calm," Mandy called above the nervous mumbling. "The emergency lights should be on in a few seconds." *Where are they? They should have come on immediately.* Several people turned on flashlights, giving at least minimal illumination to the crowd.

She felt a gust of wind at her back and a hand clamped over her mouth.

"Not a sound, and nobody will get hurt," the voice whispered in her ear. She felt a sharp prick at her throat and knew any wrong move would mean her death. The flashlights bobbed around the back of the room, but no light shone in her direction. They weren't strong enough to light the entire room.

"I'm going to take my hand from your mouth, but one sound—even a deep breath—and you're dead, and so are they. Put your hands behind your back. Carefully."

What did he mean they would die? What had he done? She put her hands back and felt a thin band encircle her wrists and tighten. A piece of tape was slapped over her mouth.

"Come on."

Mandy felt a tug on her arm and winced as the restraints bit into her arms. Wire binders were effective and illegal. They could easily slice through the wrists. She stumbled to the back of the stage. The knife, back at her throat, urged her on. The rear door opened and closed once they were through, engulfing them in the storm. Within seconds, she was drenched. She stumbled in the mud, and the voice growled at her. She could make out the shape of an anti-grav sled in the dark.

"Get in."

If she could get turned or to the ground, she could take him down. Her legs were more dangerous than her hands. She might have a chance. She leaned toward the sled, intending to kick back when something solid hit her on the back of the head and she saw stars. Her knees buckled, and she went down, but she had no chance to do anything. She felt the cold end of a hypo-spray against her neck, heard the hiss, and awareness faded.

****

Mandy awoke in the passenger's seat of the sled. Alvarez was in the driver's seat. The dim lights from the control panel lit his face—the face of the devil. He had dark hair, but she could see where the tips were still tinged with a lighter color. Her head throbbed where he'd hit her, and her arms ached, but at least he'd removed the tape from her mouth. She tried to move but couldn't.

"Ah, you're awake. Don't bother trying to move, my dear. The drug I gave you is a muscle relaxant. The effects won't wear off for a while. Sit back and enjoy the ride."

The ground rushed by in a blur as they left the compound behind. Water from her hair dripped down her neck adding to her irritation and discomfort. She figured she hadn't been out more than an hour at most, if that long. With her arms still bound behind her, sitting was awkward. She tried moving a muscle—any muscle—and thought she felt a bit of movement from her legs.

What seemed like a lifetime later, Alvarez slowed the sled to a stop. He lifted the canopy and climbed out, leaving Mandy in darkness. The wind, cold on her face, smelled of the ocean, and she thought she heard the sound of the surf over the storm. Alvarez appeared at her side, and she tried not to jerk. She was starting to feel something, but she needed to hide what she was doing.

Alvarez lifted her from the sled and dumped her on the ground. She landed on a rock that sent spikes of pain through her hip. Mandy concentrated on the pain, willing the sensation to awaken other nerves that would allow her some action. Alvarez knelt next to her and wrapped binders around her ankles.

"I know the drug is wearing off. You should be able to walk by now. Do watch your step, or you'll find yourself footless." He laughed, an unpleasantly harsh sound to Mandy's ears. She struggled to stand, using every ounce of strength she had.

The stark outline of the edge of a cliff was all Mandy could see in the darkness. Lightning flashed in the distance followed by deafening thunder. The rain had lessened from a torrential deluge to a mere soaking downpour. Both moons were cloud-covered, as if nature herself was under Alvarez's control. As they neared the edge of the precipice, Mandy heard the sea clearly, far below. She stumbled on a rock, pitching toward the edge. Barely in time, Alvarez yanked her back.

"You stupid bitch. Are you trying to kill yourself?" He backhanded her across the face, and she tasted blood.

Still groggy, Mandy let Alvarez lead her down a narrow ledge that sloped along the face of the cliff. Finally, he stopped and pulled her into a wide crack in the rocks. The darkness was complete, but at least she was out of the wind. She could see nothing until he flicked on a small hand lamp. The tiny light was barely enough to see by.

"Stay here. I'll be back." He took the free end of a metal cable secured in a ring in the rock and attached one end to her binders. "I wouldn't try getting loose if I were you. You do have such lovely hands." When he walked off, he took the light with him.

Mandy listened, peering into the darkness, trying to get some sense of her bearings. The minutes ticked by, and she thought she would scream in total madness when she heard a sound. A dim light all but blinded her, but she welcomed the brightness as a drowning man welcomes a preserver.

"Did you miss me?" Alvarez undid the cable. "Follow me. Carefully, my dear."

Mandy shuffled behind him less than a dozen steps before he stopped and moved to one side. Alvarez set the light a few feet away from her. As her eyes adjusted, she could see they were in a small cave. The space was long and narrow, roughly twice as high as wide. The floor was smooth black rock streaked with iridescent bands of minerals. Crystal?

Alvarez led her through another narrow passage into a second, much larger cavern. The dim light from the lantern was picked up and reflected back like hundreds of tiny mirrors so that the small lantern was enough to light the entire cavern. To one side, a small pool of water bubbled and flowed away through an opening in the rock. Near the pool, Mandy saw a camp complete with a portable bathroom.

"Welcome to your new home." Miguel pointed at the camp. "We have the latest in conveniences here. I'm sure you'll be quite comfortable.

"What do you want?" Mandy asked, fighting to keep her voice low and steady. Inside, her stomach churned with acid that threatened to erupt.

"You disappoint me. I thought you'd have figured everything out by now." He led her to a small camp chair, pushed her to a sitting position, and clamped her legs to the chair. He loosened the wires between the binders on her arms enough to clamp them to the arms of the chair.

"I know you're responsible for the deaths of hundreds of people, including my parents."

"Your parents were the ones responsible. The deaths lie on their shoulders." Alvarez paced the site, punctuating his words with quick, violent gestures. "I knew the gods had chosen me to carry out their work. They needed the sacrifices. I had to appease them."

Mandy tested her bonds as unobtrusively as possible. "You were ill. My father was your friend and your superior officer."

With a quickness that startled her, Alvarez jumped at her and grabbed her around the throat. "He was never my superior! None of them were. I'm better than the lot of them. I am so far above them that they should bow to me!"

Spots appeared before Mandy's eyes as darkness threatened to engulf her. As suddenly as he'd grabbed her, Alvarez released her, and she drew in gulps of air.

"It's not time yet," he mumbled. He strode away from her.

Mandy shuddered. The man was beyond insanity, and she was alone with him in an unknown cave somewhere on the island.

"I have to leave you for a while, my dear. I can't have your friends tracking the sled. Make yourself at home." Laughing at his own joke, he lit a second lantern and left.

"At least I'm not in the dark this time." Mandy released tightened muscles and stretched her fingers. As she looked around the area, she mentally catalogued everything that could be used as a weapon or a means of escape. She tried to rock the chair to tip over but discovered the legs were firmly anchored to the rocky ground.

"That's one fact about him. He's a madman, but he's thorough. He must have found this place early in order to stock up. That's where our fuel supplies have been going." She talked to keep from screaming. At one point, she thought she heard something behind her. To her surprise, the young lion cub stalked through the cave. The feline stopped at her feet and stared up at her.

"Hi. I really wish you were sentient and could understand me. Or maybe your mom or dad could, but I could really use some help. If you could bite through these bindings? Or go get help?" She closed her eyes and sighed. "I'm talking to a cat like he—or she—can understand me. I must have really lost my mind." She snorted when the cub sniffed at her pantleg, licked her hand, then bounded off. "Fine. Leave me here. But I'd really appreciate you bringing your daddy back."

Not knowing how much time she had, she listened for Alvarez as she worked on the binders. All she got for her efforts was an alarming tightening around her wrists and a trickle of blood. She quit as she heard footsteps nearing.

"That's one sled they'll never find." Alvarez dropped a pack on the ground by Mandy's feet.

"What did you do? Blow it up like you did the *Shangri-La*? Like you tried to do to the *Phoenix*? What happened, Miguel? Didn't your people follow your orders?"

Alvarez raised his hand to hit her, his face red with anger. Mandy steeled herself for the blow. Suddenly he smiled and wagged his finger at her.

"That wasn't very clever. Yes, they failed. And they paid for their failures. But I am one with the gods. I will prevail. I have a toy I'd like to show you." He pulled out a beaded metal mesh strap. The strap was about an inch wide and fifteen inches long with a large gray stone set in the center. There were connector pins on each end and along the lower length. Mandy wasn't sure what the contraption was, but she was sure she wouldn't like whatever he planned to do.

"I learned about this ingenious little device on my way from your wonderful court system to my new home. According to the government, these have all been destroyed. Strange how the only one still in existence showed up in the hands of one Master General Tyler Davis. What's even stranger is nobody, not even the honorable Master Chief Justice himself, said a word when the good general put this on me."

Alvarez dangled the strap in front of her face.

"Fortunately for me, our friends on the inside knew how to neutralize this. Unfortunately, that didn't work for Trella." He attached the collar to a small black box and activated a control. He frowned at the readout, changed some of the leads, and then nodded.

He fastened the collar snugly around Mandy's neck, adjusting the tightness until she could barely breathe. The mesh lay cold against her skin. The wire leads trailed down to the black box.

"Miguel, don't do this. You were once my friend. My father's partner."

Alvarez laughed. "Don't be ridiculous. All you meant to me was access to ambrosia. The high and mighty Amanda Ki. So pure. So self-righteous. Does your darling captain know you're a cold fish? The last living virgin of the universe, and you're mine. Everything worked out perfectly. Do you know, your name means 'worthy of the gods'? We'll see if they like your sacrifice."

"Miguel…"

"Shh. You haven't seen the best part yet. Wait." He ran his hand down her arm, then pushed a button on the box. Mandy felt a sharp sting on her neck, and a slow burn spread throughout her body.

"My little friend is tasting you, getting to know you. Soon, he will know more about you than you do. Once you have been analyzed, I'll be able to remove those nasty little binders you tried so hard to get out of. You see, with this collar, you can go wherever I want you to. Of course, you won't be able to move above a slow shuffle. He's tied into your adrenaline system. Any excitement at all, and he'll know." Alvarez detached the leads from the collar.

Then he removed the binders from her arms, and Mandy fought to remain still, gauging her opportunity. When he bent over to unlock her legs, she brought both arms down on his head, sending him crashing to the ground. She quickly removed the leg binders and ran for the outer cavern.

And the pain hit. Blinding, crippling pain that had her writhing on the floor, every muscle tied into knots. Fire raced along every nerve. Somewhere in the distance she heard screaming and realized the sound was coming from her. She cried for the pain to stop.

An eternity later the pain eased, and she lay there, gasping. Alvarez stood over her, a smirk on his face. "Did I forget to tell you about my little friend's other feature? I am sorry. You see, he knows what your system is like at rest, and any time you exceed that limit, my little friend will remind you. Oh, and he has a good memory, so each time he needs to remind you, he reminds you a little harder. That was my own little modification. Also, he doesn't like to be tampered with. The collar tends to tighten when you try that."

Tears spilled from Mandy's eyes, and Alvarez hauled her to her feet. Papa D would never have condoned the use of something like this. Not the man who had cleaned her scraped knees and kissed away childhood hurts. But what about Master General Davis? A man trained to get answers. Mandy shook her head. No. She wouldn't believe he'd do something like this. She couldn't.

Alvarez pushed her back into the camp chair. "I suggest you behave yourself. I can't have my sacrifice marred before the appointed time."

Mandy gasped. "Sacrifice? What are you talking about?"

"I mean, somebody has to pay for taking me from my destiny and stranding me here. This is my shrine now, and here I will be reborn through your blood."

Mandy looked around the cavern sparkling in the light. She had never been much of one for spelunking, but there were aspects of this cave that didn't look quite natural to her. The floor was too smooth, the walls too square and polished. Alvarez wouldn't have had time to do this much work on the cave. She wondered if he had others working with him.

"I have to go out for a while. I'm sure you'll behave yourself. Oh, and in case you get the idea of leaving these sumptuous surroundings, I've set up a little device at the entrance to the cave that's tuned to your collar. Should you try to leave, the collar will tighten until, poof, no more head. And you have such a pretty head." His laughter echoed through the cavern, bouncing off the hard surfaces. "While I'm gone, I want you to get cleaned up. You're filthy." He tossed a robe at her. "Put this on."

After he left, Mandy carefully rose from the chair. She took a couple of shuffling steps, waiting for the pain. "Calm. I have to remain calm."

She fought to keep her heartbeat slow and steady, her breathing normal. Mandy slowly made a circuit of the cavern. At the far end, across from the entrance, she found a small hole barely large enough for her to crawl into. She poked her head through and wrinkled her nose at the acrid aroma. Like an animal or animals lived there. A rustling sound came from a short distance away and, not wanting to meet the owners, even if they were her feline friends, she backed out. Mandy returned to the camp and continued her slow search. She didn't find any other exits, so she resignedly entered the fresher and did her best to clean up. The gown would be easy enough to put on, but Mandy refused to willingly do anything Alvarez said.

The gown was beautifully made and, under other circumstances, she would even admire the black silk, trimmed in deep red and belted at the waist, leaving the front open. There were no sleeves, and the material was slit on both sides from hem to arm leaving more uncovered than covered. She laid the robe down and returned to the chair. Alvarez had taken the black box with him, so she had no way to deactivate the collar, and she wasn't willing to test the truth of Alvarez's claims. She rather liked her head attached to her body. She must have dozed, although she didn't know how or how long. The next she knew Alvarez was shaking her.

"Why haven't you changed?"

"I guess I fell asleep."

"Stand up." Without waiting, he yanked her upright. Before Mandy could do anything, he pulled out a knife and slit her clothes from neck to ankle. He pulled them off her, then picked up the robe and draped the soft cloth over her, tying a sash loosely at the waist.

"Drink this." He handed her a cup filled with a thick bluish liquid.

"I'm not thirsty." Her throat was parched with dryness.

Alvarez grabbed her by the jaw and forced her mouth open, tipping the cup to her mouth. He poured the liquid into her mouth, and she gagged on the vile drink, swallowing some of the bitter liquid in the process. Finally, he released her jaw.

"We have an hour or two. I think I need to show you a surprise you never expected."

"I don't think I could survive another one of your surprises."

"Oh, but you'll like this one." He grabbed her arm and led the way to the sidewall of the cavern. "We'll need to do a little climbing, but if you're really careful, I'm sure you won't have too much of a problem."

He pushed her up onto a wide, flat rock then joined her. A narrow ledge hugged the side of the cavern wall, sloping up from the rock. The path was relatively smooth, so Mandy was able to keep her steps small, her movements slow and calm. She walked as slowly as possible, forcing Alvarez to slow his steps until they were barely moving.

He grabbed her hair and pulled until she blinked back tears. "I know you can move faster, so move or I'll kill you here and now."

Mandy's feet moved slightly faster, but her mind moved faster yet. She contemplated and discarded an incredible number of ideas in the short time they took to traverse the slope. Each one involved the demise of Alvarez, but she needed the codes to unlock the collar. The irony wasn't lost on her. All the times Alvarez wanted the codes to the company from her, and now she needed him for his codes.

Alvarez stopped and pointed to a crevice in the rock face. "This is really ingenious. You can't see this slot from the floor of the cavern. I found this by accident. I know the gods were guiding me here. Wait until you see." He pulled Mandy in behind him.

The slot opened into a small cave, not much larger

than the gym on the ship, but that wasn't what stopped Mandy. The walls were composed of the same gold-streaked black rock as the cave below, but here they were polished to an ebony sheen. Ritualistic depictions of humanoid figures and animals were embedded in the walls along with pictures of pyramidal buildings. They reminded her vaguely of drawings she had seen in ruins on Aboo.

Along the far wall, a large, black slab stood on a raised platform. Two huge basins made of the same polished rock flanked the table. The floor was laid out in a mosaic of black, red, and gold stone, like pathways, all leading to the table. Light filtered in from an opening in the roof of the cave, creating a pattern within the pattern on the walls and floor. From somewhere, Mandy heard the sound of the surf echoing faintly.

"Alvarez, I know you didn't have time to do this."

He snorted. "No, but this is perfect for my needs. When the sun hits high noon, the beam will be directly over the altar, and you will pay for your crimes. The people who lived here before us built this in preparation of my coming. This will become my throne room."

Mandy glanced at the circle of light on the floor as the beam crept inexorably toward the table. She must have slept longer than she thought because the light looked like daylight, not night.

"Come, my dear lady. We must prepare you for your debut. Today is a glorious new day. Today I will be a god. Through your blood, I will become invincible."

She bit back a hysterical laugh. Alvarez sounded like a script from a bad movie. To keep her mind off the

335

altar, she studied the cavern. The implications weren't lost on her. At one time, this planet had been inhabited. Maybe on some distant island, the people of this place still existed. Or maybe they were from another planet and used this place for ceremonies. Whatever the reason, this was the first real evidence of a civilization not humanoid. There were dozens of other races on thousands of planets, but all of them similar to humans.

Mandy was brought back to harsh reality as Alvarez shoved her toward the altar. She did everything she could to slow him down, stumbling over the gown, which wasn't difficult. Her legs refused to obey her commands, and she felt detached from her surroundings. The patterns in the cave shifted in her vision, as though they were living entities. As she neared the altar, Mandy heard another sound. One she had almost lost hope of hearing. She heard other voices and prayed what she caught wasn't her imagination and that Alvarez hadn't heard them. Mandy deliberately stumbled into him, sending him sprawling on the stone steps.

He got up and slapped her across the face, stunning her.

Chapter Twenty-Four

"Captain! Over here!"

Mandy definitely heard the quiet echo of Sarah's voice. Alvarez froze, rage suffusing his face with red.

"Sarah!" Mandy screamed, earning a hard blow to her head that sent her waning senses reeling.

Alvarez crammed a gag in her mouth, hauled her to her feet, and dragged her to the altar. He picked her up and laid her on the cold stone. "Doesn't matter if they're here or not. By the time they find this place, they will be too late."

He pulled her arms above her head and tied them to a ring in the rock, then reached for her legs. She needed to buy time for Sarah to find her. Mandy gauged her timing and kicked with all her remaining strength, knocking Alvarez to the floor. Then the pain hit. She curled into a tight ball as the agony raced through her. The collar squeezed tighter, and she fought to remain conscious, but the pain was everywhere, exploding along her nerves. She could barely breathe. After an eternity, the pain eased and she opened her eyes, blinking away the tears that flowed freely.

Alvarez stood above her, breathing heavily, anger turning his features into a hideous mask. He wiped a trickle of blood from the corner of his mouth and used that to trace a line down her chest. He jerked her legs straight and tied them to the altar then lit a fire in each of the stone bowls. The circle of light crept closer, touching the edge of the altar. Alvarez muttered something in a language Mandy didn't recognize. He pulled a long, narrow onyx knife from his sleeve and laid the weapon on Mandy's chest, the point on the pulse of her throat.

Mandy strained to hear any sound and was rewarded with a noise, but from the rear of the cavern, not the entrance. She peered down the length of the table and watched as the light drew nearer, creeping across the top of the stone.

Alvarez closed his eyes, raised his arms, and spoke out loud in the same guttural language. He opened his eyes and watched as the light reached the knife. He picked the blade up and traced an outline on Mandy's chest, drawing a thin bead of blood where he touched. He lifted the knife high above her chest and paused as Declan burst through the tunnel followed closely by Honan, Sarah, Taka, and the general.

"Don't, Alvarez." Declan spoke low and evenly, a laser pistol in his hand.

"You're too late, Captain." Alvarez sneered. "Whether I use the knife or not, she's already dead."

"That doesn't matter. Put the knife down."

Alvarez smiled and brought the knife down toward Mandy's chest as Declan fired his weapon. Alvarez spun around from the shot, blood spurting from his shoulder, the knife spinning across the stone floor. Shock registered on his face, and he stepped back.

"You think you can stop me? I am Miguel Alvarez, chosen by the gods themselves. I am all powerful!" He stepped back again, moving into the shadows at the rear of the cavern and searched for the knife.

"Move again, Alvarez, and you're dead." Declan aimed the pistol at his chest.

As Alvarez slowly took another step backward, a noise from behind startled him into turning. Suddenly, a large black cat with startling blue eyes pounced on Alvarez, batting him down with one powerful swipe of his huge paw. Alvarez screamed once, then was silent. The cat shook his head, wiped his face on the ground, then stalked forward and laid his head on the altar next to Mandy's. He huffed at her, then turned and disappeared into the shadows.

Released from their frozen horror, the rescue party advanced carefully to the altar. Pistol drawn, Declan rounded the table, searching the shadows for any sign of the cat. He reached Alvarez and knelt to check him.

"He's dead," Declan said. The man's face and neck were gone.

"What was that?" Sarah asked.

"That, ladies and gentlemen, was Mandy's kitten. Or rather, the daddy."

Sarah untied the bindings and helped Mandy sit up.

The room spun as Mandy fought for control over the drugs. "Sarah. Neck." She gasped for breath.

Sarah gently lifted Mandy's chin and let out a low whistle. "Declan, you'd better take a look at this."

Declan checked the collar. "I've read about these, but I've never seen one." He reached for the clasp.

"Don't touch that!" General Davis's commanding voice stopped Declan. "The collar's probably been programmed to kill her if anyone tampers with the connectors or even the mesh. Mandy, did Alvarez have a little black box he hooked this to?"

"Yes," she whispered, "in the lower cavern."

"Sarah, go see if you can find a small black electronic box, about six inches square. There should be several wire leads attached, a small monitor, and a touchpad. Honan, can you get me some more light in here?" General Davis gently lifted Mandy's head. "You'll be all right, honey."

Honan studied the hole in the roof. "If I can find that hole outside, I can lower a light down from the skimmer. You'll have better light control than the sunbeam."

With Declan on the inside and Honan on the outside, they quickly located the hole and sent a portable light down. General Davis set the light so the beam shone on the altar, illuminating Mandy. Sarah returned with the controller and placed the box on the table next to Mandy.

"Now what, General?" Declan asked.

"Now, we start hooking up the leads. Mandy, did Alvarez do anything to this?"

"Made the pain progressively stronger." Reality kept swimming in and out of touch. She could barely keep her eyes open. All she wanted to do was sleep. She'd feel so wonderful if she could go to sleep.

"He probably did that through the programming. These are the original leads. I'm betting he wasn't able to break all the codes, so I should be able to get in. Mandy, you have to stay awake and remain in control. Can you do that?"

"I...don' know. Gave me drug. Don't know what."

Taka stepped up and took a swab of the blood on Mandy's chest before sealing the wounds. She put the swab in her portable tester. "The result will take a couple minutes."

The general's training took over, and he became the efficient military man he was known for being. "Sarah, go see if you can find the drug to help Taka. Declan, talk to Mandy. She must remain absolutely calm, but awake. The collar is hooked into her adrenaline and nervous systems and will know when she gets excited. Honan, I'm going to start attaching the leads. You watch that line on the monitor. If that line jumps even a micron, stop me."

"Aye, sir."

Davis wiped the sweat from his hands and picked up a lead.

"Mandy," Declan spoke in low, even tones. "Remember your training. Listen to my voice and concentrate. Find that spot deep within you." He droned on, his voice hypnotic. Every time Mandy's head drooped, he pinched the pad between her finger and thumb. "Mandy, stay awake. Listen to me."

Davis connected a fourth lead.

"Stop!" Honan said, startling everyone, including Mandy.

Declan quickly grabbed her chin forcing her to look at him. "Breathe deeply. Find your center." He sensed her calmness and motioned for the general to continue.

Davis laid the offending lead to one side and continued with the rest. Finally, everything was attached but the odd one. He coded in a sequence on the pad and tried again to attach the lead. Again Honan stopped him.

"Mandy, I have one lead left that I'm going to attach. This will hurt. I'm sorry, but there's no other way. I can't cancel the collar until the lead is attached."

"No." Mandy tried to back away, but Declan held her fast. Tears tracked down her cheeks, and Declan gently wiped them away. "No choice?"

"No." General Davis shook his head, sadness in his lined face.

"Okay." Mandy steeled herself for the pain. Agony hit her with all the force of the last time and more. She curled in on herself as the others watched helplessly.

Davis's fingers flew over the pad as he entered the codes necessary to neutralize the collar. Finally, he finished. He reached over and removed the collar. "You're safe, honey."

Tears in her eyes, Mandy could only look at the man she'd adored as a child. "Why, Papa D? Why?"

General Davis's shoulders drooped, and he sighed. "I wanted to hurt him as much as he hurt you. That's not an excuse. I'm sorry, honey."

Taka stepped up. "We need to get her back to medical as soon as possible. Sarah got me a sample of the drug. The poison is a slow agent, but deadly. I need to produce an antidote."

Declan picked Mandy up and carried her out.

As the group left the cavern, General Davis paused and looked back to where Alvarez's body lay cocooned in a stasis bag Taka had wrapped around him. A pair of blue eyes in a black face stared back at him.

"I never meant for her to get hurt. She's all I have. Thank you, my friend, for keeping her safe." Shoulders slumped, he turned and followed the group.

Chapter Twenty-Five

"Taka, when are you going to let me out of this room?" Mandy complained, pacing back and forth like a caged jaguar. "You've given me every test imaginable and a few I'd rather not think about." She danced a jig across the room. "Look. I can walk. I can talk. I can move every limb. Why won't you let me out?"

"Why don't you quit your griping? You've got visitors."

Mandy sighed. Arguing with Taka was like arguing with a brick wall. She'd been cooped up in the infirmary for a horribly long week. Granted, most of that time she'd spent asleep or violently sick from the drug Alvarez had given her and Taka's antitoxin, but she was fine now. And Taka had even allowed her to put on real clothes for a change. She had hope she might be able to actually get out of there. A soft knock alerted her to her visitor.

"Come in."

Sarah strode in. "Hi! How are you doing?"

"The same as yesterday. The same as the day before. I'm fine. I wish I could get out of here. How are you?"

Sarah chuckled. "Tired. You should be grateful. There's so much work to be done, we're all wishing we could spend a week lazing around."

"Believe me, I'd trade you if I could. By the way,

not that I'm complaining, but how did you guys find me in that cave?" She really hadn't had a chance to talk to them about the cave. Taka had kept their visits to a few minutes at a time. And nobody would even talk about what had happened there.

Sarah shrugged. "That was the easy part. Hermes alerted us the back door was open, and we found one of the sleds missing. For all his genius with electronics, Alvarez never suspected these." She touched Mandy's small black earrings—the same ones Sarah had given Mandy so many weeks ago. "The last time I saw you, you still had them on. We got Chane to launch our last probe, and Hermes tracked you. We were a little confused when we got there. Hermes said we were standing on top of you, but you were nowhere in sight, then Declan remembered you saying something about the possibility of caves, so we looked around and found you."

Mandy fingered the earrings. "I don't think I'll ever take them off. Did you guys take a good look at the cave?"

"Yes. We went back the next day and got everything recorded. But is the cave and what's in there a relic of ancients long dead? Or still in use by someone?"

"Only time will tell."

"We also ran tests on some of the black rock in the cave. That's pure crystal. Chane and his crew are figuring out how to use them to power our systems instead of our dwindling fuel."

"I can probably give him some ideas on that. I might have some schematics in my files. Once I'm allowed out of here so I can access them." Mandy looked up as Declan walked in. She didn't miss the look between him and Sarah.

"I've got to go. See you later." Sarah gave her a quick hug and left.

"Seeing you in sickbay is getting to be a habit," Declan said as he leaned one leg on the bed and took her hand in his.

"One I hope is permanently broken. How is everyone? And the camp?" She rubbed her thumb over his hand.

"Going smoothly. The storm damaged some of the tents, but they've been repaired. You'll be glad to know the new weather station is up and operational. Chane and Honan went over all the wiring in our little town with a microscope. No more electronic surprises."

"Is this nightmare really over, Declan?"

He sat beside her and took both her hands in his. "Yes. General Davis and Taka both confirmed the man with you was Alvarez. You can finally put your ghosts to rest."

"What about Trish? Why didn't the general recognize her when she came on board?"

"She'd had some surgery done prior to meeting me and made sure he was never around when she was. We may never know all the answers, but we know Miguel is dead. We put Alvarez's body on the ship and set the controls for the sun. The trip will take a few years, but will eventually get there, so in a way, he did get to join his sun god after all."

Mandy touched his arm. "You'll get back out there someday, Declan."

Declan looked at her, a wry grin on his face. "Maybe. And maybe this isn't such a bad place to be grounded."

Taka stuck her head in the door. "Time."

Declan nodded and offered his arm to Mandy. "Shall we?"

"Time for what? What's going on?"

Taka all but pushed her out the door. "Time for you to get out of here. I might need this bed for somebody who's sick."

Declan escorted Mandy out of the infirmary to a curiously empty settlement. Nobody was working anywhere.

"Where is everybody?"

"You'll see."

He led her down a secondary street flanking the communal hall. A large drape spanned the end of the street, obscuring her view. Tina, O'Malley, Sarah, Honan, and Chane stood in front of the drape, grinning like a pack of hyenas.

Mandy stopped and stared at them. "All right, enough. What is going on?"

Declan nodded, and they pulled the drapery aside. The entire settlement—scientists, techs, and crew—stood in front of a neat, one-story permanent house.

"Surprise!"

Mandy stood, mesmerized as an aisle to the home opened through the crowd. "I don't believe this! This is incredible."

"Well, aren't you going to go in?" Declan asked.

Mandy moved through the crowd, hugging, joking, and laughing with all the people.

"We thought you should have the first permanent house," Declan said. "Welcome home, Mandy."

Mandy touched the walls. "This is wonderful. How

did you get everything done so fast? You've had so much else to work on."

"Teamwork," Tina said. "The rescue team was out looking for you, and we couldn't sit here and do nothing, so…"

"About darned time you all worked as a team." Mandy pushed open the door. Soft strains of guitar music with air flute met her ears. "Hermes, thank you."

"You're welcome, boss. I'm glad to have you back."

Mandy stepped inside, followed by Declan. The layout was a simple design, open and airy. Most of the building consisted of a combination living room, dining area, and kitchen. A small bedroom, bath, and study completed the layout. She circled the great room, reveling in what her friends had done. A small wall shelf next to the door drew her attention. There, prominently displayed, was the statue her father had given her so many years ago. So much had happened since that day.

Taka stuck her head in the door. "Is this a private party, or can anyone join?"

"Taka, come in! Isn't this amazing?"

Taka nodded, then gestured to Declan. "Declan, Honan needs you outside for a minute. Mandy, I'll be back in a bit. I need to talk to Sarah."

A few seconds after they left, Mandy heard a light rap on the door. "Come in."

General Davis opened the door and was propelled in by someone Mandy couldn't see but could guess at. Sure enough, Taka stepped into view. "I believe you two have something to talk about." She shut the door firmly.

The general stood, awkwardly, in the entry, his back to the door. "How are you?"

Of all her friends, the general was the one person who hadn't come to see her in the infirmary. "Fine. Taka says there was no permanent damage."

"Good."

"Papa?"

"Mandy?"

They both spoke at the same time, and then lapsed into embarrassed silence.

Davis cleared his throat and tried again. "Mandy, I never thought you would be the one hurt. I'm so sorry, honey."

Mandy looked at him. He was suddenly an old man, stooped and white-haired. He had been her knight in shining armor who could do no wrong. A hero. Finding out he was human was hard. She saw what her little girl eyes had never seen—somebody who had been deeply hurt. He had needed her and her family as much as they'd needed him.

"I know, Papa. I understand." As she said the words, she realized she did understand. Her need of him had lessened over the years, but his need hadn't.

"There's only one fact I don't understand about all this, Papa."

"Only one?"

"My father's diary. What was Alvarez after?"

"Something he'd never find. He thought your father had the codes in the diary. The diary was your father's way of keeping tabs on several groups without anyone being wiser. He could go anywhere and sit there and write, using the excuse he was writing to you. Your father worked for me for a long time, even after he supposedly quit. He was a good man and my best friend."

Mandy crossed the room and hugged him. "I love you, Papa." She reached up on tiptoes and kissed him. "I think I saw some tables full of food out there. What do you say we go join the party?"

"Only if I don't have to dance."

"Agreed." Mandy laughed and opened the door. Taka and Declan stood on the front step, like sentinels guarding a fort. "What's everyone standing around for? We have a celebration to join!"

Taka pulled the general into the gaiety of the crowd.

"Is everything all right?" Declan asked as he put his arm around her.

"Yes. Everything is fine." Mandy snuggled into his side and looked around. "What's ahead of us is not going to be easy, and there's a lot that can go wrong, but we've got a good start, and, with luck, everything will all work out."

She took Declan's arm and stepped out into the village. In the distance, she heard the faint sound of a lion's roar and smiled.

Glossary

AI (artificial intelligence) – Basically a computer that can think like—or better than—a human. They are capable of making decisions and can have basic emotions.

Cold Sleep – This is where a person is put into a coma-like state and sustained in a life pod that enables them to endure lengthy space trips.

Chrystolian Opals – also called Ki opals or Ki crystals. A special kind of rock discovered on Ki's Planet found to have special electronic properties that can be used as natural power sources.

CP or Cygnian Plague – an illness from the planet Cygnus that is usually deadly. Telltale signs include purple spots on the victim.

Fresher – a bathroom with a sink, toilet, shower (usually sonic).

Jump systems – a special type of engine in a spaceship that allows the ship to contract space so as to make the trip shorter. There are points in space (like a star or planet) that you can set coordinates for and jump to there. But there are limits so a long trip might take several jumps.

Life pod – a single-person sized unit that can sustain life for extended periods of time.

Thillo-toum – a martial art form similar to Judo

Toluba – a martial art form similar to karate

Watch your six – a term used especially by fighter pilots meaning your rear. When sitting in the cockpit of a plane, think of a clock face with the twelve being directly in front of you. Thus, the six would be behind you, to your rear.

Warrior Class – Similar to the US Marines, they

are highly trained military personnel who work in a wide variety of jobs including fighting, transportation, guardians, and more. Each job has a specific color of beading and clothing that denotes what they do.

White root – a plant found on Ki's Planet with multiple varieties. Most are harmless and have medicinal properties but one variety—the thorny white root—is highly addictive leading to psychosis and death.

~*~

Species:

Abooleans – there are many different races on Aboo, separated by tribes or clans. But all are humanoid. Most belong to tribes or classes that are denoted by their clothing and hair. Some of these include Warriors, Physicians, Merchants, Builders, and more.

Humans – though there are few humans on Aboo, there are a few. And more on other worlds and stations. How they got out into these places has been lost in time.

Masaaki – Cat people. Though humanoid (walk upright, two legs, two arms, etc.), their features are feline in appearance and they have tails.

Orilians - humanoids with blue scales, webbed hands and feet, and nictitating eyes. They mate once a year and prefer to build nest-like structures in cliffs near the ocean.

Rujaz – Bronze skin that turns bright red when angered (which happens often). Shorter and heavier than most beings due to their main planets being gravity heavy.

Surians - coal black skin and gold hair, they

mostly come from the desert planet of Jovian

Throquins – part of the mysterious Throquin Dominium. Vaguely bird-like in appearance with sharp, pointed faces and taloned feet.

~*~

Places in the series

Aboo – fourth planet in the Chalian system that is roughly the size of Mars. A mostly temperate island paradise (think Hawaii). A line of islands marches around the globe at the equator called the Maltric Chain, but there are also land masses north and south that have harsher climates. Each island contains a space dock, some larger than others. The main island, Tyreegel, is where planetary government is located. Amanda Ki owned a compound on this island.

Aino – A small planet, roughly the size of Earth's moon, uninhabitable without special living quarters and environmental suits, important only for mineral resources for the other planets in the system. Third in the Chalian system.

Aino Station – small station circling Aino. Stopping off point for miners, ore transfers. Very few amenities.

Argonia – Mountainous area (think northwestern US or western Canada) on the Apitac continent north of Tyreegel. Protected woodlands. Mostly privately owned by the Warrior tribe, they control a large portion of the continent.

Boherea – abandoned ancient city on the southern continent. Mostly taken over by the desert.

Jovani – largest planet in the Chalian system, sixth one out from the sun. Mostly desert planet. Most cities are underground with minor building above ground due to harsh sandstorms and winds.

Lanicam – ancient realm on Jovani long since overtaken by the sands. All that's left is the language, like Latin, not spoken by anyone but used by many.

Mt. Pitonas – main mountain on Tyreegel. Old, dormant volcano, largest mountain in the islands.

Pointe Noir – major space station circling Aboo. A small city of almost 5,000 people of many species and is the jumping off point for all space travel in the system.

Secundus – Fourth planet in the Xy System.

Thexadon – Fifth planet in the Xy System

Udara Station – old station in the Xy System, rarely used any more.

Xy-One – Third planet in the system, Earth-like, but largely unsettled. Two major cities—Delphi station and New Nova. Important for the deposits of Ki opals.

Xy-Three – also called Ki's Planet. Much smaller than Xy-One, but where Amanda's parents originally found the opals and white root plants. Volcanically active in the southern hemisphere

Yalla – northeastern part of the Apitac continent on Aboo. Similar to Maine in makeup.

A word about the author...

Vicky has been married forever to the one person who accepts that she lives in a fantasy world most of the time. She's even been seen at the beach building worlds for her stories. In addition to creating fun characters, fantasy worlds, and suspenseful situations, she also enjoys and is very good at things like writing policy and procedures manuals and setting up continuity and organizational spreadsheets, both of which she has actually earned money doing. She has a master's degree in library science so likes things organized. Okay, so her family thinks having the spice rack alphabetized is a bit much, but she has no trouble finding what she needs when she needs it. And just because her extensive library is cataloged and organized, that doesn't mean she's obsessive. Honest.

When not writing, Vicky can be found in the kitchen whipping up gluten-free, lactose-free, other allergy-free meals.

http://burkholv.wordpress.com

Check out Revenge Among The Stars
Galactic Danger Vol. 1

Thank you for purchasing
this publication of The Wild Rose Press, Inc.

For questions or more information
contact us at
info@thewildrosepress.com.

The Wild Rose Press, Inc.
www.thewildrosepress.com